NOT TODAY, FRED

NOT TODAY, FRED

A NOVEL

BRANDON HELMS

White River Press
Amherst, Massachusetts

ISBNs: 978-1-887043-69-4 paperback
         978-1-887043-70-0 ebook

First published 2020 by White River Press
PO Box 3561, Amherst, Massachusetts 01004
whiteriverpress.com

Library of Congress Cataloging-in-Publication Data

Names: Helms, Brandon, 1982- author.
Title: Not today, Fred : a novel / Brandon Helms.
Description: Amherst, Massachusetts : White River Press, [2020]
Identifiers: LCCN 2020004079 (print) | LCCN 2020004080 (ebook) | ISBN
   9781887043694 (paperback) | ISBN 9781887043700 (ebook)
Classification: LCC PS3608.E39235 N68 2020 (print) | LCC PS3608.E39235
   (ebook) | DDC 813/.6--dc23
LC record available at https://lccn.loc.gov/2020004079
LC ebook record available at https://lccn.loc.gov/2020004080

*This book is dedicated to
those who refuse to give up.*

Chapter 1

JUST DROPPED IN TO SEE
WHAT CONDITION MY CONDITION WAS IN

My life is chock full of mediocre days and bad days. Good days? Once every blood moon—blue moons come too frequently. The first Monday in May fell within the norm.

As I began the short walk from my apartment building to the North/Clybourn Red Line stop, the piercing wind agitating the slight hangover I had from last night's pity party of one, I felt my phone buzz in my pants pocket.

Morning! said my mom. *Have a good week!* Her clockwork Monday morning messages should have put a spring in my step, but because they were usually the only things that brightened my days, they had begun to have the opposite effect.

I began to type *You too* back to her when my face came into direct contact with a metal sign pole. Neither the post nor I wanted it to happen. I looked around to see if anyone had seen me. A woman smirking across the street answered my silent question in the affirmative. Awesome.

Without further damage to my person and pride, I was able to enter the station and navigate my way down the stairs to the platform. Somewhere between three and twenty-five minutes later—it's hard to say exactly; since I wasn't forcing my brain to concentrate, I had started to daydream—a typically crowded train pulled into the station. After I entered and the dust settled, I stood smashed between a man who appeared to be dying from emphysema and two guys around my age who were speaking at maximum volume despite their proximity.

"Shut up. No way! Did she really say that? Do you think she'd go out with me? Wait, didn't she hook up with Ryan?" the bro with brown hair queried in rapid succession.

I'm not sure he understood how a conversation worked. One must pause if one wants his questions to be answered.

"What, yeah, definitely!" answered his black-haired friend. "I dunno about Ryan. Where'd you hear that?"

Is it considered eavesdropping when you're trying not to overhear? I pretended to rub my temples while sticking my index fingers in my ears to drown out their frivolous conversation. Fred seized the moment to help me escape reality and enter his dream world of misfortune and calamity, this time transporting me to a treetop-covered precipice. A hawk screeched overhead, reminding the mountain of its presence. Something scampered under a nearby bush—message received. If I had thought it was a cobra, I would've walked toward it like a condemned man to an executioner's block, confident in my inability to outmaneuver its lateral undulations. But it was not a cobra. And even though I was seeking the end, death by snake venom sounded unnecessarily painful. No one has ever mistaken me for a tough guy.

I lifted one leg over the chasm spread out below me, but then I let it dangle over the edge, unsure whether to proceed. *Maybe I'm jumping the gun a little*, I told myself. *Maybe I should just cut another notch in my failed-attempt belt.*

Then the creature under the bush turned out to be a goddam snake after all. A hooded monster who took a semiserious lunge at me—more a range-finding jab than a fully committed cross. Always one to be easily startled, I quickly lost balance. My one foot still planted on the ground slid out from under me, and my fictional freefall began. As I plummeted downward, my mind hurled me back into reality.

The young gentlemen were still chatting away.

"Dude, she is so lame. Just ignore her for now," the brown-haired friend counseled. "She'll get over it. You don't need to apologize for that."

To my everlasting dismay, I missed whatever factoid from his buddy had prompted this directive.

Emphysema man, on the other hand, sat looking like he might expel a lung at any moment. I hoped it was emphysema, anyway, and not some deadly airborne contagion like whooping cough. Otherwise, he was patient zero, and the bros and I were going to be his first three statistics. An early departure from this world did not sound so bad to Fred, but I didn't want to be lumped into any categories with them.

As the train grinded to a halt at my stop in the Loop, I gave emphysema man a wide berth while trying to suppress a disgusted grimace. I think I failed. Then I squeezed past the young male companions—my "excuse me" going unheeded—to begin the walk to my office.

■ ■ ■

You're probably wondering who Fred is. It's a fair question.

Dr. Bhattacharya diagnosed me with cyclothymia a few months ago— a working hypothesis. As far as I understand it, cyclothymia is a poor man's bipolar disorder. More a kiddie roller coaster of emotions than a ninety-mile-per-hour neck-breaker. All I know is my steady state is a slight funk, as if a damp, black cloud is perpetually coalescing around my head and shoulders. I call him Fred. Every once in a while, I feel like I could take on the world with one hand, but on my bad days, Fred makes scraping my face on a cheese grater seem appealing.

Dr. B suggested I write down my thoughts and feelings in a journal. I like her idea, but if I tell people I'm keeping a diary, they'll make fun of me by offering to buy me glitter pens or a Trapper Keeper. That's what I would do, anyway. So I started writing this memoir instead. No one makes fun of people for writing memoirs.

As for my job, I've been an associate at a behemoth consulting firm for a few years now. You've probably heard of it. Acronyms, jargon, and argots, oh my. PowerPoint is a minor god—no project is complete without one. It's not my life's calling, but it'll do for now.

Most of the time, I'm assigned to three-to-six-month projects, and I spend most days at the clients' offices. That means a lot of car time when I'm assigned to Chicago-area clientele. At least once a week, my thoughts drift to how easy it would be to slam into a concrete barrier or glide into the path of an oncoming semi.

What kind of speed is required to take down that telephone pole? I ask myself.

Is that divider filled with sand or with water? Only one way to find out.

No, running deer and falling rocks, I will not proceed with caution.

I try to visualize aerial cliff jumps off twisting curves culminating in fiery explosions, but my subconscious knows I live in the land of flat.

Sometimes I carpool with coworkers to visit a client. Just the other week, I zoned out while driving, and a colleague asked me what I was thinking about. "Wah wah, wah wah wah," I said in my best Charlie Brown teacher voice. And then, "Nothing," when she kept prodding. A lie was more palatable than the truth. Besides, she had nothing to worry about. I only want to end my life, not take anyone with me. Assuming I reach the pearly gates, I want to appear meek, not callous.

Did you know over thirty-five thousand people die every year in the United States in traffic accidents? That's roughly ninety-six people each day. One out of every four accidents is caused by texting and driving. So my fantasy about a solo crash doesn't sound too bad in the grand scheme of things, does it?

I've spent considerable time contemplating becoming the Batman of highway vigilante justice. I'd scour the freeways for violators—in a Tesla or other high-performance electric vehicle, because the environment is more critical than my thirst for vengeance. Eating a Big Mac? Batwing shuriken to your tire. Applying eyeliner? Bat-dart to your neck. Texting your friend? Thermite grenade to your backseat. Hands at ten and two? Good, move along, and watch out for my spike strips.

■ ■ ■

In the afternoon while I was taking a short break to stare out my thirty-second-floor office window, which provides a fantastic view of Maggie Daley Park and a large swath of the Lake Michigan coastline, my office phone started ringing.

"Hello, this is James Wright. To whom am I speaking?"

"Come on, James. You know it's me."

"Have to be professional at all times. You know that, Mom."

"Yes, of course."

I heard a trace of sarcasm in her voice that I did appreciate, but I would never tell her.

"I know you're busy," she continued. "I'm just calling to check in since you didn't text me back."

Oh, right, because I headbutted a signpost. "Sorry. I got distracted this morning. I'm good."

"You sure?" She repeated her inquiry gently, so I would not get perturbed.

"Yep, I'm good. Still breathing."

"Okay," she said, with a whiff of disbelief coming through. "Call me later in the week."

"I will not."

"I love you, James."

"Love you too, Mom."

■ ■ ■

A few hours later, Manuel Ramirez stopped by my office.

"Hey, you okay, man?"

"What? Yeah," I said as I returned my office chair to an upright position.

I had been thinking hard about a project I was working on, with my face transfixed in the general direction of my open door. Whether I'm concentrating on work or concocting phantasmal endings to my life thanks to Fred, I have a tendency to enter a Zen-like state.

"You sure? You looked like you were going through a system reboot."

"How many times do I have to tell you I'm not a robot?" I was half joking. He had called me a robot before, on more than one occasion.

"That ship has sailed, *chacho*. There is no way you can convince me you're a real boy. Not unless you undergo an extensive surgery to prove you're not all wires inside."

"Boy? I see no boy here, Manny. I'm a *man*. I'm a *man*." I patted my chest twice to emphasize my status as a fully matured male.

"If you keep telling yourself that, it might come true."

"What'd you come here for anyway? Can't you see I'm busy?" I made a show of moving around the papers and files on my desk.

"Yes, I'm sure you are."

His cocked eyebrow told me he wasn't buying my performance.

"I was just stopping by because…" Then he trailed off and started looking at the floor. It's a classic Manuel mannerism when he's bringing up a delicate subject.

"Because?"

"Because," he continued, "listen, I just…"

He let his voice fade a second time. I waited for him to utter more verbal sounds, but none were forthcoming, so I started making cricket noises.

"What are you doing?" he asked.

"Cricket noises. Because of this deafening silence."

"That is not what crickets sound like."

"Whatever. What do you want to tell me? Just spit it out." I had an inkling where he was going, and although I didn't want to talk about it, I wanted to press on as quickly as possible.

"Yeah, here goes. Listen, is everything okay? Anything you want to talk about?"

"Huh? Yeah, I'm fine. Why?"

Still making minimal eye contact, Manuel asked, "Well, why did you skip going to dinner last night, but then you drank by yourself?"

"I didn't drink by myself," I said. "Why do you think that?"

"You texted me more of your inane theories on life."

"So?" I was doing my best to maintain a look of incredulity.

"You only do that when you've been drinking."

"Not true." It was true. "And they're not inane." Most of them, anyway.

"They are, but that doesn't matter," he said. "Why'd you stay in?"

"I don't know. I just didn't feel like going out. I was tired."

More truthfully, I didn't want to be around people. It's hard to be upbeat when Fred is eroding my topsoil and threatening to do structural damage beneath. Fred had been coming hard yesterday.

"You sure? Just tired?"

"Yeah, promise." *Now stop asking me about it.*

"Okay, I'll drop it. But you'd tell me if it was something more?"

"Yeah, definitely." *Maybe. Probably not.*

"All right. Good." He turned to leave but then spun around after taking a step. "Hey, there's something else."

By his tone of voice and facial expression, this second issue was not as big a deal to him.

"Okay?"

"I need to pick up furniture I ordered, and I could use some help moving it into my apartment. Are you free any night to help?"

"What's in it for me?" I was happy to help because I owed Manuel like one trillion favors, but I didn't want him to know that.

"A sense of accomplishment and a natural high from helping others."

"Hmm, I dunno. What else?"

"James, can you help or not?"

"Yep, I'm free every night this week." Like most weeks, my social calendar had zero entries.

"See? Was that so hard?"

"Nope. I guess not. Just text me when you want the help."

"Thanks. See you later."

"Adios."

You probably can't tell, but Manuel is my best friend. By process of elimination: all my other friends quit or still live in the Pittsburgh area. Actually, that's not fair to Manuel. He'd be my right-hand man regardless. Or am I his right-hand man? It doesn't matter. Either way, Manuel Ramirez is the Bert to my Ernie.

Chapter 2

FRIENDS MAY COME AND GO LIKE BUSBOYS, BUT MANUEL IS LIKE THE SCHOOL LIBRARIAN

During the second week of my freshman year at Northwestern University, I was waiting for class to start, having arrived ten minutes early, 'cause that's what I do. If you're not early, you're late. One of the lessons from my dad that has stuck with me.

A guy slapped me on the shoulder from behind and said "That's you" as he proceeded to throw a hand-drawn picture into my lap. It depicted a caricature of me falling backward on a chair. I was perplexed why a stranger would give me a drawing, but the subject matter itself made total sense.

The week before, I had been leaning back in my chair when I went too far. After I crashed to the floor, silence engulfed the room, followed by a few jeers—like the time I tried my hand at standup. I'm easily embarrassed in public settings—and private ones too—and it shows: my face, neck, and chest turn fire-engine red. This black-and-white drawing was a pretty good rendition, minus the red.

"Thanks, man," I muttered, somewhat confused. "I'm flattered, but I'm not into dudes." I didn't think for one second he was trying to hit on me, but that joke was a low-hanging apple and I didn't feel like shimmying up a tree for a coconut.

"Ha, you're a funny guy," he said, as if he had already earned the right to be sarcastic with me. Then he sat down next to me.

"I'm Manuel," he said as he shook my hand.

"James," I told him, not trying to hide my amusement and my more-than-slight irritation.

Manuel has large facial features and a square jaw, which I hear some people find attractive, but if you stare long enough, especially if your eyes start to cross, you'll notice his face isn't quite symmetrical. He's a couple inches shorter than me and thin like Gumby, but I don't know anything about his flexibility.

"I like to draw things out of the ordinary. You falling on your ass the first week of class was definitely out of the ordinary. You should keep this so you can always remember it. I can get it laminated if you want." He stated all this with a genuine smile. No undercurrent of malice coming through, just amusement.

"That's okay. I already sculpted the scene in bas-relief." I could be clever too. "Were you in University Library yesterday? I couldn't shake the feeling that someone was watching me."

"Nope, wasn't me. I'm like a ninja. You'd never see me coming."

"That makes sense. I hear there are a lot of Mexican ninjas." *Was that racist?* I wondered.

"I'm Puerto Rican."

Yeah, it was racist. Dammit. "Sorry, man," I mustered. *Is my neck turning red? Check.*

I've thought about this on a number of occasions since then, but what is the evolutionary explanation for physiological symptoms of situational anxiety? What troglodyte went on to procreate because he had a propensity for turning red and sweating like a fat kid? More to the point, why do I have so many physical tells that demonstrate I am uncomfortable in my own skin?

Manuel didn't seem to be too offended. "You wanna grab lunch after class? You don't seem to have any friends, and I always try to help out those who are less fortunate."

"Yeah, sure. Do they serve tacos in the cafeteria?" Sometimes it's best to double down when you step in it.

Manuel cracked a half smile. "I guess I deserved that for the no friends comment."

"A little, but I'm also a smart-ass."

So that's what put us on the path to becoming fast friends: a cartoon drawing, some racial jokes, and a bro lunch date. It helped that he was right. I wasn't exactly drowning in friends. I had arrived on campus a week before classes started with most of the other freshman, but I hadn't met anyone I wanted to hang out with. Homesickness had been starting to set in hard, like the bread roll I forgot I had put in my backpack.

All jokes aside, the first week had been rough. In a foreign place with no friends, halfway across the United States from my home in suburban Pittsburgh, I was missing my mom and sister, Rachel. A lot. By the weekend, the only thing helping me put on a happy face was an overriding desire to prove my dad wrong. I'd overheard him telling the neighbors I'd never hack it so far away from home and that I'd be wanting to transfer within two weeks. He even offered to put a bet on it. I wished they'd accepted; it would have been sweet revenge to get back at him for once, since I did graduate without switching schools.

When I first applied to Northwestern, I intended to major in biomedical engineering or chemistry. I was unaware, however, that every science class was accompanied by an unwanted laboratory session that was twice as long. Plus, the monotony of those multiple-hour labs was not for me. So during my freshman year, I switched to economics and got myself into the joint BA/MA program. If I couldn't find a career I would love, at least I would do something in business that paid well.

A little bit more about Manuel. He's from Brooklyn—born and raised. His sister Reina and he are the first two in their family to go to college. He doesn't speak much Spanish around me—unless he's insulting me—but at his house, his family speaks it almost exclusively. His dad worked his way up from being a busboy to a chef at a swanky restaurant while his mom took care of everything else, as supermoms do.

■ ■ ■

Now that you know how Manuel and I became besties, let's get back to more recent times. Friday had come—the day of the week when most of us are in the office instead of visiting clients. In the past on Fridays, like every other day of the week, I would eat lunch at my desk or grab something quick nearby. I tried to stay busy so I could ignore the pangs of loneliness Fred delivered every morning around eleven forty-five.

For the past few months, however, at Dr. B's urging, I had been going out with coworkers on Fridays. This particular day, I went out with Manuel and a few other associates to Catch 35, a seafood restaurant near Dearborn and Wacker. Someone had made a good choice; I could eat shrimp, fish, mussels, and lobster all day every day. There was no outdoor seating at the restaurant, but since it was early May, it was too cold to sit outside anyway.

Manuel asked the group, "Okay, so what's the best pump-up music? Like right before a game or during a run or something? What's your go-to jam? Me, I gotta go with the *Watch the Throne* album. 'No Church in the Wild' if I had to pick one song."

Manuel likes to raise impromptu surveys—he's like a human TableTopics—but I wasn't engaged at the start of his questioning. Rather, I was pondering the survival rate of diving from the top of the Marina City buildings, probably because of that old car insurance commercial. I speculated the two towers, which look like giant elongated honeycombs, were sixty stories high, so about six hundred feet, and the Chicago River was about ten feet deep. Not accounting for crosswinds or my complete lack of high-dive training (this isn't NASA, after all) and thus assuming I would land in water (by no means a guarantee), my best guess was that I had a 99.5 percent chance of severing the C5 region of my spine. I'd take those odds any day.

"Anything by Disturbed," said Richard Choi, a twenty-six-year-old guy born and raised in Naperville, an affluent suburb a half hour west of the city.

I think he's Korean, but I'm not positive, and I've known him far too long to ask. I only know he's not Japanese because his last name is mono-syllabic. He has an athletic build and sports one of those trendy haircuts where the sides and back are shaved and the top is long and combed to one side. He went to an Ivy League school for college before returning to be close to family. He's not so bad to work with—doesn't seem to think others have to fail for him to succeed—but I'm pretty sure he was one of those guys back in high school who wore one polo shirt over another polo shirt, with both collars popped.

"Or Five Finger Death Punch," Richard added.

I can't say I disagreed with Richard; I've been known to listen to his choices when the mood strikes me.

"Toby Keith or Tim McGraw," suggested Blair Powell.

From a small sample size, I generally have a high opinion of Blair, despite his first name and his tendency to wear sweaters tied around his neck. Seriously, I've seen him do it multiple times, as if he's always about to leave for the yacht club. But his acerbic humor entertains me, as long as it's not directed at me. Although his musical taste does not align with mine.

"What about you, Wright?" Manuel prodded.

I pretended to weigh his question seriously. "Sarah McLachlan, 'Silence.' Hands down." I floated it out there like a Pee Wee football pass, waiting for someone to intercept it.

"Come on, *hermano*," pleaded Manuel. "Seriously, don't embarrass yourself."

"I am serious! When she jumps to that high-pitched 'In this white wave, I am sinking, in this silence.' How would that not jack you up?"

No one acknowledged any familiarity with that golden melody, so I went on in my best falsetto. "'I have seen you, in this white wave, you are silent. You are breathin', in this white wave I am free.' Come on, you guys know what I'm talking about! She has the voice of an angel."

I was messing around with them. Sort of. The techno remix of the song is damn good.

"You can't expect us to believe that the lady who sings the song about stray dogs gets you amped up," Manuel said.

"That commercial is about animal cruelty, you heartless bastard. But fine, how about..." I paused to think for a moment. "'Adam's Song,' by Blink 182."

"Dude, you're messed up," Richard chimed in. "Isn't that song about suicide?"

"Nah, it's about apple juice in the hall, Richard," I said. "And it has an antisuicide message. The lead singer said so himself. But fine. What about 'Jumper,' by Third Eye Blind?"

I couldn't help but notice the suspicious expression on Manuel's face, but it disappeared when I looked at him.

■ ■ ■

A few hours after lunch, Manuel swung by my office.

"Hey, man, a few of us are going to happy hour—which you know will transform into more drinks and then late-night food. You in? You haven't come out in a while."

"I can't. I'm supposed to meet Rachel for dinner." A lie. "And I want to get an early start tomorrow. Need to run a bunch of errands, and I haven't been to the gym in a few days." These two statements were true, but still lies. I probably wouldn't get to either. The truth was, Fred was feeling like a soaked comforter. I needed to be alone, and I didn't want to have to tell anyone that I needed to be alone.

"Come on. I owe you a drink. And Jeff and Matt are coming out for once."

I didn't know who Jeff and Matt were, so that didn't tip the scale much. "Are Luke and Bryan also coming?" I could play the make-up-fake-names game too.

"Who?"

"Never mind, bad joke. But I can't make it, sorry," I said. "You know I'd come if I could." I followed that up with a fake sigh.

The brief look of irritation that flashed across Manuel's face made it clear he didn't believe me. I wasn't convincing.

"Alexis Owens might be coming," he said as a last-ditch effort. "Maybe you can finally make your move."

"I play the long game. You know that."

"There's a difference between a long game and not playing," he said.

Alexis was part of our incoming class at the firm, so we had gotten to know her fairly well. But she was in a different group on another floor, so I rarely saw her. A year or so ago, I rode the elevator up with her. I mumbled "Hi" and something about the weather, and then I crashed and burned on a joke my memory has graciously forgotten. Awkward silence that must've lasted forty-five minutes followed. Since then, my long game had consisted of reversing course immediately or ducking into a restroom if I saw her coming.

"What do you know?" I said. "Your strategy is to simply stay at every bar until close, hoping someone is desperate."

I had struck a nerve, which I had been trying to do.

"Fine, man. Do whatever you want. One of these days I might stop asking."

As he turned to leave, he smacked the Sidney Crosby bobblehead off my desk.

"You've gone too far!" I yelled in faux outrage as Manuel left. "You know how susceptible he is to concussions!"

If he found it funny, he gave no indication. So Manuel.

Chapter 3

RACHEL'S TURN

It was Saturday morning around ten thirty. I banged on James's apartment door, politely at first. Then again at full strength for at least a minute. No answer, and now my hand was hurting. I pulled out my copy of his keys and let myself in. This wasn't the first time I had needed to check on him.

The smell of stale beer was overpowering, and it came with a whiff of garlic and sweetness. Barbeque chicken pizza probably. It's an insult to real pizza but James's favorite.

"I'm coming in!" I yelled. "I'm here. Wake up, wake up, wake up," I called in a singsong voice. I can be an obnoxious sister, but in a cheerful way.

James's place is in a high-rise in SoNo, a newer neighborhood south of Lincoln Park. Easy to get to via the Red Line from where I live in the South Loop. Good luck taking a cab there, though. Traffic is bad anywhere in Chicago, but particularly terrible around SoNo.

The door to his lone bedroom was cracked open. No light or sounds escaped from within. I quickly surveyed his place. A half-eaten pizza sat on the coffee table, an open fifth of Jack next to it. Two empty cans of Fist City were lying on the floor, and I saw two more lying on the kitchen counter. I see this type of scene most weekends, but I'm still in college. I started to clean up, making as much noise as possible.

"What are you doing here? Go away," James moaned from his room.

"I'm not leaving. Get in the shower. I'll make coffee." There were some plates in the sink generating new forms of life, so I tackled those next.

Twenty minutes later, James came out of his room mumbling. I noticed a bruise on his cheekbone, and the dark circles around his eyes made him look like an old-timey burglar.

"Go away," he repeated.

"You're always so welcoming. It's no wonder I love you."

"Seriously, why are you here?" he groaned. He sounded so ridiculous that I had to stifle a laugh. I didn't want to be too obnoxious.

"Check your phone," I said.

"Ruh roh," he mumbled. Then he started sorting through his messages.

I had woken that morning to twenty-one messages. Nineteen were from James. All between twelve thirty and two fifteen. The first few were dumb inside jokes like "You up? You out? S'up?"

The spelling and syntax of the texts devolved in reverse proportion to their seriousness. Text seven asked how a carpenter from a small town would have developed oratory skills. Text thirteen insisted there was life on other planets, but mankind was doomed never to confirm its existence. Text sixteen queried whether…

"I really asked you whether people would miss me more if I died in quicksand versus falling through ice on a lake? What the hell?"

"I know. Not your best moment," I told him. "Quicksand is forgivable. It can catch you by surprise. Falling through ice just means you're an idiot."

"Get out."

"I know you don't mean that. Besides, I haven't finished cleaning your kitchen." I was in a cleaning groove. I couldn't stop right in the middle.

"Fine," he grumbled. "You can stay as long as you keep working. Then let's go get brunch. Until then, no talking."

"But what if I think of something that's funny?" I couldn't help myself from pestering him.

Instead of verbally responding, he used his hand to mimic a mouth closing. He was lucky I didn't punch him.

I finished in the kitchen, and then James led me to a breakfast place that sat next to a strip club. It was across the street from a grocery store. Sometimes zoning laws don't work.

We sat and ordered food, and then I began my interrogation. "So, I came over today to check on you because of the text messages. But now there's something else I want to ask you about."

"Okay."

Where to begin. Where to begin. "I don't know where to begin," I conceded. Brilliant!

"T-t-today, junior."

"Hold on. I'm thinking."

"By all means. Move at a glacial pace."

"Shut up. I was cleaning your place before you came out. Your laptop was sitting on an end table, open and on. I saw a Word document. It was about you 'seeking the end' and wanting to jump off a cliff."

It took a second for this to register with him.

"You read it?" His lips were pressed together in anger.

My turn to say "Ruh roh."

"What made you think that was okay?" he demanded.

The volume of his voice remained level, but I could tell he was raging a little inside. His eyes had morphed from blue to gray. I hesitated to answer. He was about to yell but hit his thigh instead.

Through gritted teeth he asked, "Why would you of all people betray me like that?"

I had never seen him so hostile, at least not with me as the target. "Give me a chance to explain," I pleaded.

"Let's hear it."

"I didn't mean to read it at first. Really. But I then read the parts about you wanting to jump off cliffs or crash your car, and I was worried. So I kept on reading. It scared me."

A tear or two dripped down my face. I'm not good at containing my emotions. "Are you honestly thinking about killing yourself?" I didn't want to embarrass him, so I whispered. My lip was quivering. More tears were coming down. Shoot.

"I'm fine," he said.

His face had become a mask. I couldn't read him. When did he learn how to do that?

"I'm not going to hurt myself, I promise. Just my way of venting. I started a journal, but I decided to turn it into a book that I may or may not ever finish."

"It didn't sound like venting," I told him. "It sounded like you contemplate dying. All the time." More crying.

His emotionless facade broke slightly. "I'm sorry I upset you. You know I would never want to make you cry. I'll be fine."

"Are you seeing someone? A doctor, I mean? Or taking medication? You can't make this go away with an apology." I'm not an expert in suicide, but I've looked into it before, given James's history of despondency.

The waiter came by with our food while my face was still covered in tears. I momentarily wondered if he thought James was breaking up with me. Why would I have been worried about that, given the circumstances?

"It's none of your business. But yes, I'm seeing a psychiatrist and a counselor that works with her," he said. "No, I'm not taking medicine. I told you, I'm fine. The reason I'm writing the book is because my doctor suggested that I start a journal about my life events and any destructive feelings that I may have. I don't want to write 'Dear Diary' all the time, so I turned it into a book format. My memoir."

"I'm not sure I believe you. I don't know how to process this."

"I don't care what you process." A grin appeared on his face.

"Jerk! You can't smile your way out of this!"

"Busybody! I can. What have you been up to lately?"

"No, I'm serious, James. This isn't over. I have more questions to ask you. I—"

"It's over for now. I don't want to talk about it anymore today." His voice was firm, but I was not deterred.

"I do want to talk about it," I insisted. "You mean so much to me, even if you don't care about yourself. I don't want to think about losing you!" I tried not to yell, but I was still crying. I was starting to crumble.

"Rachel, I love you, and I hear what you're saying. But I'm done talking about this now. Especially here. I'm not going anywhere."

His voice remained firm, but it had become cold as well. My resolve faltered. I would have pressed him harder if he had raised his voice. Or if

NOT TODAY, FRED   21

he had otherwise shown a lack of control. He was right, though. It was not the best time or place for an all-out confrontation.

"Okay. I'll drop it. On one condition."

"What's that?"

"You let me read what you write each week."

"Request denied."

"Fine." Shoot for the stars to land on the moon. "You don't have to let me read your book. You do have to let me write my own passages for it."

"If that will make you happy, it's a deal," he said.

Whoa. He was giving in way easier than I had expected. I was momentarily speechless. "And you promise you're seeing a doctor about this?"

"I promise," he said, exasperated.

I smiled and breathed. I think I was holding my breath for most of the conversation. I hugged him before I left him that afternoon, and I told him I loved him. Then I punched him in the arm and threatened that if he killed himself, he would never find peace. I would ask him Ouija board questions every day and conduct séances every night. He had been warned.

I know he thinks my idea to write my own passages doesn't make sense, but I'm two steps ahead of him. Whenever he reads what I write, he'll know how much I love and care about him. Call it my insurance policy against him doing something stupid.

Chapter 4

FROM THE DESK OF DR. PRIYA BHATTACHARYA

Wright, James
February 20, 20XX

James Wright is a 24-year-old man who was referred by his primary care physician, Dr. Mark Bennett.

HISTORY OF PRESENT ILLNESS: Mr. Wright indicated that approximately a year ago, he ingested a large number of over-the-counter pain medication pills in an attempt to end his life. His intake of the pills was preceded by excessive alcohol consumption. Shortly after ingestion of the pills, he forced emesis. He stated the prospect of his imminent death caused him instantaneous and overwhelming grief about how his mother would react. He did not seek immediate medical help after the incident. Last month, he mentioned the episode for the first time to his primary care physician, Dr. Bennett, who recommended that he undergo a psychiatric evaluation. Besides Dr. Bennett, he has not disclosed his suicide-related behavior to anyone.

Mr. Wright could not pinpoint any specific event or events that triggered his suicide-related behavior. He described being cloaked in a "black cloud." He notably gave this feeling a name, "Fred"—which continues to this day, but at the time of the event, he indicated he might have been particularly melancholic.

When asked if he was depressed, he paused, and his body language indicated a reluctance to answer. He did not view himself as "depressed," because he felt people suffering from depression had the negative connotation of being weak and "Debbie Downers"—i.e., generally not likable, or burdensome to other people. However, he acknowledged that his typical mood was one of mild unhappiness or discontent—as if "someone had smuggled a pea under his mattress, as the fairy tale goes." Nonetheless, he reported having occasional upswings that would last a few days to a few weeks—rare times when "Fred" is more of a "superhero cape" than an "evil nimbus." At other times, Fred weighs him down like "a bunch of rope arrows" (it appears Mr. Wright does not lack for imagination). It is at those times that his suicidal ideations are more thoroughly fleshed out.

Generally, he does not suffer from trouble sleeping or from lack of appetite. He did report fantasizing about his death, in one manner or another, multiple times per week. Typically, his ruminations focus on the legacy he will leave behind rather than on the manner of his death. Currently, he was in his "steady state," which as described above is a general sense of dissatisfaction.

He denied having had any plans to harm himself since the incident a year ago. He also denied any history of harming others or thoughts about harming others.

PAST PSYCHIATRIC HISTORY: Negative for any therapies, medications, or hospitalizations. In high school, his parents forced him to see a therapist after an incident at school, but he only attended sessions for a few months before giving up. He admitted to having had suicidal ideation prior to the incident a year ago. He denied present or past substance abuse problems. He has never been arrested.

FAMILY HISTORY: Significant for a father whom Mr. Wright described as "absent at best" and who occasionally overconsumes alcohol. He noted his sister, mother, brother, and maternal grandmother drink socially, but he does not believe they overconsume. There is otherwise no family history of psychiatric illness, suicide, or chemical dependency.

PAST MEDICAL HISTORY: Negative for any medical problems, surgeries, medications, allergies to medications, or head injuries.

SOCIAL HISTORY: Disclosed that he was born and raised in Pittsburgh but has lived in Chicago for approximately seven years. He graduated with bachelor's and master's degrees in economics and for the past few years has been working for a large consulting firm. His father is an English professor at the University of Pittsburgh. His mother was a homemaker, but after his parents divorced, she resumed her marketing career. He is the middle of three siblings, having an older brother and a younger sister. None of them suffered any history of abuse.

He reported he has not been married or engaged, and he does not have any children.

MENTAL STATUS EXAM: Mr. Wright presented as an affable young adult male who was in no acute distress. He was alert and oriented, appeared to be of above-average intelligence, and had no discernible cognitive deficits. He described mild, but prolonged, depression, a single incident of suicide-related behavior, and suicidal ideation, as noted above, as well as some anxiety. His prior suicide-related behavior, prolonged depressed state, and mild mood swings suggest he suffers from cyclothymia, but not bipolar disorder.

IMPRESSION AND PLAN: Mr. Wright is a 24-year-old man whom I would diagnose as having cyclothymia. At this point in time, he is a good candidate for medication, despite being opposed to the idea. I discussed the risks and benefits extensively. I recommended that he have a trial of medication. He agreed to take a low dose of aripiprazole (Abilify), and I prescribed 10 mg once daily. I will see him for a return visit in about 2 weeks.

DIAGNOSES:

1. Cyclothymic disorder, 301.13.

■ ■ ■

March 7, 20XX

James Wright was seen for a return visit regarding the medication Abilify. He indicated he was compliant for 5–6 days, but he started to suffer spells of nausea and dizziness and discontinued use. I explained that it may take a week or two for his body to acclimate to the medication, after which time the side effects would likely cease. In addition, after some discussion, he conceded the side effects he experienced might have been more psychological than physiological. He agreed to make a second attempt at the trial of medication (10 mg once daily).

As to interim history, he indicated not much had changed since I last saw him. He still felt "tormented by a malevolent veil of mist," and although he reported that work was going well, most days he did not find it personally rewarding. His best workdays come when he is engrossed in an analysis project and does not have time, or the requirement, to meet with clients or colleagues. As to his social life, he went out with a few friends the previous weekend and enjoyed himself, but he remained discouraged that his romantic prospects were "Dementor-level grim" (he explained for my benefit that a Dementor is a fictional entity that feeds on the positive thoughts and souls of people, which I concur sounds grim). He was not sure how to improve upon his current status quo, but he indicated a willingness to attempt to be around people more, rather than spending most evenings and weekends alone. I suggested taking small steps—e.g., going to lunch with colleagues once or twice a week or joining a recreational sports league.

He denied having any active suicidal ideation—i.e., he has not planned his death in any manner—but admitted to having passive suicidal ideation multiple times per week the last 2 weeks.

I will see him for a return visit in about 2 weeks.

■ ■ ■

March 23, 20XX

In contrast to our last meeting, Mr. Wright indicated he had been compliant with the medication Abilify. He experienced some nausea the first few days, but the adverse effects ceased after about a week. He was not sure whether the medication had an effect on his mood or outlook. I explained it may take a few more weeks before he noticed such improvements.

As to interim history, he indicated he has started to go to lunch at least once a week with coworkers, although he reported being somewhat reluctant to engage in conversation until he feels a little more comfortable around his colleagues. He is also spending more time with friends, especially his friend Manuel. He also reported exercising at the gym more, which he believed was slightly improving his disposition. He even appeared somewhat jovial, joking that he's only "five packs away from a six-pack." As for work, he reported not much had changed, but that was "not necessarily a bad thing."

He denied having any active suicidal ideation, and he believed his passive suicidal ideation was occurring somewhat less frequently since he started taking the medication.

In the aggregate, because of the medication, increased exercise, and extra efforts to be social, he reported a belief that his outlook on life was finally improving. He analogized to a darkly lit video game with poor contrast, where the character cannot proceed to the next stage without completing a task, and the task itself, let alone the solution, is not discernible. As a result, the character repeats the same actions in frustration until a discovery is made, accidentally or otherwise, and the loop is broken. Mr. Wright reported feeling stuck in such a sequence, but he was now hopeful that his efforts over the last few weeks, combined with the medication and the therapy sessions, would break his loop.

I recommended that we meet again in two weeks and, if he has remained in compliance with the medication, that we meet less frequently in the future, but that he see a therapist in my office every two to three weeks. He agreed with this plan.

■ ■ ■

April 11, 20XX

James Wright reported continued compliance with the medication Abilify.

For interim history, he reported that he continues to go to lunch with coworkers, and his reticence to participate in the conversations has decreased week by week. He also saw some friends from college last weekend, and in addition to his workouts at the gym, he has started running outdoors as the weather improves. At work, he received positive feedback from a client and one of his bosses, which he appreciated, and he is starting to consider what his long-term career plans are. They apparently do not involve "hardcore consulting for the rest of his life."

He denied having any active suicidal ideation and reported his incidences of passive suicidal ideation have declined. He indicated a continued belief that he is working toward "breaking his loop." I recommended that he start a journal to his record his progress.

Per my prior recommendation, Mr. Wright will begin to see a therapist in my office every two to three weeks, and I will see him as needed.

■ ■ ■

April 27, 20XX		
PROGRESS NOTE	CLIENT NAME: Wright, James	START: 5:01 pm
	SERVICE CODE:	STOP: 6:07 pm
SYMPTOM STATUS: maintained	DIAGNOSTIC CHANGE? No	
CURRENT SYMPTOMS: depressed state		
	LIFE EVENT? No	
MEDICATION: compliant		
SAFETY: no active suicidal or homicidal ideation		
GOALS/OBJECTIVES: Treatment Plan Goal 1 partially achieved Treatment Plan Goal 2 partially achieved		
CLIENT RESPONSE: Full Compliance		
COMMENTS: First session with Mr. Wright after he was referred by Dr. Bhattacharya. He reported no complaints today but also had "nothing positive" to report. He reported being successful in his attempts to be more social, but there was nothing in his life about which he was enthusiastic. 　　　He also reported having recently started a journal to track his mood. I encouraged him to continue and to make sure he's tapping into how he's feeling while he's writing.		
NEXT APPT: May 11, 20XX		

Chapter 5

OF ALL THE STARBUCKS
IN ALL THE TOWNS IN ALL THE WORLD

When I got home after brunch with Rachel, the first thing I did was shorten the sleep mode delay on my laptop to fifteen minutes, and then I reset my password. There would be no further accidental discoveries by Rachel—or anyone else.

Nonetheless, as you can see, I kept my promise to let Rachel write some vignettes. It was the easiest way to get her off my case, and I can always delete her portions later on. Besides, at least her break-in resulted in my apartment being clean—or cleanish, anyway. Although, I noticed a braided bracelet Rachel must have left on my counter. She has a tendency to dress like a hipster—rompers, leggings with oversized tops, vintage band T-shirts—but it works on her long, thin frame. She's medium height with hazel eyes and long, light-brown hair that she calls blond—I don't argue with her because I don't enjoy being kicked in the shin. She obsesses over her eyebrows, and if she isn't smiling, her face is fixed in deep contemplation.

Part of me is relieved Rachel now knows about my dark secret. If I had been forced to tell someone, she's the person I would have picked. We have always been able to make each other laugh, or act as mutual sounding boards. During almost every morose dreamscape Fred steers me into, I reflect on how my deletion from this world would affect my family; my ruminations about Rachel disturb me the most. She's resolute in her faith and her convictions but willing to take up new causes; I worry she would become a champion against suicide, perhaps an at-risk counselor. I hate to think my actions would change the course of her life in such a dramatic fashion. Her trajectory is bounded only by the limitations she self-imposes, and I do not want to be the underlying impetus for one.

A nontrivial part of me, however, is ashamed I have this weakness and that I let it be discovered. Something to explore with Dr. B or the therapist, because when I do serious introspection by myself, it always leads to a hangover. I know in this day and age men aren't supposed to be afraid to play the clarinet, sing chorus tunes, and discuss their emotions, but I'm not quite that progressive. Probably my dad's fault.

I suddenly realized I hadn't talked to my dad in a while. I should check in. I picked up my phone, but didn't get any further. I had nothing of significance to update him about, and he's never been much of a conversationalist. So a few more days, or weeks, or months, wouldn't hurt.

Then my phone reminded me I had six unread text messages from Manuel, which I had pointedly ignored the night before, when I was busy replacing my bodily fluids with ethanol. The first few were typical guilt trip stuff. A little name calling, a little hyperbole about how many hot girls were at the bar. The last one was oddly prescient: *If ur drinking by urself listenng to Duran Duran, I'm gonna punch you in the junk.* Did I tell him I sometimes listen to "Falling Down" and "Come Undone" on repeat? I don't care who you are, those are some freaking good songs. Besides, I threw in some "Simple Man," by Lynyrd Skynyrd, and "The Man Who Sold the World," by Nirvana, for good measure—before downward spiraling into some Tool and Breaking Benjamin.

I would've texted Manuel back, but then he would have pressured me to go out. Fred hadn't air-dried, and I wasn't in the mood to make up excuses. I wouldn't be self-medicating with liquor and beer a second night in a row, but I also wouldn't be hanging out with Manuel so he could complain that no woman would talk to him while he simultaneously made no effort to leave our high top.

■ ■ ■

On Monday morning, I bumped into Alexis Owens in line at the Starbucks near our office. Not on purpose—had I seen her ahead of time, I would've slowed down to let at least three people separate us. Or even skipped coffee altogether that morning. Now the pressure was on, and I was terrible at flirting.

"Hey, stranger," she said with a wide smile.

My God, she's beautiful. Her enthusiasm was encouraging. *Maybe I can do this*, I told myself.

"Hey there! I know. I've been visiting clients a lot lately."

I said the last part at warp speed with poor diction; I'm pretty sure it sounded like "I've viz'n cly'nz ot-ly." I took a deep breath and swallowed. Moving my lips as little as possible and cocking my head away from her, I subvocalized "ow now brown cow."

Alexis kindly forged past my incoherence. "So are you going to the office event Wednesday night? Those things can be a bore, but there will be free drinks. And heavy hors d'oeuvres, I hear."

I hadn't been planning on going to the event, but it's amazing how plans can change. "I was on the fence. But if you're going, I think I can make an appearance."

Nice—played it cool. And I had said a full sentence without skipping any syllables. Get this guy a consolation prize.

"Great! I hate it when I go to one and I'm stuck talking to client reps I don't know all night, or to colleagues I barely know," she said. "I don't mind networking. I do mind having to be on the entire time."

In the abstract, I understood what she was saying, but I'm rarely in the position she described. I spend at least half my life not wanting to talk to anyone, so the last thing I'm going to do is insert myself routinely into situations where I'm forced to chitchat with strangers for several hours. Death by poisonous snakebite sounds more appealing.

"Well, I'll do what I can to help you out." I had to tell myself to slow it down. That was ludicrous speed. "I'm pretty good at schmoozing," I overenunciated. Nothing had ever been more untrue.

"You are?"

She asked this with a little too much skepticism for my liking. I was clearly not the life of the party, but did she think I was the guy who created Dungeons & Dragons quests by himself on Friday nights? Because there was no way she could know; I've never told anyone.

"No. I'm terrible at small talk. I think you've seen that in action just now." My joke elicited a small smile. I was scoring some points. "But by comparison you'll look like a rock star. I can be your business wingman."

"Sounds like a plan, James. Bring your best C-minus small-talk game."

"I couldn't be better if I wanted."

At that point we were at the front of the line, and Alexis was ordering her drink. I was about to offer to pay, but then I worried if that would be too forward. Or chauvinistic, because she had the same job as me and could afford to pay for herself? Maybe I should have expected her to offer to pay for me in these enlightened times? Before I could make up my mind, she was already scanning her phone to pay.

We walked the short distance to the office together, and I managed to keep the conversation going with no awkward lulls. Everything was surface level, but you have to start with baby steps, right?

As I exited the elevator a few floors before her, she said to me with a smile, "Don't forget about Wednesday. I'll be counting on you to make me look good."

I was too excited about how this encounter had gone to say anything witty in response. It was going to be a good day. Suck it, Fred.

Back at my desk, I couldn't stop thinking about Alexis. She's tall—like close to my height with heels on—and thin, with an athletic build and strawberry blond hair that falls a little below her shoulders. It has some natural curls, but most days she takes the time to straighten it. Sunlight magically shines through her tresses at all times, as if she were a seraphim herself—one hundred Freds could not mask her radiance. Her cheeks have subtle dimples when she smiles, and her laugh is boisterous and infectious. But not too loud, unlike those people who seem to be shouting at you with their guffaws.

As they are wont to do, however, my thoughts took a morbid turn. I had a reverie about walking down the street with Alexis and a huge black SUV careening onto the sidewalk toward us and several other pedestrians. Using the reflexes of a jungle cat, I shoved Alexis and the others with all my might out of the path of the accelerating vehicle of death. But then I was crushed between the car and the stone wall of a building. As my life ebbed away, Alexis extolled my many positive qualities, beginning with my blue eyes and sandy blond hair—I'm attractive like a supporting actor, or maybe just an extra—and promised to name her firstborn son after me. Not a bad way to go.

Everyone daydreams, right? Some more than others. Sure, the subject matter usually isn't so macabre, but the darkness of my imagination is not dispositive of a latent fatal flaw in my code. Poe and Orwell didn't off themselves—not that I'm favorably comparing myself to them—and those guys weren't exactly beacons of levity. They both died pretty young, but that's not the point.

■ ■ ■

"So you fell off the face of the earth this weekend. No response to my texts. You must've been hiking in a remote forest? Or testing a new underground bunker?"

Manuel framed all his questions as declarative statements as he strolled into my office. I wasn't expecting him to stop by so early in the morning, but I was prepared for, and deserved, some harassment.

"Close. Reina wanted to get away with me for the weekend and wanted my undivided attention at all times. You know I'm powerless to resist her feminine wiles."

His sister is a couple of years older than us and currently single. She's physically attractive, but it's her flirty personality that guys find so enthralling—or at least I do. I'd never in a million years hit on her for real, but it's an easy button to push with Manuel. Over various breaks during college, I would drive from Pittsburgh to visit Manuel at his parents' house in New York. Reina was still living there to save money. She would purposely tease me by making lewd comments or by walking around in a towel after taking a shower. While I had mixed feelings about her behavior, Manuel had only one: rage.

Manuel punched me in the shoulder before I had a chance to evade—being seated in an office chair made it difficult to duck and weave.

"You ever go on a date with her again, I'll cut your nuts off. With a rusty butter knife."

I never went on a date with Reina. This was all a misunderstanding. Last spring, I was in New York for training, and I stopped by the Ramirez house late one afternoon to say hi to Manuel's parents. They couldn't stick around long because they were meeting friends, but Reina was visiting. I think she was bored, or otherwise her plans for the evening had fallen through. Whatever the cause, the effect was that she took me to her favorite restaurant in the neighborhood, and then we walked around for a couple hours. I had a good time and learned more about who she is as opposed to how good she looks in a towel, but neither one of us ever gave the slightest indication that it was more than platonic. Ever since then—I'm pretty sure after a phone call with Reina in which she "innocently" told Manuel how much she enjoyed my surprise visit—Manuel has half-heartedly accused me of trying to date his sister. Or maybe it isn't half-hearted. Who can say for sure?

"I gotta take you to the gym," I said. "You look like Olive Oyl throwing a punch."

"So you bail on me last weekend, you insult my sister's honor, and then you talk smack about me? You sure that's how you want this to go, *carajito*?"

I never know what the hell he's saying when he throws his Puerto Rican slang and Spanish words at me. Sometimes I look them up later, phonetically, if I'm able.

"No, Manuel. Let's start over. Sorry I didn't make it out on Friday or text you back Saturday. I just didn't feel like being around people."

"So I've noticed. You don't have to be Sherlock Holmes to observe that you've been in a funk."

The way he said it, I couldn't tell if he was annoyed or being compassionate. Maybe a little of both. I was trying to think if I'd been Eeyore more frequently lately than normal, but I couldn't recall.

"Well, today I'm not. Guess who I ran into this morning?"

"If you say Reina again, I will murder/death/kill you."

"No. Stop obsessing over your sister. It's not healthy. I bumped into Alexis at Starbucks."

"Alexis Owens?"

"Yes."

"Wait," Manuel interrupted. "You mean you didn't do that lame thing where you slow down to a crawl so that she doesn't see you?"

"No, I didn't do that lame thing where I slow down to a crawl," I mocked in my best impression of Manuel's voice. It sounds like him if he were part Wookiee and had a speech impediment. "I probably would have, but I didn't see her. So I had no choice but to dazzle her with my charm."

"So you blew it?"

"Manuel, you're a terrible best friend. I *almost* blew it. The first few things I said were unintelligible. But she was stuck in line with me, and I eventually regained my faculties of speech."

"Well, I suppose forming words is one-tenth of the battle," he said.

"Exactly. It's important to be able to do more than nonverbal gestures." I'll have to include that when I write my Guide to Dating Women: *Expect to be required to do more than point and grunt.*

"Anyway, I told some jokes, she smiled at me, my heart simultaneously melted and leaped into my throat. No one vomited. Things went well."

"Awesome, man." He seemed to say this with pure excitement—no trace of sarcasm. "So you asked her out?"

"Not exactly, no."

"What? You finally talk to her, you're not making an ass of yourself, and you don't ask her out? How long is your long game?"

"Well," I said, "I didn't—"

"Seriously," Manuel said. "Take some chances once in a while. You've been secretly pining over her for like three years."

"What I was going to say, you horse's ass, is that I didn't ask her out because she sort of beat me to it. She's going to the firm client event on Wednesday and wanted to make sure I was going too. So I'll see her there."

"Okay, fine." He paused to collect himself. "Rant retracted. I hate those client appreciation things, though," he said with disdain. "Have fun. I'd rather spend an evening alone with Graham reading Shakespeare."

Graham is an associate principal with whom Manuel and I have both worked. He's desperate to make partner. He has the appearance of someone you think is going to be hilarious, but he's not funny at all. If you were playing a role-playing game in which you had to assign points to various attributes, Graham's humor score would be 0. It doesn't stop him from trying to tell jokes, though. And he has a habit of reciting Shakespeare at inappropriate times, which is basically all the times.

"You're going too," I informed him. "You have to."

"The hell I am. I'm not going to that ass-kissing festival."

"When did we start using the word 'ass' so much?" I had just noticed our proclivity.

"I've been trying to cut down on the worst swear words. Something has to take their place. Ass it is."

"That's sound logic, my friend. But you have to go because I need you, Manny. I need a wingman. I don't want to be following Alexis around like a lost puppy all night. I probably can't do that anyway, because clients will talk to her. I won't be that guy that eats food by himself at a high top all night, trying to make eye contact with anyone that walks by. Or the guy that gets lit at the bar while he tries to talk to whoever has to squeeze next to him to order a drink." I lose sleep over being stuck in those types of predicaments.

"First, don't call me Manny. Second, how often do you fixate on being the lonely guy at the bar?"

"What frequency could I tell you that doesn't result in you making fun of me?"

"No frequency."

"Okay then. I concocted those scenarios on the fly, just now. My mind works very quickly; you know that. I excel at improv—"

"*Callate*." Manuel said. "I'll go, but only because I feel so bad for you."

Joke was on him. I have no shame when it comes to getting my way, so his pity was wasted. "Excellent. Mission accomplished. See you Wednesday night... Now get out."

"Hold on. I have something to tell you. It's—"

"No, Manuel. This conversation was about me only. No stories about you. Save it for Wednesday."

He started laughing to himself. "You're lucky I'm your friend."

Then he left, but only after knocking my Troy Polamalu bobblehead off my desk. Such beautiful hair should never be exposed to dirty carpet.

Chapter 6

TUESDAY, WEDNESDAY, BREAK MY HEART?

The rest of Monday and all of Tuesday sped by, and then time slammed on its brakes Tuesday night, like one of those techno dancers who vogues at hummingbird speed only to jerk his or her body into a pantomime of a three-toed sloth. It's cool the first forty-five times they do it, but then you realize they're just standing in place moving their arms. That's why they all need sweet nicknames like Glytch or Rypcord or Flynch—I made those all up; I'm not cool enough to know any hip-hop dancers, but I do know there's always a *y* replacing an *i* for some reason. But there's nothing awesome about insomnia. My mind wouldn't stop racing about the myriad ways I was going to blow my chance with Alexis.

On Wednesday morning, I woke up with a headache and raccoon eyes. Lack of sleep is hard to hide when you have alabaster vampire skin. My dad used to joke that I needed suntan lotion in the womb. Hardly fair on his part, considering he's halfway responsible for my condition. I hear that pale skin is all the rage in China, but I have never been to China. If Alexis rejects me, maybe I'll move there. If the local women are not intoxicated by my bleached complexion, I could always jackknife off the Great Wall.

Needless to say, I was a bit of a mess at lunch. On the way to the restaurant, at least twice I reconfirmed with Manuel that he was still going to the event. I let it be known that our continued friendship depended on his attendance.

We were sitting in Gage on Michigan Avenue—Manuel, Richard, Blair, me, and a girl named Samantha Carlson, whom I only vaguely recognized. Woman, I mean, not girl. I don't mean to be chauvinistic. My longtime default was to call a group of males "guys," and females "girls"—regardless of age. It streamlined everything. But I had a female college professor who did not appreciate my limited gender lexicon, and she grew weary of reminding me of its inadequacy. Every once in a while, despite her robust efforts, I lapse back into it.

Anyway, back to lunch. Gage is one of my favorite places—crowded bar in front, table seating in the back, and the venison burger is crazy delicious—but my stomach wasn't into it that day. Manuel was expounding on why Yankee Stadium was the best place to watch a baseball game. I don't think the rest of us cared all that much, none of us being diehard baseball fans, but you're not going to find anyone who's lived in Chicago for any length of time to agree that the experience of Wrigley Field can be surpassed by another baseball stadium. It's in the heart of a safe and affluent city neighborhood; it's surrounded on all sides by bars, restaurants, and brownstones equipped with bars and rooftop bleachers; it's easily accessible by the Red Line; the outfield bleachers consist solely of seats in direct sunlight—no supercilious bars with umbrella tables; and no one goes home until at least three hours after the game (because of the surrounding bars).

"Seriously, Yankee history alone is enough to top Wrigley."

"Move on, man," Richard said. "You aren't going to win this one. None of the rest of us have been to Yankee Stadium. And we don't need to go, because we have Wrigley."

"Fine. You're all wrong, but whatever," Manuel said. "So, Sam, James has a big night tonight. He's hoping to win over Alexis Owens at the client event."

I visualized a Batwing shuriken lodging in Manuel's neck.

"Oh, I think I know her," Sam said hesitantly. "Blond, pretty, super nice?"

Pretty? Super nice? Try again. She's beauty and compassion personified.

"Yes," I muttered without opening my mouth, still firing laser beam eyes at Manuel's stupid face. I didn't see any visible effect, but one of these days I'm going to pull off some kind of telepathic or telekinetic power. It's my destiny.

"James, I didn't know you were into women," Blair jested.

At least I think he was jesting.

"I thought you were the asexual type," he continued, needlessly in my opinion. "Like you can appreciate why people are interested in sex on a scientific level, but it's never piqued your interest personally—raised your flagpole, so to speak."

"I don't understand your subtle innuendo. Please explain." No Bat-darts for Blair, just punches to the throat by Kevlar-encrusted fists. I don't like being caught in anyone's comedic crosshairs, so I said this a little more aggressively than intended.

"Relax, relax," Richard said. "I don't think Blair meant any harm. We're just intrigued that you're into someone."

Blair's smug face suggested he meant exactly what he said.

"So why Alexis?" Richard asked.

I could have told them about how she's always armed with a ready smile, regardless of whether she's tired or stressed. Or about how she can be positively giddy when she's happy. I could have recalled the time I saw her surreptitiously give the janitor an envelope of money because his son had been in the hospital, whereas I didn't know the janitor's name let alone that he had a son with medical problems. Or I simply could have explained that when I'm in her presence, life felt like a lazy river on a sunny day with Fred nowhere to be seen—instead of a sulfurous swamp through which I had to slog. But I wasn't about to divulge the extent of my feelings to them.

"I don't know," I said. "I think she appreciates my asexuality. She's into me not being into her." There was still an evident edge to my voice.

"Damn, okay, we'll drop it. Sorry I brought it up." A little late there, Manuel.

"Well, good luck tonight, James," Sam said diplomatically. "I'm rooting for you. Maybe I'll see you there. I haven't made up my mind whether I'm going."

"Thanks, Sam. I hope to see *you* there. You would be better company than these losers."

I wish I had come up with a better insult than "losers," but my eloquence sometimes suffers when I'm angry or embarrassed. At that particular instant, I was both. Blair's comments would have been irksome to anyone, but they annoyed me so much because they hit close to home. I love women as much as anyone—an appropriate context to avoid saying "girls"—but I haven't dated anyone since college. Heck, I haven't had a single date in more than a year. Manuel jokes that I should join a seminary, but I like theology less than I do chemistry labs.

The truth is, Fred is the ultimate antiwingman. If he's not persuading me to stay home, he whispers doubts in my ear all night long like Wormtongue. I often find it easier to give in to him ahead of time, rather than have to deal with him in the presence of other people.

■ ■ ■

The firm event was at an open-concept bar and restaurant on Michigan Avenue, within walking distance of our office. Our marketing people were getting better; the particular bar is a trendy place to host an event, and most of the area was reserved for us. I walked over with Manuel fashionably late—fashionably late because I had to wrap up a conference call first, and with Manuel because there was no way I was going alone. Like I said, I lose sleep worrying about being the lonely guy at the bar. The first thing we did was head to an open spot to order some bourbon on the rocks. I needed an artificial confidence booster.

"Alexis is here," Manuel whispered discreetly into his left shoulder, as if he were a Secret Service agent with an earbud. "Five o'clock, by the pillar."

I began to scan the room nonchalantly. Target acquired. She was talking to three guys whom I didn't recognize; they must have been clients. Did I need to be worried about any of them? None of them seemed that attractive, but one had just made her laugh. Fred was coaxing me to abort the mission, suggesting it was doomed from the start. I did my best to ignore him.

"It looks like she's busy at the moment. Let's walk around and see if there's anyone worth talking to."

"Copy that. Proceed," Manuel ordered.

"I like the spy thing you're doing right now."

"I knew you would. That's why I'm doing it. Now move out."

"Roger."

We left the bar area walking diagonally away from Alexis, but in a manner that allowed us to insouciantly keep an eye on her. Maybe not so casually, because I almost walked straight into Sam.

"Hey, you're here. Good to see you."

"Yeah, you too!" said Sam as she gave us both a quick hug, which I appreciated.

Sam is a tiny little person, but the way she carries herself makes her seem much larger. She has mocha skin, voluminous ringlets of dark hair that drop to her shoulders, and large doe eyes.

"Have you talked to Alexis?"

So nice of her to ask.

"Negative. We're doing some reconnaissance and threat assessment first. Then I need to do an internal review of my talking points. Contact is phase three. Also, we just got here."

"I didn't know you guys had a full-scale operational plan," she said, playing along. I was really starting to like this little lady. "Is that what you did after lunch?"

"I'm only going along with the secret agent stuff for his benefit," Manuel uttered, throwing me under the bus. "I wouldn't even be here if it wasn't for James and his quest for love."

"Yeah, yeah, I know, you're too cool for school," Sam said. "You'd never pretend to be a spy for your own amusement."

Anyone who makes fun of Manuel gets a gold star in my book.

"Right, never," Manuel confirmed.

"Don't let him fool you, Sam. He has Nerf guns and walkie-talkies in his apartment. Last week he wanted to build a fort."

Sam was looking past me and apparently missed my stellar jokes.

"It looks like Alexis is about to break from that group of guys, James," she said. "You might need to skip to phase three in a hurry."

She was right. Alexis's drink was empty, and she was turning toward the bar. Her acquaintances did not appear to be going with her. I needed to act fast. I downed most of my drink so I would have a plausible reason to be at the bar, and I started my approach while humming the *Mission: Impossible* theme song. Then, in a slight panic, I started subvocalizing "Red leather, yellow leather; red leather, yellow leather." Don't judge me.

I caught up to Alexis as she was setting her empty glass down.

"Well, look who it is." I managed to say this with appropriate volume and enunciation. As to inflection? That's anybody's guess.

She turned and smiled. "Hey, you're here!" she exclaimed. "I was looking for you earlier, but didn't see you."

She...was looking...for me. Did you hear that, Fred?

"I had to finish a client call before I could leave the office." *Stop and breathe, James.* Words were supposed to have distinct sounds. "Did I miss anything?" I asked with methodical enunciation.

"Nope. These events are pretty much always the same. Although those guys I was just talking to weren't so bad."

Damn. I had been hoping they were lame so I could shine by comparison.

"Well, what are you drinking? I'm buying."

"It's an open bar. The firm is paying."

"Exactly. I can at least flag down the bartender."

A smile. Point for James! "Okay. Vodka soda with a lime," she said.

"Three shots of Jack it is."

"Ha ha, very funny."

She said this while lightly shoving my upper arm. I'm no body language expert, but wasn't that a sign that maybe she liked me? I wished I'd had time for a second drink before I bumped into her; my sweat glands were starting to kick into high gear. Does Xanax prevent excessive perspiration? I should talk to Dr. B about that.

We collected our drinks and walked away from the bar to meet up with Manuel and Sam. They seemed to be getting along well; there were arm touches and gentle pushes aplenty. I made a mental note to interrogate Manuel about their "friendship" at a later time.

"Alexis, I know you know Manuel, and this is Sam. Sam, Alexis."

"Hey, Manuel. Hi, Sam. I've seen you around before. Nice to officially meet you."

Alexis seemed so comfortable in her own skin. I was a little jealous, but mostly just impressed. I wondered if she was naturally outgoing, or if it was practiced. Either way, I wished I had that skill.

Out of nowhere, Julie, an associate principal I've worked with on several occasions, tapped me on the shoulder.

"James, I'm glad you came to this client event. You're listening to my feedback to interact with our clients more. There are some people from Blue Cross you should come meet."

Just like that, I had to leave Alexis behind. Apparently fate was on Fred's side and not mine.

■ ■ ■

I eventually escaped Julie's clutches and was talking to Manuel while scoping out Alexis's location.

"Hey, the thing I wanted to tell you the other day," Manuel was saying. "It has to do with—"

Richard interrupted him by lumbering over with his arm around Blair.

"Help me," Richard pleaded in a stage whisper. Then, a little more quietly, "Blair is trashed."

"James, what's up, homo?" Blair almost yelled at me. "Hey, Manuel."

Trashed indeed. "Quite a greeting," I said.

Apparently we were the only ones who had heard Blair's outburst, which was extremely fortunate for him. I'm pretty sure a bigoted comment like that gets you fired these days. I assume getting super drunk at corporate events also is frowned upon.

"You're not," Blair slurred.

"What happened?" Manuel asked Richard, ignoring Blair's nonsensical response. "The event's only been going on for an hour and a half!"

"Blair got here early with a couple other guys, before the event even started," Richard said. "I think the others wisely left. I've been trying to get Blair to drink water, but he keeps chugging drinks instead."

"Shots!" Blair shouted. "Shots, shots, shots!"

Blair was so obnoxious that I was tempted to stand back and watch him put his job in jeopardy. But his yell gave me an idea.

"Get Blair to the bar in a minute," I instructed Richard and Manuel. "I'll make sure he drinks water."

"Good freaking luck," Richard said, "but okay."

I caught a bartender's attention and asked her for four shots of grenadine and water, and a tonic water with a lime. Then I pointed discreetly to Blair and asked that if he ordered any more drinks, she only give him tonic water.

"Not a problem," she said. "That guy's been pissing me off all night."

I could only imagine.

As Richard and Manuel saddled up with Blair, I handed them shot glasses. Richard was about to argue with me, but I mouthed "water" to him.

Blair downed his shot without suspicion, and then I handed him the tonic water.

"Let's hang out here for a few minutes," I told them. "I need a break from small talk." This was true, but I was also grasping for a way to keep Blair away from others.

"Sounds good," Richard said.

"Hrmmph," grunted Blair. But he stayed put.

For the next twenty minutes, we employed various tactics to keep Blair glued to the bar. At one point he tried to shove Richard, but his impaired balance and coordination undercut his effort. As Blair's eyes began to droop and he slumped against the bar, Richard and I guided him as casually as we could to the exit, while Manuel went off in his own direction.

We got to the door and Richard asked, "What do we do next?"

"This is as far as I go," I said. "Do you know his address?"

"Yeah, he lives on Seminary in Lakeview."

"All right. Put him in a cab and tell the driver where to go. Or go with him if you want. But I'm done being a Boy Scout."

■ ■ ■

Finally rid of Blair, I grabbed a real drink and then redoubled my efforts to intercept Alexis, without making it look too intentional. I was only able to do so a few times over the next hour or so—once even without premeditated movement on my part. None of the opportunities gave me a chance to talk to her in private for more than a few minutes.

As the event drew to a close, Shakespeare Graham approached a small group of junior associates, of which I was one, and as he patted one of us on the back, he quoted, "'Listen to many, speak to a few.' Am I right?"

I had no time for his nonsense, so I crept away from the group like a pickpocket. I was mentally chalking up tonight as a moderate success when Alexis called my name.

"James, hey, you're still here! Good! I thought I might have missed seeing you leave."

So she was keeping tabs on me as well, eh? Presumably in a much less creepy manner than I was.

"Yep. I was just about to grab a cab," I said. "Manuel left a few minutes ago."

"Which way are you headed? I live in Lincoln Park."

"I'm on the way, in SoNo."

"Do you want to share a cab?" she asked me, clearly miffed I hadn't asked her.

"Yeah, sorry. Let's do that."

"Okay, great. Let's go."

On the ride north, we chitchatted about various people we had met and random office gossip we had heard. I tried to stay in the moment—isn't that what people say you should do?—but I also couldn't stop thinking about how this was exactly where I wanted to be. In Alexis's presence, with her undivided attention. No man had ever been luckier.

"This is me," I told the cabbie as we pulled up to my building and I struggled with how to say goodbye.

I had spent the last thirty seconds analyzing the options. It would have been way too presumptuous to go in for a kiss, and besides, I didn't have the gumption to pull that off. A handshake seemed way too formal, a close-quarters wave far too effeminate. Ultimately, the decision was easy, because she leaned over to give me a one-arm hug at the same moment I had decided that was the best course of action.

"I had a good time. Thanks for convincing me to go."

"Yeah, me too!" she said. "But I thought you said the other day you were already thinking of going?"

She had a sly look on her face, so I knew she was messing with me, but I still started to turn red. "I've said too much," I blurted, intentionally awkwardly.

I began to open the car door, but then I turned and asked, without worrying about the consequences—I had no idea my brain was capable of such an achievement—"Do you want to go to dinner this weekend?"

What have you done? my mind screamed belatedly. *Too soon!* Beads of sweat started to form on my brow. It was like Fred had mainline access to my sweat glands.

"I'd love to," she said.

Oh, thank God. I can breathe.

"But I can't. I have plans already. Do you want to go out two Fridays from now?"

I was about to make a lame joke like "I have to check my calendar first," but I fortunately stopped myself. She'd been nothing but direct with me, and there was no question I wanted to see her again. And there sure as hell wasn't anything on my social calendar.

"Yes, sounds good. I'll check in with you next week if I don't run into you."

"Okay, great. Have a good night, James."

"You too."

I handed her money for the cab ride and jumped out. All in all, I would give the night an A. If it had been a Dungeons & Dragons quest, I couldn't have scripted it any better. I was smiling like an idiot as I walked past lobby security and got on the elevator.

Chapter 7

RETURN OF THE MACK (RACHEL AGAIN)

The Friday after I confronted James had arrived. The weekday weather was unseasonably warm for mid-May. But in true Chicago fashion, the temperature was plummeting toward the forties for the weekend. Boo. Hiss.

James had asked me to go dinner with him. I couldn't remember the last time he had initiated weekend plans with me, so I was tensed for bad news. I've come to expect the worst when something out of the ordinary happens involving him. When he greeted me in the entrance to Girl & the Goat, my fears were replaced by a state of bewilderment.

"Hey, Rach!" James exclaimed as he hugged me. "Thanks for coming."

"Who are you? Where's James?"

"Ha. You're so witty. A brother can't be excited to see his baby sister?"

"Brothers in general can be, yes. But not you. You're kind of freaking me out."

The first thought I had was James was on drugs. And not of the prescription variety. But I dismissed the idea as too preposterous. I had never had a reason in the past to suspect drug use. I shouldn't have jumped to conclusions then.

"Okay, fine. I know I can sometimes be like Sadness from *Inside Out*."

He had picked an analogy I recognized. I am a huge Pixar and Disney fan.

"But I've had a good week for once," he said, "and I wanted to tell you about it. But more importantly, I realize I don't always check in to see how you're doing. Like you do with me. So I want to hear how school is going and about life in general."

We had definitely entered the twilight zone, but I was truly touched. I know James loves me and cares about me, but he's not always good at relaying his feelings. I'm sure part of that is because he's a guy. A bigger part is because he's *James*. Evil stepmothers are more liberal with their praise. He's not unlike Dad in that respect, but I would never tell him that.

"Thanks, James. That's very sweet of you. Let's get a table, or a drink if there's a long wait. I'll tell you all about me."

"Works for me," he said. "I'm still getting used to you being able to drink legally in public."

"It's a nice change of pace."

No one would confuse me for the partier type. Nor would they suspect I drank alcohol before turning twenty-one. I usually don't drink enough to get drunk, but I enjoyed my first glass of wine in high school and never looked back.

The walk-in wait appeared ominous, but it did every time I was there. The restaurant had been a smashing success since it opened. The inside was full of wood and earth tones, with an extra-long bar on one side and modern sleek design elements. But it was the award-winning food that packed the house every night. The eclectic menu had something for everyone. James and I are not picky. We eat almost everything. No, let me rephrase that. We enjoy all cuisines, but we have high standards for food.

We ordered drinks at the bar to help pass the time, but Lady Luck was on our side, and we were seated within fifteen minutes. So far, there had been no indication James had repeated his one-man binge-drinking session.

"So," James began, "how's your junior year at the University of Chicago going? Have you figured out how to save the world?"

My program of study is public policy, with a focus on environmental science. My dream job would involve evaluating and establishing long-term renewable energy programs for US cities that are lagging behind. Governments at every level should be harnessing natural energy sources and protecting the environment.

"Couple more weeks and then yeah, whole world saved," I replied. "No pollution, world peace, cancer cured."

Sarcasm never comes as naturally to me as it does to James. I had to force that one out. James waited for my truthful answer.

"It's going well. I'm looking forward to my internship this summer. It's with a company that created a thermal battery. It's an artificial ice composition intended to be integrated with air-conditioning systems. In the summer, it can be used as a substitute for the air conditioners to save on electricity. It should be good experience learning how energy start-ups function and grow."

"That's awesome, Rachel. I'm excited for you. Is it paid or unpaid?"

"It's unpaid, but my school is giving me a stipend."

The stipend is key. I could always ask Mom or Dad for some money. Sure. But I like that I'm starting to be a little more independent.

"Even better. I'm proud of you."

He was smiling. That happens on the rarest of occasions. I couldn't tell if it was genuine or mocking.

"Thanks, James. You mean it?"

"I do. I'm jealous you know what you want to do from the start, and you have a plan to execute your dream. I wish I had a dream, let alone a plan."

I'd never heard him talk this way about work. I always had the impression his consulting gig was going well.

"What do you mean? You have an awesome job. There are a hundred things you could do if you ever want to leave."

I have a general idea what he makes. Money isn't a priority for me, but I'd be more than happy with his salary.

"I know it's a good job," he said, "and I know I could go somewhere else if I wanted. You know what I mean, though. I've never had a passion for business consulting. Who in their right mind does? It pays the bills, which is good because of my expensive tastes. But maybe one day I'll find what drives me, like you have. If only I could get paid for writing Amazon reviews. That would be sweet. Who knows, maybe I'll blog or something. But you—you have your passion. Stick to it no matter what."

"Thanks. I will. I'm as motivated as ever. I need to be, because this school year has not been easy."

Sometimes I feel like all I do is study, go to class, study, go to class, study, go to sleep. Then repeat.

"Junior year can be the toughest. Don't worry; you'll make it. Things still going well with your roommate…"

"Sarah?" I offered.

"Yeah, her."

He never remembers her name. Poor Sarah.

"Yep, no problems there. We're both so busy that we hardly ever see each other. And neither one of us dates all that much. There have been no awkward mornings when I wake up to a random dude standing in my kitchen."

"Shush, I don't want to hear about 'awkward mornings.' Ever. As far as I'm concerned, you'll be a virgin until forty. I only want to know if there's a guy I need to rough up."

"Okay, tough guy. Lips are sealed. But enough about that. Tell me, what was so good about your week?"

"Have I ever told you about—"

"Wait!" I said. "Let me guess what your good news is." He paused, which I took as acceptance. So I started guessing. "You got a raise?"

"No."

"A promotion?"

"No."

"You bought a new suit?"

"No," he said with a smile. "That would make me happy, but it wouldn't make my whole week. Just half of my week."

"Okay. Then it has to be a girl?"

"We have a winner," he said.

My instincts had told me that from the start, but I'd shrugged them off. As far as I knew, James hadn't been on a date for a year or two. It's hard to get out there and meet someone when you refuse to "get out there."

"All right, who is she? Would I approve? Would Mom approve? Tell me everything." I might have been hyperventilating.

"Slow your horses." James laughed. "One question at a time."

I waited for him to say more. He was purposefully remaining silent, drawing it out.

"James! Details! Now!"

"Okay. Have I told you about Alexis? The girl at my office?"

"The one you avoid at all costs?"

Everyone knows about her. Bus drivers and Red Line conductors know about her, from James.

"Yeah, her," he said.

"Didn't you once walk into a Victoria's Secret store just so you could avoid her on the street?"

It was comical how he had faceplanted into a pane of glass. Plowed right into the revolving door. Divine intervention is the only explanation for why she didn't notice him.

"You have me mistaken for someone else."

"No, the whole scene is coming back to me. I was with you. You almost broke glass with your face."

"These aren't the droids you're looking for," James said as he waved his hand in a slow arc.

"Whatever you say. So she's the woman? What happened? Tell me everything. Now."

I was desperately trying to recall as many details about her as I could. It was no use. All I could remember was blond hair, and she was physically fit. I was instantly jealous of her physique.

"I don't know. Are you sure you want to talk about this? Tell me more about school."

"James, if you don't stop stalling, I'm going to kick you in the nards." I didn't like resorting to such base threats, but it was not an idle one. James knew that.

"Okay, okay. I thought you'd never ask. The short version is I talked to her early in the week without stuttering, we hit it off at a client event Wednesday night, and we're going on a date a week from now." He was practically giddy while telling me this.

"I'm so happy for you! You have to tell me the long version."

James proceeded to recount the whole story. When I thought he was glossing over a particular part, I made him stop and elaborate. If I have to deal with his moodiness, he has to deal with my enthusiasm.

"Well," I said. "She sounds pretty great. I hope next Friday goes well too."

"Thanks."

"It's about time you dated someone normal. Or any person, for that matter."

"Shut up," he said with a smirk.

"Remember that weirdo Melanie you dated in college? She had some screws loose. Like seven screws."

"She just had a strong affinity for unicorns and dolls. She wasn't that weird."

I just stared at him.

"Okay, she was weird," he said. "And a little creepy. Her dorm room looked like a children's psych ward."

"How would you know what a children's psych ward looks like?"

"Stop challenging me. Go back to fawning over Alexis."

"No."

"Fine. I can assume what a children's psych ward looks like."

"Sure. What about the wannabe Valley girl you dated for a little while in high school? What was her name?"

"Brittany," he said.

"Right, Brittany. 'Like, so, what do you want to do, James, like, I dunno, go to the movies, or something?'"

"She wasn't so bad," he protested. "I liked that she talked so much, even if it did grate on the ears. The less talking I had to do, the less likely it was that I spoke incoherently."

"Is that your ideal companion? Someone who talks so you don't have to?"

"Back then? Yeah."

"Didn't you get catfished right after college too? Didn't she say she was—"

"Enough," he said. "No more about my past dating life."

"All right. Well, good luck with Alexis. If it goes well, you'll have to let me meet her soon."

"Not a chance."

"James!"

"Fine. Maybe. Let me get through this date first."

"Okay."

I have to say, he seemed like a whole new person. No signs of his depression were showing. There was no indication he had had any suicidal thoughts. Alexis must be a miracle worker.

Chapter 8

UNWELCOME CONCERN

My phone was ringing Saturday afternoon. The ringer was the *Halloween* theme song, which meant it was Andrew, my brother and superior in age only, I like to say. I couldn't imagine why he was calling.

"Hello?"

"Hey," he said.

Nothing followed except awkward silence.

"So, what's up, Bro-bani Yogurt?" I'd been waiting to use that one.

"Huh?"

"Bro Jackson?"

"Huh?"

"Broba Fett?"

"Why are you making stupid bro puns?"

Totally wasted on him. It's like he sucks all the joy out of life.

"Never mind, Andrew. What can I do for you?" I could count on one hand the number of times he'd called me, and none of them were to shoot the breeze.

"Mom said she talked to you a couple weeks ago."

Another awkward pause followed.

"Yes, this is true. I talked to her more recently too."

I usually talk to her at least once a week. She brought me into this world and raised me for eighteen years before I spread my wings and left the nest; the least I can do is check in regularly.

"Was there something in particular you wanted to discuss?" I asked.

"Not really. Mom mentioned you were a little depressed and said I should call. So why are you down? Tough week at work or something? You didn't lose your job, did you?"

I'm going to have to have a talk with my mom. She wasn't doing me any favors here. I'd rather stand naked in front of a room full of strangers while they audibly critiqued me than talk to Andrew about my suicidal fantasies or any other problems.

"No, I didn't lose my job, but thanks for immediately jumping to that conclusion. I'm fine. Don't worry about it."

"Yeah, Mom said you would say that. Is it a girl thing? Are you coming out of the closet?"

What a scumbag. "I'm actually doing pretty well right now."

Fred had been threatening to make an appearance the night before, but he couldn't overcome the high I had still been riding from Wednesday night. I hadn't gone more than a half hour without thinking about Alexis.

I was about to add a snide comment but held my tongue. My mom and Rachel tell me I'm too confrontational with Andrew. I don't think they realize the complete lack of empathy he demonstrates, at least toward me, but that doesn't mean I should avoid the high road.

"Thanks for asking, though," I said. "What's new with you?"

"Same old for me. Working all the time per usual, but Leslie and I have a few trips planned. We're going to the Keys for a long weekend in a few weeks, and then we have a destination wedding in Turks and Caicos at the end of June. Should be a good time."

He recited this all offhandedly, as if everyone could afford to take multiple beach vacations in a short period of time and pay exorbitant prices. I bet he'll be staying at a Four Seasons for both trips and tips everybody a single dollar bill.

Andrew is a senior associate at a giant international law firm. He tells everyone he meets that he's "pretty much a lock to make equity partner in a few years." On a coordinate grid, the probability approaches 100 percent (the y-axis) as time approaches ninety minutes (the x-axis). He's probably right because he's always excelled at school and work, but that doesn't make it any less obnoxious. Leslie, his wife of three years (or is it four?), used to be an associate at an equally large law firm. Now she's in-house counsel for an international corporation. Because they make a combined ungodly amount of money, they have no sense of a budget: if they want something, they buy it. But they also have precious little time to enjoy all their wealth. Once, when Leslie was complaining about this "predicament" at a family holiday party, I lightheartedly offered to experience life on their behalf, at their expense. She looked at me like I was a kindergarten class wall covered in smeared boogers.

"That does sound like a good time," I patronized. "Does the beach have Wi-Fi?" I couldn't help myself from throwing in a barb.

"Funny," he deadpanned. "Don't worry; my phone can always act as a mobile hot spot." He was dead serious when he said that, as if he already had planned to have his laptop on the beach. "So you're sure you're good, sport?"

Sport? I'm only four and a half years younger than him, and he's not a sixties dad. "Yeah, I'm good. Thanks."

"Okay, good. I was worried we'd have to come visit you in some mental hospital. Or install a padded room in our condo to take care of you." He was being facetious, but with a strong trace of his true feelings.

"I would never want to be a burden to you, Andrew." I would also never want to live with him. "Mom could always upgrade the wrestling room at home for me. It's already mostly padded."

Andrew had started wrestling in junior high, and he somehow persuaded my parents to convert the small bedroom in the basement to a practice gym, installing a wrestling mat on the floor and padding halfway up the walls. Despite being much younger and thus much smaller, I was often Andrew's practice buddy. There was nothing chummy about it. On his particularly vindictive days, that room morphed into the Seventh Circle of Hell.

"Yep, that's true. Well, I should get going..." He trailed off.

No misinterpreting his intentions there. Our short call, which he had initiated, must have been approaching one tenth of an hour—Andrew's standard unit of measure for billing clients. I would have been offended, but it's not like I wanted to drag the call out any longer.

"Sure, thanks for calling. Say hi to Leslie for me."

"Will do. Later."

"Bye," I muttered, I think after he'd hung up.

I felt much better. Thanks, Mom.

■ ■ ■

Unlike with Rachel, the consequences my premature death would bring Andrew do not cause me much heartburn. I surmise he would grieve genuinely but fleetingly. At my funeral, in true *American Psycho* style, he would enthusiastically eulogize me as the Paris to his Hector, rather than as the Cyrus the Younger to his Artaxerxes that I really am. He would even quote a Phil Collins song for good measure. I think he sometimes invites the comparison intentionally.

In the more distant future, he would toast me at a holiday dinner with some form of backhanded compliment, or reminisce about how I was always hopelessly trying to match his prowess in sports and academics. Andrew suffers from a god complex. I diagnosed him last year.

If I'm being honest with myself, which I should be since this is my cathartic memoir, I try not to flesh out in my mind's eye how Andrew would react. I have a lot of pent-up anger toward him because of how he treated me as a kid—and continues to treat me as an adult—so I assume the worst about him. That, in turn, only makes me more downcast. We're brothers; we should be there for each other. What alarms me more than anything is that maybe I'm right about him—maybe he would barely miss me. So facing reality isn't an option; cracking jokes about it is the way to go.

I've considered trying to talk to him—to try to repair our relationship—but I'm not sure how he'd respond. And once I'm on this train of thought, it doesn't take long for my dad's voice to pop into my head. "Suck it up, James. Stop being so weak. Your brother was never a crybaby like you." I think that was his idea of a motivational speech. He certainly expressed those sentiments enough times that I didn't need a poster to remember them.

Fred seems to be bringing in a cold front despite the good week I've had. That usually means holing up in my apartment until the storm has passed.

Chapter 9

TUNNEL VISION

Five days before my date with Alexis, I arrived on time (that is, five minutes early) for a Monday team meeting. There was only one other person in the conference room, Elizabeth Foster. No Liz or Beth for her. You refer to her by all four syllables, or you do not refer to her at all. She shouldn't have to remind you.

Elizabeth is notorious in the office for wearing low-cut and formfitting blouses, sweaters, and dresses, and she magnifies the effect by propelling her ample bosom upward and forward with what I assume are bras two sizes too small. The result, while striking, is the sexual discrimination equivalent of a Vietnamese punji stake pit for the unwary male coworker. This day was no exception. Treating her like Medusa and using only my peripheral vision—a piece of broken mirror would've been ideal—I observed that Elizabeth was wearing a skin-tone blouse that plunged ever so downward and an unbuttoned royal blue sweater that was doing nothing to protect her modesty.

Don't look at her boobs, don't look at her boobs, I chanted like a mantra in my head.

"Good morning, Elizabeth."

I looked right at her boobs. Dammit! It was almost impossible not to when she was sitting down and I was standing up—it was a matter of basic geometric optics. I could hire a physics expert to defend me. But everything was okay. She was still looking down at her phone. No one would be contacting HR, but I reminded myself to get it together.

Elizabeth typed on her phone for at least thirty more seconds before setting it down and looking up.

"Hi, James. How are you?"

She used the facial expression and tone of voice of a restaurant hostess who just had customers walk in five minutes before close. Was she always this pleasant? I hadn't been alone with her enough times to know. That's probably a good thing because if one listens to the gossip, and I do, one hears rumors she's an EEOC Jedi Master with two or three sexual discrimination claims pending. They're probably all valid, knowing this place, but it wouldn't hurt to stay on my best behavior.

"I'm doing great," I proclaimed in my cheeriest of voices as I took a seat across from her.

I wasn't being entirely truthful; Fred was bugging me, but I felt compelled to be obnoxiously upbeat in light of Elizabeth's asperity. Kill 'em with kindness, as they say. I take the same approach at restaurants to minimize my intake of spittle.

"I'm excited to be wrapping up this project. The drive has been a real drag." My nerves might have caused me to slur all of those words together. Who can say?

"I know," she said as blandly as pad Thai with no spice. "Plus, there are no good restaurants or bars out here. Or maybe it's that no one on this project ever goes out." Pure acidity in every word.

I'd been keeping my eyes at or above a ninety-degree plane to avoid being turned to stone, generally focusing on Elizabeth's right eyebrow or the empty space to the left of her head. But when she made that comment, my concentration wavered as I tried to ascertain whether her complaint was directed specifically at me or at the team as a whole. While I was pondering, I noticed her pull both sides of her sweater together, as if she felt the need to cover herself. A pointless gesture, as her sweater would be back in its original position within seconds. I knew I hadn't been looking at her chest—at least I hadn't been registering it if I had been—but I was feeling self-conscious, and my neck was turning red. It didn't matter that I wasn't looking at her cleavage; she thought I was looking, or wanted me to think that was what she was thinking, like a game of wits with a Sicilian when death was on the line.

"Are you okay?" she asked me. "You look a little blotchy," she pointed out in a not-helpful manner.

She knew what she was doing—if she was acting intentionally. But that didn't matter now. *Pull it together, James. Eyes no lower than ninety-five degrees.*

"I'm okay. I think I ate some bad shellfish last night. The blotchiness has been coming and going." I had no idea if food poisoning could result in skin irritation, but I was grasping at straws.

Just then the door opened, and four more people walked into the room. Just in the nick of time. I may have to rethink my early-arrival policy for team meetings, at least ones where Elizabeth is on the team. I was fairly certain there would be no HR contact coming from that episode, but I was going to need a beer at lunch.

■ ■ ■

Later that day, I walked into the office Manuel shares with another associate named Miles Parker—a not unusual arrangement at our company for junior associates, although I had somehow managed to get my own. Miles is not my favorite person. He has dark messy hair and is gaunt, like he's perpetually on a hunger strike. I can only assume he dresses in Gothic clothing when not at work. I have suspicions Miles is a domestic terrorist or a cannibal. That day, like most of the times I visit Manuel, Miles thankfully was not around.

"Dude, have you ever had to interact with Elizabeth Foster?" I asked Manuel.

"I have." He said this without looking up or otherwise pausing to note my presence.

"At work?"

"Yes." He was still looking down, like he was trying to find Waldo.

"Did you get the feeling that maybe she was trying to set you up the whole time?" I paused to give him time to respond, but he remained silent. So I went on. "You know, like purposely trying to catch you checking her out?"

"Yes!" he exclaimed as he jumped up. "She's like the Temple of Doom! So many booby traps!"

I couldn't help but laugh in the face of his sudden enthusiasm, which I now understood he had been setting up. "I know. I know. I had a meeting with her today, and—wait. Was that pun on purpose?"

"Heck yeah it was." Manuel's Cheshire Cat grin revealed how proud he was of himself. "That one's been in my back pocket."

"It's pure gold," I admitted. "But you were just hoping one day someone would mention Elizabeth Foster in your presence? Just so you could say 'booby traps'?"

"Well, come on. It was a foregone conclusion someone would," Manuel said. "But I didn't have to wait for just her name to come up. I could've used that joke with several other female coworkers—and one male coworker."

"I see." Apparently, Manuel was an avid observer of the female body, and of at least one male body, HR risks be damned. "Don't tell me who. I'd rather discover them on my own and then confirm with you, instead of you telling me all at once. You know, like you did with the five remaining Cylons."

Manuel laughed. "Are you ever going to get over that? It's been years now."

"No," I said. "I will forgive you, but I will never forget." I suppose it's partly my fault I never watched the rest of the episodes, but *Battlestar Galactica* requires some serious tenacity to finish.

"Speaking of female coworkers, though, what's going on with you and Sam?"

"What do you mean?" Manuel was trying to act blasé, but I had caught him off guard. I can read him like a children's smiley face book designed to teach emotions. Right then Manuel was surprised with a touch of embarrassed.

"Come on. I saw the way you guys were acting at the client event last week. You're either dating or hooking up, or one of those things is about to happen."

"You're crazy, *chacho*. I wouldn't dip my pen in the company ink like you're trying to do. Besides, how could you have noticed anything? You couldn't stop staring at Alexis all night."

Shakespeare's "the lady doth protest too much, methinks" popped into my head, and I quickly dismissed it. I hate that phrase because it's a catch-22. You either remain quiet, which prompts people to assume you're guilty of whatever allegation is being bandied about, or you deny it, which also spurs people to assume you're guilty. It's a worthless argument.

"Incorrect, my dear Watson," I replied. "As you may recall that night, I was focused more on my surroundings than on Alexis specifically. Like a member of the League of Shadows. You see, I needed to scope out the most opportune times to talk to her. During some routine surveillance, I happened to notice you and Sam rarely left each other's side, and there was a lot of smiling and laughing happening."

"So we talked to each other and had a good time. Big deal. I know you don't have firsthand experience, but that's what people do when they're out at a bar."

"A lot. You talked to her a lot." He was starting to collect himself, but I wasn't going to let this go easily.

"Fine, whatever. It's not like I went home with her." His lie betrayed him. Time to close this case.

"Are you sure about that?" I asked innocently.

"Yes."

"Because I saw you leave with her." Boom goes the dynamite!

"Now I know you're crazy. I walked out the front door by myself."

He tried to state this emphatically but couldn't quite pull it off, although in his defense, his face hadn't turned bright red like mine would have. Then again, his Puerto Rican coloring spares him some of the indignities that my cadaverous epidermal layers do not.

"Aha! That's what you wanted people to think. But I saw Sam lurking outside in the cab line, and you joined her. Then you both got in the same cab. Busted!" This Perry Mason moment was exhilarating! I could see why he did it for nine years.

"What are you, the office Gossip Girl?"

"I wish, Manny. Think how much power I'd have here." Seriously, Gossip Girl was damn near omniscient and had leverage over everyone. I was suddenly reminded I hadn't watched long enough to find out who Gossip Girl was. Maybe she was a Cylon.

"Fine, you win," Manuel said. "We've been hanging out for a few months, and we made it official a few weeks ago."

"Wait a second. You've been hiding this from me for months?" How could I have missed this?

"Not exactly. I told you once when you were drunk, but I figured you would forget."

"That was a safe bet."

"Yeah, seems so. I was going to tell you again at that client event, but Blair got in the way. We've also been pretty sneaky on purpose, and I'm not giving you any other details. If you tell anyone else about us, I'll burn your house down."

"I don't own a house." He should have known this.

"*Vete pa'l carajo.* You know what I mean. Seriously, dude, please, don't tell anyone," he pleaded. "Neither one of us needs the office to know. We have no idea how the partners would react."

"Have no fear. I will protect your secret just as Bane protected Talia al Ghul's identity."

"What the hell are you talking about?"

"*Dark Knight Rises?*"

His face showed no sign of familiarity.

Spoiler alert. "Bruce Wayne entrusts Miranda Tate with control of his company and his fusion reactor? But Miranda turns out to be Ra's al Ghul's daughter? And then she literally stabs Batman in the back? The whole time Bane keeps her true identity a secret." I feel like I have to explain everything to him sometimes. It's exhausting.

"Why would you reference that now?"

"Because I just joked I was a member of the League of Shadows. This is all perfectly linear!"

"Your brain is wired funny, *mano.*" More Puerto Rican slang I needed to look up. "But thanks for keeping it a secret. Although if you noticed something that night, it's possible someone else did." He paused to think for a moment. "If anyone asks you about us, please deny it rather than pretend you don't know anything. The latter is never persuasive."

"Cool. I can do that. Do you want me to pretend to be dating Sam to throw people off?"

"No. Nice try."

"I can be very convincing."

"Get out of here."

I looked for something to knock over before I exited, but his office lacked any personal touches, so I left sans dramatic flourish.

As I walked back to my office, I daydreamed about Manuel and me walking down the street. He was asking me to promise I would take care of Sam if he died young. Not to date her, he clarified. Just make sure she, and any kids they may have, would have enough money to live comfortably. I made that vow and was about to ask for a reciprocal pledge from him, but then my subconscious stopped itself. I hadn't even been on a date with Alexis yet; not even dream fantasy me wanted to get too ahead of myself. Besides, if I ever marry, it will probably be of the mail-order variety.

■ ■ ■

Wednesday came, and so far I had not run into Alexis. I supposed I'd have to be a man about this for once and intentionally visit her in the afternoon. I considered just texting her, but that would have undercut the significance of the potential date. The occasion required a bit more gravitas.

That afternoon, after a pretty hectic morning, I worked up the nerve to visit her. By worked up, I mean I had a beer and a shot at a late lunch. Alexis was just hanging up the phone and looked a little frazzled—stunning still, but not quite herself—when I stepped into her office. "Hey there. I was just stopping by, but I can come back if you're busy." I had done some mouth exercises on the way to her office; I think I got all my words out in a coherent manner.

"Hey, umm, no, I could use a break. For a few minutes anyway. It's good to see you."

She was smiling while she spoke, but her voice didn't match the words. Was she forcing the smile? Or was her stress restraining the smile? Was she annoyed I was there? *Stop thinking so much, James.*

"You sure? I don't want to interrupt whatever it is you're working on. I mainly just wanted to make sure we're on for Friday." Knots immediately formed in my stomach. It was one thing to ask her out under the cover of darkness after imbibing a small distillery. It was another to confirm our plans in the light of day.

"Okay, if I'm being honest," she said, "I'm slammed right now. So I don't have time for a break. But we're definitely on for Friday! I was starting to worry. I hadn't heard from you since last Wednesday."

Dammit, I knew I should've texted her. "I was playing hard to get. That's what I do."

"I should've known. You play games, huh?"

No, that wasn't what I wanted her to think. Why did I always have to make jokes? "Nah, no games. I actually typed around ten texts to you over the weekend, but then I deleted them all."

"Ha! Come on. You don't have to try to make me feel better."

She was coming off genuine. How could this radiantly beautiful person have had the slightest doubt about whether I was interested in her?

"Nope, not trying to make you feel better," I said. "I was nervous. Even right now, I'm like five seconds away from sweating." *Come on, James. Is that the mental impression you want to leave behind?* "But I'm excited about Friday. I made reservations at Piccolo Sogno for eight p.m. Does that work?"

"Perfect."

"Great. I'll get out of your head now. Hair—I meant hair." She just smiled as I fumbled with my words. "It sounded like you got twenty-five emails while I was here."

"Thanks, sorry. See you Friday!"

I'm pretty sure I floated all the way from her office to mine, with Fred completely absent. I could get used to that.

Chapter 10

FRIDAY I'M IN LOVE

I woke up Friday morning with a dilemma: shave or not shave? If I shaved, maybe Alexis would appreciate I had made the effort to be clean cut for our date. But the ladies also love a five-o'clock shadow, right? My reddish-blond facial hair is too fair to be visible unless I haven't shaved for several days, but I do look grittier when I've let it grow—although not gritty in a Wolverine type of way; more like a baby-faced hockey player trying to grow a beard for his first playoff series. After an internal debate that lasted far too long, I went the traditional route and shaved. I figured there was no way Alexis's interest in me was contingent on her thinking I was a bad boy.

I went to work and spent most of the day embroiled in various tasks, but I can't tell you specifically what I did. My mind was fixated on my date with Alexis that night, alternating between pure excitement and sheer dread, like a kid in line for his first haunted house. To help ease my nerves, I made an imaginary list of anecdotes and stories in case the conversation lulled. No one's ever said I'm not prepared.

I departed work around six—one detail I do remember—and headed home to shower and change. The first thing I did when I walked in my apartment was blast Sublime from my speakers, and the second thing I did was crack open a beer, because what I got was the makings of an anxiety attack. I didn't want to be too buzzed when I met Alexis, but I definitely needed something to take the edge off. Also, it was after six thirty on a Friday night; when your grandma starts making her vodka tonics at eleven in the morning and your mom refers to Friday night—all Friday nights—as scotch night, it's sacrilegious not to have a drink in hand. Alcoholism does not run in my family, just an appreciation for fine spirits and craft beers.

I tried on essentially my entire closet. Too formal and Alexis would think I was pretentious. Too casual and she'd think I didn't care about our date. And women say men have it easy. That is likely still true, but the scales are evening out. I eventually settled on dark jeans, a dress shirt, and a light-gray blazer with a blue windowpane print. I opted not to go with a tie or pocket square. It was a first date, not the Kentucky Derby.

Piccolo Sogno was brimming with people when I arrived twenty minutes early. I hadn't planned to be quite that prompt. I hate fighting for a spot at restaurant bars, or worse, loitering by the hostess stand like an apprentice learning the fine art of guiding people to tables, but I also can't stand killing time at my apartment when I have somewhere to be. I'm the kid who tied his shoes and put his backpack on before his mom was even downstairs to drive him to elementary school. Luckily, I found a seat at the bar and ordered a glass of barbera in relatively short time.

Surrounded by couples, the bartender distracted by other customers, and refusing to perfunctorily stare at my phone, there was nothing to do but drink my wine. I finished the first glass and was contemplating a second when I saw Alexis walk in. She didn't notice me at first, which was good because I was shamelessly staring at her. She looked incredible, sporting a puffed-up ponytail and wearing a black, high-waisted dress that stopped slightly above her knees—just high enough to show off her slim and toned quad muscles. Her calves needed no assistance, but her black high-heel shoes were doing their job anyway. Have I mentioned she has fantastic legs?

I took a deep breath, subvocalized "She sells seashells down by the sea shore," and made my way over, the beer and wine keeping the frayed ends of my nerves in check. She noticed me about ten feet away and flashed a bright smile. Fred had been on the fringes, but I could feel him disintegrating like the Nazi who "chose poorly" and drank from the wrong Holy Grail.

"Hey! You look great," I told her as I walked up and gave her a hug. "I like your dress!" *Did that come off genuine? Or was it creepy, like she should worry whether I will later try to make her skin into a lamp?* No apparent signs of distress materialized on her face. So far so good.

"Hi. You don't look so bad yourself. How'd you hear about this place? The patio is beautiful."

The interior of the restaurant isn't bad, but the experience is entirely different if you dine on the back patio, which is one of the best in Chicago. It's a garden oasis in the middle of the city, with lights strung through the tree limbs above you. I needed all the romantic help I could get.

"I'm a connoisseur of restaurants and bars with outdoor areas," I said. "This is one of my favorites."

"Oh, so you bring all your first dates here?"

Did she have a past life as a lawyer? How was she able to keep twisting everything I said, even if it was playful? I could tell she was joking, but I wanted to reassure her this was not a repeat performance on my part.

"Nope. First time here on a date, I promise. I have been here before with friends, and I took my mom here once when she visited. So technically my second date, I guess. But that one was purely platonic, I swear." *An Oedipus complex joke? Come on, James. You're better than this.*

"I'm just messing with you. You seem so relaxed," she said. Thankfully, she did not qualify her comment with *unlike all the other times we've spoken.*

I'd had a few drinks—that was why I was laid back, but I refrained from blurting that out.

"It looks beautiful, though," she said, referring to the courtyard. "I'm excited to eat here."

"Great. I hope you like it as much as I do. I'll let the hostess know we're ready."

They sat us in the middle of the patio, and we decided to order a bottle of Chianti. I needed to be careful. I didn't want to move from a delightful buzz to slightly drunk before she'd even finished a glass of wine, so I employed a ratio of three sips of water to one sip of wine, hoping that would do the trick.

We talked a little about work and some recent office gossip before Alexis hit me with a blunt question about my professional goals: "So are you hoping to make partner one day? Or are you just biding your time until you figure out your next step?"

People in my office remain tight lipped about their intentions, particularly when they're as junior as Alexis and I are. It's no secret that at least

75 percent of us will be gone by the time we're in serious consideration to make partner, but no one wants to lose their job and a steady income prematurely by openly discussing future plans that don't involve the firm. For this reason, Alexis's question unnerved me a little. Nevertheless, I swallowed down my suspicion that she was a mole sent in by the partners to divine my loyalty to the firm. Let's be honest: I had to assume no one cared that much.

"I haven't given it enough thought," I told her. "Some days I like what I do, but I can't say I have a passion for consulting. I'll probably just keep working until they force me out or tell me I'm being considered for partner. I do my best decision-making by deferring on all decisions. How about you? Did you always dream that one day you'd grow up to be a fancy business consultant?"

She smirked. "Not a chance. I wanted to be a professional beach volleyball player. I still do, but I knew I had to give up on my dreams when I stopped getting taller—and when I came to grips with the fact that I stopped getting better."

I temporarily lost focus thinking about her in a bikini on a volleyball court, sweat glistening on the small of her back, sand sticking to parts of her long, toned legs. *Now is not the time, James.* I willed myself to pay attention. She didn't seem to have noticed my wayward thoughts.

"How long did you play?" I asked her, trying to recover.

"Through high school and college. I went to Pepperdine, but I rode the bench most of the time. Almost all the other girls were taller and way more athletic than me."

I pinched my thigh to prevent the bikini thoughts from resuming. "Oh, come on," I said. "You must've been really good to play at a division-one school. That's impressive." She had more athletic chops than I did.

"Thanks," she said. "It wasn't a big deal. It was fun, though; at least I can say I was on the team."

"I don't care what you say. I couldn't have played D-one anything, so you have me beat. Though you've done a good job at avoiding my original question. What are your long-term work plans?"

She grinned. "Caught me. Probably not making partner, that's for sure. Don't get me wrong; I like my job. I could be happy making it a career. I just feel like I should be doing something more meaningful with my life. Working for a nonprofit maybe."

"What kind of nonprofit?" I was curious about her plans, because I always respect when people demonstrate a willingness to put others before themselves.

"I'm not sure exactly. Lately, I've been thinking of starting my own. I want to help single moms and high school dropouts develop vocational skills so they can find jobs—more than just those places that teach people how to make pastries. Something like training to be veterinary technicians or IT techs." I'm not sure what my facial expression was telling her, but before I could respond, she said, "I know, it sounds dumb."

"It doesn't sound dumb at all." I knew I liked her for more than her beauty. "I actually love that idea. Maybe I'll work for you when they force me out. If you'll have me, of course."

"Ha, sure, you can be my first underpaid employee."

Every time she smiled at me, I envisioned a gold star going up on my chart, and when I earned enough stars, it would mean she was ready to be with me for good. I am not mature when it comes to relationships, or life in general. This is probably not an earthshattering revelation to anyone.

"I'll take it," I told her. "I've thought about starting my own nonprofit, but I've never gotten past the 'thinking about it' stage." That was probably putting it euphemistically. I daydream about a lot of things, and not all of them are my imminent death.

"What would it be?" she asked. "Saving penguins? Feeding children in war-torn regions? Or something a little less dire, like making sure any pledge who wants to be in a fraternity can afford to be in one?"

She laughed at her own joke, which I found charming. If you can't amuse yourself, what the heck are you doing with your life?

"Well, I've had a lot of dumb ideas; I won't bore you with those. But there's one idea that keeps sticking. It's sort of like a Big Brother program. But not—" I stopped myself midsentence, unsure whether I wanted to reveal this idea.

"But not?" Alexis asked, drawing out the "not."

Dumb move, James. Now I had to tell her. "Well, it would be focused on kids who have...special needs, I guess is the best way to put it."

"Special needs? Like autism?"

"No, more like depression, anxiety, low self-esteem. Those kinds of things." The cringing face I made telegraphed that I suffered from some or all of those afflictions.

"Hmm, that's a worthy cause. What makes you want to get into…" She trailed off as my embarrassment became more pronounced.

I took a deep breath and did my best to forge ahead, while Fred suggested I was tanking fast. "It's not something most people focus on," I answered. Reminding myself to remain vague and away from my personal demons, I continued. "I think there are a lot of kids who suffer from those types of mental issues, and they can be scared or embarrassed to share them with friends or parents. They might be more comfortable talking to a caring but neutral volunteer. It's probably a stupid idea."

"No, no, it's a great idea. I totally agree with you."

I couldn't tell if she was truly on board with the idea or was just trying to help me move past this delicate subject, but I welcomed her efforts all the same.

"Thanks. Sorry, I didn't expect to talk about this tonight. It wasn't on my list of preapproved topics."

"It's okay. It's interesting. And what preapproved list are you talking about?" Alexis asked mischievously. "Did you prepare for our date?"

"Huh? Nothing. There's no list. Forget I said that." I was getting self-conscious and starting to ramble. "Let's move on to something else. Like, do you have any siblings?"

"Don't worry about it. There's no need to apologize. I like your idea. To answer your question, yes, I do have siblings. Two younger sisters."

"Are they still in school?" I was starting to regain my composure as my internal temperature dropped from surface-of-the-sun levels.

"One's in college, and the other is finishing high school. But I want to know more about your list," she said with a smirk. "What else is on it?"

"There's no list!" I said in a mock yell. I don't think anyone appreciates when I do that as much as I do myself. "You misheard me."

She gave me another smile. "I guess I'll let this list thing slide, for your sake."

Phew. And it appeared I hadn't done too much damage insinuating I struggle with mental illness. "Thank you. So tell me more about your family. Where's your sister going to college? Where does the rest of your family live?"

"My youngest sister, Amanda, still lives at home with my parents in downstate Illinois, close to U of I. Much to my parents' dismay, my middle sister, Ashley, and I both decided not to go there and instead went far away for school. Ashley's going to Vanderbilt in Tennessee."

"Three A names, huh? Do your parents both have names that start with A?"

"Nope. They're just quirky."

"Are you close with your sisters?"

"Yeah, I'd say so. I'm closer with Ashley than I am with Amanda because of our ages, but we're a pretty tight-knit family. My parents are goofy and happily married, so our house has always been a fun place to be."

That was something to which I was not accustomed. I had heard of these mythical families where everyone gets along and the parents stay together, but I had rarely seen them in nature. What would it be like to celebrate a holiday in one place, with everyone there? What do parents talk about when they're not yelling at each other or complaining to their kids about each other? Whom do you punch if you don't punch your brother? Whom does your dad belittle if it's not you? Oh, the things I did not know.

"What about your family?" she asked. "Are your parents still together?"

"My family is the opposite of yours, so we're keeping the universe in balance. My parents divorced when I had just started high school, which is really the opportune time for your parents to divorce. I think if child development research has shown anything, it's that kids going through puberty are the best at handling stress and big life changes."

She snorted when I said this, after just having taken a sip of water, and a little came out her nose. I didn't think my joke was that funny, so she either had a soft spot for jokes about adolescence, or the wine was kicking in a little.

"I mostly lived with my mom when it was all said and done, but my sister and I spent alternate weekends and the summer with my dad. Nowadays, I'm much closer with my mom than I am with my dad."

"I'm sorry they're divorced."

"Please, don't be. It was a long time ago, and for the best."

"Hmm. Why do you think you're closer to your mom than your dad?"

She presented the question in such an innocent manner, seemingly purely out of curiosity, that I didn't take any offense to it. I did wonder, though, whether she asked everyone such probing questions when she was just starting to get to know them.

"I think I could write a book in response to your question. The short answer is probably because I'm more like my mom, and because my dad isn't good at being considerate—long-term, that is. He's great when you first meet him. You'd probably get the opposite impression from how I'm describing him, but you can't rely on him for any length of time."

"Okay. Thanks for answering," she said with tenderness. I shrugged it off. "So you just have one sibling? Your sister?"

"I also have an older brother. Andrew lives with his wife in New York and works for a huge law firm. Rachel lives here and goes to the University of Chicago."

"Are you close with them?"

"I'm super close with Rachel. She's awesome: talented, smart, funny. You'd love her."

"Sounds like it. I'd love to meet her."

"My brother, though? Not so close. We're a few years apart in age." As if that explained everything. I had jumped down enough rabbit holes on the date; there was no need to explore with her why, in the age of technology, Andrew and I communicated less frequently than medieval pen pals.

"What about his wife? Do you like her?"

This question caught me off guard a little. I don't think about Leslie much. "You know, I have to say I don't know. They've only been married for a few years, and I haven't spent a whole lot of time with her."

I needed to find something positive to say about her before it started to sound like all I did was rag on my family. "She seems to make Andrew happy." Nice job, champ. "Obviously, if I was closer to Andrew, I'd know her better."

It was time to shift the focus back on Alexis; who knew what other skeletons she'd unearth if we stuck to my past. "Enough about me for a second. You went away to California for college. What brought you to Chicago when your family is downstate?"

A transitory shadow passed across Alexis's face. It seemed like an innocuous question to me. Curious. Or maybe she just swallowed a burp. Maybe it wasn't that curious.

"I don't know," she said many seconds later. Then she hesitated again before continuing. "Had to put my degree to use somehow, right?" She smiled when she said it, but it seemed contrived. "Also, I wanted to be back by my family. I didn't want to live down in Southern Illinois—I wanted to experience big-city life—so Chicago was the obvious choice. And where else can you find all these restaurants?"

I smiled back at her, but my antenna was picking up some serious static. Her answer made sense, but there was something off pitch about it. Or maybe this was all in my head and I was concocting something out of nothing.

"That's true," I said. "It is great for restaurants. Well, now that you're here in Chicago, where do you and your friends spend most of your time? What do you like to do?"

"Well, for one, I'm in a book club. We meet tomorrow, now that I think about it."

"Nice!"

"Oh, are you in one too?"

"No." I didn't mean to be quite so excited. "I just think it's cool you're in a book club."

"Oh, thanks."

Calm down, nerd. "What book are you discussing?"

"I'm blanking on the title," she told me. "It's about two brothers in Ethiopia who both became doctors, only one came to America and the other stayed where they were born."

"Sorry, I can't help you." I'd read like five different fantasy books in a row. Maybe it was time to branch out. "Is it good?"

"It's fantastic—but very sad at times too. I'd recommend it. You can borrow my copy if you want."

"Thanks. Maybe. I don't read sad books all that often." My life had that genre covered. I didn't want her to ask me why I refrained from reading tales of woe, so I blurted out another question. "So what else do you do besides book clubs—and volleyball?"

"Well, you asked me where I hang out a second ago. My friends and I go to trivia night at State on Tuesday nights pretty much religiously. We're good, too, I might add." She granted me a genuine smile this time; I could already tell the difference. "And otherwise—I don't know—I read, I go to movies, and I get outside as much as I can. Normal stuff."

"That's cool. I am not good at trivia," I said. "My brain isn't wired to remember a ton of facts." I'm all RAM, no ROM.

Some awkward silence began to set in for the first time that evening. My mind entered panic mode and spit out the first question that bubbled to the surface. "So, uh, how come an amazing woman like you is single?"

Oh no. What had I done? A cardinal sin of first dates.

The darkness that crossed her face this time was more a lingering solar eclipse than a fleeting shade. My question was dumb, but it shouldn't have registered that much of a reaction. There was something I was missing. A recent breakup? A boyfriend who was mauled by mountain lions? A voodoo curse? The possibilities were endless.

"I don't know," she said with another forced smile. "Maybe you'll find out."

I wasn't sure how to interpret her comment. Did she mean I'll get to know her better—all sides of her? Or was she implying there would be no second date and thus she would remain single?

"Just kidding," she said with a playful smirk.

So it was the latter. At least she was joking. I hoped.

We finished our entrees and polished off the bottle of wine—keeping the conversation fairly banal compared to how it had begun—before deciding we had no need for dessert. What to do next? Should I have presumed she wanted to hang out longer, or was one dinner more than enough time with James Wright for her liking? *Be bold*, my alcohol-infused blood told me, *be bold*.

"Any chance you want to stay out longer?" I mustered. "I have tickets to an improv show at eleven if you're interested." *Way to go, James. You took the shot.*

"That sounds great!" She didn't even stop to think about it, so her enthusiasm came off genuine, or she was a tremendous actress. "I haven't been to a comedy show in the longest time."

All right, all right, all right. You're still in the game, James. As we got up and walked to the street to grab a cab, I noticed my legs felt a little wobbly. Alexis was slightly flushed but otherwise was showing no signs of intoxication. Of course, my observational skills were a little impaired by that point.

We both grabbed a beer before the show—improv places always have bars in-house; I assume they help with the crowd reactions even more than with the profit margin—and the conversation carried on without any additional awkward lulls. I even made her laugh a few times, possibly more a product of her own alcohol consumption than my wit. The show itself was okay. There were some genuinely hilarious moments, but it was definitely no Second City performance. I didn't mind at all, though; I was finding myself listening to Alexis's rich laugh rather than focusing on the show itself. There wasn't a thing I didn't like about her so far. I was even amused by her incredibly personal questions.

She took my hand in hers as we began to exit after the show, and she kept holding it until we hopped into a cab. I loved her directness. When we arrived at her apartment building, which loomed over the Lincoln Park Zoo, I asked the cabbie to wait for me, and then I walked Alexis to her door. Another lesson from my dad that stuck, although I never saw him so much as open a door for my mom.

"I think this was probably the best first date of my life," I declared. No reason to hold back at that point.

A wide smile appeared. "I don't know if I can go that far," she joked—I think. "But you have definitely earned a second one."

That was good enough for me.

Before I could think about it too long and waste the opportunity, I went in for a kiss. To my great relief, she did not turn away or slap me. The kiss was a modest one by today's standards, especially in light of the amount of alcohol we had consumed. Not bad for my first kiss in, well, I don't want to say how long. No teeth were gnashed, and my tongue made no unexpected attempt to breach her oral cavity. Has a kiss ever been described more eloquently? Perhaps only Shakespeare described it better:

"Then move not, while my prayer's effect I take. Thus from my lips, by yours, my sin is purged." Yeah, he did it a little bit better. Shakespeare Graham would agree.

I said good night and glided like Tinkerbell back to the cab. "Tonight was a good night, man," I informed the driver. "Ten out of ten."

"That's great," he said. "My shift isn't over until four a.m., and I start my other job at nine a.m., but I'm so very happy for you."

Not even that nuclear blast level of sarcasm could bring me down. Stay dead, Fred.

Chapter 11

May 11, 20XX		
PROGRESS NOTE	**CLIENT NAME:** Wright, James	**START:** 5:03 pm
	SERVICE CODE:	**STOP:** 6:11 pm
SYMPTOM STATUS: maintained	**DIAGNOSTIC CHANGE?** No	
CURRENT SYMPTOMS: depressed state		
	LIFE EVENT? No	
MEDICATION: compliant		
SAFETY: no active suicidal or homicidal ideation		
GOALS/OBJECTIVES: Treatment Plan Goal 1 partially achieved 　　　　　　　　　Treatment Plan Goal 2 partially achieved		
CLIENT RESPONSE: Full Compliance		
COMMENTS: Second session with Mr. Wright after he was referred by Dr. Bhattacharya. He reported no complaints today. Said he had limited suicidal ideation since our last session, which surprised him because he calls himself the "Walter Mitty" of suicidal fantasies. Had been successful in his attempts to be more social. In fact, he went to a client event and spent time talking to a woman named Alexis. Appeared enthusiastic about a potential date with her. 　　　He continued to journal and has enjoyed the writing process.		
NEXT APPT: May 23, 20XX		

■ ■ ■

May 23, 20XX		
PROGRESS NOTE	CLIENT NAME: Wright, James	START: 4:56 pm
	SERVICE CODE:	STOP: 5:54 pm
SYMPTOM STATUS: maintained	DIAGNOSTIC CHANGE? No	
CURRENT SYMPTOMS: depressed state		
	LIFE EVENT? No	
MEDICATION: compliant		
SAFETY: no active suicidal or homicidal ideation		
GOALS/OBJECTIVES: Treatment Plan Goal 1 partially achieved Treatment Plan Goal 2 partially achieved		
CLIENT RESPONSE: Full Compliance		
COMMENTS: Mr. Wright appeared upbeat today and reported he was in a better than normal mood. He reported his suicidal ideation remains less frequent than before he began coming to therapy. He also noted having gone on a date with Alexis that went well in his eyes. Although he joked that at some point his current reality will reveal itself to be a long suicide dream "once my top stops spinning." He also has continued to journal about weekly life events. His disposition as a whole appears to have improved with each office visit.		
NEXT APPT: June 12, 20XX		

Chapter 12

I'M WALKING ON SUNSHINE (WOW!)

On the following Monday—the second to last in May—I walked into Manuel's office. "S'up, bro-fasa," I greeted him as I entered.

"Come again?"

"Bro-fasa. Like Mufasa, but with 'bro.'"

"Ah. It's a stretch, but I'll allow it."

"Nice. How do you feel about 'bro-bani yogurt'?"

"That one's good," he verified for me. "Chobani yogurt is very popular these days."

"Finally! Someone who likes my bro puns."

"I didn't say I like them," Manuel interjected. "I was merely acknowledging your effort."

"Shush, Manuel. Don't speak. I didn't hear anything you said after 'That one's good.'" Then I noticed Manuel wasn't alone.

"Hey, Miles. Good to see you," I said to Manuel's officemate.

He's the definition of a wallflower when he's around, which is almost never as far as I'm aware, so I sometimes forget he has a right to be there. He's also alarming. If anyone is going to mow down coworkers in a hail of gunfire, it's this guy. Don't ask me how I know; I just do. I don't need to be bitten by a radioactive spider to activate my spidey sense.

"Hey there," Miles quickly responded before immediately turning back to his monitors. He had two, and both of them were twice as large as the typical office monitor. His awkward demeanor combined with his oversized displays led me to suspect Miles was an online gamer afterhours. I should be a detective.

I made eye contact with Manuel and jerked my head toward the door so he would know I wanted to talk to him somewhere else. If his officemate had been anyone other than Miles, I would've just asked Manuel out loud to go outside. But Miles could take it the wrong way, and I had no desire to be on his murder list—I had no doubt Miles had a list of people he was planning to chop up and make into sausage.

"What's wrong, James?" Manuel asked. "Is that a facial tic?"

He knew damn well what I wanted. I glanced in Miles's direction, but he was oblivious to what was going on. I repeated my head jerk and threw in a finger point toward the door for good measure.

"James, are you okay? Are you having a mild seizure?"

Manuel knew about my unverified but rational fear that in the not-so-distant future we would rue the day that no one took a preemptive strike against Miles—a calculated decision to prevent what certainly would be a future domestic terrorism attack. If there were ever a time to employ the one percent doctrine, this was it. Yet here Manuel sat, in the presence of the enemy, messing with me.

I'd been standing there in silence for too long. Miles was surely growing suspicious and was possibly reaching for a homemade bomb or a bottle of face-eroding acid. I didn't even have any Batwing shuriken on me for self-defense.

"No, Manuel, it's not a seizure. Just a cold shiver." Because future killer Miles was walking over my grave. "Would you like to get some fresh air? Maybe get some coffee?"

"Sure," Manuel answered with a smile. "I could use a break."

"What about you, Miles? Coffee?" *Please say no. Please say no.*

"Hmm? No, I don't drink coffee." *Just the blood of the innocent.*

"Okay, thought I'd offer." I walked out of the office without waiting for Manuel to get ready, and he caught up to me in the hallway.

"You're so ridiculous," he told me. "Relax. He's not a bad guy. Just a little odd."

"That's what they said about Tom Riddle."

"Who?"

How did he not know who Tom Riddle was? "Never mind. The guy gives me the heebie-jeebies. Plain and simple. So thank you for prolonging my interaction with him."

"No problem."

"For real, though, don't ever try to open one of his drawers or cabinets if you need a pen or something. They're probably rigged to explode. Or you might find a human hand he's been nibbling on."

"So he's a terrorist and a cannibal?"

"Maybe."

"I'll keep that in mind, James." He was patronizing me, I could tell. "So you seemed like you were in a good mood before you noticed Miles. Your date went that well, huh?"

"Yep. I texted you that over the weekend. I told you, and I quote, 'Alexis is amazing and we are going to get married.' Remember?"

Manuel laughed. "Yeah, I remember. But I thought you were exaggerating to be funny."

"Well of course I was exaggerating. I'm not going to elope after a first date. Come on, Manny. But I was serious that it went well. If it hadn't, you wouldn't have heard from me. At least not until I was blackout drunk at my apartment."

"That's true. There is no middle ground with you, so marriage or death by acute alcohol poisoning makes sense."

"I can't tell if you're mocking me," I told him, "but it doesn't matter. What matters is Alexis and I are going out again Wednesday night."

"That's awesome! So tell me the details. Did you go home with her?"

"Manuel, don't be so uncouth. A gentleman does not kiss and tell."

"She gave you a handshake at the end of the date, didn't she? Isn't that second base for you, *chacho*?"

"Joke all you want. You're not going to trick me into giving you any details. Nice try, *guapo*."

"You know what that means, right?" Manuel asked.

"No, and I don't care. You should assume I meant it facetiously."

We walked to get coffee—at a location farther away to kill time—and I filled him in on the rest of the date. Before we arrived back at the office, I asked him about Sam.

"Things are good, man," he whispered.

We were in the danger zone, as Manuel called it—an amorphous perimeter encircling the office in which he was unwilling to discuss Sam for fear of being discovered—so he told me this in a hushed voice.

"We still hang out all the time," he continued, "and we text all the time. I'm trying not to rush into it too fast, but it's hard not to. She's so cool and easygoing. She even plays video games."

"That's great, man." I was happy for him, which was easier for me to be when I was happy myself. Or happyish, anyway. One date with Alexis hadn't solved my entire smorgasbord of problems. "Sounds like you hit the jackpot. Don't try to play it too smooth." A girl who's attractive, witty, easygoing, and plays video games? That's like finding a unicorn in the woods, or the golden ticket in your candy bar—or a family where everyone gets along!

As we walked out of the elevator and went in separate directions to our offices, Manuel said, "Don't worry about me, *pana*. I got this. Just worry about you and Alexis."

"*Sí, señor.* Whatever you say. Mark my words about You Know Who, though. You open one of his drawers, you lose a hand, *guapo*."

"You should really go look that word up. It doesn't mean what you think it means."

"You should go look it up," I taunted in my Manuel-is-a-Wookiee-who-can't-speak voice. I couldn't tell if he heard me.

■ ■ ■

"You're a sight for sore eyes," Alexis said as we met up in our office lobby after work on Wednesday evening. She once again looked effortlessly effervescent. "It's been a long week, and there are still two days left."

"It doesn't sound like my week has been nearly as taxing, but I'm excited to see you too." And not just because I had gotten to the lobby entirely too soon and had to say hello and goodbye like a Walmart greeter to multiple coworkers leaving for the night. "Does dinner and a movie still work?"

I think I made those seven words sound like one. *Slow down. Take a breath, James. If you blow this, the worst that can happen is that Fred makes you…oh, wait. Never mind.*

"The restaurant for sure." She must have understood me despite my verbal apraxia. "Let's play the movie by ear; I probably have to do more work tonight."

There's an upscale Irish pub called D4 in the nearby Streeterville neighborhood, and it's right around the corner from a movie theater. We took a cab to the restaurant and ordered pints when we sat down. "So what's good here? I've never been," Alexis said.

"Manuel always gets the pulled pork sandwich. I can vouch for it. But you can never go wrong with the fish and chips or the shepherd's pie. I've never had any of their salads, but the ladyfolk seem to like them." Ladyfolk? I had never used that word in my life. I don't even know where I learned it. Probably from that professor in college. The brain does funny things when one is talking to a beautiful girl.

"I've been eating like a bird all week. Shepherd's pie sounds fantastic."

"Not this guy. I've been eating like a pig all week. I'm not proud." I was playing this up somewhat—a little hyperbole never hurt anyone—but I do need to start watching my diet. I'm no longer an eighteen-year-old who has wrestling or lacrosse practice for two and a half hours every afternoon.

"It doesn't look like you have anything to worry about from where I'm sitting," she divulged with a wink.

I recommend an Alexis for everyone; she does wonders for your self-esteem.

"I think the same could be said about you." I would have winked back, but I'm physically incapable—one of my many genetic flaws. All I can do is lift my cheek up high enough on the right side that I think my eye is closing. It's not an attractive look.

"How far do you run each week?" I asked.

"How do you know I'm a runner?"

"You don't get toned legs like you have by dieting or doing yoga." I managed not to stutter, but I don't think I enunciated every word, and spots of red were flaring up all over my upper torso like a war games simulation. "And there are only like six weeks a year here that you can play beach volleyball in Chicago, so that's not it." Full body blushing was going on now, and I definitely strung some of those words together. At least she probably knew I was being truthful and not just trying to sweet talk her.

"So you were checking out my legs?" She smiled impishly at me.

"You know damn well I was," I said with a grin, my full-body rosacea be damned. "You looked amazing in that dress. I couldn't stop thinking about it. I'm still thinking about it." I had gotten all the words out clearly, and now she was blushing a little! Success. "But honestly, I'm curious. Are you a runner?"

She was still blushing. I had scored some points. "I am. I swim and bike a little too, but mostly run. I do play volleyball in some recreational leagues—more than six weeks a year, I'll have you know—but not frequently enough to stay in shape. Running's great because I can just throw on some shoes, shorts, and a sports bra and go."

That was a picture I would have liked to capture with oil paints, charcoal, or sidewalk chalk. Through sheer willpower, I forced my brain not to degenerate midconversation into another sexual fantasy. I should look into meditation.

"We should go for a run sometime," I said with a smirk. Man, I'm immature.

"Ha, why? So you can see me in a sports bra and spandex shorts?"

"What? No, of course not." I was so full of it. "I also happen to enjoy staying in shape, thank you very much. And nothing beats running along the Lakeshore path."

That last part was true; I love running along Lake Michigan with the various packs of runners. What could be better than zipping through parks and harbors with the lake on one side and skyscrapers on the other? Especially when you get passed by a fit woman wearing spandex shorts?

"You're so full of it." Was she reading my mind? Nah. She was laughing, though.

"I'm hurt that you would think so little of me. But I forgive you. So why are you so stressed at work this week?"

Alexis vented to me for a while about the overbearing client she was currently working with and the duds from our firm who were also staffed on the project. "I didn't work as hard as I did to get where I am just to have some jerk client and a clueless partner ask me to do a thousand things they don't need and will never look at. You know?"

"I do know. Unfortunately." Her complaint was basically my job description. Both our job descriptions. "At least there's probably a way out for you." I was starting to relax a little as the conversation transitioned to talk of work.

"What do you mean?"

"You can talk to anybody," I said. "I bet clients love working with you. You won't be stuck with the junk work for much longer."

"Maybe." She wavered, but she knew I was right. "But the same is true for you."

I appreciated the token effort on her part, but there was no comparison between her people skills and mine. She was an experienced hostage negotiator, and I was a call center worker in India. "Thanks. We'll have to agree to disagree."

We continued talking about work over our food, mostly joking about difficult clients and insufferable partners. Then the waiter stopped by. I ordered another beer and asked for the check before joking, "If I have any more after this, I may have to start thinking about AA."

Scalding fury flashed on Alexis's face in stark contrast to the half-smile she had been wearing a moment ago, as if an evil spirit was lurking just behind her visage. "You shouldn't joke about something like that," she scolded me. "Alcoholism is serious."

She admonished me so gravely that at first I thought she was joking. But her expression remained grim. "I'm sorry. Didn't know it was a big deal."

Her face finally softened. "Sorry, I didn't mean to get worked up. But I know someone who's an alcoholic. It's not something to joke about."

"No need to apologize. I won't do it again."

"Thanks."

I resumed our office gossiping, trying to move on from my tongue lashing, when the waiter came over with the check. Alexis tried to pick it up.

"Get out of here," I chastised her as I snatched it away. "I got it."

"Hey! You paid for the first date. It's my turn." She tried to rip it from my grasp, but I was too quick for her.

"Nope, you're wrong. You don't get to pay until at least the fifth date."

"Whose rule is that?" she asked with mock ire. "I have the same job as you. I should be allowed to pay."

"One of the rules of life according to Patrick Wright. The lady doesn't pay until after the fifth date, and even then it's not guaranteed. Patrick Wright is my dad, in case you were wondering."

"Thanks. I was able to put two and two together. No disrespect to your father, but I don't agree."

"That's because you're smart."

"I'll let you pay tonight," she said, "but that doesn't mean I'm agreeing to your five-date rule."

"Don't worry; you'll have it your way soon," I told her. "It's only a matter of time before you're telling me, 'Farm boy, fetch me that pitcher' when the pitcher is hanging only six inches above your head. Then, after that, you'll say, 'Farm boy, dig that hole,' and then 'Farm boy, polish that saddle.' And I'll say 'As you wish' every time like a schmuck. I know how these things work."

She chuckled. Half a gold star. "You're such a nerd." Then she shifted gears. "I hate to say it, but I don't think I can do a movie tonight. I should do some work before I go to bed."

"What if I let you pay for the movie?"

"Ha, it's not that. I really do need to work. But I don't want to rush home. It's so nice out—feels like summer already, even though we're just entering June. Will you walk with me to the Red Line? I can transfer to the Brown Line at Fullerton."

"As you wish." That triggered the smile I was hoping for.

I had no intention of letting her walk home by herself from the Fullerton stop. It wasn't dangerous—far from it—but it was another code of conduct instilled in me from a young age. Patrick Wright has his faults, and he may not practice what he preaches, but he taught me a few important lessons.

After we jumped off the train and walked to the path leading to her apartment building, she turned and put her hand on my chest. "I like you, you know."

How did she do it? So calm and collected when she told me things that would have turned me into Porky Pig. I was no idiot, though; she was all but telling me to kiss her. So I obliged. Electricity shot through me from my lips to my toes. I noticed how full her lips were before our tongues met like star-crossed lovers. I could have continued kissing her for hours, but eventually I came up for air, although all I could smell was her intoxicating perfume.

"You're growing on me. That's the best I can say." I was getting better at flirting. The only direction I could go was up.

"Shut up," she said as she playfully pushed me. I caught her hand and held it to my chest and kissed her again, while my right hand caressed her cheek. When had I learned to do that? I had no moves.

Sometime between thirty seconds and one hour later, we stopped kissing. "I like you too. A lot. We should go out again this weekend," I suggested.

"I agree. Thanks for tonight." One more kiss, this one a peck, and then I opened the door to her building for her. My heart was beating faster than those guys who whack buckets outside every sports venue ever. I could have gone for a run right then, but I settled for walking home.

There was no man flying higher than I was at that exact moment. Not even Fred could reach that altitude.

■ ■ ■

My mood had soured precipitously, however, by the time I had walked home. I should know better, but I continue to underestimate how effective Fred can be. He made me wonder whether Alexis was telling the truth about why she had to skip a movie and head home. Maybe, for whatever reason, she was still mad at me about the AA joke? Or maybe she just didn't like me as much as I liked her? Could this have been our second and last date?

I needed to get an objective opinion on the night's proceedings, but Manuel's would have to do. I texted him when I got in. *Hey man, what are you doing?*

I didn't expect an instantaneous response—I was willing to give him thirty seconds to a minute—so I turned on the TV and flipped through the channel guide. There was nothing good on the first fifteen channels I checked, so I texted Manuel again. *Manny manny fo fanny. Text me back yo.* Then I resumed channel surfing while keeping my peripheral vision trained on my phone to spot any incoming messages.

After being patient for an exhaustingly long three minutes—no, that is not an oxymoron—I texted again. *Second date with Alexis went well. I think. But I need to get your thoughts.*

Finally, like an endless ten minutes later, he texted me back. *That's great, man.*

That was it? That was all he had to say? I waited for more, but it didn't come. *Can you talk?* I asked him.

A few minutes later, he sent, *No. Busy.*

What about now? I asked him a minute later, just in case he had wrapped up whatever it was he was doing.

I'm with Sam, he messaged me 119 seconds later. I was counting. *Tell me tomorrow,* he said, after another delay.

That's how you treat your best friend?

Yes. Go away. That message came in a little quicker. I needed to keep up the pressure.

I just need a few minutes, I said. *You can put me on speaker. I don't care if Sam hears.*

I'm turning my phone off.

I typed some curse words but didn't send them. One of us needed to handle the situation maturely. I then immersed myself in a video game so Fred would stay out of my head.

Chapter 13

IS ALIEN ABDUCTION REAL?

I met James for lunch on Saturday afternoon. Before I followed him to Chicago for school, I would visit while he was going to Northwestern. He always took me to an "encased meat emporium." It was a hot dog place that specialized in exotic sausages and amazing duck fat fries. To my horror, the owner closed it down right after I moved. Such a bummer! For nostalgia's sake, James was meeting me at a somewhat new hot dog place in Lincoln Park. Its menu offered alligator, duck, and kangaroo sausages. It might be the only place in Chicago that could stake that claim. Sorry, vegetarians and vegans. I respect what you're trying to do, but I am not one of you.

I took the train and met him at the restaurant, where he was already waiting for me. I assumed he'd been there for at least fifteen minutes. I would like to be punctual all the time, but no one's as anal as James. Mom jokes he was even born a few days early.

When I saw him, he was already springing up to give me a big hug. His face was plastered with a giant smile.

"I don't like this, James." I told him matter-of-factly. "You're freaking me out."

"What do you mean?"

"You're in a good mood for the second time in a row? What cranial operation has been performed on you?"

He immediately looked angry. "I can't win with you guys. If I'm moody, you check on me constantly. If I'm happy, you question why. How do you and Mom want me to act? Should I just take lithium and be a brain-dead zombie all the time?"

He had a point. I hadn't thought of it like that before. Although I would never question our family's vigilance in monitoring his well-being. He's my brother and I love him, and he's shown in the past he's not fine if left unchecked. We have reason not to trust him. But I could see how our supervision could get tiresome.

"You're right. Sorry, James. I should be excited you're still doing well. Correction—I am excited."

"Thank you. Apology accepted. Just stop being the Eye of Sauron all the time."

I knew this reference! James forced me to read *The Lord of the Rings* when we were kids. "We're not doing it to be evil, James. Or to rule you. We care about you and want to make sure you're okay."

"Fine. Look, I know this is uncommon for me, being in good spirits and all. So I won't give you too hard a time. I just want you guys to back off a little."

His concession was exactly my point. We have reasons for monitoring his every move. Nonetheless, I had learned my lesson and made no jokes about aliens kidnapping him. Even though it was so tempting. I didn't want to ruin the half grin that had already returned to his face. When he's happy, his eyes smile more than his mouth. I so rarely get to see him happy.

"Thank you for your generosity. So tell me, why are you all smiles today? Your date must have gone well?" No need for guessing this time.

"You're very astute. They both did. About as well as they could have gone."

"Both? You've already gone on two dates?"

"Yes, that's what the word *both* means. Two."

"Shut up. Did you hold doors for her and slide in her chair for her?"

"Of course I did. Who do you think I am?"

"Just checking. Did you talk about me?"

"We did."

"All good things?" They better have been.

"Of course."

"Good."

"But we didn't talk about you for long."

"Whatever. Did you kiss her?"

"I'm not going to answer that."

Drat. I embarrassed him and asked the question too soon. But he couldn't contain his beaming smile. It was adorable. I always knew if some-one gave him a chance, she'd be pleasantly surprised. She'd just need to get past the sullen first impression he often makes.

"Fine. But what I really need to know is, is wittle James-y in wuv?"

I could see his neck and face turning red. Another endearing feature of his, although he doesn't view it that way. I suffer from the same pale skin malignancy. I know it can be a real pain in the arse.

"No, little James is not in love," he said. "I do like her, though. A lot. So fingers crossed this keeps going well." Fingers crossed indeed. "Although I wouldn't mind getting your thoughts on a couple of things that happened, just to make sure I'm not reading them wrong."

James then told me all about his two dates as we gorged ourselves on exotic meat sausages. I wonder if that's the first time that sentence has ever been written? And I reassured him that it sounded like things were going great. Then we walked around for a while because the abnormally warm weather had continued. But I wasn't able to stay too long. I had a ton to do for school, and there weren't enough minutes in the day. When we finished eating, James walked me back to the train station.

I didn't say anything about my concern for him as I left. I simply re-minded him how happy I was that he was happy. I don't think he minded me repeating it.

Chapter 14

HELLO, IS IT ME YOU'RE LOOKING FOR?

Friday was here again, the first Friday in June, which meant the guys were out to lunch—Manuel, Richard, Blair, and me. And psycho killer Miles. Manuel claimed he had no choice but to invite him. I wasn't buying it. The more time I spent around Miles, the more likely my demise at his hands would become. I was not good at hiding my aversion to him, and every time he looked at me, I felt like he was wondering which part of me would taste best.

Out of a healthy fear for my life, I wasn't talking much. That may seem ironic given my suicidal fantasies, but I want to choose when and how I go—I don't want Miles of all people to make the decision for me. It appeared no one else was talking either, which prompted Manuel to whip out one of his mental discussion topics.

"So I was flipping through channels the other day," he said, "and I stopped on ESPN2 because they were showing a Ping-Pong match. Last time I checked, ESPN stood for 'Entertainment and *Sports* Programming Networks.' Ping-Pong is not a sport. I mean—"

"What do you mean it's not a sport?" Richard asked. "Why not?"

"Of course you think it's a sport," I said sardonically to Richard. I purposely provided no rationale.

"Why? Because I'm Asian? So I must love Ping-Pong?" he exclaimed.

I know you're Asian, dammit. You were supposed to tell me which nationality! That was the whole point! "No, not because you're Asian," I said matter-of-factly, covering my tracks. "Because you're not good at real sports like football, baseball, and volleyball."

This was objectively true. We both had played in office leagues for flag football, softball, and volleyball when we started working for the firm. Richard was voted as the worst player in each—I did some informal polling—but he made everyone laugh, so we tolerated his lack of ability.

"Ah. Fine. That's valid," he said. "Man, am I bad at volleyball." Here was a man who knew his limitations. "But that's not why I think it's a sport," he said. "It's a sport because it requires physical skill and some stamina, it's competitive, and there is objective scoring. Therefore, it's a sport."

"But you can be good at Ping-Pong without being athletic," Manuel countered. "You can improve your Ping-Pong game by drinking beer midgame. You don't need to work out—ever—to be good at Ping-Pong. So no, it's not a sport."

"I think Ping-Pong is on the fence," Blair said, "for the reasons both of you said. There can be no dispute, though, that poker is not a sport. I don't care how many damn poker tournaments are shown on ESPN. It's not a sport. When what you do is substantially controlled by fate, it's not a sport. And if everything you do is done sitting down, it's not a sport."

"I can agree with those two rules," Richard said. "Plus, if you can eat nachos while playing your 'sport,' it's not a sport. Although I do want to remind you all the E in ESPN is for 'Entertainment.' I sometimes watch those poker tournaments."

"No one cares about the sad things you do when you're alone," Manuel said.

Miles had been silent this whole time but was clearly paying attention. I would have joked that Call of Duty and Magic the Gathering were not sports, but as I said, I didn't want to give Miles any fodder for putting me on one of his human grocery lists. Also, I had played Magic the Gathering in junior high on the down low with some friends who shared my desire to keep our activities clandestine. It was fun, but I would never tell Miles that. And just because it was fun doesn't mean it's a sport.

"I second the motion to deny poker as a sport. Although I think the IOC is currently considering it for the Olympics." What a crock that is, considering the IOC recently considered eliminating wrestling—one of the oldest and truest forms of sport in the history of mankind—from the

Olympics. "However, I submit that NASCAR and other forms of race car driving are not sports."

"I think you'll lose this one," Manuel instantly said.

"Really," Blair said. "How is one of the most popular sports in the country not a sport?"

I guess I shouldn't have been surprised Blair liked NASCAR, but how did someone with a bourgeoisie name like Blair even grow up to like country music and NASCAR?

"Hear me out." I largely could use the same arguments these guys had just made. "You sit the entire freaking time. There's no need to work out, and no stamina or strength are required. You need more stamina to drive in Chicago rush hour. You could even take a phone call during the middle of the race if you wanted to; in fact, aren't those guys on the radio the whole time? Same thing as a call. They're probably ordering pizzas for every pit stop. More importantly, you're substantially dependent on the quality of your car, not your own physical skills. The only thing you need—and I mean the *only thing*—is a quick reaction time. If that's the threshold for a sport, then fly swatting is a sport. Or Whac-A-Mole." Not to mention the fact that NASCAR is terrible for the environment. There are a lot more productive things that could be done with 216,000 gallons of gas a season than having cars drive in circles for hours.

"My dad and uncle work in NASCAR pit crews," Miles mumbled.

Are you kidding me? This was the first time Miles had spoken all lunch, and he dropped that bombshell?

"The drivers absolutely have to be in shape so they can be focused for hours at a time in a two-hundred-miles-per-hour car. My dad says their workouts are crazy. They also train for years to hone their reaction times. It is definitely more involved than Whac-A-Mole."

He spoke every word dispassionately like a sociopathic robot—*My CPU is a neural-net processor; a learning computer.* I had surely secured my spot as victim number one on his inevitable murderous rampage. I needed to fix the situation tout de suite. Otherwise, my family was going to receive my head in a box. *What's in the box? What's in the box?*

"What do you have to say to that, James?" Of course that came from Blair. I was tempted to mimic his comment, but that would have been childish. Also, I hadn't practiced how his Wookiee voice would sound.

"Nothing. I stand corrected. Thanks for the schooling, Miles." I tried to sound jovial when I said that, but he and I both knew he would one day be eating my liver with fava beans and a bottle of Chianti. I needed to kill him with kindness from there on out.

"All right then," Manuel said. "NASCAR is in, poker is out, and Ping-Pong is a maybe."

Waking up to Miles in my apartment had been a maybe before that lunch. But thanks to Manuel's "innocent" invitation, I put the odds of a Miles home invasion north of 90 percent. I was going to have to install a security system when I got home.

The guys were still talking, but I had entered Fred's dream world. I was in my apartment coming to, and I realized my wrists and ankles were tied to a kitchen chair with rope. I couldn't see anyone, but I could feel the presence of someone else in my apartment. Someone with malicious intent.

"Comfortable?" a meek male voice inquired from behind me. "Ropes too tight?"

It took me only a few seconds to recognize the mocking voice as Miles's. A second later he walked into my line of sight, wearing a Magic the Gathering hooded sweatshirt and black gloves. Then I noticed my apartment was covered in plastic, just like a *Dexter* kill scene. This was not good. No bueno.

"What do you want, Miles? Why are you here?" I did my best to be authoritative, but it was hard to do so in my predicament. "You can have my D&D stuff. I'll tell you where it is. And all my fantasy novels. Just let me live."

"Shut up, James. You sound pathetic. I don't want anything you have. My dad and uncle want me to teach you a lesson. They don't appreciate your views on NASCAR. And I know you mock me behind my back. So it's time to pay."

"Your dad and uncle want you to do this? Or you want to do this, Miles?" Apparently if he was going to kill me, my subconscious wanted him to be clear on the reason.

"Stop. Talking. James. You think you're so clever." Miles was still using his monotone voice, exponentially increasing the sinister atmosphere.

I tried to reason with him. "You don't have to do this, Miles. Please, just let me go. I won't tell anyone."

"I know I don't have to. But I want to." Quick as a dark elf—my subconscious assumed that was Miles's favorite D&D race for his characters—Miles picked up and threw a steak knife at me. It missed my face by millimeters.

"Miles!" I strained to scream "Stop!" But my mouth suddenly felt like it was full of marbles, limiting me to nonverbal guttural sounds.

He turned to search my kitchen for another projectile weapon. This was my only shot to go out my way, not his. As quickly as I could, I hopped the chair—and me in it—toward the floor-to-ceiling window. Then with all my might, I launched myself. As I was breaking through the glass, my mind hit the eject button on the dream and thrusted me back into the real world.

"James, what do you think Miles should do?" Manuel was asking me a question, but I had no context. Had he not noticed I was not paying attention? The nerve of that guy.

"Huh?" I responded. It was my best play at the moment—needed to buy some time.

"The problem Miles is having with his project," Manuel said. "You dealt with a similar problem last year. Any ideas what he should do?"

I hate you so much right now, Manuel. What the hell was he talking about, and why was he putting me on the spot? I had no choice but to come clean. "I'm sorry, I spaced out for a minute there. What's the issue?"

Miles didn't answer. He only shot me a steely gaze and waited for Manuel to summarize. I was relieved to note there were no knives on the table for Miles to grab.

I did my best to troubleshoot Miles's issue—turned out I did have some ideas for him—and then I shut up for the rest of lunch, which could not end quickly enough.

■ ■ ■

Manuel stormed into my office about an hour after we got back from lunch. "What's your problem, *carajito*?" he demanded.

"What do you mean 'my problem'?"

"Miles. Why were you such a jerk to him at lunch?"

"I told you he weirds me out with his Columbine mystique. You know this, but you invite him to lunch without asking anyone else?" I said this as both a statement and an interrogative.

"Yeah, exactly," Manuel said. "I felt bad for him because he never goes to lunch with anyone, and the whole time you're openly hostile to him. So I ask again, what's your problem?"

"I wasn't openly hostile," I objected. "I was quietly inimical." Like a racist grandma when her grandkids bring a non-Caucasian to a family party.

"Your dislike for him was palpable. It's one thing to ignore him when you stop by my office. It's another thing to be a jerk to his face."

"Like when you ignored my text messages about Alexis the other night?"

"No, not like that. I was busy, and you were being annoying." Annoying? Maybe a little. "Today, you were just rude. I doubt he ever goes to lunch with us again."

That seemed like a favorable outcome. I was about to quip exactly that, but Manuel was rarely angry, and right then he was furious. *Maybe I should shut off my default defensive mode,* I told myself, *and listen to him.* "Was I really that bad?"

"You barely acknowledged his existence most of the time, and when you did, you sneered at him. Then you ignored his story about a difficult client when you actually had experience that could help him."

"I didn't ignore him on purpose, Manny. I was spacing out, and it co-incidentally occurred while Miles was speaking." This was all true, but as I said it, I knew it sounded like a shabby defense. "Also, you know me well. Miles doesn't. Maybe he didn't notice I wasn't being friendly."

"Helen Keller would have noticed your hostility," Manuel said. "Look, did Miles say anything to me? No. But he would never speak up; he just doesn't do that. Does he seem more dejected than usual? Yes, undeniably."

"You think I should apologize?"

"Come on, man. Why do you think I'm here?"

"You're walking off some of your calories from lunch?"

"Go freaking apologize," Manuel said.

"What if I just act friendly to him next time and pretend like today never happened? Everybody wins." And I wouldn't put myself within a few feet of homemade pipe bombs and an angry terrorist.

"Shut up, James. You know I'm right. Go. Apologize. Now."

"Fine. I'll go apologize. But I'm not doing it in front of you, so get lost."

"I have to go to the bathroom anyway. You better apologize."

"Number one or number two?"

He just stared at me.

"I need to know how much time I have to work with," I said.

He left without answering. So Manuel.

I dragged my feet down to Manuel's office—Manuel's *and Miles's* office, I mentally corrected myself—and knocked on the doorframe since the door was open. "Hey, Miles, you got a second?" *It's okay if you don't.*

I must've startled him, because he visibly jumped in his seat before turning around. "Oh, hey. What's up?" He declined to make eye contact with me, which, if I'm being honest, made me feel pretty damn terrible. I was already starting to see him in a different light, as if Manuel's confrontation had cleared my brain's cache of Miles browsing data.

"I just wanted to say sorry about earlier. I wasn't super friendly at lunch."

He didn't say anything back. I thought I was making him uncomfortable. Or was I just telling myself that because I was uneasy and I wanted to end our encounter quickly? Hard to tell, but it was probably the latter. But why wasn't he saying anything? The silence was unsettling. I briefly considered turning around and sprinting away like a cartoon character.

"And I'm sorry about the NASCAR comment," I said, just to fill the void. "I didn't know your family works in the industry."

"I don't care about your thoughts on NASCAR," he snapped at me, with more force than I was expecting. "It's not the first time, though."

I wasn't sure what he was referring to. I was pretty sure I had never talked about NASCAR with him in the past. I thought that day was the first time I'd talked about it with anyone. "What's not the first time?" I asked.

"Today wasn't the first time you weren't 'super friendly,' as you put it," Miles said. With emotion, I should add. "You've never been friendly."

My first instinct, which is always my first instinct when I'm accused of something, was to fight back. But I took a second to compose myself and let the impulse wither and die. Was I growing as a person before my very eyes?

I can't say I was used to hashing out problems with other guys, though. How did one go about it? Awkwardly, I assumed, which was the path I treaded most often anyway. "Well then, I apologize for all the other times. I never meant to be rude to you. But to be honest, you've never been that welcoming yourself. You always keep your back to me when I visit Manuel. I just assumed you didn't want me to talk to you."

"I know." Miles briefly made eye contact with me, which was progress, but went back to staring at the floor. "I've always assumed you were an ass." I would have been offended, but he snickered when he said it. It made me chuckle too.

This was starting to feel a little like *The Breakfast Club* to me, but I'd gone this far. Couldn't back out now. "I am one, that's true," I said with a grin. "But I never tried to be a jerk to you," I said. "I'm sorry I've been one all this time." *I was just worried about you blowing everyone up.* I managed to hold that back.

He seemed to be relaxing a little. I wouldn't have been able to point out a specific change in his body language that told me that, but whatever I was picking up, it encouraged me to press on. "If we're clearing the air, though, you sometimes give me the creeps, Miles. Like you're gonna go postal on everyone." Panic momentarily surged through me. *Was this it? Had I gone too far? Was this the tipping point for his mass destruction?*

But then he laughed—a full laugh, as if I had told a good joke—and I breathed again. "That's what my sister tells me all the time. She says I'm too intense. Don't worry; I'm not going to shoot anybody."

"That's a relief," I joked, although the small part of me that had misjudged him also felt relieved. "I'll let HR know to stand down."

"You contacted HR about me?" he asked, sitting up in his chair, suddenly flustered.

"No, man. Of course not. I'm just kidding." He slumped back down. "But seriously, I'm sorry I wasn't friendly in the past. It'll be a whole new me going forward."

"Thanks. I'll do the same. Sorry I assumed you were an ass." His demeanor had made a 180-degree turn from the beginning of the conversation.

"No problem. See you later, Miles."

With that, I turned and strolled back toward my office thinking I had just lived through a Lifetime movie. But I felt good about it. After all, Miles might be a kindred soul. Neither one of us was a social butterfly; we both probably could have benefited from each other's company years ago. Two outcasts trying to find common ground and a sense of place.

Chapter 15

Two weeks into June and I am still riding high from Alexis. We've been talking and hanging out quite a bit. So high, in fact, I have been having the urge to call my dad. That almost never happens, mainly because we don't have much of a relationship these days. Our bond is weaker than London dispersion forces. That's a chemistry joke for you.

Indeed, my dad is by far the biggest disappointment in Fred's induced gedanken experiments. An end to my life would only register as a minor blip on his lifetime EEG, the minutest of deviations in his neural oscillations. Not because he doesn't care about me—he does, he says—but because all extrinsic influences in his life induce only the scarcest of responses. My parents' divorce came as a surprise only to him. Then he was back to his usual routine within a few days, minus an emotional punching bag. Needless to say, he does not actively participate in my life.

I'd go into more detail, but I don't want to spoil my good mood. Certainly not because of him. Besides, I think you're starting to get the gist by now. He has never been a supportive or positive influence in my life—or even just an interested party.

Anyway, my attenuated association with my father notwithstanding, I plopped on the couch and took a break from my journaling so I could give him a call this Thursday evening.

"Hello, this is Patrick," he stated formally, as if his phone was not telling him his second-oldest son was calling. Maybe he didn't know; maybe I was not one of his contacts.

"Hey, Dad," I muttered like a timid little mouse. I cleared my throat and declared in a lower octave, "It's James." That was better.

"Hey, son, how are you?" he asked, more cordial now. I gave him the benefit of the doubt that he knew what my phone number was, or at least that he had saved it in his phone and knew it was me calling.

"I'm good. How are you?"

"Hey, hold on for a second," he said. "I'll be right back."

I then waited for three to four minutes in silence. I was considering hanging up when he finally picked the phone back up.

"Hey, I'm back," he said. "Where were we?"

No explanation for the delay? "Dad, where'd you go? Comcast has a faster response time."

"Huh? Oh, nothing. So what's up?"

He was not going to say sorry or provide any explanation for putting me on hold? "Seriously, civilizations have risen and fallen while you were gone."

"Don't be a smart-ass, James. You're always busting my chops. I'm here now. So what's going on? Why'd you call?"

Fine. I would smash this down and shove it deep inside like I did everything else with him. Isn't that what everyone says you should do with your negative emotions? Compress them, and bury them, and crush them down some more—until you have a diamond-sized kidney stone?

"Just calling to say hi. We haven't talked in a while." This call was already reminding me why.

"Oh, okay," he stated with perplexity. The idea of a call with no express purpose must have been foreign to him. "So what's new?"

"Well, work's going well." Why not start things off with the mundane stuff. "I'm staying pretty busy, and it seems like my bosses like me." Some of them, anyway.

"That's good. You should know, though."

"What?"

"Your bosses. If they're not giving you feedback, you can't just sit quietly like you normally do. You need to be assertive and talk to them, ask for feedback. Need to know where you stand."

That's the thing. I don't care where I stand. "Sure. Right," I said to appease him.

"I mean it, James. That's the only way you'll move to the next level. What are you now?"

"Hmm?"

"Your job title. What is it?"

"Associate."

"Yeah, so the only way to move up from associate is to know where you stand and to work on your shortcomings."

I regretted bringing up work. I hate talking about work. Office gossip and complaining about bosses? Sure, count me in. But work itself? No, thank you. And now that he was on the track, it was going to take an earthquake to derail him.

"Okay, I got it."

"You do want to move up to the next level, don't you?"

Maybe? That evening it seemed like an okay prospect. The next day? Who was to say; that was so far away. "Yeah, I think so." Dammit. Why did I waffle? Rookie mistake, James.

"You think so? You need to know so. You need to be laser focused. Look at your brother Andrew. He wants to make partner, and he's on pace to do that. By being dialed in. He'll be making a million dollars a year soon. Don't you want to be successful like that?"

"Sure, yeah."

"Son, you have to go for it if you're going to make it in this world. All out. You have to go all out. No one's going to help you get to the mountaintop. You have to provide your own drive. You have to want it, and you have to go for it."

Why was the call transforming into a life-coaching session? I had no one but myself to blame. I had initiated the call, and I had failed to prepare for it ahead of time. "I hear you. I have to want it. I do want it."

"And you have to go all out! That's the key. You never go all out, James. You have to change that, or you'll never come out on top. You have to fully commit."

I was so angry at myself. I knew better. I needed to change the topic before he drowned me in aphorisms. "Okay, I got it, Dad. But I also wanted to tell you. I'm seeing someone." Would that be enough for him to jump the track?

"Oh yeah? You're dating someone?" To his credit, he didn't sound completely taken by surprise.

"Yeah, her name's Alexis."

"Oh good." A pause. "I thought maybe you were going to say a guy's name."

Credit withdrawn. I was instantly pissed and humiliated. I shouldn't have let him affect me like that, even if he was my dad.

"Come on, James," he said when I didn't respond. "I was just joshing with you."

"Sure, Dad."

"James, don't be so sensitive. You're going to sulk now because I made one joke?"

"No, it's fine."

"Really, James—"

"Dad," I interrupted, "it's fine. Move on."

"Okay. I was just joking. So tell me about…" He trailed off.

"Alexis?"

"Yeah. Tell me about her. How did you meet her?"

"She works at my firm. I used to see her around every once in a while, but we went on a date last month and hit it off."

"Have you gone out since?"

"Yeah, we've been on a bunch of dates since then. And we talk and hang out a lot."

"That's good. That's good. Hey, you remember that flighty girl you dated in high school?"

"Brittany?" I said. How the heck did he remember her?

"Yeah, her. Alexis has more between the ears than she did, I hope?"

"Yeah, Dad." Are you kidding me? I was telling him about a person I was dating now, and he had to remind me I dated a dumb girl in high school? I'd had enough. "Hey I'm getting another call," I lied. "I should go."

"Oh, all right. Remember though, you have to go all out. Like your brother."

"Nice talking to you, Dad."

"Sure. Thanks for calling."

I was still seething after I mercy killed our conversation, so I texted Rachel. *Hey, what are you doing?*

Watching TV, she said moments later. *You?*

Just talked to Dad.

You did? He call you?

No. I called him.

Really? You never call him.

I know. There's a good reason for that, I reminded her and myself.

So what'd you guys talk about? How awesome I am?

No. You didn't come up.

☹

I told him about work first. He wanted to know whether I was "going for it" like Andrew is. I think he wishes I was an Andrew clone.

Maybe. What'd you tell him?

Who cares. Doesn't matter. But then I told him I was seeing Alexis, and guess how he responded?

? I don't know.

He expressed gratitude that I'm not dating a guy.

Oh. Sorry.

So annoying. He's such a dick sometimes.

Don't say that. At least he showed some interest. He usually doesn't.

True. Infanticidal fish show more interest in their young.

You want Dad to eat you?

No. You're gross. And disturbed.

You said it!

Whatever. You want to get lunch tomorrow and bitch about Dad?

I'll meet you for lunch. I'm not sure I want to complain about Dad the whole time.

Fine. I'll take one out of two. Talk to you later.

Good night.

I had wanted to say more to her—a murderous rage was coursing through my insides from the call with my dad—but I didn't want to talk on the phone. I burden Rachel enough with my problems; there was no need to compound it with a lengthy phone call about our dad. And I couldn't guarantee I wouldn't shed some tears if I discussed him at length with her. Texting allowed me to avoid that shameful possibility.

■ ■ ■

That night, as I was lying in bed staring at the ceiling, unable to quench the wrath my dad had set ablaze, Fred popped up out of nowhere like a sniper in a ghillie suit. I was suddenly sitting at a small table in a dark room with no windows. A black box sat on the table. My curiosity demanded I discover what was inside, so I removed the lid to reveal a red button and a blue button. Instructions on the inside of the lid told me I couldn't leave the room until I pressed one of the buttons. If I selected the blue button, my dad would die. If I chose the red button, I would die. I checked the other side of the box for a possible third button, but this was Fred's psychotic dream world, and he never offers happy endings.

As I agonized over my decision for an eternity, I was tempted to slam down both buttons at the same time and be done with it. But in the end, I knew the right choice—the only choice. The illusion ended as I brought my fingers down on the red button.

Chapter 16

THERAPIST NOTES, CONTINUED

June 12, 20XX		
PROGRESS NOTE	**CLIENT NAME:** Wright, James	**START:** 5:31 pm
	SERVICE CODE:	**STOP:** 6:34 pm

SYMPTOM STATUS: maintained	**DIAGNOSTIC CHANGE?** No
CURRENT SYMPTOMS: depressed state	
	LIFE EVENT? No

MEDICATION: compliant

SAFETY: no active suicidal or homicidal ideation

GOALS/OBJECTIVES: Treatment Plan Goal 1 partially achieved
Treatment Plan Goal 2 partially achieved

CLIENT RESPONSE: Full Compliance

COMMENTS: Mr. Wright reported he continues to see Alexis, and their relationship is generally going well. As for work, he noted everything is good, except he had misgivings about how he treated a coworker and had been treating him in the past. He noted they cleared the air, and he hoped to build upon their conversation.

      We spent considerable time discussing a phone call he recently had with his dad. Mr. Wright noted his dad has a history of being uninterested in his life, or worse, condescending. I advised him to be more direct with his father in the future, to state explicitly how he feels when his dad pushes his buttons. He seemed reluctant to follow my advice.

NEXT APPT: June 27, 20XX

Chapter 17

MOM COMES TO VISIT

By the third week in June, I was in love. Well, I think it's love, but what do I know about the subject? Alexis is the first woman I've dated for more than a few weeks. What I do know is since the beginning of June, I've only noticed Fred's presence a handful of times, most notably the night I spoke to my progenitor. Seeing or talking to Alexis every day has kept the vaporous beast at bay. Like the severe acne I had my freshman year in high school that resisted nearly all treatment, he was not missed.

I'm taking Friday off from work because my mom is coming to town. She'll stay with me for the weekend and then with Rachel for the week. Apparently, Rachel's internship is stressing her out more than she expected, so my mom wants to help by doing domestic chores for her like cooking and laundry. I complained I would appreciate the same services, but it got me nowhere. I always knew Rachel was her favorite. At least I rank above Andrew in the pecking order. I think.

My mom is neck and neck with Rachel when it comes to reasons for not acting on my Fredicidal ideations. She is the quintessential mom: slow to anger, quick to forgive, endlessly fair, patient, and loving in all things. When we were young, these traits revealed their shortcomings only in board games. She purposely sold Park Place and Marvin Gardens for pittances to the person in last place, wildly upending the balance of the game (and eroding the basic tenets of capitalism).

It seems strange to write about given the recent but growing disconnect between Fred and me, but if I ever did kill myself, I know it would devastate her. She gives everything for the three of us; we are her world, and she feels our pain so acutely. I wish I lived closer to her so I could see her more often, but my desire to put hundreds of zip codes between my dad and me won out.

■ ■ ■

My mom arrived Thursday night, and on Friday morning we met Alexis for brunch before Alexis flew to Nashville for a bachelorette party. She and Alexis immediately hit it off. I was surprised by how well, but I guess I shouldn't have been. My mom is the best, and how could you not like Alexis?

"I know you have to leave for the airport any minute," my mom said, "but has James told you about the time he was too embarrassed by a girl to say 'thank you'?"

"No, I'm pretty sure he has not," Alexis said, with her eyes wide open in mock surprise.

"Mom, I don't know what story you're digging up, but Alexis should be leaving—"

"No, it's okay." Alexis cut me off while casting suspicious squinty eyes at me. "I've got a few more minutes," she told my mom with a wink. How many ocular gestures can one person make? It was such a sad life being limited to blinking.

"Okay, wonderful. James was in sixth grade—"

"It was fourth grade, Mom," I interrupted.

"Huh?"

"It was fourth grade. Not sixth grade."

"I thought you didn't know what story I was referring to."

"I figured it out. It was fourth grade."

"You figured it out, huh? I see. So James was in fourth grade," my mom continued, "and this cute little girl named Gretchen had a crush on him. James was always popular with the girls in grade school. Did he tell you that?"

"No, he sure didn't," Alexis replied while poking me in the ribs. She must have been out of ophthalmic gesticulations. "But I can believe it." My face and neck had gone from coral pink to crimson—like a cut from shaving that wouldn't stop bleeding.

"Oh he was such a handsome little boy. Didn't smile enough if you ask me, but so darn cute. The girls on the playground were always trying to kiss him on the cheek."

"Yes, I peaked in third grade. Enough, Mom. Get back to the story, or Alexis will miss her flight."

"I thought you didn't want me to tell the story, honey."

"I prefer the story to any improvisation on your part." Who knew what tangents she could go down.

"Okay, then let me tell it," she said, before pausing to see if I would interrupt again. I didn't. I wanted this over. Otherwise, her stupid story would be the only thing Alexis remembered about me while she was in Nashville. "So back to Gretchen. She was an adorable little girl with red hair that she always had in a ponytail, and she was always wearing the cutest little dresses. James, did she like to wear dresses, or did her mom want her to wear them?"

"Come on, Mom! I don't know, and I don't care." I really had no idea. I barely even recalled her wearing dresses.

"Okay, okay. As I was saying, Gretchen liked James. And she knew he was a Steelers fan."

"Every kid was a Steelers fan, Mom."

"Shush. So she comes to school one day with a card signed by a player. I can't remember which player; it's on the tip of my tongue—"

This story was never going to end. "It doesn't matter," I informed her.

"Hmm?"

"The player on the card. It has no bearing on your story," I told her. "Please continue."

"Well, that's rude. Anyway, Gretchen brings a Steelers card to school. I think her dad got it signed for her. And how does James respond?"

"I believe I thanked her appropriately for her gesture," I lied, "but I didn't like her back. So I then gently explained to her that while she was a lovely girl, I was not the one for her, and there were plenty of other fish in the sea. She was dismayed but ultimately understood I was not ready to be tied down."

My mom laughed, and I'm pretty sure Alexis snorted.

"Oh no you didn't," my mom said. "James stood there as speechless as a statue. Didn't say a word. Eventually Gretchen walked away embarrassed."

"You weren't even there, Mom," I said. "How would you know?" Gretchen might have walked away embarrassed, but she and her friends later made fun of me for an extended period of time. I definitely remembered that.

"Is that not how it happened, James?" she asked rhetorically. "Your friends and the teacher told it that way." I refused to answer. There was no need to add details or length to her story. "So the next day, I had to call her mother and thank Gretchen on James's behalf."

"So you've always been smooth with the ladies, huh?" Alexis wisecracked.

"Your flight is going to leave without you," I said. "You should get going now. Don't they say you should get to the airport at least three hours in advance?"

"I wish I could hear more stories, but James is right. It was a pleasure to meet you, Mrs. Wright," Alexis said as she stood up.

"You too, dear. I'm so glad I got a chance to meet you before you left for the weekend. James has said so many good things about you."

"Wrap it up," I said, poorly disguised as a fake cough.

My mom and Alexis hugged, and then I walked Alexis and her suitcase to a cab outside. For the record, I offered to drive her, but she wouldn't hear of it when she learned my mom would be in town.

"Have a great time. I'll miss you. Ignore any and all dudes that hit on you," I advised. I had been trying my best not to think about exactly how many grimy sleazeballs were going to be flirting with her, buying her drinks, and trying to dance with her. Maybe I should have bought a plane ticket and protected her honor from a distance—but no, I couldn't have ditched my mom.

"Ha. You have nothing to worry about, James," Alexis said. "But now that I know you've been a ladies' man since grade school, I have to worry about you!"

"Yeah, yeah. I'm the one who has to worry. I knew I should've bought you a promise ring to mark my territory."

She snorted this time; I was sure of it. "Very funny. Your territory. Do you want to inspect my outfits to make sure they're not too revealing?"

"You'll let me do that?" I asked her with fake sincerity.

"No! Get out of here. But seriously, James, you have nothing to worry about. I'll miss you the entire time." Then she kissed me in a way that told me she meant it. That would have subdued my angst for no more than five minutes, despite her passion.

"I don't know. I'm not persuaded. I think I need another one of those." She obliged.

"All right," she said as she took a breath and stepped back, "I really am going to be late now. I'll let you know when I land. Have fun with your mom. She seems like a great lady!"

"Okay, be safe. Talk to you soon." Then she was gone, heading to the land of bars, cowboys, live bands, and competing bachelor and bachelorette parties. I had nothing to worry about. Nothing at all.

I strode back into the restaurant and noticed my mom was just sitting back down in her seat. "Were you spying on us?" I was half surprised and half amused.

"Of course not," she said with forced indignation. "How dare you accuse me of such behavior." The red on her neck revealed her embarrassment. It's no secret which of my parents gave me my genetic tell. "But that was some kiss you two had." Then she winked at me. Why can't I wink if she can?

"Mom! Never speak of this again."

"Really, it was sweet—"

"Never again!"

"Whatever you say. I like her, though. You did good. Don't mess this up; she could have her pick of men."

"Thanks for the added pressure, Mom. But yes, I know. She likes you too, by the way. I have no idea why."

■ ■ ■

After brunch, we headed to Michigan Avenue to walk around, more to enjoy the weather than to buy anything. We occasionally stopped in the designer stores, but my mom wouldn't let me purchase anything for her. Unlike me, she doesn't have expensive tastes. She's always been content shopping at places like Target and TJ Maxx. Even when I had bought pricy things for her in the past without asking her, she ended up returning them, so I gave up trying to impress her. I can't even begin to imagine the heartburn my mom's frugality has caused Andrew all the years he's been working at his law firm. That makes me a little happy.

After lunch at Shaw's Crab House—my mom's a sucker for seafood, too, and she at least let me pay for that—I tried to persuade her to go to the Art Institute, but she wasn't biting.

"Rachel told me how much fun those architectural boat cruises are. It's so nice outside; do you want to do that?"

I couldn't say no to my mom, so I took a river cruise for the second time in four weeks. It turned out not to be a bad thing, because I apparently paid much more attention to Alexis than the buildings the first time.

■ ■ ■

That night, we ate dinner at Carnivale, a Latin fusion restaurant in the West Loop, where my mom spotted couples dancing in the bar area—a common scene at that place.

"I used to do that with Charles," she said, somewhat wistfully.

My parents divorced about ten years ago, when I was still in high school. My dad has dated floozies ever since, but my mom went several years without a date. By choice, mind you—she's a catch by anyone's standards: attractive with shoulder-length blond hair and blue eyes, fit for her age, caring, intelligent, and easily amused. And she can cook. But she spent over two decades married to a guy who it turned out lied more often than he told the truth, so the last thing she wanted to do was rush into another relationship.

Charles, an elementary school principal, was recently divorced when he met my mom about three years ago through a mutual friend. He was a nice enough guy on the few occasions I met him—he and my mom only dated for about a year—but I always thought she could do better. Apparently she did too.

"You and Charles used to salsa dance?" I asked skeptically. "Like more than once?"

"We did! Don't look so incredulous. Well, I did, anyway. Charles had two left feet, but he was always willing to try; I appreciated that. I don't think your dad took me dancing once in almost twenty-three years of marriage."

I never knew my mom liked to dance, though I guess that isn't something a son is supposed to know about his mom. "When'd you learn to dance?" I asked her. "And whatever happened with Charles?"

She laughed and said, "I had a life before you came along, you know. I was young once."

I wanted to know as little as possible about her dating history and the early years when she and my dad were in love, so I cracked a joke. "Before Andrew came along, you mean, right? He's the one who ended your party lifestyle? Then you had to have me, because Andrew was such a big disappointment?"

"Exactly. Then I had to have Rachel for the same—"

"Hey! I see what you did there."

"I love all three of you equally," she said. "You know that. And you know I wish you wouldn't say so many negative things about your brother. He loves you, even if he isn't good at communicating it." If my mom has blinders for anything, it's for my brother's lack of empathy—and his general dearth of redeeming qualities.

"All right, no more Andrew bashing," I said. I do plenty of it on my own time. "But back to Charles. What happened? He seemed like a decent guy."

"He was. He was always a perfect gentleman. That was never an issue. He was funny too. Besides you and Rachel, no one has made me laugh more." I was glad she gave Rachel and me the credit we were due, but I had a hard time believing Charles was as witty as us. "He might have been a little lacking in the passion and romance side of things, but even that wasn't a problem for me."

She trailed off without elaborating this last point. I was glad she didn't try; I was getting ready to cut her off.

"The thing that ended it for me," she said, "was that he wasn't over his first wife. She divorced him rather than it being mutual, and I could tell he'd go back to her in a heartbeat if she ever asked."

Sometimes as a kid, and even as a young adult, you forget your parents are people. Or the realization never dawns on you in the first place. Parents are people who have lived a quarter to a third of their lifetimes before you were even here. People with feelings, dreams, fears. And lust. Gross, gross, old-person lust. They've been around as long as you can literally remember, you've embarrassed each other countless times, you've ruined their belongings, you've made them unbelievably proud, and you've loved each other unconditionally—but you've never known who they are. Perhaps you never even realized you lacked the understanding as to what makes them tick.

Then you have conversations like the one I was having with my mom, and you get to see a new side of your mom or dad. You begin to understand their world, while often about you, is not always about you. You begin to note and appreciate their more subtle qualities, like a fine wine, or in a movie when a minor character reveals him or herself to be much more than what you first assumed. *The Usual Suspects* comes to mind.

"What let you know he was still hooked on her?" I was truly curious.

"I don't think there was any one big thing," she said. "I just noticed many little things over time. He still had a couple pictures hanging in his house that featured her, he had a box of her stuff in his basement... What else? He kept his ring in a little ceramic dish on his dresser, as if he might wear it again someday." I didn't want to know why she knew the contents of his bedroom. "And he would sometimes say things that made me wonder," she said, somewhat mysteriously.

"So how did you end it?"

"Basically by telling him what I just told you. He took it pretty hard, but he also seemed to agree with me and after a while almost seemed relieved. I know I made the right decision for me. And for him. He needed time to figure out who he was without his ex and without anyone to distract him from that journey."

"Are there any prospects on the horizon?" If I kept asking questions like that, I was going to start hearing hints about my mom's sex life, and I did not want that. But I was also interested to learn more about this aspect of her life of which I knew so little.

"There might be," she said coyly. She didn't say anything more.

"What, are you going to make me beg?"

"Nope. I don't want to tell you just yet."

"What? Why not? This morning you interrogated Alexis and then spied on us making out."

"I did nothing of the sort! But she is a lovely young woman. I don't want to tell you about him because it's early. If it gets a little more serious, I'll tell you all the grisly sexual details."

Ugh. I had asked for that, but I didn't want it. "Let's get the check," I told her. "Time to go home."

■ ■ ■

Our Saturday was more low key. I showed her around my small neighborhood, and we visited parts of Lincoln Park to run errands before going to a movie that night. I cooked breakfast for us Sunday morning while she got her stuff together to go to Rachel's.

"James, you're going to drive me to Rachel's?"

"Of course, Mom. What kind of a son do you think I am?"

"A good one. I was just checking."

"The best?"

"Tied for best. Before we leave, I want to talk to you about your mental state."

She tapped my forehead as she said this. It would've been an annoying gesture if anyone else had done it; with her, it felt loving. But I can't say I was thrilled we were going to discuss my depression. I had been hoping we could avoid it all weekend. And for the rest of my life.

"I'm fine. I know you employ Rachel as a spy, so you must know that." As much as I love Rachel, her constant meddling can be a little overbearing; she does not excel at hiding her intent. Although I secretly agree that her oversight is a necessary evil.

"We're all concerned about you. You're my son. I'll do whatever it takes to keep tabs on you and to make sure you're okay. You know I wish you hadn't moved so far away. And you took Rachel with you!"

"Okay, okay. I know. And like I said, I'm fine. I'm more than fine. I've been happy since I started seeing Alexis. When was the last time I could say that?"

"That's what has me worried, honey. What happens if the relationship doesn't work out? Are you strong enough to handle it? Do you have a support system in place?"

I could feel Fred maniacally laughing in the back of my mind like Dr. Claw, and I didn't like it. "I'm as strong as I've ever been, Mom." I wasn't sure how reassuring that comment was to her. "And I do have a support system. Rachel's here, Manuel's here, and I'm seeing Dr. B. I got it covered."

"You know you can call me day and night? I keep my phone by my bed."

"I know, Mom. I know."

She hugged me for a long time, probably the longest she had in years, and she cried a little too. My mom isn't much of a crier, so it's notable whenever she does it. "I love you, James," she whispered. It was easy to take that kind of love for granted; I needed to remind myself to savor the moment.

"I love you too, Mom."

Then I drove her to Rachel's place.

Chapter 18

YOUR GRANDPA'S CLOTHES AND THE GREAT OUTDOORS

I rendezvoused with Manuel Sunday afternoon for a late lunch. For whatever reason, he wanted to go to a thrift shop afterward. Sometimes it's easier not to ask when it comes to Manuel's intentions.

"*Hermano,*" he greeted me as he sauntered in—of course I beat him to the sandwich place right by his apartment—"*Qué tal?*"

"You're in a good mood. You see Sam this weekend?"

"*Si. Si.*"

"And?"

"And what?"

"You're not going to give me any update? You guys are hanging out like every single night."

"*Chacho,* you sound like Reina right now. We're good; everything's going great." I was pretty sure his face just flushed a little. "But you still have to keep it a secret. Neither one of us wants to be office gossip. *Entiendes?*"

"I got it, man. Tell everyone. No problem."

"Funny. What about you? You still aren't mopey, so you must've seen Alexis this weekend."

The mopey comment stung a little. I know I'm not always happy-go-lucky, but I try to minimize my exposure to others when Fred is coming down on me. I hate thinking of him indirectly raining on other people's parades. "Nah. I told you Alexis was going to Nashville for the weekend. Remember?"

"Oh, right. Did she meet a rock singer and leave you?"

"No. We're still a thing, I think. She comes back tonight. But based on her text messages, it sounds like she got hit on by the entire city of Nashville."

"Well, whatever you're doing, keep doing it. It seems to be working." He paused momentarily and then asked with a furrowed brow, "So if Alexis was flirting with guys all weekend while you were here, why are you in a good mood?"

"I can't just be in a good mood, Manny?"

"You? No." Then he tacked on, way too late, "No offense."

"Oh, of course, none taken," I said. Has anyone ever prefaced or followed a statement with "no offense" and not offended someone? "My mom was staying with me. That's why I'm not mopey."

"Diane Wright was in town? Why didn't you tell me? I love your mom."

"Her orders. She said, 'Keep Manuel away from me.' I thought it was harsh, but she's my mom, so—"

"Shut up, man. Seriously, I would've loved to see her." My mom's always been fond of Manuel too. Probably mostly because his presence increased my small circle of friends by one.

"Relax, she's still here. She's staying with Rachel during the week; we can meet them for dinner one night. We just had a mother-son weekend, that's all."

"Good. You're off the hook, for now. Hey, before I forget, I want to put together a camping trip this weekend, since July Fourth is around the corner. Are you free? Do you think Alexis would want to go?"

"I'm free and definitely interested. Wait—are you trying to set up a double date?"

"Ah, you're too predictable, *mano*. I told Sam you'd make some stupid joke about it being a double date."

Maybe I'm predictable, but in my defense, who wouldn't have made a double date joke in that circumstance? "Well, glad I could prove you right. It just so happens Alexis and I were looking to get away somewhere. Not with you and Sam, of course, but I'll check with Alexis. I think this could work."

"Sure, no problem. We were thinking of going to the Michigan dunes."

"Cool. I camped near St. Joseph a couple years ago and loved it there. I think I could sell that to Alexis."

"All right. It's a plan." Then he corrected himself unnecessarily. "Tentatively. A tentative plan."

■ ■ ■

After eating, we rode the train to a secondhand store. "So what are we doing here?" I asked Manuel.

"For starters, I'm always on the hunt for costume accessories. You know this." I did know this, even though I've only been on a handful of thrift shop outings with him. His closet is full of random stuff, and if you're ever in urgent need of a costume, Manuel is your guy. He's like one of those year-round Christmas stores that I despise—doesn't everyone?—but for Halloween.

"And I also want to get some stuff for camping," he said.

"Have you been camping before? What kind of stuff do you think people wear? It's not ruffled tuxedo shirts and oversized pleated khakis."

"No, I've never been camping in a tent," Manuel said. "But how hard can it be? Don't you wear flannel shirts, old jeans, and anything made by Carhartt? And a toothpick in your mouth; can't forget that."

"I think you're conflating camping with rodeos. But I guess you're technically not wrong about the rest. I would advise against flannel, though; it's going to be like eighty degrees this weekend." Just thinking about wearing long-sleeved flannel was putting my sweat factories into action; they are always prepared for maximum output at the drop of a hat. "I'll mostly bring shorts and T-shirts and a couple swimsuits. Oh, and a sweatshirt or two for at night," I told him. "Zero flannel shirts."

"Your loss, *muchacho*. I'm going to look like a rugged lumberjack. Sam won't be able to keep her hands off me."

■ ■ ■

On Wednesday night, I joined Manuel, Rachel, and my mom at a tapas place in River North. Rachel and my mom were already at the restaurant when I arrived, which I have to say caused me to have a minor identity crisis. My distress must have been palpable, because Rachel started to laugh when I walked toward their table.

"I told you, Mom," Rachel joshed. "You owe me five dollars."

"I absolutely do not. I never took your bet. The whole world knows James can't stand being the second person to arrive."

I looked at each of them slowly, with quasi scorn, mainly to give myself enough time to think of a good comeback. "Technically, I'm the third person to arrive. And punctuality and reliability are highly desirable traits. I don't know why you two would mock me for having them. No one ever failed a quiz or missed their son's recital for being too early."

Rachel and my mom, respectively, did those two things, although I don't think they cared too much. Rachel has never received a final grade other than A through all levels of school, so her one missed quiz was no biggie. As for the cello recital my mom missed, I had failed to practice for the stupid thing, so it was in everyone's best interest that she did not attend.

As I was speaking, Manuel stepped up behind me and slapped me on the back, hard but not hard enough to be noticed by others.

"Hey, bud," he said, all chummy, as he slipped past me after assaulting my person.

You're good, Manuel, but I'll get you back. This was going in the vault.

"Mrs. Wright, so good to see you," Manuel exclaimed.

My mom said something similar, and they exchanged a hug. It was a formal kind of hug where the participants formed a collective X with their arms as they approached each other, but then my mom gave Manuel a little extra squeeze before letting go. I'm going to have to have a chat with her about the appropriate way for a mom to hug her son's smart-ass friend.

He then turned to my sister and gave her a similar hug while stage whispering, "*Hola*, Rachel, *eres hermosa, como siempre.*"

Then he capped off his Spanish nonsense with a kiss on each of her cheeks. The gesture was probably not suspect to my mom or Rachel— it was probably even appropriately affectionate to them—but he's never greeted someone like that in my presence the whole time I've known him. I saw through him like the off-white bathing suit I used to wear as a preteen.

The majority of the dinner conversation was unremarkable. Manuel's parents were happy; the restaurant his dad worked at was doing well; his mom was volunteering at their church and was jogging multiple days a week; and Reina was excelling at a Big Four accounting firm. I asked Manuel if Reina was dating anyone, and he pointedly ignored me.

The only offbeat part of the evening occurred on my way back from the restroom. Before I was in eyesight of our table, I got a premonition that the three of them were talking about me. I would have dismissed the portent as idle paranoia, but they hurriedly changed the topic of conversation and raised their voices as I came within earshot.

I was more than a little perturbed they were talking about me. I presumed it had to do with my present mental state and whether I had shown any continued signs of depression. Since I hadn't been—I thought—there was nothing to worry about. Still, they could have asked me directly. They didn't have to talk behind my back. Suspicion always haunts the guilty mind, however, so I did my best to play along with their feigned dialogue.

■ ■ ■

The week seemed to drag on, as workweeks do when you're looking forward to a trip. But the end finally arrived, and Alexis predictably had no qualms about going camping with Manuel and Sam, so the four of us drove to St. Joseph Friday evening. There was no point in leaving earlier—aside from my internal clock's relentless desire to leave as early as possible for everything—because of the Friday afternoon traffic that clogs up I-94 East coming out of Chicago. I'm pretty sure half of the city owns a lake house in Western Michigan, and I am conspicuously among the other half.

By the time we arrived at the campground and Manuel parked his car, it was after nine thirty, and light was fading fast. None of us were experienced outdoorsmen; half of our gear probably still had tags on it. Except for Manuel's gently used clothes, of course.

Much to my surprise, tent technology had come a long way since I was a kid. By "when I was a kid," I mean when my dad was a kid, because he refused to replace things that "ain't broke." Instead of having to weave rusty, ill-fitting metal poles through moldy canvas that smelled like an overflowing toilet on a cruise ship, I quickly snapped together two shiny poles that consisted of smaller poles held together with a threaded elastic rope. I even resisted the urge to use them like nunchakus. After I strung them through the tent fabric and popped them up, I was done! Given my newly acquired survival skills, I figured I should look into scaling Mount Everest next. If guys in their seventies could do it, it couldn't be that hard.

The four of us had a beer, but we didn't hang out too long before separating to our respective tents. It was colder than I expected; I was glad I had brought some long-sleeved shirts in addition to the two sweatshirts I mentioned to Manuel. Although cozying up to Alexis in our tent would help.

Once in the tent, Alexis purred softly to me, "I'm happy we're here, James," as she nuzzled her nose against my neck.

"Me too," I said quietly. "When my girlfriend was in Nashville last weekend, all I could think about was having her back, right next to me." Thanks to some earlier practice, I managed to say this line articulately and without it seeming forced.

We hadn't had a relationship talk. I had concocted a dozen different ways to broach the subject, but I had never executed any of them. I figured this weekend was as good a time as any to bring it up. Especially because it was damn near impossible to exit a tent quickly. She would have had to find the zipper in the dark, unzip the flap (actually two flaps on that brand-spanking-new tent), and then step out as if she had just driven a Fiat for a thousand miles. So long story short, she was stuck with me now.

"Your girlfriend, hmm? So we're an official couple now?" I could tell she was trying to provoke me rather than sincerely question our status, but I still wanted to explain to her, at least try to explain anyway, how important she was (and is) to me.

"Aren't we? When I'm away from you, I can't stop thinking about you, and when I'm with you, I never want to be anywhere else. I know we only went on our first date like a month ago, but I knew I liked you the day I met you three years ago." I had never bared my heart to anyone whom I wasn't paying to listen to me. Must have been the fresh air. I prayed it wasn't a mistake.

"That might be the sweetest thing anyone's ever said to me. I feel the same way, James," she said. "It is kind of crazy. I mean, it's only been a few weeks, but I want to spend every minute with you." Huge internal sigh of relief. I envisioned Fred floating away with his head hanging. "Whenever we leave each other, I start looking forward to the next time I'll see you."

"Well, you make me happy. It's as simple as that." If she only knew how significant that was for me. Happiness, something I had never experienced before her. A fun day here and there? Sure. But happiness? Prolonged contentment? Never. Not with Fred around.

"You make me happy too, James. So happy. And thanks for bringing me here." Then she pressed her beautiful lips against mine. A hundred watts shot through me; I was starting to become familiar with that sensation, but it still caught me by surprise.

■ ■ ■

A family of what must have been twenty kids unceremoniously woke us up at the crack of dawn the next morning. Well, their cacophony combined with the lower back pain I should've expected would come from sleeping on the ground. Perhaps I should roll back my designs for Mount Everest. Start with Mount Kilimanjaro instead.

After shaking off our rude awakening, we spent most of the day at the beach getting sun, which was fine with me. When you have the same pallor as Gollum, you take all the color you can get, even if it's red. Around midafternoon, Sam and Alexis went for a long walk along the beach, which provided Manuel and me a chance to catch up. We tossed a football while we talked, though; two guys lying on the sand together, sunbathing and chatting, raises questions and eyebrows. I don't mind if random people think I'm gay, but I do mind if they think Manuel is my type.

"So, things still good with work and Sam?" I asked Manuel as I caught one of his wobbly ducks. "She doesn't seem to be annoyed with you—so far, anyway."

"They are, *mano*. Life is good. Work is busy but not crazy, and everything with Sam is so easy. We have a good time every time we hang out, which is almost all the time. Ouch." I had thrown a pass a little hard, and it bounced off Manuel's hands. "But she tells me when she's too busy or has other plans. And I know that when she tells me something like that—like that she has to work late one night—it's the truth and not her playing games. On the flipside, when I tell her I have to stay late at the office or I'm meeting a friend, she doesn't give me a hard time. She just tells me to have fun or that she misses me—and not in a needy or guilt-trippy way."

"That's great, man. Awesome, actually."

"Yeah, I have no complaints," he continued, unprompted. "The only thing I'm worried about is moving too fast. I've had girlfriends before—you know that—but nothing that felt as serious as this. When am I supposed to propose to her, if it goes that far? Do I move in with her before that? These are things I need to know."

"I gotta say, you're asking the wrong person," I said. "I don't know the answer to any of those questions. But I think the fact you're thinking about them means this relationship means more to you than the ones you had in the past."

"Yeah, that was more me thinking out loud than asking you questions. A few months ago, your idea of a date was talking to the lady who answers the phone at the Chinese restaurant by your apartment."

"I'm going to ignore that," I said, but it was a tiny bit true. She has a beautiful voice. "I hope things with Sam keep going well for you, though. I like her a lot." That was the truth. I didn't have a lot of data to go on, but so far I had always enjoyed talking to her. And, I could see the effect she was having on my best friend. How could I not like her? "But did you tell her you're Puerto Rican? And does she still want to be with you?"

The racial jokes never quite died out between us. Manuel's are way funnier than mine, but I wouldn't do them justice if I tried to write them down. They're usually more about his delivery and parodic skills than the actual words, although he does enjoy referring to the whiteness of my skin as bioluminescence. If only—at least then I'd have a superpower.

"Maybe you've never heard of 'tall, dark, and handsome'?" he asked as he tried to whiz a pass at me. It was way too high, and I had to run after it. "Also," he went on when I was back within hearing distance, "ladies love a little Latin flavor. A little spice in their life. Very few women I know go crazy for plain vanilla frozen yogurt like you, *mano*. Especially when those guys' life accomplishments exist only on their Xbox."

That stung a little. "You're not tall, Manuel. No one under six feet has ever called themselves tall." It was a weak comeback, but it was all I had at the moment. Some women like vanilla frozen yogurt, right? It's perfect for adding any kind of topping!

"All right, fine, but I am dark and handsome. And there's no denying my proud Puerto Rican heritage. Or my swagger."

I'm not usually in the business of ignoring a person's use of the word *swagger*, but before I could say anything, Manuel asked me about Alexis, so I let it slide. That time. "We're good. Not quite on the same level as you and Sam, I think. But things are upwardly projecting. She's here, after all, right?"

"Yeah, true."

"Although…" *Should I bring up this nagging feeling? Nah.*

"Although what?" he asked as he bounced a pass into the sand five feet in front of me.

"It's nothing," I said. "Sometimes I get the feeling there's some secret she's hiding. But I'm probably just making something out of nothing."

"You can be paranoid sometimes."

"This is true." But I can be a grade-A sleuth too. In this case, though, my mind had probably mulled over the few times Alexis's reactions had thrown me off—like when I joked about being an alcoholic—far more often than it should have.

"Any idea where things are headed?" he asked. "I know your mom likes her, so that's positive. But do you think you're moving toward being a couple?"

"If you had asked me yesterday, I wouldn't have been sure. We talked about it last night, though, and we're definitely boyfriend-girlfriend now. So I can tell relatives I'm not single, and it will be the truth." I have a couple of aunts who were starting to harass me about my bachelor status, and not because they were worried I was a playboy. "Actually, she even invited me to a wedding in a few weeks, and her parents will be there. If she's willing to let her close friends and family meet me, she must be comfortable with me."

"Well then, congratulations are in order. Well done. I'm a fan of Alexis. She's good for you."

"Thanks, Manny."

"But James," he cautioned, "whatever you're doing, don't be yourself. That can only lead to disaster."

"Thanks, Manny."

"I mean it. Whatever drug you're giving her, or whatever lies you're telling her, keep doing it."

"Thanks, Manny."

"And stop calling me Manny."

"Okay, Manny."

Chapter 19

BEHIND ENEMY LINES

In early July, a couple of days after the camping trip ended, I was back in the office and unusually light on work. That was fine because I couldn't stop thinking about how much fun the trip was—and how gorgeous Alexis was, particularly without makeup and running water. She even naturally smells good! My thoughts, as they typically were doing lately, started to drift slightly erotic in nature.

I began to daydream about Alexis walking toward me on an ocean beach wearing only a diaphanous beach cover-up. The last rays of the sunset played off the water and danced on her tanned skin. She directed a flirtatious smile at me as she started to slide the gauzy material off one of her shoulders and lasciviously licked her top lip…

"James, perk up," some obnoxious voice barked at me. "This is no time for la-la land!"

"Hrrrmm?" I said, as I jolted forward in my ergonomic office chair—perfect for grinding out long hours in front of a computer screen or for ill-timed forays into dreamland. I was temporarily discombobulated. My left hand reflexively moved to cover my groin area. Without knowing my exact status down there, it was better safe than sorry to add some cover—the tailored fit of the modern man's dress slacks was less than ideal for concealing ill-timed arousal.

Francis Mason, the wannabe drill sergeant harassing me, is one of the most polarizing partners in the office. He looks just like Sgt. Slaughter fifteen years after he quit wrestling. Francis is single-handedly fighting the work-life balance movement, demanding long hours from his subordinates and expecting availability seven days a week. Half the partners love him because they can look reasonable by comparison, and a vocal minority of sadomasochistic associates adore him because they are sad, sad people with no outside interests. In my humble opinion, life is entirely too short to devote the majority of it to office work. Something tells me, however, that his wife doesn't mind him being at the office eighty hours a week.

Did you know Europeans are *guaranteed* twenty to twenty-five paid vacation days a year? Saudi Arabians get twenty-one days, Ethiopians have fourteen, and even China mandates five days for its citizens. In the United States? Zero mandated paid vacation days. I think we have our puritanical ancestors to thank. Thanks for nothing, forefathers.

"James. Seriously, son. Snap to it."

Apparently, I didn't address him quickly enough. I was all clear down below, so I moved my awkwardly placed left hand to a less conspicuous position.

"Uh, so sorry, sir," I mumbled clumsily. "What can I do for you?"

I say "sir" to almost no one. Not out of a lack of respect, but because I'm not in the military, and the practice seems to have fallen out of style. Francis is an exception, because he seems like the type of guy who would pursue one's termination with zeal if one did not kowtow to him. I avoid obsequiousness as much as I can, but my desire for nice things trumps that particular point of pride.

"Conference room in twenty minutes. I'm putting together a team for an upcoming project. You're on it."

I suppose I was a little flattered he had chosen me, but I was more concerned about what that meant for my future free time. Four months ago, I didn't have an active social life. That sentence is probably even more accurate if I removed the adjective "active." But now that Alexis—I mean, my girlfriend—had metaphorically pulled the curtains open and let the sunlight in, I'd rather take my chances as a tribute than be worked like a District 12 coal miner.

I arrived at the conference one minute early and noted Elizabeth Foster was not present. A small relief. There were only three people: Francis, Richard Choi, and an engagement manager named Yasmin Gadhi. I had never worked with Yasmin, but people seemed to like her. Although I couldn't recall specifically why I had that impression; maybe something Manuel had said. Yasmin wears a hijab, and every time I've seen her, she's been impeccably dressed in designer clothes.

"Sit," ordered Francis as I entered the room.

"Y-y-yes, sir," I stammered like King George VI. *Pull it together, James.*

I almost saluted Francis but managed to refrain from doing something so blatantly derisive. My dad says I'm the type of person who's good at pissing people off. Parenting style aside, he may have a point. So I'm hypervigilant not to earn a reputation with management as being a smart-ass—although I'm probably failing at that. After all, vinyl floors disguised as hardwood fool no one.

"The firm is starting a nine-month project for a multistate manufacturing company, and the client wants consultants from multiple offices with varied experience levels. You three will be working with me as the Chicago contingent. We won't be starting in earnest for another month or so, but there will be some work leading up to that. Once the project ramps up to full speed, I expect frequent travel to a number of facilities. From what I hear from others, you three are particularly promising, so I have no doubt you'll be up to the challenge, provided you have the proper dedication and fortitude. I'll contact you in the upcoming weeks with more information. Any questions?"

None of us asked any, because Francis posed his question as he was standing up to leave. From all that military vernacular, I was expecting him to dismiss us rather than leave himself.

"That's it? We're just conscripted into a nine-month project without any details being provided to us?" Richard asked rhetorically after Francis had left. It's not uncommon to be given assignments without much notice, but usually the news was not delivered as if we were fresh recruits appearing for boot camp. "I guess we won't be taking any vacations for a year."

"No kidding. I'm thrilled to be staffed with a real live G.I. Joe," Yasmin deadpanned. She has a prominent nose, round cheeks, and full eyelashes, which seem to be trademarks of Pakistani women, although I can't say I'm an expert on the subject. "Who needs nights and weekends?" she joked. *James does. That's who. James does.*

My brain wasn't fully registering what they were saying, because it was currently fabricating another suicide dream sequence. Guerrilla terrorists had commandeered every floor of the office. They carried AK-47s and wore crisscrossed bandoliers holding grenades. Displeased with the progress of hostage negotiations, they began to execute random employees. Blair was one of the first to go. I couldn't watch Alexis, Manuel, and my other friends die without putting up a fight. Drawing from a well of combat experience that in reality I have never received, I yanked a knife from the ankle of the nearest guerrilla fighter and stabbed him in the neck. I then wrenched his AK-47 from his body and began to systematically neutralize all opposition. Just when it looked like I was going to clear the floor of enemy combatants, two hand grenades landed near me within a few feet of each other. In an effort to save as many people as possible, I pushed Francis down on one and dove on the other. In the aftermath, the office decided to install an enormous oil painting of me in the lobby to commemorate my valor. On the anniversary of my death, like clockwork, Alexis would lay flowers and a six-pack of IPAs beneath my portrait.

"Knock, knock. Earth to James. You in there?" Richard asked. "You're not worried about having to work directly with Sgt. Slaughter for so long?"

"Huh? Yeah, of course I am. That man is a maniac."

"Where'd you just go, spaceman?" Yasmin chuckled. "I look down, I look up, and you look like you've entered some kind of trance."

"Ha, I dunno. I zone out sometimes. At least we can commiserate together in the trenches these next nine months." I meant that too. I was already a fan of Richard from our lunch outings. Yasmin was new to me, but I liked my first impression of her. I wished my brain would cut off the military references though.

"That's true," Richard concurred. "You guys couldn't have asked for a better teammate than me."

"Humble, huh?" Yasmin teased with a half smile. "Good to know."

■ ■ ■

As I headed back to my office, I couldn't help but worry whether that daydream was a harbinger of things to come. I'd been flying high for over a month thanks to Alexis, and the frequency of my suicidal fantasies had dropped precipitously. But was my reprieve from Fred only temporary? Was I doomed to return to my previous prolonged state of discontent?

This whole writing exercise sprang from a recommendation to keep a journal, so maybe I should do some reflecting. Put things in perspective. Take stock. Stop stalling.

I'm young and in good physical health; those are definitely favorable characteristics. I also have a respectable job, so add a few more points. My mom and sister are loving and supportive, and I have a dad and brother who are not terrible all the time; those amount to a big net positive. I have a girlfriend who's a real-life girl—giant uptick. And she's gorgeous, intelligent, funny, enjoys the outdoors, and has kept Fred away like an invisible dog fence; those are all icing on the cake. Last but not least, I have some good friends, most notably Manuel, who takes my crap and dishes it back. In the aggregate, those are some pretty significant positives.

I don't want to explore the negatives—I hate giving Fred the chance to creep to the forefront when he's been dormant—but I should do so anyway for completeness. Until recently, I had been hounded so relentlessly by an all-encompassing feeling of gloom that I bothered to name it. That's a bright-red warning flag. I also have less-than-stellar relations with my dad and brother, which undermine my mental health. Not so good. Finally, while I have a job that pays well, it's not my passion in life; I don't see it as a career. And I have no idea what would fulfill me. I think life would be easier if I had something that excited me when I woke up in the morning.

So there it is. Roughly one quarter into my life, and I'm objectively... not sure. Even keel? Doing all right? Let's say Alexis pushes the positives slightly ahead. So don't worry, be happy, James—I know, easier said than done.

■ ■ ■

Tuesday morning, the week after Francis informed me he was going to ruin my life for the next year, I walked with my head down and in a fog as I traversed the first-floor lobby where my office is located. Then I shambled into the elevator that was about to close. I went to lean against the back wall when a husky but sensual female voice greeted me.

"Hello, James."

Startled, I reflexively pushed myself away from the wall and stood up straight. Then I twisted my head and looked up to see Elizabeth Foster across the elevator from me. Before I could stab out my eyes with a pen to prevent petrification, I noticed her jet-black hair was in a loose but attractive bun. Unconsciously, my eyes moved downward, and I saw she was wearing a gray skirt suit and what appeared to be tissue paper for a shirt. On closer inspection, however—my eyes seemed to be stuck in some sort of tractor beam—I observed her top was actually made of fabric, but it was a thin veil of gauzy material that revealed the coloring and contours of her cream-colored bra beneath. Her breasts looked resplendent from where I was standing.

Then it dawned on me what I'd done.

"Goo—good, good morning, Elizabeth," I stammered.

As I was doing so, she briefly flicked her eyes downward at her chest and then directly at me, signifying she had caught me. The left side of her mouth pulled upward into a smirk, confirming she had me dead to rights. Houdini couldn't have escaped this trap.

"How, how are you doing?" I muttered.

I folded my arms and discreetly pinched the hell out of my side so I could focus on anything other than my intense mortification. Some other time, I should investigate whether pain is effective at reducing the intensity of one's humiliation. I will certainly have plenty of opportunities in the future to explore.

"I'm well, James. Are you all right this morning? You seemed a little distracted a second ago." Her voice remained seductive with its low timbre. While she was speaking, she removed whatever item was keeping her hair in place, letting her shimmering onyx locks fall around her shoulders. Then she shook her head to assist her hair's migration.

"Uh, yeah, you caught me off guard. I, uh, didn't know anyone was in the elevator. I wasn't paying attention when I walked in. Long night, you know? A few long nights in a row. I'm way overdue for some sleep. Could

sleep for days." Why was I babbling to her? I'm not a babbler. People sometimes need the jaws of life to extract a sentence out of me.

Oh no. No elevator button was alight. We'd just been sitting there on
the first level for what felt like forty-five days. Caterpillars metamorphosed
into butterflies in less time. I bolted forward too quickly and pressed the
button for my floor with a complete lack of dexterity, my hand movements
resembling an octogenarian with rheumatoid arthritis. Then I stepped
back to where I was and observed Elizabeth smiling.

"So," she said as a full sentence. "I hear you and Alexis Owens are a
couple. Office romance is your thing, hmm?"

The combination of her facial expressions and tone of voice rendered
me dumbfounded. I had no idea what her endgame was; I was totally out
of my league. I also wanted to know how she had heard that information.
Alexis and I hadn't taken pains to keep our relationship secret—certainly
not the way Manuel and Sam had—but it's not like we were broadcasting
its existence. I had only written notes on the backs of a few bathroom doors
across the city.

Before I responded, Elizabeth wiped invisible dust away from her
blouse, just below her clavicle. But I was ready for any such overtures and
kept my eyes to the space slightly right of her head. I had walked into the
elevator an unwary sheep, but I was now a caged orangutan itching to
make my escape. Did you know they can pick locks and unwind screws?
It's true.

"Yep, we're dating," I answered, as impassively as I could. I didn't want
to give away any further emotions. My discomfort must have been palpable.

By the grace of all the gods, the elevator door opened on my floor a
moment later, apparently where she was also getting off. I was tempted to
jolt out first and sprint for cover—anywhere to get away from her—but
it's been ingrained in me to let others out first, so I held the door as I let
her pass. "Have a good day, James," she purred as she brushed by me. The
whole of the elevator door was available for her egress; there was no need
for her to invade my personal space. I did like her perfume, though.

She began to sashay down the hall. I waited an inordinate amount of
time before I began to follow her, my office being in the same direction she
was traveling. After she finally turned a corner and exited from view, all of

my muscles relaxed, and I could feel the heat of my shame emanate in all directions like a tiny supernova.

■ ■ ■

"Manuel!" I shouted as I walked into his office without knocking. "I'm toast. Stick a fork in me. It's all over!"

"Slow down, *mano*. You're fine," he said, not trying at all to placate me.

Then I saw Miles. "Hi, Miles." I greeted him calmly, as if I hadn't walked into his office like a professional gambler who just lost to the wrong bookie.

"Hey," he said.

"I don't know what you're worked up about," Manuel told me, "but I have to run. Sorry." So callous of him. It's like he wasn't taking me seriously at all.

This would not do. No, it would not. I needed to vent before I hyperventilated. "No! You can't! I'm pretty sure HR is on their way down right now to find me. I need to hide. Or leave for the day and never come back."

He grabbed my shoulders and jokingly slapped me. "James, get a grip. You'll be fine. But I have to go."

"What's so important, Manny, that you can't help a friend?"

"Sam and I are going to get coffee." He whispered this, so his danger-zone rule must have still been in effect. Then, with more volume, "You'll be fine. We'll talk when I get back."

"You're turning your back on me for caffeine? Starbucks will still be there in fifteen minutes." Or an hour. I didn't know how long I needed to uncoil my knotted intestines.

"Yes. Goodbye," as he shoved past me.

"If you walk out that door, you're dead to me, Manny."

"See ya," he replied as he stepped out the door. So much for my ultimatum.

I lingered for a second hoping he would return, but he was gone for good. Walked right out of my life without a second glance. Our friendship destroyed in a blink of an eye. I was about to take a step to leave when Miles spoke up.

"So what happened?" he asked. "You kind of look like you've seen a ghost."

"No, that's just my general hue, Miles. Stark white like a bedsheet." I almost said, *We have that in common*, but I managed to hold my tongue. Miles wasn't accustomed to my good-natured mockery. "But I was caught by surprise by a temptress, and now my career is over."

"You're going to have to explain that one," he said.

It should have been plain as day, but I humored him. After all, he hadn't bailed on me, unlike my Puerto Rican ex-best friend. "Elizabeth Foster—you know her?"

"Maybe? I think so," he said unconvincingly. "Describe her."

How do I broach this delicate subject? Miles was not exactly in my circle of trust, so I needed to tread lightly. He could be an HR spy, after all. "Fairly tall, long black hair, full figure."

No lightbulb was going off in his head. "I'm going to need more than that," he stated.

"Well-dressed, carries herself with an air of superiority."

"Still nothing."

Dammit, Miles, come on! He had left me with no choice. "Huge boobs, nice ass. Tends to flaunt them."

"Got it! Yeah, I know her. What'd she do to you? Or should I say, what'd you do to her?"

"I did absolutely nothing, Miles," I told him. "Don't you dare insinuate that I did." He put his hands up to signal truce. "I got on the elevator this morning," I continued, "and she appeared out of the shadows like a trickster demigod. Before I knew what was happening, her feminine wiles left me transfixed, staring at her beauty."

"By beauty, do you mean her boobs?"

How did he know? "Yes, Miles. I do."

"Well," he said, trying to find a silver lining, "I'm sure she didn't notice. You're probably blowing it way out of proportion."

"Oh, she noticed. Trust me. She noticed." If there was a camera in the elevator, she was probably obtaining the footage right then.

"Come on, you can't know that. I doubt she told you that."

"She did! More or less, anyway." There was no other way to interpret her eye movement.

"Hmm." He seemed to be thinking deeply about my predicament. Take notes, Manuel. This is how a friend operates. "Is there anything I can do to help?"

"Yes," I said instinctively. But then I needed to think of something. *Come on, brain, work faster. I got it!* "If she does file something against me, could you write an affidavit on my behalf?"

He seemed dubious. "I could probably do that. What would you want it to say?"

"I don't know. We can cross that bridge if and when we come to it. Maybe something about how I'm an Eagle Scout and in my spare time I volunteer at a women's shelter."

"Are you an Eagle Scout?"

"No, Miles. But it's not like you can get in trouble for lying in an affidavit. Everyone knows that." I hoped he knew I was joking with him. Otherwise, any real affidavit he did write was going to be extremely damning for me. "But like I said, we can talk about that later, if necessary."

"Okay, but do you help at a women's shelter?"

"Huh? No, let it go, Miles."

"You're the one who said it."

"Fine. We can talk about it later." I needed to get to my office, since I hadn't actually been there yet that morning. "There is something you could do right now, though, if you don't mind. It's minor."

"Sure," he said immediately. "What is it?" I liked how he was still willing to help me despite my suggestion for him to commit perjury. Like I said, Manuel, take notes.

"Could you look out into the hallway and make sure Elizabeth isn't out there?" I asked.

He stuck his head out the door and looked right and then left. "Oh crap," he said.

That didn't sound good. "What is it?"

"It's Elizabeth. She's walking this way. And Kathy Mannino from HR is with her."

No! This couldn't be happening. Not even Fred could fabricate a nightmare that swift and hellish. Then Miles saw my face and burst out laughing.

"There's nobody out there, is there, you punk?"

He wasn't able to answer for a while, because he was doubled over laughing. I eventually joined in with a little chuckle. After all, I do love when people amuse themselves to such a degree.

"Well played, Miles. Well played. I'm leaving."

"See ya, Eagle Scout."

"I'll be at the women's shelter if you need me."

Chapter 20

THERAPIST NOTES, AGAIN

July 13, 20XX			
PROGRESS NOTE	**CLIENT NAME:** Wright, James		**START:** 5:05 pm
	SERVICE CODE:		**STOP:** 5:53 pm
SYMPTOM STATUS: maintained		**DIAGNOSTIC CHANGE?** No	
CURRENT SYMPTOMS: depressed state			
		LIFE EVENT? No	
MEDICATION: compliant			
SAFETY: no active suicidal or homicidal ideation			
GOALS/OBJECTIVES: Treatment Plan Goal 1 partially achieved Treatment Plan Goal 2 partially achieved			
CLIENT RESPONSE: Full Compliance			
COMMENTS: Mr. Wright was in good spirits during this session and reported having been in an optimistic mood for over a week. He attributed most of this to his blossoming relationship with a woman named Alexis. His suicidal ideation remained infrequent, and it is noteworthy he did not joke about its inevitable recurrence, or about Fred's inexorable return, which he typically does to qualify his reports of positive feelings. His view on work remained largely the same, although he was concerned about an upcoming project that could consume most of his free time for the foreseeable future.			
NEXT APPT: August 2, 20XX			

Chapter 21

MAWAGE. MAWAGE IS WOT BWINGS US TOGEDER TODAY

The end of July had come, about three weeks after our camping trip and two weeks after my Elizabeth Foster elevator encounter. No one had fired me so far, and no one had notified me that a sexual discrimination complaint had been filed. I was probably safe—I assumed my office had a lot bigger fish to fry than me—but I was still a little freaked out.

The past few weeks, I had been spending almost all my free time with Alexis. I wouldn't go back and change anything, but I was starting to miss Manuel and Rachel—and I was feeling guilty about not seeing them. At least my conscience was a little assuaged because they themselves had been busy—Manuel with Sam and Rachel with work.

Despite my misgivings, I couldn't make time for them yet. On Wednesday after work, I was waiting for a haircut. The wedding to which Alexis had invited me was coming up, and I wanted to make a good impression on her family and friends. Long hair and scraggly sideburns were not the way to go. I was at a generic salon chain rather than a barbershop because I had no interest in banter about baseball and the recent past when America was great—as if it had all gone to pot in these modern hedonistic times.

There were a few magazines lying around, so I swiped a *Cosmopolitan* or a *People* or something like that—I wasn't paying attention to the cover. I flipped past what had to be twenty pages of advertisements to an article about the ten things irresistible people do. Maybe there was something I could use; I was feeling pretty good, but I assumed it was only a matter of time before Alexis tired of me.

Number ten started by telling me that alluring people derive their irresistibility from within, from an inner confidence. I might as well have stopped reading then. Fainting goats have more innate confidence than I do, at least when it comes to dating; although Alexis recently had done wonders for my self-esteem. But I read on, having nothing else to do while I waited. Two of the ten items suggested treating people with respect and treating them how I would want to be treated. Common sense; I could do that. But another one said irresistible people don't try too hard. One could argue that merely reading that dumb article was trying too hard. Then number four told me to be authentic. The article was pissing me off. If I was not self-assured to begin with, and if I tended to try too hard, how could I change those aspects of myself and *to thine own self be true*? Not only was this article stupid, it was also paradoxical.

Number one instructed me to be a positive person, as if anyone chooses to be a sad little hermit. I don't drink by myself with the lights off because I think it's a cool thing to do. I do it because Fred is a debilitating sonofabitch. None of this was going to help me with Alexis, but I had reminded myself why I don't read magazines.

■ ■ ■

Be at your place in 30 minutes, Alexis's text informed me.

It was Friday evening; I had just gotten home from work and needed to shower and change quickly. Alexis's grade school friend Hannah was getting married the next night, and Alexis was the maid of honor; Friday night was Hannah's rehearsal dinner. I suppose it was also her fiancé Kyle's rehearsal dinner, but no one cares about the groom.

Showered and clean but not dressed, it was critical that I conserve energy from there on out. No wasted movements. The last thing I wanted to do was work up a sweat in a suit, which was a legitimate fear in the summer in Chicago. My German genes weren't designed to handle temperatures over seventy-five degrees, especially when the humidity was high. I needed to save my linen suit for the next night, so I went with a light-gray Hugo

Boss suit and a John Varvatos charcoal tie with mini white dots. I looked like James Bond, without the movie star looks and personal trainer body, and much more prone to hyperhidrosis.

Pulling up now, said another text from Alexis.

Damn, I had to rush now. I hoped the cab driver would have the AC blasting, because my sweat factory was about to come online. Heat and anxiety do that to me every time. I felt a bead of sweat form on my brow as another trickled past my left sideburn. That was not how I wanted my interactions with Alexis to commence.

"Hi, beautiful," I greeted her as I stepped into the car. "You look fantastic."

She was wearing a pale-yellow cocktail dress that immediately raised my internal temperature. At that point, it was the last thing my overtaxed internal cooling system wanted.

"Hey you," she said as she pecked me on the lips. "I love, love, love your suit." Then she noticed what I assume resembled a waterfall cascading down my face. "Are you okay? You look a little flushed."

Dammit. It was as bad as I thought, maybe worse, but I was thankful she put it euphemistically. "I'm okay; just overheating a little." Then I turned to the driver. "Could you blast the AC?"

"It's on already," he barked at me.

I felt nothing. Exhaust pipes provided more cooling air. "I know, but could you turn it way up? I'm running a little hot at the moment." I watched him turn the dial from 1 to 2. "No, way up, please. Max that sucker out." With a huff, he grudgingly complied.

I then went silent for a little while as I put my body on standby mode, basking in the cool air surrounding me. I could literally feel my pores close up as my sweat-producing factory workers went on break. They could go on strike forever, for all I cared.

"You okay now?" Alexis asked. "You want to stop for a slushie or bag of ice?" Her voice and facial expression were registering as 75 percent joking, 15 percent concern, and 10 percent "what the hell is wrong with this guy?"

A walk-in freezer would have been good. "No, yeah, thanks, I'll be all right. No need for a slushie. My body has a set temperature range it finds comfortable, and today is above that range." I needed to get the attention off me and my profuse sweating. "How are you doing? Excited to see your friends?"

"I'm great! Another workweek done, and now it's party time. I'm so excited for Hannah, and definitely psyched to see her family and our school friends—and my parents, of course."

"Besides your parents, whom do I need to look out for?"

"Don't be silly," she said. "My parents can't wait to meet you. But as to who you should look out for? Hmm." She hesitated for a second and twirled some hair with her right hand. "My friend Jane definitely wants to meet you. Other than Hannah, she's my oldest friend."

"Jane? That's easy enough to remember. I need a refresher on your parents, though. Your mom was a stay-at-home mom, but now she works part time at a bakery?"

"Right."

"And your dad is a doctor at Carle Foundation Hospital?"

"You got it."

"Internist?"

"No, endocrinologist."

"Oh yeah. Diabetes and thyroid stuff. And he loves U of I sports."

"You don't need a refresher," she told me with a smile. "You got this."

Too bad I didn't know anything about U of I sports—who did? The only thing I knew about diabetes was that it's fun to say it as diabeetus.

■ ■ ■

The rehearsal dinner was held at an Italian restaurant in Little Italy. After some schmoozing with various people whose names I do not recall, Alexis introduced me to Jane as guests were getting the signal to sit down at random tables. I instantly could tell I was going to like Jane, because she picked up a second glass of wine before she sat down, making sure there would be no gaps in her alcohol intake.

Jane is short, like five-foot-nothing short, with dark hair and dark eyes and tan skin that is the deepest of browns. I bet she's one of those people who darkens within seconds when exposed to the sun, whereas I blister and peel and then crumble to ash. She is also in good shape, which it seems everyone associated with Alexis is.

Jane grabbed a seat on my left, and Alexis sat to my right, and next to her was her friend Michelle, whom Alexis hadn't seen in years. With Michelle distracting Alexis and the noise in the room inhibiting cross-table talk, Jane began her inquisition with minimal impediments.

"So, James, Alexis has told me a lot about you. It's nice to finally get a chance to hang out." There was a smile on her face, but she had the suspicious eyes of an investigator. I had a momentary impulse to check my pockets for contraband.

"Yeah, me too," I said. I'm fairly certain that evening was the first time Alexis had mentioned her name, but I didn't want to seem rude, and maybe I forgot. "You went to elementary and high school with Alexis?"

At least that's what I meant to ask her. I should've seen this coming, but I was nervous having to talk to Alexis's friends. Jane's perplexed expression confirmed I garbled all of my words.

"Sorry, you went to school with Alexis?" I repeated with exaggerated enunciation.

Comprehension dawned on her face this time. "I sure did. All the way since preschool." Her voice had a little bit of southern twang to it I never noticed with Alexis. "I think up until high school, we had almost every class together, and we played volleyball together growing up."

"You must have been the setter." I forced myself to slow down my speech again, as if I were narrating an audio book.

"Ha, you're right. Whatever gave me away?"

"Lucky guess."

"So what's your story, James?" she asked. "Tell me about yourself."

Breathe in and out, James. You can do this with proper enunciation. "Well, I'm a Scorpio, so I'm secretive and intense—you know, supposedly like every other person born in early November." She granted me a forced smile. *Why do I always make inane jokes? Maybe I should tell her I tell a lot of stupid jokes? No, she'll figure that out soon enough on her own.*

I proceeded to tell her briefly how I knew Alexis and where I was from before she asked where my family lived.

"My parents are both in Pittsburgh, but not in the same location. In fact, never in the same location." *They're like time travelers*, I thought. *They can't occupy the same space without destroying each other.* I forewent telling her that analogy though; I didn't want to have to explain I got it from a D-plus action movie, or that I had watched the movie like a bazillion times. "They're divorced," I simply explained.

"I'm sorry to hear that," she said in consolation.

"Don't be; it was a long time ago, and it's for the best. Everyone is happier now that they are not together."

"Who's everyone? Do you have siblings?"

I answered in the affirmative, and Jane proceeded to pepper me with questions about Andrew and Rachel. I did my best to humor her, even answering her more probing inquiries. My thinking was that if I won over Jane, I would in turn build up goodwill with Alexis, which would directly lead to Alexis wanting to marry me. It was just like the game Mousetrap—everything was connected. You just needed to set the pieces up correctly and then hope nobody nudged the game board or breathed in its general direction.

Playing twenty questions had been fun, but I was curious about her story. It was time to turn the tables a little. "So where do you live now?" I asked. I assumed it was not Chicago, since I hadn't met her before tonight.

"Well, unlike almost everyone else Alexis and I went to school with, I don't live in Chicago." I definitely should be a detective. "I know, weird, right?" she added. I'm not sure what she was reading on my face to make that comment, but she had an entertaining way of speaking that I could have listened to all day. "I graduated from U of I and then moved to St. Louis; that's where my dad is originally from."

"That's cool. I haven't spent much time in St. Louis. What do you do there?"

"I'm a biochemical engineer. In a nutshell, I work on scalable biochemical processes to increase food production." She described some of the details, but my eyes glazed over, like they did the tenth through two hundredth time my grandpa retold the story about the first time he saw a television set. It was in a storefront. Imagine that.

"Really? That's awesome. I respect that. I originally studied biochemical engineering and chemistry in college, but the labs did me in. Too monotonous and time consuming."

Alexis turned to me and told me her parents were running late but should be there soon, and then she excused herself to the restroom. This apparently was the opportunity for which Jane had been waiting.

"So," she said, "there's another question I want to ask you. How are things going with you and Alexis, hmm? What are your intentions?"

"Are you interrogating me?"

"Yes," she said with a grin. "Answer the question."

"Well, we're dating. You know that. As for future plans, we haven't talked about it much ourselves, but I can tell you I like her a lot, and when we hang out, there's nowhere else I want to be."

"Oh my gosh, I love that answer. Gold star for that one. But what about other girls? Are you seeing anyone else?" Her facial expression hadn't changed, but I could tell it was still a serious question to which she demanded an answer.

If only she knew how absurd that question was when applied to me. Dating multiple girls? Not even my subconscious could concoct that scenario for my daydreams. "Nope, no one else. Alexis is it for me."

"Okay, good. She needs something stable."

Huh? Alexis needed stability? Subtle warning bells were ringing in my head. "What do you mean?" I asked. "Why does she need stability?"

Jane looked a little flummoxed, and I think she swore under her breath. She must have let something slip that she shouldn't have.

"Alexis was engaged a year ago. Her college boyfriend. He's the reason she came to Chicago in the first place. He had a job lined up here."

I had known there was something off when I asked Alexis on our date why she'd moved to Chicago. But in light of the nature of this news, I couldn't revel in my gumshoe proficiencies.

"They'd been dating since junior year," she carried on, gossip seemingly being second nature to her. "But she had to call it off. It took a toll on her." Then she looked up to see Alexis approaching the table. "I shouldn't have said anything. Don't repeat what I told you to her!"

I was totally stunned; I needed something else, anything else, for now. "What was his name?" I asked in a hushed voice.

"Bill," she hissed. "Now shush!"

What the hell was I supposed to do the rest of the night? I felt like I had just regained consciousness with a bomb vest strapped to my chest, and nobody had given me any instructions on how to remove it.

In the corner of my mind, Fred was coalescing from the floor like T-1000.

■ ■ ■

"Mr. Owens, so nice to meet you," I told him as I shook his hand. It was a perfect handshake, which I appreciated. Firm grip, one-and-a-half shakes, and then a small delay before a clean release. I hate when guys with small egos clasp early so that I'm stuck with the tips of my fingers wrapped up in their whole hands. I do not appreciate being forced to feel dainty.

"Great to meet you, James," Mr. Owens declared in a baritone voice that matched his substantial size.

He was a few inches taller than me and considerably bigger, but almost none of his bulk was lipid in nature. He was just a big guy.

Mrs. Owens, on the other hand, had features similar to Alexis, and her looks belied her age. This was promising news for future Alexis, and for me.

"Nice to meet you as well, Mrs. Owens," I said as she leaned in to give me a one-arm hug and a cheek-to-cheek side kiss. I am in favor of those as well.

"Yes, we're so pleased to meet you, James," Mrs. Owens said. She had the same hint of southern twang that Jane had. It was pleasant to the ear. "Alexis seems to be very fond of you."

Alexis had just walked her parents over to me; they had missed the dinner portion of the evening due to gridlock, but everyone was still mingling at the restaurant. Normally, I would have been a wreck in that situation—a chaotic jumble of nerves and self-doubt—but several hours of drinking, and my practice run with Jane, had unwound most of my knots. Even with preparation, some of my uneasiness was trying to force its way out.

"Mom!" Alexis exclaimed. "Knock it off!" It appeared my mom wasn't the only one who liked to embarrass her children, whether intentionally or otherwise. But I appreciated the boost of confidence.

"Oh, sorry, dear," Mrs. Owens said while winking at me roguishly. Am I the only person in the world who can't wink? Can you train yourself to wink? I need to search the internet later for some videos.

"Yes, I've been waiting to meet the two people who raised such a fantastic daughter." I caught Alexis rolling her eyes at me. It was cheesy, I admit. But I approach parents like I do cream cheese on my bagels: I'd rather spread it on thick than not cover the entire surface. "Sorry you had such a horrible drive up here. Could I get either of you a drink?"

"Yes, that'd be wonderful, thank you," Mrs. Owens said. "I'll have a glass of red wine—cabernet or pinot noir if they have it."

"And I'll have a beer," Mr. Owens chimed in. Well, more a foghorn than a chime. "Anything dark and heavy is good with me. No light beer."

"So one of those lemonade-infused beers?" I joked.

"Exactly," he said, as he laughed after only a brief quizzical look. One point James. I could get along with anyone who enjoyed sarcasm.

When I returned with drinks in hand, Mrs. Owens and Alexis were talking to another guest, so I handed her mom the glass of wine and approached Mr. Owens. We forced small talk about Illinois and Pittsburgh sports for a while before we discussed my family, and I made a benign joke about my dad never understanding a happy wife means a happy life.

"Well, I don't know about your dad, but as long as you put Alexis's feelings first, things should work out just fine. Of course, if you don't, I can get up here in a few short hours with my guns. I have a mix of handguns, rifles, and shotguns."

Although I was 99 percent sure he was messing with me, blood still drained from my upper body and pooled in my feet. My pallid skin, now devoid of all life-sustaining elements, had turned ashen gray. Perhaps my ancient genetic precursors avoided death by looking like death?

But then Mr. Owens cuffed me on the back and chortled. "I'm just joking, James. Sorry, I couldn't help it. I've always wanted to do one of those angry dad bits and never had the chance. You're not gonna faint, are ya?"

Maybe? I wasn't sure. Was I feeling weak? *No, pull it together, James. You're a grown-ass man. You're not going to faint in front of all of Alexis's family and friends.* "Nah, I'm okay, sir." At least I thought so.

"Okay, good. Let's go refill our drinks."

■ ■ ■

I woke up Saturday morning unrefreshed. I had tossed and turned basically until dawn because of the news from Jane. Fred was in his glory concocting various fantasies in which my relationship with Alexis, and usually my life as well, went up in flames. That bastard can be unrelenting. He had reared his ugly self almost out of nowhere, with a vengeance.

In the wee hours of the morning, through tears (it shames me to admit), I had written at length about all my worries and how frustrated I was that Fred never let me go too long feeling like life might be permanently improving. It was an epic homage to misery and self-pity. But then I became incensed with my self-indulgent sorrowing and, vowing never to let Alexis see me like that, deleted all of it.

Anyway, let's move on from my episode of weakness. I've dwelled on it long enough. Alexis had bridal party duties all day, which I was led to believe involved hours of makeup, hairstyling, some crying, some reminiscing, some nervous banter, some crying, and then some picture taking accompanied by some more crying. Alexis's fully occupied status meant my day was wide open until four in the afternoon, when I needed to be at Holy Name Cathedral. That was a lifetime for Fred, so it was crucial to make myself busy.

I ate a few bites of leftovers for breakfast—I've never been discriminating in what I eat in the morning, although the time I ate chicken noodle soup for breakfast crossed a line for my college roommate—and then I ran to the Lakeshore trail to clear my mind. While waiting for cross traffic to clear before I reached the trail, Fred subtly encouraged me to jump in front of a delivery truck. That would have been a terrible idea—no option for an open casket with that type of demise.

Once I was on the trail surrounded by the immense blue lake and modern high-rises, with people of all shapes and colors behind and in front of me, peace enveloped me. Nothing could bring me down there. Not even when I was passed by the guy who looked like he was more equipped for hot dog eating contests than running; I just assumed he was sprinting his final leg, or he had Kenyan and Ethiopian ancestors.

I usually run four or five miles at a time, but I ran seven that day and walked an eighth to keep Fred in the periphery as long as possible. Then I meandered back in the direction of my apartment. I could sense Fred lurking behind corners and up on rooftops, so I ambled somewhat aimlessly as I peeked into the various business windows and then people-watched to kill extra time.

I finally returned to my apartment and took an extra-long time showering and getting dressed—it was necessary to keep the perspiration at bay. Then I hailed a cab and was dropped off outside the church.

■ ■ ■

Inside, the cathedral was probably the most beautiful church I've seen outside of Europe. The central walkway to the altar consisted of a terrazzo floor with an ornate design, while the two side paths were lined with impressive marble columns that supported grandiose arches. The ceiling itself was dark wood covered with gold inlays everywhere, and enormous stained-glass windows lined both the first-floor and second-story walls. An enormous wooden cross with a fully sculpted Jesus carved within it hung above the altar. It was truly majestic and divine.

I saw Alexis, who gave me a big hug and a cheek-to-cheek "kiss" so she wouldn't smudge her lipstick, but she quickly left me to hole up in a secret room with the bride until the ceremony. Then I noticed Jane. Before I made my way toward her, I did some mouth stretches and whispered *Mary Mary, quite contrary.*

"Hey there," I said. "How'd this morning go for you?" So far, so good on the diction front.

"Hey, not too shabby!" she said. "No hangover at all. You?"

"I've had better mornings. Feeling okay now. May I sit with you?"

"You may. On one condition."

"What's that?" I asked.

"You can't ask me about Bill. Not now, anyway. I'll maybe tell you more later at the reception. I feel like I'm betraying Alexis if I do, but I'm the dumbass who brought it up—oops, sorry, I cursed in church—and I also feel like I can't leave you in the dark. But no matter what, I don't want to talk about it here where people can overhear. Deal?"

I had to force my eyebrows not to furrow, because she had just talked about him without me prompting her. I had assumed she wouldn't tell me anything more. "Deal," I said. "I ask no questions now, and you tell me everything later."

"No! That's not what I said." But then she saw my smirk and softened. "Later, maybe. And only if I can do it without anyone else noticing."

"Okay, deal."

We sat on the bride's side and waited for the mass to begin. The temperature was moderately cool in there, but the groom, Kyle, appeared to be a little red-faced. God knows I felt for him, so I tried my best to send him cooling thoughts telekinetically.

Out of the corner of my eye, I observed Alexis walking down the aisle. My first impulse was to tell her chauffeur groomsman to step back, lest he incur my wrath. Then she smiled at me as she passed, and I forgot all about the groomsman and his well-fitting tuxedo that made it clear he was bigger and stronger than me. I didn't want to have to fight him anyway; it was a wedding after all. Show some class, random groomsman.

The second the mass ended, church employees hustled all the guests out to State Street because a subsequent wedding was about to begin. Alexis and the rest of the wedding party boarded one of those stretch SUV limos to go take pictures somewhere while Jane and I joined the rest of the guests piling into multiple shuttle buses.

■ ■ ■

The reception was located in the Crystal Gardens at Navy Pier. I usually avoid that part of the city like the plague: it's full of tourists who don't know where they're going, generic chain restaurants, and people who can't drive in the city. Basically, I have no reason to visit Navy Pier and a hundred reasons to steer clear. I understand why out-of-towners flock to it, and I'm not judging them, but I want nothing to do with it.

That all said, the garden venue for the reception was beautiful. It was a colossal atrium with glass walls and ceiling, filled with palm trees, hanging vines, and circular planters with fountains that spurted water from one planter to another in aquatic arcs.

The bridal party wasn't present yet, and I didn't see Alexis's parents, so I was sticking close to Jane. I grabbed a "signature drink" for each of us— some overly sweet raspberry prosecco concoction I assumed was normally used to attract hummingbirds—and told Jane, "So, I don't want to press the issue, but this is probably the best time to ask about Bill."

After a trivial internal struggle, Jane relented. "Look, I'm only going to tell you this and then nothing more, got it?"

I nodded my head.

"Okay," she said. "Alexis and Bill were engaged for a while."

"Wait," I said, as I had just realized something. "I don't remember ever seeing a ring on her finger." I knew I hadn't seen Alexis every day for the past few years, but I felt like I would've noticed an engagement ring.

"Yeah," Jane said, elongating her enunciation of the word. "Bill never bought her one. He was supposedly saving up for it, but he was never good with money."

"Oh." I immediately felt bad for Alexis.

"Anyway, Alexis broke off the engagement because Bill is an alcoholic. She didn't want to end it, but eventually he left her no choice. She struggled with her decision for a long time. That's all I'm telling you."

I had a million questions. Did they still talk? Did he go to AA? Did he go to AA before they broke up? Was there a traumatic event that broke the camel's back? Or was it death by a million cuts? What was Bill like? Was I better looking? Funnier? What did Bill do for work? How much money did he make? Could he wink? Could he teach me how to wink?

But I let them each evaporate on my tongue like Communion wafers. Showing some surprising self-restraint, I simply told her, "All right, thanks. Let's go get real drinks."

■ ■ ■

The bridal party arrived only a few minutes before the guests were instructed to be seated for dinner, and then Alexis sat at the head table with the rest of the wedding party. She delivered a short but touching maid of honor speech. I remembered Andrew hadn't asked me to give a speech of any kind. Probably prescient of him, as I would've struggled to express sentiments of love or good-natured humor—the two staples of a good wedding toast. Anyway, after the cake cutting, I finally was able to spend some time with Alexis.

We were on the dance floor during a slow song when she asked, "Is everything okay? You've been a little distant tonight."

The entire night, I had been failing to stop my mind from fixating on Bill, like Jack Torrance's incessant typing about being a dull boy. Despite my one-track thoughts—no doubt spurred on by Fred—I figured I was killing it in the acting department—at least well enough to receive praise at a rural high school production. Apparently not, or Alexis was adroit at seeing through me.

I almost blurted out *It's okay; let's talk later*, but that would've been an asinine and selfish answer. Although Bill was tormenting me to the point of *redrum*, I didn't want to spoil the wedding for Alexis by bringing him up. Saying *Let's talk later* would only have freaked her out or caused her to demand that I tell her what was going on, and then I would've been stuck telling her anyway. So, I mentally burned my thoughts about Bill and tried to erase any concern from my face.

"Yeah, I'm okay," I finally replied. "My stomach is just acting up. I haven't been distant… I was just trying to give you a little space, since you haven't seen so many of your friends in a while. Sorry if I seemed that way."

My explanation did not seem to mollify her. I knew this because she immediately asked, "You sure? You'd tell me if something was bothering you?"

Now there was no way to win. If I told her I knew about Bill, I ran the risk of ruining her night. If I answered affirmatively, I would be lying to her. The option that did not involve bringing up Bill still seemed to be the best one. "Yup, I'm sure. I would tell you."

To my great relief, the band started playing "Don't Stop Believin'," and one of Alexis's friends grabbed her to air guitar and sing along. Alexis proceeded to dance the rest of the night, while I alternatingly danced with her and snatched beers from the bar—and at all times wondered about the mysterious Bill. When the after-party drifted from a bar to the hotel suite Mr. and Mrs. Owens had paid for—I hadn't suspected they were the partier types—I headed home to lie sleepless in my bed the rest of the night.

■ ■ ■

On Sunday morning, Hannah's parents hosted a brunch at the hotel where most of the guests were staying. It crossed my mind to skip it, but the fact that Alexis's parents would be there grounded my thought before takeoff.

Thankfully, Mr. Owens was my kind of guy; he wanted to get on the road and drive home as soon as possible, which meant they did not linger for an extended goodbye. Alexis and I said our goodbyes to Jane and her other friends, and then we went for a walk down Michigan Avenue toward Millennium Park.

"So are you going to tell me what's bothering you?" she asked. "Or do I have to torture it out of you?"

I guess I need to go to acting class. I couldn't even fake my mood for a full day. "What kind of torture are we talking about? You tie me up and tease me?"

"Ha, nice try. Something way more painful than that." When I didn't say anything for a few seconds, she play shoved me and yelled, "James! I'm serious! Tell me."

I knew what I wanted to say, and I knew it would have been easier if I just blurted it out instead of dragging things on, but that knowledge didn't make it easy. "Okay," I said, to give myself some time. "I feel dumb for worrying about this, but it's been bothering me since I found out. And it's not your fault it's bothering me. You didn't do anything. It's just—"

"James! Get to the point!"

I would've cut me off too. "All right. I found out you were engaged to a guy named Bill last year," I divulged. "And it bothers me you haven't told me about it. Like maybe you aren't over him."

I swear I saw fury ripple across her countenance, but then her face became a mask of tranquility so quickly that I must have been mistaken. No one could control their emotions that expertly, unless they were a Mexican ninja. And I know only one of those, and he's not even really Mexican or a ninja. Or good at controlling his emotions.

"Who told you that?" she asked. She was eerily calm—like a night at a summer camp minutes before a psycho wearing a hockey mask murders everyone while they sleep in their bunks.

To avoid throwing Jane under the bus, I needed to tread lightly. Fortunately, I had given it some thought the past two sleepless nights. "I thought I heard one of your friends mention it at the wedding table, but I couldn't quite make it out." This part was pure fantasy. "But then later I heard another of your friends, a tall brown-haired guy, mention how you seem to be doing well and seem to be over Bill." This part was true, but I didn't hear the friend say Alexis's name specifically, so I wouldn't have understood the reference without Jane's information. And he dropped his voice considerably when I came near, the significance of which would have been lost on me without Jane's disclosure.

"Was it Mark?" she asked.

"Who?" Oh, she was referring to the brown-haired guy. "The brown-haired guy?" I asked.

"Yeah."

"I'm not sure. Maybe. I can't remember his name."

She stayed quiet for a while, and I could tell the cogs were turning. I began to worry that she was more concerned about uncovering the rat than she was about addressing the situation and assuaging my fear.

"So you heard I was engaged before. Anything else about it?"

Now red flags were raised, and sirens were flooding my cerebral cortex. Why was she asking me questions? Why wasn't she explaining? "That's basically it. I told you, I couldn't hear much either time. It's not like your friends would tell me about this directly." You're welcome, Jane. "I only overheard bits and pieces, but enough to put together that you were engaged. Am I wrong?" I was starting to lose my cool a little.

"No, you're not wrong," she conceded, seemingly relieved. Was it because of my feigned lack of knowledge? "It's not something I like to relive all that often." She didn't seem prepared to say anything else.

"I get that. I'm sure it wasn't an easy thing to go through. Can you tell me a few details, though?" I required something more, or I was never going to sleep again. I figured I might as well tell her that, because it could help my cause. "I couldn't sleep last night because of this."

"I really hate talking about this subject."

I waited to see if she was going to say more, and I was about to ask a question when she offered a few more details. "I was engaged, and yes, his name is Bill. I ended it last year, because he had problems he couldn't overcome. I loved him very much, so it was not an easy choice. I still love him, as a person." Was it my paranoia, or did she tack the "as a person" on at the end as an afterthought when she realized how it would sound to me without it? *Get out of my head, Fred!* "I think that's all I can say at this point. You're going to have to be patient with me."

"That's fine. I can do that. But you'll tell me more when it becomes less painful?"

"Yes," she said. I had left my request extremely open-ended, so I hadn't extracted much from her.

Then I gave her a hug, but it didn't seem to help. We walked for a little while longer before both claiming we needed to get home to do some work and run some errands. I had a better shot at surviving a fall from the Marina City buildings than I did of sleeping that night.

Chapter 22

HIDDEN SECRETS

Still reeling from the Bill revelation six days after the wedding, I could not get any sleep because of the fictional Bill I had crafted in my head, and he was becoming fast friends with Fred. I was even starting to hate the name Bill; it was beginning to sound dirty, like a dollar bill lying on the floor of a seedy bar bathroom. Dirty-bathroom-floor Bill.

I had no intentions of writing another masterpiece of self-wallowing, so that week I had taken to going for three-a.m. runs to clear my mind. If the practice continued for any length of time, I could do an experiment to evaluate how physically fit yet mentally unstable a person could be at the same time.

I had to work through lunch on Friday, so I came up for some air in the afternoon and popped into Manuel and Miles's office to say hi.

I saw Manuel first because he appeared to be getting ready to leave. I had to figure out a way to stop him.

"Hey, don't leave," I instructed him. Would that do the trick?

"Sorry, man. Have to run."

No, it would not. "All right, just wait one minute," I said. "I have to tell you about something with Alexis that's been driving me crazy."

"Really, I gotta go. I'll talk to you later." Then he proceeded to brush past me.

"Fine, whatever, Manny," I said. "You wanna hang out tonight? Drink some beer, play some video games? Something like that?"

"Can't. Sorry. Plans with Sam," he stated as he exited the office.

I didn't even have time to protest that he always had plans with Sam. I couldn't remember the last time I had hung out with the guy one-on-one. Normally, I wouldn't have cared, because I'd been hanging out with Alexis. But with her being busy over the coming weekend and Manuel unavailable, I was looking at a whole lot of me time I did not ask for and did not want.

"The whole weekend?" I yelled after him. No response back.

I hung back for a second after Manuel departed. To Miles, I must have looked like a lost puppy.

As I was about to say goodbye and walk out, he waylaid me.

"Hey," he said. "I was probably just gonna play video games and drink beer by myself tonight. You want to come over?"

Not too long ago, I had suspected Miles of being a terrorist or a cannibal. I doubt people are ever both, though, right? If you're blowing people up, you can't eat them too. Some parts will be charred, others will be raw, and you risk destroying the prime cuts. Damn, that's dark even for me. Anyway, look how far Miles and I had come! He was asking me to hang out!

I clearly had no legitimate reason to decline—he had just witnessed me beg Manuel to hang out to no avail—but I didn't need to have one either. Miles had been growing on me, and I was curious to see what his place was like. Besides, Miles time sounded better than me-by-myself time, even if there was a slight risk of dismemberment.

"Yeah, that'd be great. What time?"

"Any time after work is okay with me."

"All right. How about I come over around seven thirty, and we can order pizza?"

"That works for me," Miles said.

■ ■ ■

I bought a bunch of Half Acre Daisy Cutters and arrived at Miles's place at 7:25 p.m., right on time. I didn't think we were going to drink all the beer, especially if he had some already, but I figured I would bring a gift like at a housewarming party. That was the appropriate thing to do? The adult thing to do?

Miles lives in a three-story walk-up in Wicker Park, which used to be Hipsterville, USA, but now it's almost as gentrified as every other neighborhood on the North Side. I don't often make my way this far northwest of the Loop, but my favorite brunch spot in the city, Bongo Room, is located there. There's something wrong with you if you don't like red velvet pancakes covered in a white chocolate drizzle.

Miles buzzed me in, and I climbed the stairs to his second-floor apartment. My trepidation about being blown up or cut into freezer-size pieces was mostly gone, but I had no idea what to expect. Did he live alone or have a roommate? Were his walls painted black and adorned with upside-down crucifixes? Was his TV bigger than forty-two inches? This last question was the most important. If the answer was no, I might have to leave right away; who can play video games on anything smaller than forty-two inches? Then I remembered the size of his office monitors, and my apprehension flew away like the jacket I dropped semi-intentionally as a kid from the top of an amusement park ride. My father was not pleased with me, but then again, he never was.

"Hey," Miles welcomed me as he opened the door. Then "Oh, uh, thanks," as I handed him the beer. That's how you present house gifts, right? You shove it at them the first chance you get, with no explanation? I'm pretty sure that's what the books on manners recommend.

"Hey," I said. "Thanks for having me over."

"Yeah, no problem. I'll put some of these in the fridge, but it's already stocked with other beer too."

"Okay, cool."

I felt like I was on a first date where I didn't care what the outcome would be; the date itself would be a good time, so there was nothing to worry about. But I had to get past the awkward introductory stuff first before I could move onto why I had come there: to play video games, refute (or confirm) Miles's criminal behavior, and forget about Alexis and Manuel not wanting to hang out with me—and get to know Miles better, of course.

I followed Miles to the kitchen, and he handed me a cold beer. "I like your place," I told him.

I hadn't seen much of it, but it appeared to be nice. The door from the exterior hallway opened into the living area and a kitchen that was attached in sort of an open concept arrangement. There was a decent amount of light, hardwood floors, neutrally painted walls, modern appliances, normal furniture, and, more importantly, no visible body parts or bomb components. My preconceived notions were way off.

"Thanks. I'll give you the quick tour in a second. Are we still ordering pizza? We should probably call that in before we do anything else. I'm starving."

"Fine with me."

"Do you like deep dish?"

I lived in Chicago, didn't I? "Yeah, works for me. Lou's?"

"Sure."

"Okay, good. Whatever you want on it is fine with me, but make sure you order the Malnati salad too." I could eat that salad seven days in a row. The sweet vinaigrette combined with the salty gorgonzola are what tie everything together.

"Got it," he said.

After placing an order for delivery, Miles showed me around his place.

"All right, this is the kitchen, as you know. You came in through the family room or whatever you want to call it." Then we moved toward the hallway. "First bathroom's on the right. It's the guest bathroom and the one my roommate Steve uses."

It was a nice bathroom with updated fixtures, but it was not going to win any cleanliness awards: uncapped toothpaste and soap residue marred the countertop, there was a scattering of those paper flaps from unwrapped Band-Aids lying on the floor, and a dirty sink and an overflowing trashcan complimented the rest. It appeared hygiene was not high on Steve's list.

"Mm hmm," I said with a nod, like a guy at an open house who had no intention of making an offer—he had only come out of curiosity and the prospect of free cookies. I am one of those guys. I bet realtors love guys like me.

"Steve's bedroom is on the left."

Steve's door was closed, so I obtained no further insight into this shadow figure. Was he a terrorist and he roomed with Miles to deflect suspicion from himself? There were no sounds or smells emanating from his room, so if he was soldering wires or packing ball bearings into pressure cookers, he was good at covering his tracks. Or maybe he wasn't home? Yeah, that was probably the likeliest scenario. This was one case where I required more clues before reaching a conclusion, or, as the Scottish say, I needed more "scoobies."

Then Miles led me to his bedroom, which appeared to be a much larger master bedroom. Most of the stuff I saw was the typical stuff you see in a normal bedroom: queen-sized bed on an unassuming frame, nightstand, dresser, and a picture of Soldier Field on the half wall that was adjacent to the second bathroom. It was the opposite wall that drew my interest.

On either side of a window were two large bookcases. On those bookcases appeared to be comic book memorabilia of all kinds: action figures, masks, folded capes, you name it. Two shelves in particular were occupied by Batman stuff. I, of course, moved in closer to inspect those items.

Oh my god, oh my god, oh my god! "Miles! What are these?"

"Damn, dude, you startled me. Calm down. What are what?"

"These!" as I grabbed what looked like an authentic Batwing shuriken. There were nine more inserted into a foam lining inside a wooden box.

"Oh yeah, those are cool," he said.

Calling them cool did them a disservice; they were works of death-dealing artistry. "Where'd you get these, man? They're amazing." I knew he owned them and they had been sitting in his room for who knows how long, but how was he not more excited about those perfectly contoured pieces of black metal?

"My friend and I made them," Miles said. "Well, he really made them, but I was with him. He has a studio where he does metalworking and machining."

"So, he can make more if he wanted to?" I asked this nonchalantly, as if I didn't want to order them in packs of a thousand.

"Yeah, probably," Miles said with indifference.

"How many do you think he could make in a week? Five, ten, fifty?"

"Dude, I have no idea. You want me to text him and ask?"

"No, not yet, thanks." I didn't want to undermine my position in any future business negotiations by appearing desperate. "Do they work, though?"

"What do you mean?" Miles asked.

What did he mean, what do I mean? Batwing shuriken have one purpose: to be flung with maximum velocity so they lodge in your enemy's neck or groin. "Do they fly straight?" I clarified. "Do they stick into things? Have you tried throwing them into a dartboard or something?"

"I don't know, man. They've barely moved from that box since I've had them."

Blasphemy! How could he have not used these? He hadn't been curious enough to even throw one? "All right. First order of business after we have a few more beers is to test these bad boys out." I suspected Miles thought I was joking, because he didn't say anything.

"What about thermite grenades?" I asked him. "Do you think your friend could make those?"

"Thermite grenades?" Miles asked, with either skepticism or unfamiliarity.

"Yeah, thermite grenades. Handheld incendiary devices." That should clear things up for him.

"I have no idea. I doubt it. I'm pretty sure looking up how to make a grenade will get the NSA after you."

"Nah," I said, "they can't track you that way. There's no way." I said this without thinking, and then I realized they could probably do exactly what Miles had just said. The real question was whether they cared enough to come after you. A few internet searches does not a criminal make. I am living proof of that.

I spent a few more minutes inspecting his memorabilia while he waited patiently. At that point, he was probably worried about me trying to pocket something and take it with me. I might've taken a Batwing shuriken if I hadn't made such a big deal about them. But after I acted like a ten-year-old girl at a Disney concert, he would definitely have known I was the culprit if one went missing. I would have to get the contact information for his friend before I left that night.

■ ■ ■

I had been at Miles's place for like three hours—we had eaten pizza and played some video games, and the first-date awkwardness was gone—when I heard a door open down the hall. Miles was sitting right next to me, but he did not react. Then a door closed; I thought it was the bathroom door. I didn't say anything because maybe I was hearing things, and again, no reaction from Miles.

Then a toilet flushed, hands were washed under a faucet, and doors were opened and shut in rapid succession.

"Miles, who the hell was that?"

"Huh?" he said, still playing the video game. "Who was what?"

He seemed to have absolutely no idea that a third person was in the apartment with us. Was I hearing things? Was I going crazy? On top of all the other mental issues I had going on, I didn't need to add hallucinations to the pile. For real.

"That noise," I said. "Someone just went to the bathroom, and then either went into one of your bedrooms or exited out your back stairwell."

"Hmm? Oh, that was Steve."

"He's here! What the hell's he been doing this whole time?"

The guy was quieter than a field mouse in outer space. Why wouldn't he have said hello when he heard Miles giving me a tour of the place? Or when he came out to relieve himself before scurrying back to his hobbit hole? He must have read the same manners books I had.

"I think he's working."

I stared at him with raised eyebrows to indicate my disbelief.

"That or playing a video game on his computer; he wears headphones most of the time," he explained. "He's a software programmer and barely leaves his room. He's actually not a bad roommate for that reason."

I supposed that made sense, but it was still weird. "What kind of programming?"

"Now? I have no idea. He used to work for a defense contractor on classified stuff. He can't talk about any of that. I'm not sure who he works for now. To be honest, I think he might be doing some mercenary stuff on the side, because every once in a while, a strange person will show up at a weird time and pay for a thumb drive. Other times, he leaves in the middle of the night, when nothing is open, comes back a half hour later, and goes straight back to his room. Oh, and every once in a while, he buys a new hard drive and throws out a melted one."

"Miles, are you kidding me? Your roommate is a creepy, silent hobgoblin who might also be a hacker?"

"I wouldn't go that far—"

"Wait a minute," I said, "wait a minute." I needed to get back to the important stuff for a second. "You think your roommate could be committing cybercrimes, but you're worried about doing a couple internet of searches on how to make thermite grenades?"

"What? Yeah, man. I want nothing to do with terrorist stuff." How could I have been so wrong about him? "And Steve is harmless. At least I think he is. As far as I know, he only does small stuff like hacking school websites or creating fake social media profiles."

"It sounds like you have no idea, Miles. People don't pay money in the middle of the night so that someone's Facebook account is hacked. They just wait until their friend leaves the room with their laptop or phone open. How'd you meet Steve?"

"He's a friend of a friend. He seemed nice enough when I met him," he answered with a shrug.

"Does he only come out of his room to go to the bathroom? What does he do about food?"

"Yeah...he spends almost all his time in his room. Pretty much only comes out to go to the bathroom. I'm not even sure if he showers."

I was getting the heebie-jeebies just being there. "Seriously, what does he do about food?"

"Oh, sorry. He has a small fridge and a microwave in his room." Then he trailed off for a second. "Now that I'm talking about it, it does seem a little weird. Our kitchen is only like twenty-five feet away."

Exactly my thought. The situation was getting stranger by the second. I felt like Miles should have been more concerned about the person who slept down the hall from him—much too close for law enforcement to come to his aid in time, should Steve decide to try to eat him.

"Dude, if the feds ever come after him, he's probably going to point the finger at you," I said. "He probably put incriminating evidence on your laptop just in case you're ever tempted to rat him out. You ever think of that?"

"No, I have not. I think you're being a little paranoid."

"You're not being paranoid enough! You don't want to go to federal prison because of that guy. Guys like you don't do well in prison."

I assumed. I had no idea. I doubt I'd fare any better. "Also, have you ever checked what he keeps in that fridge? Or your freezer? There are probably human heads in it."

"Ha ha, come on, man. Relax. If you saw him, you wouldn't be worried about him physically harming anyone. He's a tiny little guy, like 130 pounds soaking wet." Then he stood up. "I need another beer. You want one?"

"Sure." I didn't know how Miles had learned that I am mollified by beer, but he had made a smart tactical decision. Seriously though, if I were him, I would be wiping my hard drive—once I figured out how to do that—and getting a new laptop ASAP. I would also lock my bedroom door at night and put a camera in the hallway above my door—one I could watch on my TV or laptop from the safety of my room. Maybe throw in a wall-mounted turret gun for good measure.

■ ■ ■

Miles and I ended up hanging out until almost three in the morning. Steve only came out one other time while I was there, and it was to go directly to and from the bathroom again.

"Well, Miles. I better get going, man. This was fun."

"Yeah, definitely. We should do it again sometime."

I stood up and started to bring some beer cans and other trash to the kitchen. Then Miles said, "Hey, I don't mean to pry, but what's going on with you and Alexis? Are you guys a couple?"

I hadn't realized Miles knew so little about Alexis and me; I had assumed because he shared an office with Manuel, he knew everything. "Yeah, we've been dating for a few months now."

"I thought so."

"Yeah, sorry, I thought you knew. We've been moving pretty fast, I guess. Although we slowed down lately."

"Oh. Did something happen?" He asked it hesitantly, like he was trying to hide his curiosity. I appreciated the effort.

"Umm, I guess. Sort of. She has a fiancé I didn't know about."

"Are you kidding me! She's engaged and she's dating you? That's messed up, man."

"What? Oh, no. I said that wrong. She used to be engaged, like a year ago. I didn't find out about it until her friend told me last weekend."

"Oh. That's not as bad, but that sucks, man. Sorry."

"Yeah, thanks. It's okay."

"Is she over him?"

That's the question we all want answers to, Miles. "I don't know. I don't think it will be a big deal in the end. But it does make me worry about where we're headed, you know? I thought we had gotten close, but apparently not close enough. So maybe she isn't over him. Who knows?"

I had no idea why I was opening up like that to Miles. He was a pretty unassuming guy, which made him easy to talk to, but I still barely knew him. It was probably just because I needed to get that stuff out, and Manuel had let me down, so here I was: telling Miles about my problems with Alexis, while Creepy Steve devised weapons of mass destruction or hacked credit card accounts twenty feet away.

"I don't know Alexis well," he said, "but I'm sure it'll be fine. She doesn't hang out with him still, or talk to him, does she?"

"I don't think so," I said. "I mean, it's not like I check her phone or log into her email or anything, so it's possible she talks to him or sees him. But I have no reason to think she does." Maybe I should have Creepy Steve hack Alexis and find out?

"Yeah, so then I'm sure everything's fine," Miles said.

"Thanks. Anyway, I should get going. Thanks again for having me over."

"Sure, anytime. See you at work."

As I walked outside, I realized I had forgotten to throw some of his Batwing shuriken. Dammit.

■ ■ ■

The following Wednesday afternoon, Manuel dropped by my office. Apparently he had not totally forgotten about me.

"Hey, everything okay, man?"

"Yeah, why?" I said without looking at him.

"I don't know. I haven't heard from you in a while."

"Oh."

"And because you're doing your best not to look at me."

"Hmm."

"Are you mad at me for something?"

Was I? I realized I was just directing my frustration with Alexis, and life in general, at him. "Nah, not really," I told him. "Honestly, the world is bringing me down. You turn on the news or walk down the street, and everywhere you look, people are so awful to each other. There's no faith in anything. People hate whole groups of people simply because they're different. No one's asking the question, How do we make this life better for everyone? Sometimes I think the universe should just end this whole thing with an asteroid blast."

"Hmm. Well that's not morbid at all," he deadpanned, "but I hear what you're saying."

"Yeah, I know it's a little gloomy, but I've been thinking about this kind of stuff for a while." Way too much, to the point where it was probably unhealthy. "A cataclysmic end might be for the best."

"Okay, well, I think I'm going to skip over arguing why the world shouldn't end in an apocalypse," he said. "But are you honestly telling me everything? Nothing else is bothering you?"

"Well, I also found out last weekend Alexis has an ex-fiancé that she didn't tell me about."

"Hmm," Manuel said with a furrowed brow. "How long ago was she engaged?"

"Like a year ago."

"How'd you find out?"

"Not from her, that's for sure. Her friend told me after having a few drinks."

"I'm not sure it's that big a deal. Why is it bothering you?" he asked.

That was not a demonstration of how empathy worked. "I dunno. I need to think about it more. I think a big reason is the fact that before I started dating Alexis, things were kind of bleak in my life—"

"Yeah, no kidding, *chacho*," he said, a little too enthusiastically for my liking. "I was going to stage an intervention if you dropped any further into the darkness."

I really, really need to look into an acting class. "Shut up," I said. "But yeah, I was down in the dumps. Alexis changed all that. I was actually happy for a change."

"*Was*? You used the past tense."

"Slip of the tongue. I am happy, super happy. Alexis is amazing. I guess I'm just a little worried about why she didn't tell me about it. Maybe she still has feelings for him or something."

"You've been dating her for what, like two or three months? Maybe she was getting around to telling you," he said. "Or maybe there was never a reason to tell you because she doesn't think about him?"

"Yeah, you're right," I said, with less conviction than I was feeling. The back of my mind was telling me, *Be afraid; be very afraid.* Certainly coming from the place where Fred was hanging out. Sowing doubt is one of the many things he performs with éclat.

"Everything is probably fine. I just need to see her again; I've barely had any time to talk to her because of Francis."

"Yeah, I hear working for him can suck," Manuel said, "which is why I avoid him like the plague."

"You have no idea, Manny. No idea. But thanks for checking on me. I appreciate it."

"No problem, *mano*. I'm always willing to grab a beer and talk."

Is he, though? Fred posed in the back of my mind. *Only if he doesn't have plans with Sam.* I shook him off; I wasn't going to let Fred in. *Go back to playing solitaire, or whatever it is you do, Fred.*

"I know. Thanks. Now get out of my office."

Manuel chuckled and walked out the door. Then he popped his head back in.

"Seriously, if you ever need to talk, just call me."

"Can I call Reina instead?"

"You're an ass."

Chapter 23

SLEEPING ON JAMES'S COUCH, JUST LIKE OLD TIMES

Imagine my surprise when James called me in the afternoon, just to hang out. I couldn't believe he was willing to spend a precious Saturday night away from his beloved Alexis. Whatever the reason, I took it. They had been inseparable almost since they started dating. If I wasn't so happy for him, I would have been annoyed. Especially because it was mid-August, which meant Chicago had precious few days of summer left. No more summer meant no more outdoor beer gardens and restaurant patios.

Seeing him that night was perfect timing. Besides missing James, I needed a laid-back evening. I had gone to a happy hour the night before with coworkers and then met some friends later in the evening. It wasn't until 3:00 a.m. that I realized I had skipped dinner. Chugging water and eating a frozen pizza at 4:00 a.m. didn't stave off my hangover Saturday morning.

After I didn't feel like death anymore, I ran a few errands and then started to make my way toward James's place. He had suggested we walk somewhere nearby for food and then go back to his place to watch a movie.

When I arrived at his apartment, no one answered the door. I checked the handle, and it was open. In I went.

"Hello? James? It's Rachel," I called out.

I heard a muffled "Be out in a minute." He must have been in the bathroom.

The place appeared to be clean! I was shocked. It seemed having a girlfriend was the right motivation for James not to live in squalor. As I snooped around, I didn't notice anything out of the ordinary. No signs of excessive drinking or melancholy. Except for the slow-paced song playing, which I did not recognize. The refrain had something to do with familiar faces going nowhere.

"Hey," he said as he came out of his bedroom. "How are you?"

"I'm good! My hangover is gone as of an hour ago."

"That long of a hangover, huh? Must've been a good night."

"It was. I went to happy hour with coworkers and then met Sarah and some other friends. And I forgot to eat food for a long stretch of last night."

"Sarah?" he asked. "Brown hair, English major, likes boy bands?"

"She's my roommate, James."

"That's the one."

"Yes, you've met her several times now."

"I know. I was just testing you. You want to head out for food?"

"Sure." As we started walking, I asked him, "So what'd you do last night? How did you escape Alexis's clutches? I never see you anymore."

"Nothing last night. I had to work super late and then the same most of today. Work is out of control right now. I'm not sure I can keep up this pace for the next nine months." Then as an afterthought he added, "I think I'm going to see Alexis tomorrow night for dinner. She's been busy, too, and has a ladies' night tonight. Which is fine with me, I guess. I kind of need to decompress."

"And you were overdue for hanging out with me?"

"Yes, of course that," he said with a smile. "So what's new? Job is still going well?"

It was going well, and I was loving it, but it isn't exciting to write about. As we ate, I told him mostly about work, and about the few dates I had had, none of which had gone well. Guys my age seem so immature. I'm not looking to hook up, which is the opposite of what 99 percent of them want to do.

As we were talking, I began to notice James wasn't as jovial as he had been in the recent past. Either in person or through his text messages. He was not in a James-level funk. Certainly not as gloomy as he was in the era I call Pre-Alexis. But something seemed off kilter. It took me a while to realize he hadn't mentioned Alexis once. Unless he was giving pithy answers to direct questions about her. The jig was up; I was onto him. Time to get the full scoop.

"So, besides your hectic schedules, how are things going with you and Alexis? Usually every time we talk, you can't stop raving about her."

He started to speak but then paused to reflect. A rare course of action for James. It's not that he typically speaks out of turn. He just normally doesn't backtrack when he has something to say. "On the whole, I think things are going really well," he said. "Being with her is easy. I can be myself and not worry about her judging me. She's caring and smart. And likes my jokes." Another rare pause, then, "She makes me want to be a better person."

"But?" I asked.

"But what?"

"You started by saying 'on the whole.'" I'm a good listener. "I was waiting for you to make some kind of qualifying statement, but everything you listed was positive."

"Yeah, I guess these past few weeks haven't been the best."

"Did you guys have a fight or something?"

"No. Not a fight. It just hasn't been a great couple of weeks."

That wasn't much to go on, but we were making progress. "Because you were so busy?" I asked.

"No. Well yeah, but that's not it."

"So what is it? Did something happen that you haven't told me?"

Something registered on his face. I had a clue to chase down now. "Nothing bad happened, no. But I found out Alexis was engaged."

"Oh." That was kind of a big deal. "How long ago?"

"About a year ago, to a guy named Bill."

"How'd she bring it up? It doesn't sound like an easy conversation to have."

"She didn't. Her friend told me."

"Hmm. Are you upset she didn't tell you?" They had only been dating a few months. It wasn't crazy she had not told him yet, but I held my tongue.

"Yeah, I guess so. And about how she reacted when I asked her about it."

"Ah. How did that go?"

"Well, not great," he said. "We talked on Sunday afternoon about it, and she didn't say much. We haven't talked about it since."

"Have you tried to?"

"No, not really. I've only seen her a few times over the past couple weeks. Sgt. Slaughter is taking up all my time."

"Huh?"

"Oh, a partner at work. He's driving me into the ground. Plus, I had to travel this past week."

"That sounds not so fun," I said.

"It's not. The only silver linings are my coworkers Richard and Yasmin. They make the project slightly bearable."

"Well, at least you have that."

"Yeah."

"Back to Alexis and Bill. Are you worried maybe she still has feelings for him?"

"Bingo. Give this girl all the money."

"Is there any reason to suspect she does?"

"I dunno. No? Maybe?" he said. "Except...except when I told her I knew about Bill and that I was worried about her having feelings for him, she ignored that aspect of it. She didn't try to reassure me at all. Instead, she started interrogating me about who told me and what exactly I knew."

"Erm," I said eloquently. Taking a defensive posture from the start was no good. But I didn't know the full context either, since I was not there. I would never take her side over James's, but I didn't want to jump to any extreme conclusions without hard evidence. "Did you tell her everything you know?"

"No. I would have, if she had wanted to talk about it, instead of ignoring the substance and asking me what I knew and how I knew it."

That made sense to me. "So what didn't you tell her?"

His expression was growing glummer by the second. I hated seeing him sad. "Bill's an alcoholic," he said. "Apparently, she gave him every chance to get better, but he couldn't do it, so she eventually left him. Her friend says it tore her up for months afterward. Even Alexis admitted she still loves him." He halted for a second and then said, "All of that wouldn't be so bad. But the fact that she hid it from me, and she didn't immediately come clean when I asked her about it, makes me wonder what else I don't know. Like maybe she still talks to him? What if he's able to get sober? Would she go back to him? I need to talk about these things with her. But I don't want to push her away by bringing them up."

I was not afraid to say we were over my head at that point. I have only had a few relationships. None were that serious.

"James, I don't know what the right answer is. I can say that I understand why you're worried about this. If I were in your position, I'd be concerned too. Hopefully, Alexis decides to talk to you about this sooner than later."

"Thanks, Rach."

"But, like you said, you need to give her time. And while you wait, you can't let this fester inside you. I know you."

"What, me? You're saying I let things gnaw at me?" He flashed a grin. That was a positive sign.

"Yes, I am. But give me a hug."

"I can do that."

"Love you, Rach," he told me as he released from the hug. "Thanks for always being there for me."

"Love you too. I will always be here for you. The same way you are for me."

"I know. I'll tell you whenever Alexis and I talk again about this. Let's go back and pick a movie."

The rest of the night seemed like old times. It was moments like that one that made me happy I decided to follow James to Chicago. Although I do miss Mom a lot. I miss Andrew too, but I would have never seen him even if I lived in New York. He's way too busy.

However, I don't like that the traces of a specter are back in James's life. I thought Alexis was exorcising his demons, whether she knew it or not. Now she seems to be feeding them. That is not a good omen.

Chapter 24

ROUND ONE, FIGHT!

I fist-bumped Raul, one of Alexis's lobby security guards, as I entered her building Sunday night, and he let her know I was there. After seeing each other enough times in the lobby, we had moved past saying hi and started having real conversations; it was getting to be more awkward not doing so. Then one day, while I was waiting for Alexis to come down—I was way too early, imagine that, and didn't want to be a pain while she was getting ready—some lady in her seventies started screaming at Raul unjustifiably. Something to do with maintenance work not being done properly, but Raul had nothing to do with scheduling or overseeing maintenance. I know this because he told me. We had a pretty good time mimicking her outrage after she left. Well, as she was leaving; we had started laughing before the elevator had closed all the way. I think she saw me wag my finger the same way she had.

Anyway, Raul and I were now quasi friends, and seeing him helped me compose myself a little. Although at that moment I was way more excited to see Alexis than I was worried about dirty-bathroom-floor Bill.

When I approached her door, I was about to knock when it swung open and she jump-hugged me. A more robust man would've caught her in stride, but I teetered for a second before regaining my balance. Then she began kissing me aggressively, which I was not prepared for but heartily welcomed. Her hello had temporarily driven away my residual concerns about Bill.

"Hi, James-y," she purred. "I missed you."

"I missed you too."

Then I carried her inside. As a gentleman, I have to skip over what happened next.

■ ■ ■

Sometime later, we opened a bottle of wine, and I started chopping vegetables while Alexis did other prep work. She tried to persuade me to let her do it all herself, but she was making homemade pasta and sauce from scratch and cooking various shellfish—I couldn't just stand around doing nothing.

However, I was moving in slow motion. The past hour had dispelled much of the worry that had followed me there, but her ardent greeting caused me to think it was a good time to talk, so I was tempted to bring Bill up again. Then I remembered my promise to be patient. I didn't want to jeopardize the evening after its exhilarating beginning. Nonetheless, my natural inclination toward impulsivity commenced a war with my restraint.

On top of that, I was assessing my feelings about Alexis in general. Right then, like every time I was with her, a happiness approaching bliss coursed through my veins like white water rapids. Was it love? It felt like love. It had enough staying power to be love. And if it was love, shouldn't I have told her I loved her? I didn't want to wait. Yet the shadow of Bill caused me to hesitate.

So there it was again. No steps could be taken, no progress could be made, until Bill was addressed. And then thrown down a back-alley stairwell and buried in wet concrete. Figurative Bill, of course, not real-life Bill. I'd be fine if real-life Bill just moved to Antarctica or took up refuge in the International Space Station. The space station was actually the best option; besides being unable to visit or communicate with Alexis, Bill's muscles and bones would atrophy and his immune system would weaken in the zero-gravity environment, which would increase my odds of being able to take him in a fight. Let's hope he has always wanted to be an astronaut.

As my internal struggle lingered, Alexis and I finished cooking and then ate. Everything was delicious. I guess I can add culinary skills to the list of the many things at which Alexis excels.

After cleaning up, we migrated to her couch to look for a movie to watch. She had her legs draped over mine, and while she was flipping through options with the remote, I paused to appreciate her. I don't stop often enough to be grateful for the life I have and the people and things in it. I didn't want to do the same with Alexis, so I soaked in the little things she does that warm my heart, like the dimples that appear when she is truly smiling, the way she twirls her hair with her right hand absentmindedly, and the semi–smoker voice she has even though she has never lit a cigarette in her life.

"Hey," she said in mock accusatory fashion, "are you paying attention?"

"Huh? To the movie options? Yeah."

"What'd I just say then, Mister?"

I had no idea. "*Monty Python and the Holy Grail*?"

"Nope. You're the only person alive who wants to watch that repeatedly."

That was not true; I bet there are lots of people several generations older than me that would watch it on repeat. In fact, old people always complain about how TV and movies these days are rubbish.

I was about to make some silly retort when Alexis's playful expression was replaced by a more somber one. "Really, what's been on your mind? You've been in your head like all evening."

The abruptness of her mood shift had me on alert, and her accusation that I'd been withdrawn had me on the defensive. Overly vigilant, defensive James was not who I wanted to be right then. So I took a moment to breathe.

"Honestly, I was distracted by you. I was watching the way your nose sometimes twitches when you're looking at something."

"My nose doesn't do that," she kind of snapped at me.

It does; I had just been watching it. It wasn't the first time I had noticed it and I found it charming.

"And don't joke around with me," she said. "More and more lately, you seem like a Gloomy Gus, and I want to know why."

I was telling the truth to her, but I could tell if I reasserted what I was doing, it would fall flat. My hackles were also up in response to her calling me a Gloomy Gus. First of all, someone named Gloomy Gus didn't sound bad at all; he might even be fun to share a beer with. Second of all,

I thought I was doing a tremendous job of not seeming aloof because of Bill; if she saw right through me again, those acting lessons were on like Donkey Kong. Third of all, I was kicking ass at not talking about Bill, and now it seemed like I had no choice but to mention him.

Besides, I'd been riding the honesty train lately with everyone, it seemed, so maybe I should stay aboard for this station stop. "I was truly having a great night with you, so I'm sorry that I've seemed distant. I didn't know I was coming off that way. There's absolutely nowhere else I want to be."

"Then what is it?" she asked. "What are you thinking about?"

"I don't know. I guess—I guess it's just that I can't be 100 percent free with you."

"Why? Why can't you be free?" She derisively put air quotes around *be free*. I have a severe pet peeve about air quotes. "What does that even mean?"

"There's something between us. You know what it is," I stated in a more hostile tone than I intended.

"What? Tell me," she demanded.

"Bill."

"I knew it! I knew you were focused on him! It's like all you can think about since the wedding."

Now I was starting to get a little pissed off. I think it was perfectly acceptable for me to be hamstrung by that news and the way she hid it from me. Bill wouldn't even have been an issue if she had told me about him earlier. I'm mature enough to understand that people have relationships that don't always end cleanly. Isn't that why people are always throwing around the word *closure*? What I didn't understand was how in three months of seeing each other on an almost daily basis, and me sitting there contemplating whether it was the right time to tell her I loved her, she hadn't felt it was necessary to tell me about Bill—and apparently still didn't think it was appropriate to discuss.

"Look, I do think about it a lot. That's true. But I've been trying hard to put it on the back burner like you asked, including tonight. I wasn't going to bring him up at all until you pointed the finger at me."

"You didn't have to mention his name. It was written all over your face."

I detest having people, any person, tell me what I'm thinking. Even if they're right, it's not their place to make those assumptions. She had done it to me twice, within seconds. But I didn't want to fight with her. I really didn't. So I again, uncharacteristically, paused to breathe and to let my blood drop from a boil to a simmer.

I wanted to divert attention away from my behavior and onto Alexis's past with Bill. If we were going to be talking about him, I would rather have learned something instead of being harangued about my supposed gloominess.

"Like I said, I've been trying really hard to ignore him. I'm sorry I wasn't as successful as I thought. But you can tell it's bothering me; it's eating me up a little inside. Can't you tell me anything about Bill? Something that might make me feel better?"

I think she was expecting me to strike back. Or at least not be so calm and candid. Whatever the reason, she seemed momentarily taken aback by my response. Then she decided she wasn't done being haughty.

"I don't know what's so hard to comprehend, babe," she said. I had never been called *babe* in such a condescending manner. "I told you I don't want to talk about Bill. That means I don't want to talk about Bill. Nothing about him. At all. Why can't you respect that?"

"Okay, I get it."

"Apparently you don't! Or we wouldn't be having this conversation!" Her voice was getting a little shrill at that point.

Rage was bubbling back up inside me like a septic tank that was close to capacity.

"What is it you're hiding, Alexis?" It turned out I couldn't hide my frustration any longer, and the volume of my voice rose. "Forget about me. Why is this such a big deal to you? Why are you avoiding talking about Bill at all costs?"

"I don't want to talk about him!" she nearly screamed at me.

The force of her objection pushed me back like a Sith Lord attack. "Fine. You don't want to talk about it," I said with icy coolness. "But I don't want to stay here being accused of being a Gloomy Gus."

I almost cracked up at the ridiculousness of that sentence, but I managed to keep it together. Gloomy Gus must be Debbie Downer's brother and Stinky Lee's first cousin.

"I think that's a good idea. You should leave. I don't want to see you right now."

I was intending to get up and go anyway, but her words were like a Batwing shuriken to my heart. I had to make a joke to describe this, because while I'm sitting here writing about it, it's still too painful to think up a more accurate simile.

"Okay. I'm going," I told her, and then I stood up to leave.

After I exited her apartment, I took baby steps halfway down her hallway and halted, hoping she would come out to get me.

She did not.

I could feel Fred on my periphery, silently laughing with his shoulders heaving, like Sagat in *Street Fighter II*. Man, that guy pissed me off when I was young. My dad and I spent hours on his SNES trying to beat the game on every level with every character. Sagat's reaction after winning irked me the most, even brought me to childhood tears when I was especially frustrated. At least in the game, you could restart and fight him again. I was not sure where things would go with Alexis.

■ ■ ■

As I trekked home, I imagined dirty-bathroom-floor Bill running at me from a dark alley. He was wearing a sullied tracksuit that led me to think he had been thrift shopping with Manuel. His face was amorphous and opaque because my brain hadn't settled on his features; all I knew was that if this were a movie, he would have had a scar running across his left eye. In one hand, he was brandishing a paper bag with a whiskey bottle inside it. I somehow knew his other hand held a crumpled picture of Alexis, even though I couldn't possibly see it based on the distance between us. He was shrieking incoherently except for a few words like "Alexis," "belong together," and "interloper."

Since I had a few seconds to prepare, I did a short kata before entering into my Keysi Pensador fighting stance, which involved dropping into a slight crouch and putting both hands near my head to protect my face, with my elbows out. I was going to unleash hell on his shapeless face.

Now within striking range, Bill threw his right hand in a long arc, attempting to bring the whiskey bottle down on my head. With both of my elbows already up, I lunged toward his attack, easily blocking the downward strike with my left forearm and quickly countering with a short jab to Bill's face with my right hand.

The blow momentarily staggered dirty-bathroom-floor Bill. Using the opportunity to gain a further advantage, I planted a solid front kick to his solar plexus. The force of the kick pushed him back several paces and he dropped the bottle, which shattered on the concrete. With the immediate threat of his weapon neutralized and this early exchange demonstrating I was superior in hand-to-hand combat, it was time to play with him before I finished him off.

I closed the distance and extended a left jab, which caused Bill to retreat a step or two and throw his hands up in defense. At the same time, I lunged with a right cross but instead of landing the blow, I used my newly achieved proximity to tie him up in a Muay Thai clinch. While I engaged, I could feel the enormous strength advantage I held over him. Imagine what I could have done if he had spent one or two years on the space station! Then I launched a knee to his unprotected gut before whipping him like a rag doll toward a nearby building wall.

He appeared to be pinned to the wall, by exhaustion or confusion, while he attempted to regain his bearing. I began to approach, contemplating whether I should throw a spinning back head kick and end the fight with style points or rough Bill up some more with knees to the body. While I pondered how to continue the onslaught, I noticed him attempting to pull something metallic from his tracksuit pocket.

From my right and Bill's left, I heard, "Hands up!"

Apparently moving with the stealth of an Apache warrior, a police officer had gotten the jump on both of us. Before I had time to think up a diversion to allow me to extricate myself from the situation, I saw Bill was still trying to wrestle the metallic object from his pocket.

"Drop it!" the officer ordered.

Bill appeared to have no intention of complying. He was turned slightly toward me and away from the officer, and from my vantage point, I could see the object was not a gun. Rather, it was a chrome flask with what looked like Alexis's image on it. I couldn't let Bill die because of his obsession with Alexis—after all, I was afflicted with the same disease.

The officer shouted another warning, but his tone of voice and body language indicated he was about to shoot. Applying my years of fictional training, I propelled myself forward like a champagne cork, throwing my body between the gun and dirty-bathroom-floor Bill. The bullet caught me square in the chest. With no body armor on, the round ruptured my heart and exited my back, leaving behind a gaping hole.

Loss of consciousness was coming fast. In the remaining seconds before I departed Fred's phantasmagoria, I realized Alexis would no longer have to grapple with whom to love. She would forever wonder, however, what might have been had she had the opportunity to marry the hero who saved Bill. And every time future Bill thought about taking another drink, he would remember the time I whooped his ass and then died to protect his life. Just like the Dark Knight was willing to do, before Harvey Dent screwed everything up.

■ ■ ■

While I was lying in bed an hour later, unable to sleep, a text message popped up on my phone. I had been hoping she would text me and I was positive it was her, so I twisted like an anaconda to grab my phone sitting on the nightstand next to me.

I'm sorry, it said. *I shouldn't have yelled at you.*

Then, before I could type back, *I missed you so much, and it was so great to see you. But I didn't want to talk about Bill.*

I know, I told her. *I'm sorry. I didn't want to bring him up. I was missing you like crazy too. I'm sorry I seemed distant or removed. I won't be in the future.*

Okay, we both messed up. We were going to have a little fight sometime. Everyone does at some point.

Do they? My past relationships had never lasted long. I had no idea when it was normal for people to have their first fight or how frequently they occurred. *I'll make it up to you*, I told her. *Whatever you want me to do.*

Anything? ☺.

Yes, anything. I liked where this was going.

A repeat of earlier today then. With some added twists thrown in, but I won't tell you what they are in advance.

I had no idea what she was trying to convey, but I was going to enjoy formulating ideas in my head between then and the next time I saw her. *Sounds like a plan. Like I said, whatever you want.*

Excellent. Good night, stud muffin.

Good night. I still couldn't bring myself to text a pet name; I feel so dumb using them. Maybe I just need to go with something and stick with it until I no longer cringe when I say it.

It was a quick exchange, but I was relieved she had texted me. Her words should keep Fred away. I hoped.

Chapter 25

I'VE BEEN NOTHIN' BUT MYSELF SINCE THE DAY I WAS BORN, AND IF YOU CAN'T SEE THAT, IT'S YOUR FAILIN', NOT MINE

The *Star Wars* Imperial March began to emanate from my phone. It had been so long since I'd heard that ringtone that it took me a second to realize it was my dad calling. It was around eight o'clock Wednesday evening. I was reluctant to answer but did so anyway, given the peculiarity of the event.

"Hello?" I answered, pretending not to know who was calling. Two could play that game.

"James?"

"Yep. It's me. How's it going?"

"Good. You?"

"Good."

"Good." Then he didn't say anything. Did I need to ferret out why he was bothering me? I mean, why he was calling me?

"You there?"

"Yeah, sorry. Thinking to myself. I want to bounce something off you. Kim is tired of hearing me talk about it."

"Who's Kim?"

"The woman I'm seeing."

He stated this like we actively participated in each other's lives—as if he divulged his thoughts and feelings to me.

"Of course, Kim. How could I have forgotten." Maybe he was right; maybe I did antagonize him at every opportunity.

He plowed through my comment like a thirteen-year-old driving hard to the basket through a bunch of nine-year-olds. Andrew did that all the time to my friends and me, in case you were wondering. "I'm dealing with a scenario at work. I got your brother's opinion, but I want yours as well." Probably because Andrew didn't give him the answer he wanted.

"Okay. So what is it?"

"Let me cut to the chase. A few years ago, I started helping another professor with a workshop she's been running. Initially, everything went smoothly; we were on the same page. But in the past year or so, we stopped seeing eye to eye. She has some crazy ideas on what we should be covering and what the emphases should be. And I can't seem to get her to see things from my perspective."

I knew where this was headed. "So you want to take it over and do it your way?"

"Well, no. I want to do the program the right way. But she seems unwilling to make the right changes."

"So what are you asking me?"

"I want to know if you think I should find a way to spearhead the workshop and make the changes that need to be made." Had I not just said that? "All I care about is that the students get the best quality instruction they can for their money."

Sure he did. As long as "the best quality" meant his instruction. I just assumed for the moment that his ideas were better than his colleague's; obviously, I had no way of knowing. "Dad, I have no idea what that would entail. What would you have to do to carry out a hostile takeover?"

"Well, for one, I wouldn't phrase it that way. But I'd probably have to go over her head to the department chair or the dean."

"Would they look kindly on you doing that? Wouldn't you alienate the other professor and her friends?"

"Well, that's the rub. I think I have more clout than her, but I'm not sure how the department chair or the dean would react. I'm not worried about her supporters—I'm not even sure who they are."

"If you don't know how the department chair or dean would react, then I don't think it's worth the risk," I said.

"That's what your brother said."

Oh no. I must have been wrong, then. Andrew could never know I agreed with him.

"What's the benefit to you anyway? Why do you want to take over the workshop?"

"Well, for one, I enjoy teaching it. But two, it's developed a good reputation over the years, and it's popular with the students. If I'm the primary person in charge, it'd be an extra feather in my cap."

There was the ulterior motive. I knew there had to be one. "All right, well, I stick by what I said. If you don't know the extent of the risks, I wouldn't make a move."

"Maybe you're right. I'll think about it."

We both knew he'd ultimately do whatever he wanted to do, others' opinions be damned.

"Hey, Dad?" As long as we were engaging in this rare exchange of ideas, I might as well ask him for some advice.

"Yeah?"

"I have a question for you. A relationship question."

"Oh, okay. Is this about that girl you were telling me about?"

"Yeah, Alexis." I was surprised he remembered any details from our last call. "We're still dating."

"Good for you." Was he patronizing me or sincerely congratulating me? I always assumed the worst with him. "I was wondering the other day if you two were still together." Sounded like he was doing both.

"Thanks." *I think.* "So I'll cut to the chase too. Here's my problem. Alexis and I are getting pretty serious, but she was engaged last year, and she doesn't want to talk about it. In fact, she hid it from me until her friend told me about it. I want to hash things out with her, but she refuses to talk about him. I'm a little worried she still has feelings for him. What do you think I should do?"

"If I'm hearing you right, this isn't a problem. It's an opportunity."

"Hmm?" My eyebrows assumed their skeptical slanted arch.

"It's an opportunity. You don't need to talk to…"

"Alexis."

"Right. You don't need to talk to Alexis. You need to prove to her there is no competition. You're the alpha male, and she should have no reason to think about her ex-fiancé."

"So you're saying I need to meet him in an alley and fight him?" Because I just did that. Sort of.

"Probably not, but maybe, if that's what it takes. You need to man up and show you're the better guy."

I couldn't tell if his advice was genius—albeit poorly worded—or a lot of machismo baloney. Was he saying I should just focus on how I interact with Alexis and how I treat her, and not worry about what Bill does or what she thinks of him?

"Maybe you have a point," I told him.

"Of course I have a point. When has your old man steered you wrong?" *I don't know, like all the time?*

"What's this guy like?" he asked.

"I have no idea. I only know he's an alcoholic."

"There you go. You're not one, so that's one big way you're better for her than he is."

He was technically right, I think. "Thanks, Dad. I guess I'm not worried about the ex-fiancé per se. I'm worried about how I act because I'm not sure how she feels about him, and about me. It's making it hard for me to be myself around her."

"What do you mean 'hard to be yourself around her'?"

He was going to make me spell it out? "I'm doubting myself around her, worried she's thinking about him and not me. She keeps accusing me of brooding."

"You're not getting all depressed again, are you?"

"What?"

"Moping around. Your woe-is-me attitude you sometimes have. You're not going back to that, are you? Because then you'll definitely lose her."

I had so many emotions in response to his words that they canceled each other out and left me unsure how to respond. I said in monotone, "No, I'm not getting mopey. Thanks for asking."

"Good. I don't want to hear either that you're on one of those anxiety or depression medications that everybody's on. People want the easy way out; they want a pill to solve all their problems."

This call was going downhill fast. "Nope, not on those. Anyway, I should get going. Working crazy hours lately."

"That's good. Like I said before, you have to go all in and be laser focused."

Ugh. I needed to terminate the call immediately. "Okay, bye, Dad."

"Take care, son."

The next time I start feeling guilty about not calling him more often, I'll remember this call. Why couldn't he, just one time in my life, make me feel a little better about myself after I interacted with him? Every compliment has to be undermined by two criticisms. Every piece of fatherly advice washed away by scorn. Is it any wonder I have the problems I do?

After I hung up with him, I spent some considerable time fuming while trying to stymie the tears that were dotting my eyes. I texted Manuel to help my efforts. *Hey, do you think your dad would adopt me?*

I received a response a couple minutes later. *Huh? You're not even a minor. Why are you asking?*

Because my current patriarch is no good.

What do you mean?

Sorry, he's no bueno.

No, jackass. I mean how is he no good? Is he visiting you or something?

No. Just got off the phone with him. Stellar conversation.

Well, sorry can't help you, he told me. *I don't want to share my inheritance. Also, if this is an elaborate ploy to get closer to Reina, I'm going to kick your ass.*

You're too cynical, Manny. Give people the benefit of the doubt unless you have a reason not to.

I have many reasons not to give you the benefit of the doubt.

I walked right into that. *All right, I'll talk to your dad without your blessing. What's his number?*

Bye, James.

Later.

My short conversation with Manuel made me feel minutely better, but I was still pretty worked up. Thankfully, my refrigerator had a few beers in it.

Chapter 26

CHILDHOOD NOSTALGIA: JAMES HAS ALWAYS BEEN THE BEST

It's been a week since James and I had dinner. Based on his text messages, he continues to be overwhelmed with work and engrossed in the Bill saga otherwise. Because James is dejected about Bill, I want to write about one of my favorite James stories.

It's a sad story, but it says so much about who James is as a person. It's also a story James probably thinks is a secret only he holds. It goes back to when I was in grade school and James was in junior high. Andrew was a freshman in college. Our parents' marriage was deteriorating, a truth evident to anyone who had more than passing contact with them. At the time, I did not have the capacity to understand why our parents were acting the way they did. In retrospect, I can fit some pieces together.

My whole life, Dad has been emotionally detached, particularly with Mom. He is also overly critical to the point that he is almost incapable of praise. He is an equal opportunity employer when it comes to that aspect of his person. More specifically, though, over time he seemed to lose interest in Mom. And anything having to do with her. Unless it was to criticize her. That rejection and denigration built over time and clearly impacted Mom. It would have affected anyone in her shoes.

When James and I were young, it did not seem to bother her as much. Or she just accepted it without much fight. But as we got older, her response was to lash out at him. As if her anger grew more concentrated year after year. Mom has a tendency to harp on things longer than necessary. With Dad, she honed that skill to an art form. By the time of the story I am building to, rarely a day went by when they were not yelling at each other or ignoring each other.

One particular day, Mom and Dad were really going at it. She was screaming about him never helping with household chores like dishes and laundry. Yardwork excluded, because he loved doing that. Dad was yelling about her being perpetually unhappy and nagging. He claimed her negativity brought down the whole family. When they finally separated (Mom to the garden and Dad to his TV upstairs) and the turmoil dispelled, I saw James quietly slip into the kitchen. He started scrubbing some pots and pans.

I had stopped whatever I was doing during the melee. Reading a book, I think. I was probably in a form of shock when the fight was over, so I just watched quietly from the couch while James cleaned. When he was done, he slipped down to the basement. I was now curious. From the top of the stairs, I covertly watched him sort laundry and put a load in the machine. Before that day, I had only ever seen Mom use the laundry machine. Still, in isolation, James cleaning the kitchen and doing the laundry wasn't that remarkable. Not enough to stand out in my mind years later.

What makes it memorable is that his actions started to form a pattern. A few weeks after I spied James cleaning and doing laundry, Mom scolded Dad for not helping her bring in groceries. That prompted another battle. James didn't do anything then. But the next time Mom came home from the grocery store, James greeted her at her car to assist.

When I grew older, I began processing these memories from time to time. I first surmised James was simply covering for Dad. He was either making Dad look good or he was helping Dad escape a dreaded nagging. Or both. James's opinions changed by the time he started college, but when he was growing up, Dad was his idol. My initial hypothesis, however, was wrong. Or it was incomplete.

I take Mom's side generally, but she was not blameless for the unrest. In the tinder and brushwood environment that was our household, any act or omission could have sparked a fire. Although it seemed like a minor thing, Mom was notorious for driving Dad's car and not moving the seat back. I'm positive her neglect was intentional. I observed James on more than one occasion rectify the situation for her. More significantly, she had a tendency to forget to remind Dad about schedule changes. I think she intentionally chose not to tell him. Either way, he'd arrive a half hour early to pick up James from afterschool sports practices. Or he'd be forty-five minutes late to a Saturday game. It drove Dad nuts. James took pains to notify Dad himself through written notes at home. Or he would leave messages at work.

James undertook all of his labors as imperceptibly as he could. He never mentioned them to Mom or Dad. Nor did he seek to curry favor. Without seeking affirmation or commendation, James was single-handedly trying to save our parents' marriage. He was trying to eliminate the minor gripes and obstacles that prevented our parents from addressing their core problems. From seeing and treating each other like people instead of adversaries. The pain and anxiety James must have felt, bottled up as a thirteen-year-old. It breaks my heart just thinking about it. Especially because all these years later, he's never been thanked for what he tried to do.

James, now you know that I know.

Chapter 27

RETURN VISIT WITH DR. BHATTACHARYA

Wright, James
August 24, 20XX

James Wright was seen for a follow-up visit. It has been several months since I last saw him, but he has been seeing a therapist in my office bi-monthly. He reported continued compliance with the medication Abilify during the interim months.

Work was going well for him until the past few weeks. He reported having started a new project with a partner whom he described as not be-lieving in having a life outside work—the "Jacob Marley of business con-sulting." For now, he reported accepting the increased hours and workload, but he expressed doubt at being able to sustain the pace long term. Now that he has worked to develop an active social life, he has no interest in "forging his own chains" of foregone fun and life experiences.

As to interim social history, he has continued working out at a gym multiple times per week and has continued to see friends at lunch and on weekends.

He also reported a relationship with a woman named Alexis that has been going on for several months, and his face lit up when he told me. He indicated that she makes him happy and that he had started thinking about the future more because of her. When pressed for details, he indi-cated he never gave much thought to marriage before, but he had started to think about it now. Yet he clarified that he had no present plans to marry. His expression dimmed, however, when he noted they recently had a fight because she refused to discuss a prior relationship she had hidden from him, one in which she was engaged. For now, despite his misgivings, they agreed to table any discussion of the previous relationship.

He also spent considerable time discussing a conversation he recently had with his father. They don't communicate often, and he reported that this call reminded him why. He reported feeling that his father has never been supportive of him and in fact usually chips away at him with subtle and not-so-subtle swipes. He contemplated whether a continued relationship with his father was best for him; I will revisit this on his next visit and will discuss it with his therapist.

He denied having any active suicidal ideation and reported a continued reduction in passive suicidal ideation, particularly since his relationship with Alexis began. Although the relationship and its effects are positive for Mr. Wright, I suggested that if the relationship ever deteriorates, he should contact my office immediately to discuss coping mechanisms. I explained it is best to have a contingency plan with the hope that one never needs to implement it.

Per my recommendation, Mr. Wright has agreed to continue seeing a therapist every two or three weeks.

Chapter 28

IS THERE ANYBODY OUT THERE?

Two weeks had passed since Alexis and I had our first fight. It was fun making up, but I'd rather not fight again. I hadn't reintroduced the topic of dirty-bathroom-floor Bill, but I had also only seen her a handful of times. I'd been working most nights and weekends because of Sgt. Francis Slaughter, and she'd had a hectic work schedule too. The few times we were together, we had a good time—at least I had a good time; I'm starting not to trust my assessment of her—but having to ignore Bill made me feel like our dendrites and axons were there, but an invisible wall was blocking some of our synapses.

While I wanted to see her more often—preferably every day and night—the time away was probably for the best. Distance made the heart grow fonder, right? Also, the more times I was around her, the more often I'd be conflicted about not discussing Bill, and the more chances she'd have to call me Gloomy Gus. I know me, though. My patience won't last forever. I only hope she will be ready to talk before my dam bursts.

Anyway, on the last Friday in August, we were out to lunch. Richard and Alexis couldn't make it, but Manuel, Sam, Blair, Yasmin, and I were at South Branch. It's on the other side of the Loop from our office, but with an outdoor patio set next to the river and tucked between skyscrapers, it was worth the cab ride.

Blair kept shooting glances at me like he wanted to say something, but he turned away as soon as I returned his gaze. It almost seemed like he wanted to pick a fight with me, but I had no idea why. Besides, if he knew what I had done to Bill (albeit in my mind), he wouldn't have been so quick to start something. I had mentally perfected that front kick, and I was working on an ax kick.

The others seemed to have run out of things to say, and with Blair and me engaged in some kind of weird lambada with our eyes, the conversation had lulled. In stepped Manny with his ever-present list of topics.

"I went to the Art Institute the other day," Manuel informed the group, "and when I was in the Modern wing, I saw a Salvador Dalí painting I can't stop thinking about. It depicted an arid landscape, with an old man featured in the foreground and a man in a suit in the background lifting a piano with one hand. Only the piano looked like it was melting and was dripping downward as the guy in the suit picked it up. There were a couple other things in the painting, but I can't remember them. I hate to use the name of the genre to describe the painting itself, but the whole scene was so surreal that I just stood there staring at it."

Manuel had barely finished speaking when Blair piped in, impertinently. "I know where this game goes. You want us to tell you what our favorite paintings are?"

"Well, yeah," Manuel answered defensively.

I wished he'd been confrontational instead, especially since I liked the topic he'd presented. I'm a huge fan of surrealism myself, so I appreciated Manuel's painting choice. *Time Transfixed*, a painting of a tiny locomotive flying through a fireplace by the surrealist René Magritte, is one of my favorite paintings. It just so happens to be part of the Art Institute's permanent collection, in the same section as the Dalí painting Manuel described. But it's not my all-time favorite work of art.

"It doesn't have to be a painting," Manuel said. "Sculptures, mosaics, or whatever would work too. I'm not sure if Dalí's my favorite artist, but that painting is up there. What about you guys?"

Yasmin jumped in quickly to respond. "I have one!" she announced. I love how animated she always is. "It's not my favorite, but I just learned about it: *Arabs Crossing the Desert* by Jean-Léon Gérôme. The juxtaposition of the colorful clothing and horses against the desert backdrop is so striking. Plus, I feel like you don't see a lot of Arabs in Western art."

I had never heard of the painting or the artist, but I did like her casual use of the word "juxtaposition." One of my favorite fantasy series when I was a kid was the Apprentice Adept collection, and one of the books was titled *Juxtaposition*. I've had a special affinity for the word ever since. Because Yasmin recommended him, I did intend to look up works by Gérôme when I got back to the office. I had found over my weeks of working with her that her enthusiasm can be infectious, and she has good taste.

"I can't say I know that much about art. I rarely go to museums," Blair said. "But I do happen to have a favorite artist. He's British, but I can't remember his name. I saw one of his paintings in a magazine once and thought it was awesome. It was like a really cool cartoon. Thorne was his last name, I think."

"Thorpe?" I suggested. "Mackenzie Thorpe?"

"Yeah, that sounds right," he agreed grudgingly.

"That's a good choice. I can't argue with that."

Blair fired me a look that said he didn't care one way or the other about my concurrence, but I won't let him ruin Mackenzie Thorpe for me. I love Thorpe's paintings and his sculptures. Blair's description of his art wasn't that far off. He has a series of works that feature a faceless cartoon boy who wears a black cloak, and objects around him are shaped like three-dimensional hearts. The one I love the most is titled *Reaching Out*, and it has the character hanging from a tree by one arm, stretching to reach a heart-shaped fruit. The tree, which is barren except for the lone heart fruit, is on the edge of a cliff, and the heart fruit hangs over a bay. A full moon illuminates the sky and sparkles on the water below. I like to think the boy is searching for love, and he's willing to go to any length to obtain it. Yes, I tear up when I think about what the boy must have endured to reach that point of desperation. No, you can't judge me for it.

"I'm embarrassed to admit that, like Blair, I'm no art critic," Sam said. "I know what I like when I see it, but I couldn't tell you specific artists or works of art." She hesitated for a moment, and her eyebrows furrowed, so we knew she was trying to recall something. "Okay, I thought of one artist, but I don't know who he or she is. He or she does a lot of black-and-white drawings. One is of a hand holding a glass globe, and the reflection of the person holding the globe appears inside the globe. Another one shows people walking endlessly up and down stairs, which all somehow lead back to the same place."

"M. C. Escher," Manuel told her. "I forget his name a lot too. You've got good taste."

"Thanks," she said.

"I have a two-way tie for my favorites," I said. "The first is Thomas Eakins's *Gross Clinic* at the Philadelphia Museum of Art. It's huge and depicts a nineteenth-century medical professor instructing students during surgery on a leg. There are spectators in the crowd in stadium seating. It's unbelievably realistic; you could spend hours examining every person's facial expression. It gives you an idea of how ghastly medical procedures were just over a hundred years ago."

"Man, you were primed and ready for this particular survey by Manuel, huh?" asked Sam. "It's like he set you up."

I appreciated her comment, but it made me feel a little self-conscious about my geeky excitement; I would have toned it down if I could.

"Ha, seems like it," I said. "Most of the time I'm not even paying attention to him, so I usually have no idea what to say when it's my turn."

Someone, most likely Manuel, kicked me under the table, but it was a glancing blow.

I temporarily forgot I owed them a second favorite, but Yasmin was there to remind me. "What's your second one?" she asked. "I liked your description of the Eakins painting so much, you better not let me down on your second choice. What do you got?"

"Yeah, sorry about that. I'll try to live up to your expectations. The story of how I saw it is a little pretentious, though, I admit, so you'll have to bear with me." I'm pretty sure Blair rolled his eyes as I made my disclaimer. "When I was in college, I spent one of my spring breaks visiting a friend who was studying abroad in Rome. The Sistine Chapel is amazing, obviously; nothing compares to it. But my favorite was at the Galleria Borghese. It's the *Rape of Proserpina* by Bernini. He was only twenty-three when he sculpted it out of marble. I'm not even big on sculptures, but the skill required to create this statute is astounding. It shows Pluto abducting Prosperina and taking her to the Underworld. You can see every striation of the muscle in his legs as he bears her weight and as she tries to fight him off by shoving his head away. You can see the indentations in her thigh where he's gripping her with all his force. It's so lifelike that you can almost see it in motion before you. I could've spent all afternoon inspecting it, but the museum kicks you out after two hours."

"It sounds amazing," Sam said. "Maybe you and Alexis can go see it together sometime?"

"Yeah, maybe," I said.

Or maybe she'll go with Bill, Fred whispered from the dark fringes of my mind.

■ ■ ■

"Manuel," I announced as I strolled into his and Miles's office later that afternoon, "am I crazy? Or does Blair have some kind of problem with me?"

Then I saw Miles.

"Hey, Miles," I said.

Manuel began to talk while I was greeting Miles, and Miles replied "Hi" back, so I missed Manuel's words.

"What was that?" I asked him.

"I said, I don't know what you're talking about, but I don't have time right now. I have to run to a meeting and then make some calls after that."

No, that answer would not do. "Come on," I said. "I just need like ten minutes to vent."

"*Lo siento, mano.* Can't do it."

"Five minutes, then?"

"Nope, I don't even have one minute," he said. "Besides, whatever beef you and Blair have going on, you need to get over it."

He had no idea what had transpired between Blair and me. Why the hell was he telling me to get over it? "Whose side are you on?"

"Your side. Always your side. But I gotta go," he repeated as he stepped out of his office.

I started to speak, but before I could get any words out, he asked, "Are you about to tell me our friendship is over?"

How did he know? "What? Of course not," I assured him.

"James?"

"Yes?"

"Were you?"

"Get out."

"Later," he said. And then he was gone.

"So what about Blair?" Miles asked, snapping me back to the present.

Miles, coming through again. Pull your friendship notes back out, Manuel. "You know him?"

"Yeah."

"He's a dick."

"I don't know," Miles said with an expression that told me he was quickly constructing a Blair pros and cons list. "He's not that bad."

"Yeah, maybe not. But he was a dick today."

"How so?"

"I dunno. He kept giving me weird looks." I felt dumb as I was saying it.

"Oh, okay," Miles said in a voice one would use with a deranged person.

"Cool. Glad we're on the same page. I feel better now."

"That's it?"

"Huh?"

"That's what you call venting?"

"Ha, yeah, you don't want to see me pissed off. Watch out."

"I'll keep that in mind," he said wryly. "By the way, you're probably a little crazy."

"Hmm?" He had lost me. His comment was coming from three base-ball fields away. "What's that?"

"Your question," he said. "Are you crazy, or does Blair have a problem with you? I don't know how Blair feels about you, but you're definitely a little crazy."

"You're probably right."

"I know," he said.

"What are you doing tonight?"

"Nothing. You?"

"Nada. You wanna see a movie?"

"Sure."

"Cool." It seemed like Miles was always down for hanging out. Unlike Manuel. "Good talk. Let's touch base in a couple hours."

"All right. Later."

■ ■ ■

Early Saturday afternoon, I decided I needed to text Manuel. I wanted to see if he was free that night. Bail on me once, shame on him, bail on me twice, double shame on him.

Manuel, where you at?

I waited a reasonable amount of time for a response, say thirty seconds, and then texted again, *Chacho mano señor quesadilla, what are you doing?*— basically all the Puerto Rican Spanish words I knew. Then I added, *I'm ron'ry.*

This time I gave him a little more time to respond, at least one minute.

Mexican Ninja, I am in need of your drinking prowess and maybe your sword skills. Let's get drunk tonight and then fight crime. Or just get drunk. Ur call. I could go either way.

If that didn't grab his attention, I had no idea what would. Despite my efforts, he did not text me back within a few minutes, so I started to clean things around my apartment while I listened for my text message sound to chime. There were a few false alarms—it's amazing how many things can sound like a text chime or a vibration when you're desperate for human-electronic-human interaction—but finally he sent me a message a half hour later.

You're so needy mano. You're like my abuela. What's up?

The second I heard the text come in, I pounced on my phone like a cougar stalking its prey in the jungle. I typed back to him within a heart-beat, *I need some Manny time. What can you do for me?*

Before he responded, I sent a second text: *Also, I'm over the Blair thing. So you can stop worrying about that.*

A few minutes later, much too slow for my liking, he said, *Good, kiss and make up, whatever it is.*

What? Kiss and make up? Sonofa—whatever. What I cared about was what he was doing that night. He had blithely ignored that critical part of the conversation.

Fine, doesn't matter, I told him, *but WHAT ARE YOU DOING TONIGHT? Inquiring minds want to know.*

After an everlasting delay of about fifteen minutes, he texted, *Sorry, out with Sam's sister. We're doing some shopping around Michigan Avenue.*

Why was he out with Sam's sister and not Sam? Weird. And shopping? Since when did Manuel go shopping? Although I was ready to do anything to get out of the house.

Mind if I come down and tag along? I could use some fresh air.

He responded quickly this time. *No, sorry. Ring shopping—just window-shopping, not buying. Then meeting Sam for dinner later.*

Had he just casually dropped ring shopping into a text? As in engagement ring shopping? This was how I found out Manuel was thinking about proposing to Sam—through a freaking text? And only after I had badgered him?

No bueno, Manny. This is how you tell your best friend you're going to propose? You're better than that.

The responses came back quicker now. *I'm not doing it right now, just getting idea of cost, etc.*, he said. *I'll tell you more later.*

I'm busy later.

Not the most mature response, I know, but I was ticked off. My happiness for him, which would be overwhelming later, was currently overridden by my annoyance at how I had discovered the news.

But congratulations, I said, reluctantly.

From the abyss of my consciousness, Fred told me I was a loser with no friends. I need to develop the chemical equivalent of Magneto's mind-shielding helmet, and then I need to inject it directly into my brain. Maybe then I could stop Fred's communications for good.

Thanks, mano, he replied. *Promise I'll tell you more this week. Hang out with Alexis tonight or Miles again.*

I was tempted to tell him to eat some male genitalia, but that would have been rude. I wasn't that annoyed with him. In fact, that irrepressible happiness was already starting to shine through. Manny's a great guy, and he was thinking of marrying a fantastic girl. Good for them. I hoped they got married, bought a lake house, had lots of babies, and then let me use the lake house because they didn't have time to use it because all their kids joined the school band and also played baseball on traveling teams.

Not a chance, Fred goaded. *You're destined to be alone, and your friends won't have time for you.*

■ ■ ■

Manuel's suggestion—or maybe more so Fred's castigations—encouraged me to text Alexis. *Hey you,* I sent her—still hadn't settled on a cute nickname. *Miss you. What are you doing?*

I had to wait even longer with her than I did with Manuel to get a response, but I was smart enough to know not to pester her. Manuel and I have years of mutual, friendly antagonism. Alexis and I have like a four-month relationship, the last few weeks of which have been much rockier than the start, and I generally do not act like a smart-ass with her. Well, I am a more subdued smart-ass with her, anyway.

About a half hour later, while in my room, I thought I heard my phone vibrating on my coffee table. I sprinted into the other room and dove over my couch to grab it like a Secret Service agent with shots being fired.

Hey there, said the first text from Alexis. *Miss you too.*

That was good to know. *What are you up to?*

At work ☹. *Too many projects. You?*

I'm at home. Trying to figure out what to do later. Did you do anything fun last night?

Sort of. Saw some friends for dinner. Wasn't out late tho. Had to do work.

Glad you saw friends, I told her. *Sucks that you have to do so much work. What kind of odds am I looking at to see you tonight?*

Not good, she answered, *sorry. Think I'll be in the office most of the night and then probably finish up working at home. Sunday will be mostly work too.*

Hmm. Maybe I could help her out and see her at the same time? *I could come over and cook for you?*

That's sweet of you, but I don't think it will work. I don't know exactly when I'll be back and I'll probably be hungry before I leave the office, so I'll order delivery here.

Boo, I responded. *Hope you finish things up quickly. Any chance we can do dinner sometime during the week?*

Definitely. I miss you tons.

Miss you too. Good luck with work.
Thanks. You too.

Well, I was zero for two, and I didn't want to give Miles the option of striking me out. Plus, two nights in a row was too much for our fledgling friendship. Also, I definitely had no desire to go back to his place before I knew more about cyberterrorist Creepy Steve, who might be moonlighting as a cannibal.

I supposed I would just have to do some work that afternoon, and then either work or drink that evening, or do both.

■ ■ ■

I woke up Sunday morning around ten thirty. First impression before I attempted to stand was that my body was functioning properly with no repercussions from the night before. Then I tottered to the bathroom, and all hell broke loose. My head was pounding, my mouth revealed itself to be drier than a saltine cracker dragged through a sandbox, and my stomach began growling for food. The day was going to be a rough one.

After I texted with Alexis the day prior, I worked until 9:00 p.m. or so, but I couldn't bring myself to do anything more. Francis had me approaching the burnout stage, at least a temporary one. So I turned off my phone—I didn't want to repeat a night of texting like the one that had prompted Rachel to read the beginning of my manuscript—and started guzzling the nectar of the gods. All the nectars. Whiskey, vodka, beer—I drank pretty much everything but gin. Why anyone likes drinking fermented Christmas tree water is beyond me.

I remembered turning a movie on around ten thirty in the evening, but my memory was pretty shot after that. It was time to investigate my apartment for clues as to what had happened the rest of the night, right after I downed some headache medicine.

At first glance, things appeared not so bad. Sure, there were beer cans lying around, and some leftovers were sitting out on my kitchen counter, but those messes were easily remedied. I just needed to call Rachel over. Ha! Then I noticed a notepad on my coffee table. That seemed out of place.

I'm not a good artist, but I had apparently made an effort that night. Most of the images were of knives and katana swords skewering stick figures that were supposed to be Bill. If I were a six-year-old who had drawn these illustrations in kindergarten, they might have raised some alarms. But as a young adult who had never physically harmed another person unless in self-defense? I saw nothing wrong with them, other than that they were of poor quality.

Then my eyes fell upon a hole in one of my walls. It appeared to be the size of a fist. Then I looked at my right hand and observed dried blood on my knuckles. I'm no forensic expert, but I figured I could put that case to bed.

That seemed to be the worst that had happened that night. I could patch up that hole; I've done it a couple times before. By my estimation it was a no harm, no foul night—like a game of Russian roulette where you forget to load a bullet in the chamber.

Chapter 29

September 7, 20XX		
PROGRESS NOTE	CLIENT NAME: Wright, James	START: 5:29 pm
	SERVICE CODE:	STOP: 6:32 pm
SYMPTOM STATUS: maintained	DIAGNOSTIC CHANGE? No	
CURRENT SYMPTOMS: depressed state		
	LIFE EVENT? No	
MEDICATION: compliant		
SAFETY: no active suicidal or homicidal ideation		
GOALS/OBJECTIVES: Treatment Plan Goal 1 partially achieved Treatment Plan Goal 2 partially achieved		
CLIENT RESPONSE: Full Compliance		

COMMENTS: Mr. Wright appeared slightly despondent today, much more downcast than he appeared in our previous meetings. He attributed his mood to stress at work and an ongoing issue with his girlfriend involving her reticence to discuss a prior serious relationship.

He noted "Fred" had been making frequent "visits," typically when he was thinking about his girlfriend's ex-fiancé, which he said was all the time. Until they discussed the prior relationship and allayed Mr. Wright's fears that she still had feelings for the ex-fiancé, Mr. Wright was worried Fred would continue to drop by "like an annoying neighbor." Mr. Wright had fabricated various fantasies in which he beat up or embarrassed the ex-fiancé and then sacrificed his own life to save the ex.

He also reflected on his general sense of the world, expressing sentiments that more and more people have antipathy or enmity toward others, rather than love and concern. He attributed some of Fred's recent activity to this overall impression.

Near the end of the session, Mr. Wright noted his best friend Manuel was thinking about proposing to his girlfriend. He was excited for Manuel but also apprehensive that he would be seeing Manuel less and less. He joked that "Ernie needs his Bert." Although he also noted he had been spending time with a new friend named Miles.

NEXT APPT: September 21, 20XX

■ ■ ■

September 21, 20XX

PROGRESS NOTE	CLIENT NAME: Wright, James	START: 5:33 pm
	SERVICE CODE:	STOP: 6:39 pm

SYMPTOM STATUS: maintained | DIAGNOSTIC CHANGE? No

CURRENT SYMPTOMS: depressed state

LIFE EVENT? No

MEDICATION: compliant

SAFETY: no active suicidal or homicidal ideation

GOALS/OBJECTIVES: Treatment Plan Goal 1 partially achieved
Treatment Plan Goal 2 partially achieved

CLIENT RESPONSE: Full Compliance

COMMENTS: Mr. Wright began today's session by expressing frustration about work: his long hours had continued, and he was not seeing much worth in what he does.

He reported his social life was faring slightly better. Although his best friend, Manuel, remained somewhat aloof, he had been spending a little more time with Alexis and with Miles. However, his free time was still largely hampered by his work obligations, and his relationship with Alexis remained encumbered by her continued silence regarding her ex. Mr. Wright referred to the ex as "dirty-bathroom-floor Bill," which I indicated was not a healthy development for him.

NEXT APPT: October 4, 20XX

Chapter 30

IF YOU WANT TO DESTROY JAMES'S SWEATER, HOLD THIS THREAD AS HE WALKS AWAY

Three weeks into September, and I had been derelict in my duty to remind James by written missive that I cared about him. I had a chance to redeem myself on Saturday afternoon, because he was coming to my place for dinner. Alexis was coming too! I was excited to spend more time with her. The Bill issue aside, she seemed like an awesome lady. I wanted to know her better. To cap things off, my roommate, Sarah, had plans, so everything was working out.

I heard a hard banging on my apartment door, followed by a yell.

"Open up! It's the IRS!"

I purposely took my time answering the door. I even stopped to rearrange a couple of things on a shelf before I opened it.

"I'm pretty sure the IRS doesn't arrest people," I said. Then I cracked the door open only a few inches.

"You'd be wrong about that. But I'm pretty sure the IRS only works during tax season too. They don't seem to do anything else. But you're never in trouble, so saying FBI or police wouldn't have been realistic."

"I pay my taxes too, dummy. The IRS isn't realistic either. I'm an all-around upstanding woman. A real pillar of society."

"This is true, so let me in. I'm in need of food. And beer. This is your chance to add to your list of benevolent acts."

His smile appeared and disappeared rapidly. I sensed he was not in the best of moods. He had also said "me" instead of "us."

I held the door semiclosed and peeked around him. "Where's Alexis?"

"She already slipped past you. We've been training in ninjutsu, the art of the ninja. Let me in."

"Seriously, she's not coming?"

"Is she not behind me? She must be getting better at being a ninja than I thought."

"James. Is. She. Coming. Or. Not?"

"It would appear that she is not."

"That's all you're going to tell me?"

"Yes."

"Then you're not getting in."

"Fine. I'll tell you more if you let me in and give me a beer," he said.

"You promise? You're not crossing your fingers or anything?"

"I promise."

"You may enter," I told him as I opened the door.

"You're ridiculous, you know that?"

He came in and immediately headed to my refrigerator. I don't drink beer that often, but I had bought some IPAs earlier in the day. I'm an awesome sister. Truly the best.

"I hope you're in the mood for meat loaf and mashed potatoes, because that's what I'm making."

"That sounds perfect. I haven't had meat loaf in forever."

"Yeah, neither have I. I suddenly had a craving." Mom used to make it all the time when we were kids. Sure, the name doesn't suggest culinary greatness. I suppose it's not aesthetically pleasing either. But it's delicious!

"Where's your roommate, Sarah?" he asked.

"You mean Sarah?" I said too quickly. I had been preparing to have to correct him.

"Yeah, that's what I said. I've met her a bunch of times."

I thought briefly about flicking his forehead or smacking his arm. "She has other plans."

"Oh." Then he said nothing for a little while.

"So?" I prompted.

"So what?"

"I upheld my end of the bargain. You are now inside my apartment. You are now drinking a beer. Now it's your turn."

"It's nothing, really. I should've just told you before I came here, rather than make a big deal out of it."

I waited for him to continue.

"We had a fight last night," he said when he got the hint. "We decided we needed a day apart today. The end. So what's going on with you? How are the first few weeks of your senior year going?"

"Nice try, buddy. You're not getting off that easy." What did he expect? I am a Grand Inquisitor. "Start from the beginning. And don't skip over anything."

"Okay. I'll tell you about the fight, I promise. But we always talk about my stupid problems. Tell me about what's going on with you first."

"James, we made a deal."

"I know, and I swear I'll tell you. But I don't want you to feel like all I do is talk about Alexis. And lately, only complain about Alexis."

"All right, fine. Let me finish cooking. It's almost done, and then we can talk."

"Cool. While you were talking, Alexis just appeared behind you."

Like an idiot, I spun around to see what was there. There were no signs of Alexis.

"Just kidding. She's not a ninja, dummy," he said.

James helped with the finishing touches, and then we sat down to eat.

"So, Rach, I've been trying to get it out of you since I got here. What's new in your life? How did the internship end?"

Sometimes I truly could punch him.

"I'm really happy about how the internship went. You know that, because I told you a bunch of times. I learned a ton."

"But you still don't think it's a place you would work after college?"

"Nah. For one, I don't think there's a space for me. They don't have a lot of extra capital for hiring new people. Two, I want to be involved in a broader project. Something like urban planning for a city to make it eco-friendly."

"Always saving the world," he said.

"Exactly." If he wants to think I'm Wonder Woman, I am not going to try to convince him otherwise. "Three, I'm not sure I want to work right away after college. I'm thinking of doing a gap year and traveling. Assuming Mom and Dad would subsidize me, that is."

"Like a backpacking around Europe kind of thing? Or something else?"

"No, something else. I'd be backpacking, but I want to go to developing world countries. Maybe India. I want to see firsthand what realistically could be done to protect the environment. And what can be done to improve the lives of the people. Ideally, those two goals should work hand in hand."

"Well, that's pretty impressive, Rach. I think you should do the gap year thing."

"Thanks." I appreciated his enthusiasm. "But please hold your applause until I actually do it."

"Of course, of course. I may join you. Quitting my job and traveling through remote locations for a year sounds pretty sweet."

"You're welcome to come. But you should probably keep your job," I cautioned.

"Yeah, that. So," he said as a filler, "any dates lately?"

"I've had a few dates, but nothing serious. One guy was a real piece of work."

"What'd he do? What's his name? Where does he live?"

"Relax, killer. It was no big deal. Besides, what are you going to do if I tell you?"

"You don't want to know any of the details. Plausible deniability."

"Mm hmm. Sure."

"Really," he said. "I recently met a terrorist cannibal. Sort of met him, anyway. A real psycho."

"Shut up. You're ridiculous, and playtime's over. You have to tell me about Alexis."

"Hmm. So you haven't forgotten about that, huh?"

"No, I haven't."

"Okay. We got in a fight yesterday because I asked her about Bill. I told you about him, right?"

"Yeah, it's come up once or twice." Or a hundred times.

"I know, I'm just messing with you. I couldn't take it any longer, though." He did not explain any further. It was more than a little annoying.

"What couldn't you take any longer?"

"Us never talking about Bill. It was driving me crazy, always skating around the issue, like a giant hole in the middle of an ice rink."

"Nice analogy," I said. "A tad literal, but I'll allow it."

"Yeah, I've had better. But really, I accepted her request not to talk about it. It took every ounce of my willpower to contain myself, but I did it. I kept hoping she would finally bring it up, but she never did. As far as I can tell, she poured concrete around her feelings for Bill and then dropped them in the ocean."

"That one's a little better. But why are you focused on analogies involving water?"

"Do you want to hear the story or not?"

"Okay, sorry." I mimed locking my lips and throwing away the key. "I do."

"All right then. So it's been like six weeks since I found out about Bill. Not that anyone's counting."

"Of course not."

"And the whole time," he said, continuing without pause, "not once has she offered to talk about him. Not once! Even though she knows I'm dying to talk about it. I specifically told her that it's holding us back. So, I had to take matters into my own hands. Like Gandalf would do."

"He takes things into his own hands? I thought he delegates everything." He conscripted a hobbit for a dangerous mission, for goodness' sake. Twice! Two different hobbits!

"Hmm. You have a point, but Gandalf's still a boss."

"Okay, if you say so." I had to get this conversation back on track. "I thought she asked you to be patient. You didn't think it could wait a little longer?"

"Whose side are you on?"

"Oh, come on. I'm just trying to make sure I'm seeing the whole picture." James isn't the most patient person. It's possible others could have respected Alexis's wishes longer. I wanted to get the full scope.

"Fine. I see where you're going with this. Yes, I'm insanely impatient. I know that's what you're thinking."

That was remarkably close to what I was thinking.

"Normally," he said. "But not this time. So stop thinking that."

He was staring at me. "Stop it!" he insisted.

"Okay. You weren't impatient. I'm listening. So tell me why you had to talk to her about it yesterday."

"The reason I had to bring it up is because I'm starting to unravel. At first one thread at a time, but the momentum is building. I can't keep the facade up any longer. Not around her, anyway."

He looked so exposed and helpless when he told me this. I wanted to bear hug him immediately, but I held back on the affection. I was worried it might cause him to close up.

"What do you mean? What disguise are you putting up?" I understood, I thought. But I wanted to know for sure. I wanted him to tell me in his own words.

"Pretending it's not bothering me! I can't ignore it anymore. Every time I look at her, all I see is dirty-bathroom-floor Bill."

"Huh?"

"That's what I call her ex-fiancé. Trust me, he deserves the nickname."

That little fact was a little weird. He had never met her ex-fiancé Bill. So why give him a derogatory moniker? And declare that he deserved it?

"Okay," I said, glossing over the strangeness. "But why has it been eating at you so much?"

"Because at this point, it's bigger than her just not telling me about him. The fact that she can't talk about him, now, over a year later... It's messed up. Honestly, it's scary. Whether she still loves him or not, she can't get over him. If she can't get over him, we're doomed. We might as well break up. I'd probably never do it if that were the case, but I should."

"That all makes sense. I definitely get it. You're right—if she can't talk about him now, she's not over him. Something about him anyway." I had no need of her side of the story to agree with James.

"So how did you bring it up with her?" I asked.

It was necessary for me to know how the fight ended. If it was a relationship-ending one. What I really needed to know was how vigilant I was going to have to be with him going forward. Periodic texting or phone calls every thirty minutes?

"We were hanging out at my place. We were supposed to watch a movie, but neither one of us left work before eight p.m. By the time she came over, we were both too tired to sit through one. So instead, we were just sitting around talking, and she said something about life being too short to work like this. Like, to work so much."

"Yeah, I got it." The meaning was obvious.

"Right. Something in my brain caught when she said 'life is too short.' I decided right then and there I needed to bring up Bill again. We needed to talk about him. And then throw him in a pit and set him on fire."

Violent imagery aside, for once James's explanation for how he linked one thing to another thing made sense to me.

"Got it," I said, to show I was being an active listener. "How exactly did you bring it up?"

"I demanded, 'Tell me about Bill. Now! Everything! Or else this relationship is over!'"

He said this with a straight face, but of course I knew he was joking. "Come on, James. Everyone knows ultimatums only get you what you don't want."

"Yeah, that's not how it went. I made her drag it out of me. That's my go-to method when I want to talk about something, but I also don't want to talk about it, you know?"

The fact that it was happening right now appeared to be lost on him. "Okay. So how did that go?"

"Well, I eventually said I wanted to talk about Bill. She immediately tensed up and flexed her fists. Then she visibly cooled, and I'm pretty sure I saw an anger cloud emit from her."

He never lacks for imagination. That is for sure. "What does an anger cloud look like?" I asked, just to be a pest.

"Oh, you'll know it when you see it. It's pretty distinctive."

Sometimes I wish he wasn't so quick on the draw. It can be infuriating trying to one-up him. "So she tensed, and then she blew smoke from her ass?" I said. "Then what happened?"

"I won't give you a full play-by-play. Mainly, I don't want to keep saying 'she said, and then I said, and then she said,' and so on, and so on, and so on."

"I appreciate you sparing me the nitty-gritty details."

"You're welcome," he said. "Essentially, she accused me of not listening to her and with being obsessed with Bill." He turned to look at me and then stated with a serious face, "I obsess over no man, Rachel. No man." Then he returned to a normal conversational tone. "So anyway, I got defensive and said she wasn't over him and probably still loved him. There was some yelling, some loud sighs of frustration, some yelling, and eventually I accused her of seeing him behind my back."

"Do you have any evidence of that?" I was starting to have a little déjà vu from the last time we talked about this subject in person.

"Before yesterday? A little bit. She's been using work as an excuse not to hang out a lot lately—and so have I; don't get me wrong—but sometimes it doesn't seem genuine from her. Like maybe she had other plans and was using work as a cover. I can't put my finger on anything other than it rang hollow a couple times."

"But no concrete evidence?"

"Right. Only circumstantial."

"But after yesterday?"

"I'm almost certain she's seen him lately. The way she reacted to my accusation said everything. She looked guilty. She stuttered before responding. She never stutters; she rarely even looks flustered. So I knew I had sunk her battleship."

"Huh?"

"It was a direct hit; that's what I mean. She's been seeing Bill, and now I know it."

Right, the board game. "I got it. So after being flustered, what did she do?"

"Told me I was being insecure. Swore she hadn't seen him. Predictable stuff. What else could she do if she wasn't going to admit it?"

Or if she was telling the truth? But I held my tongue. I knew better. Plus, I suspected James was onto something. If Alexis was complaining about something he did, I would have been less inclined to believe his side of the story. But that wasn't the case here. James was bothered by something she was doing. Or I guess in this case not doing. He may not always be in touch with his own emotions, but he's excellent at reading other people.

"How did the fight end?"

"Sort of similar to our first fight. She decided to leave around the same time I was going to ask her to leave. At least we're on the same page when it comes to kicking each other out. So we have that going for us."

"You guys didn't break up?"

"No. We're still together. We both apologized by text today, but we agreed it was too soon for her to come with me here tonight. Emotions are raw."

"I can see that."

"I'm supposed to see her later this week sometime."

That was a huge relief. I didn't have to go into full-on disaster recovery mode with him. "Okay, well, I'm glad you're still together. Aside from the whole Bill thing—"

"Dirty-bathroom-floor Bill," he said.

"Yes, aside from that. She seems to be good for you. I know how much you like her."

"For now. If she keeps ducking the issue, eventually I'll have to keep throwing it in her face until she breaks up with me. 'Cause we know I won't break up with her."

It was terrible of me to think it, but I hoped that if they broke up, it wouldn't be for at least ten months from now. I'm too busy with school to be a good monitor of James.

That doesn't mean I'm not watching, brother.

Chapter 31

HALLOWEEN: I WANTED TREATS, BUT I GOT TRICKED

The rest of September and almost all of October were largely the same. I woke up and went for a run or to the gym, then rode the train to work, and then stayed at work until late in the evening. After all that wonderfulness, I came home each night and did more work, or I went to bed exhausted. The weekends weren't much different. This was not what I had signed up for. I should be doing the bare minimum of work between 9:00 a.m. and 5:00 p.m., and in return my bosses should be paying me a boatload of money. All the money. Don't they know that's how it's supposed to go? What happened to the American dream? Who's going to pay for my lake house, and my pension, and my eventual plastic surgery?

This unsustainable work schedule certainly has been leaving me distressed, but that is not hard to do. Being distraught is like my life calling. Fred has been salivating because of this development, whipping up torrential rains and hurricane winds in a nonstop barrage. Like a Florida native, nonetheless, my mind has barely been registering his appearances. I simply have been too exhausted. Too tired even to write at night like I had been doing. Every time I tried, which wasn't that often because of my fatigue, everything I typed read like a crappy Emily Dickinson poem. Something tells me, however, Fred is just waiting for the right moment to come busting through like an ethereal Kool-Aid Man.

I haven't seen Manuel much the past few weeks, but I know he's getting close to proposing. He picked out an engagement ring, with guidance from Sam's sister, but he needs to save up a little more money before he passes the point of no return. He didn't tell me how much it costs and even I am not tactless enough to ask him, but based on the picture he showed me, I'm guessing you could get a sedan with a base package for less money. Some people like to drive to work; other people like to be armed robbery targets—different strokes for different folks. I can't criticize, though; I like shiny things too, and I'd probably do the same thing in his shoes.

Alexis and I have only been seeing each other a few hours a week lately, but we've managed to steer clear of Bill, mainly through extreme bodily passion. We don't spend much time talking, if you catch my drift. Our time apart has stoked the fires of our sexual attraction hot enough to melt tungsten. What I mean to say is… Oh, you get it and want me to move on? You understood from the start and you are now annoyed? Okay, I'll change topics.

By the way, tungsten has the highest melting point of all the known elements at 6,192 degrees Fahrenheit. Now when that question comes up at your next trivia night, you'll know the answer, and you'll be reminded of me and my sexy times with Alexis. So, you're double welcome.

Really, I should be uncontrollably pissed off about dirty-bathroom-floor Bill and Alexis's continued refusal to discuss him. But I'm not, mainly for the same reasons Fred has remained ineffective. I simply haven't had time to be upset about Alexis's continued circumvention of the issue. Of course, our intense lust has helped to quell my fury.

This coming weekend, however, is Halloween weekend. Manuel will be hosting a party, and then we'll do some late-night bar hopping. There is no way I'm going to let Francis and this untenable work schedule ruin this particular Saturday night for me. Moreover, despite Francis pushing us like sled dogs in the Iditarod and my general tendency to mutter around him like I'm missing my red stapler, I have developed quite a rapport with him, if I do say so myself. This is how, yesterday, I managed to get out of working tonight and all day tomorrow:

Me: Hi, uh, sir, umm, may I talk to you about this weekend?

Francis: Hrumph. What is it?

Me: Umm, I may not be able to do any work after Saturday afternoon, sir. I have some, uh, well, serious things going on this weekend.

Francis: "May not be able to," or you cannot work after Saturday afternoon? Which is it?

Me: Probably more of the former, sir.

Francis: Do these "serious things" involve a family emergency?

Me: They do not, sir.

Francis: Do they involve you wearing a costume and drinking alcohol?

Me: They do, sir. If, uh, all goes according to plan, that is.

Francis: Fine. Come in earlier than usual on Monday.

Me: Thank you, sir.

[I threw another coal on the fire like Bob Cratchit and then ran out of his office.]

Francis smirked when I mentioned "serious things," and then he was outright smiling when he asked me whether I'd be wearing a costume, so it wasn't all that bold of me to respond in the affirmative. I appreciate the time off this weekend, but it is a sad state of affairs that I even had to have the conversation.

Here is why having Saturday night off and Sunday to recover are absolutely necessary:

First, Alexis will be coming out, and she promises me her costume will not disappoint. As I just noted, our ardor lately has been unbridled, like a wild stallion and an amorous mare romping through a valley untouched by humans, and I look forward to seeing the sexy ensemble she shrink wraps onto her lithe and sporty frame, whatever it may be.

Second, Manuel's Halloween parties are legendary. I've already recounted his fondness for hand-me-down costume accessories, but that is just the tip of the iceberg. The guy spends weeks making playlists, decorates like a champ, and spares no expense on high-end liquor and beer. For only those reasons—nothing to do with his personality, I assure you—his parties are always well attended.

Third, I spent an inordinate amount of time planning and assembling my costume this year. I'm going as Link from Zelda, which isn't original, I know, but I'm hoping a flawless execution will make up for its mundaneness. Aside from growing out my hair and sideburns, I found online some workable boots, a foam sword, a Link belt, wristbands, and a bandolier; I purchased some white tights at a drugstore; and Rachel helped me make a green tunic and hat. She is talented in all areas. In fact, I should have persuaded her to do the whole thing, because I ended up measuring the tunic too short. It stops just a hair below my butt, affording me scant leeway for bending over. My ego is okay with the mistake; I've spent a lot of time the past few months running and doing lunges and squats. This is the time for my lower extremities to shine. I think people will be simultaneously impressed and embarrassed for me, and whether they laugh out of amusement or out of pity, they'll still be laughing.

■ ■ ■

I started to get ready for the party on Saturday around five thirty, which wasn't all that early considering I was supposed to be at Manuel's place at seven to help with any finishing touches. The rest of the guests weren't scheduled to arrive until nine. As I began to get dressed, I put just the tights on first and jumped around like a ballet dancer. I looked pretty damn good, but I had the grace of a newborn giraffe. It was a smart decision to buy some extra pairs of the tights to take with me to the party and the bars; there was no way I was going to make it through the night without tearing at least three of those bad boys.

Then I put the rest of my gear on. Hot damn, I made a good Link. I didn't bother with a shield because I would have tired of carrying it after t-minus twenty-three seconds, but I wished I had taken the time to make or buy a pan flute. Oh well, there was nothing else left to do at that point but drink a beer and whack things with my foam sword. So that was what I did for literally the next twenty minutes. Finally it was time to leave for Manuel's place, so I went downstairs to get a cab.

As I walked through my lobby, my ID and credit card fell out from where I had tucked them into my waistband. I could leave my keys with the front desk, but I hadn't thought about phone, money, and credit card storage ahead of time. I was bending over to grab them when I heard a security guard in my lobby catcall whistle me and yell, "Nice ass, James!" It had begun.

"You're welcome, Rob. I dropped that stuff on purpose for you."

"You shouldn't have."

■ ■ ■

Manuel lives in a River North high-rise in a one-bedroom apartment. He could have probably bought three engagement rings by now if he weren't paying for that place, but his one-thousand-plus-square-foot abode does offer some fantastic views of the city, and he is minutes away from some of the best nightlife Chicago has to offer.

As I leaped off the elevator like the hero I was dressed as and walked down the hallway toward his apartment, I could hear some spooky Halloween sounds emanating from within, along with some kind of incense smell, maybe a smoke machine. I knocked once and entered, finding myself engulfed by pirate ornamentations. There were some palm trees on walls, plenty of skull-and-crossbones flags, a few treasure chests sprinkled around the place, a sandpit in a corner, chocolate gold coins scattered throughout, candles brimming over with wax, and rum everywhere. I had to give him credit; he was a master of his craft.

"James!" he yelled, walking from his bedroom. "Welcome, me matey. You actually put together a good costume this year!"

"Arrrr, thanks for noticing, buddy."

"You're welcome."

"I put a lot of effort into it, with Rachel's help. Need to look good for Alexis. Check this out." Then I quickly turned around and bent over to pick up a gold coin.

"*Fuera de acá!* You're obscene."

"Yeah, but how does my butt look?"

"*Chacho*, if you ask me that question ever again, our friendship is instantly over."

I thought that was a little harsh of a reaction, but it's not like I hadn't issued drastic threats to him before—like on a weekly basis. I then observed the full scope of Manuel's attire. He very much resembled Captain Jack Sparrow; his attention to detail was unparalleled. Though I thought he had overdone it on the makeup just a tad.

"Your costume looks awesome as usual, man," I said.

"Thanks."

"But are you competing in a drag competition later? Are we going to Boys' Town tonight? It's okay if we are; I just want to get in the right mind-set."

"Huh? What do you mean?" He seemed genuinely perplexed.

"You're wearing more foundation than a teenage girl with acne."

"Shut up. It's just the right amount. You'll see."

"Mm hmm. I will see," I said as I grabbed a beer from his fridge.

Just then, Sam walked into the apartment and saw me first. "Hey, James!" she greeted me. "Great to see you." Then she gave me a big hug.

"Great to see you too." She was dressed as a sexy female pirate, so I told her so. "You're the hottest swashbuckler I've ever seen."

Manuel barked "Back off" at the same time as Sam responded, "Thank you! You're looking pretty good yourself."

I refrained from putting on the same show for her that I had for Manuel. I had some boundaries.

Sam then directed her attention to Manuel. "Hi, lover," she said as she approached him. Then she halted in her tracks. "Whoa. You didn't tell me we were supposed to dress as cross-gender pirates."

I spit out the beer I had just sipped.

"Are you serious?" Manuel said. "You too? It can't be that bad."

"It is. You went way overboard with, well, with pretty much all your makeup. We need to go fix *this*," Sam informed him as she waved her two hands in a circular pattern around his face.

"Fine. *Chacho*, finish cutting those limes on the counter and then check my list, which is also on the counter, to see what else needs to be done before people get here."

"Got it. Drink all the rum. No problem."

■ ■ ■

By the time Alexis arrived a little after nine o'clock, I was feeling pretty, pretty, pretty good thanks to the rum punch Sam and Manuel had formulated. I'm fairly certain the recipe was two parts rum, one part punch, and three parts poor life choices.

Besides my natural predilection for being early, I usually arrive at house parties at the designated time because I prefer to maximize my access to free alcohol. I have observed over the years, however, that not many people share my enthusiasm for slamming booze before anyone else shows up. Tonight was no exception, and only a few people had walked in before Alexis.

I had been keeping my eye on the door while I chitchatted with the first arrivals, so I noticed Manuel's door open and Alexis begin to appear. At that precise moment, a fourth-dimensional being chose to act on our three-dimensional universe—there could be no other explanation—to either decelerate the earth's centripetal motion around its axis or to grant me the temporary ability to see the world at twice the normal frames per second, as if I were a golden-mantled ground squirrel. Look it up. The effect was that Alexis entered Manuel's apartment in a slow-motion glide, affording me ample time to note and analyze every luscious part of her.

Starting at the top, her hair was in the same puffed-up ponytail I had loved on our first date, only she had added some glitter to it. Her shirt was a Pepperdine volleyball uniform, but the neckline had been cut to provide some truly spectacular cleavage. Four inches of spandex lovingly embraced her athletic hips and thighs, while white tube socks climbed up the lower halves of her sinewy calves. I knew she was carrying a winter coat with her, but in light of the more important details my mind was recording, it did not deem the coat's appearance noteworthy.

Then the dimensional interloper lost interest, because Alexis said in a normal-speed voice, "Hey babe! You look awesome!"

"You too! You look incredible. I think you dropped something in the hallway, though." Alexis turned around to look, which provided me with the view I was looking for.

"There's nothing out there—" Then she twisted back around. "You're terrible," she said as she came over and kissed me. "But I should've expected that from you."

"Yes, you should have. Let me take your coat, and then I'll make you a drink."

"Thanks. I have to ask, though. Are you an elf? Or Peter Pan?"

"You don't know what my costume is?"

She scrunched her face and then said, "No, sorry. It looks great, but I don't know what you are."

"We're breaking up."

"Shut up!" she said as she play shoved me.

"Make your own drink. You'll find rum here, and there, and over there…"

"Come on. Tell me what you are. Please, James-y," she purred demurely.

"I'm Link from Zelda. I am the hero who protects the lands of Hyrule."

"That's a video game?"

"We're breaking up."

Then she leaned in and kissed me again. "Are we still breaking up?"

"You've earned yourself a temporary reprieve, but tomorrow, we're playing a Zelda game."

"Deal. Now go make me a drink, farm boy."

I had to laugh. "As you wish."

■ ■ ■

Within an hour, guests had filled up Manuel's place, and within two hours, people were getting sloppy. Masks and handheld accessories had been discarded, and those few shortsighted folks who wore outfits unconducive to expelling waste had abandoned their guises entirely. Oh, and people were drunk.

I was in the process of cinching up a bag of trash to take to the garbage chute in the exterior hallway when Alexis approached me with panic on her face.

"I'm sorry, James. I have to go. I'm sorry."

Then she turned and bolted for the door with her coat in hand. I was a little slow witted thanks to rum and beer, so I didn't respond immediately. I was also holding a bag of trash, so I couldn't just run after her.

"Wait!" I yelled, a few nanoseconds too late. She was out the door before I could figure out what to do next.

I tied the trash bag up quickly and then ran to the sink to wash my hands. I briefly considered just dropping it and sprinting for the door, cleanliness be damned, but I was in a room full of people. I should've done it anyway, but I was worried someone would freak out and cause a scene because of my lack of sanitization. By the time I stepped into the hallway, the elevator doors were closing. Stairs were an option, but Manuel lived on the nineteenth floor. Unless that fourth-dimensional was going to come back, there was no way I was going to make it down in time to catch her. Instead, I stood frozen in the hallway, wondering what the hell had just happened.

We had been having so much fun—lots of joking and teasing. She kept kidding that I was dressed as Peter Pan or a fairy and that my costume was indecent from behind. I told her she was jealous that my spandex-covered butt was getting more attention. And not once had I been tempted to mention Bill.

Dirty-bathroom-floor Bill. That's why she left! She must have gotten a call or a text from him. It was so obvious, I didn't bother trying to think up alternative theories. But why would she have run out so quickly? Why couldn't she at least have had the decency to spend thirty seconds explaining to me why she had to leave? What could Bill have said to make her jet out of there? And why did it smell like freaking vomit out in the hallway? Oh, I could answer that last one. It was because somebody had puked out there.

I called her phone, but she didn't answer—not the first time I called, nor the seventh time. Then I texted her. *Where are you going? Why did you leave?*

I didn't expect to get a response anytime soon.

Humiliated, confused, and raging inside, I returned to Manuel's apartment. Even though the trashcan was sitting in the middle of the floor, no one had taken ten seconds out of their party schedule to put it back in place, so I handled that and washed my hands again. Then I plucked a near-full bottle of rum and sat by myself in a corner.

Manuel walked over. "*Qué pasa?* Where's Alexis?"

He apparently didn't see her turn her back on me and then run out of there like a German villain had called her and threatened to blow up multiple city blocks if she didn't answer various riddles.

"She left," I said, knowingly vague and unhelpful.

"What do you mean she left, *mano*? Did you guys get in a fight?"

"Nah, man. She just ditched me. Ran right out of here with no explanation. Pretty sure she went to see Bill."

"Come on, you don't know that. Maybe someone she knows is in the hospital or something."

I knew he was trying to be helpful, but I didn't want him to try to put a glossy sheen on her dastardly deed. "If that were the case, she would've told me that before she left. Or texted me by now to explain she was headed to the hospital. But she didn't tell me squat. Treated me like I didn't matter and sprinted out of here."

"Sorry, man."

"It's probably your fault," I told him like a pissed-off toddler. "She probably couldn't take your decorations any longer."

That made him smirk. "You take that back right now, or you hand over that bottle of rum."

Not a chance. If she was going to run out of here with no explanation, I was going to get blackout drunk. "Nope. I'm going to drink all of this. Then I'm going to dive down your garbage chute."

"Ha. As your friend, I have to advise against that. Your ass is too big."

"You're not a good friend, Manny."

"I'm your best friend, *chacho*."

"That's the saddest part about this."

"Come on," he said as he pointed toward the kitchen area. "Let's do a shot of Jack before you drink more of that rum."

"Good idea."

■ ■ ■

I woke up at about eleven thirty Sunday morning and propped myself up on an elbow. At first I had no idea where I was, like one of those dreams where you're supposedly at your house or school but nothing looks right. Then the fog lifted a little, and I realized I was on my couch. Relieved I was not lying in an alley or a dumpster, I lay back down and closed my eyes for a few more minutes.

Then I pieced things together as best I could. I had no recollection of how I had gotten home or when. That was confidential information drunk me was not sharing. I vaguely remembered Manuel being annoyed with me, but no specifics were rising to the surface. Then I wondered where Alexis was, and the image of her running away from me came flooding back.

Where was my phone? I started flailing my arms like a car dealership windsock, but my exertions did not produce the whereabouts of my hand-held device. I then stood up slowly and took some gingerly steps around my apartment.

My phone was not in any of the usual places, and having taxed almost all my energy, I gave up and sat down in a chair. Before I closed my eyes, however, I spotted my phone on the floor several feet away, partially concealed by my couch. I stared at it for a long time, but that morning was not the day that my telekinetic powers took root. Teleportation also escaped me. Then I tried calling it names and yelling at it.

It didn't budge. Looked like I would have to do it the old-fashioned way. Why was everything so hard right then?

I slid out of the chair like a pile of ooze and crawled on my hands and knees to pick it up; then I rolled upward onto my couch. Zero missed calls. Sonofabitch. I had one missed text, but it was Manuel, not Alexis: *James, it's Sam. We dropped you off after everyone else left. You were pretty belligerent and refused to sleep at Manuel's. Don't worry, he's not pissed. We're sorry Alexis ditched you.*

I didn't want Sam's pity, but I appreciated her and Manuel's efforts to take care of me. I texted him back: *Manuel, thanks for getting me home. Please thank Sam too. Sorry if I was a pain in the ass.*

I could have messed things up a lot worse. I would have to apologize to them both in person.

You were, he texted me back instantly. *The cabbie hated you. We had to tip him extra. But don't worry about it. I understand. Let me know when you find out what happened to Alexis.*

Manuel must have been talking to Miles about how to be a good friend. *Thanks,* I sent him. *I will.*

Scanning my other messages, I was elated to find that I did not send any texts after I asked Alexis where she was. Before I considered what I was doing, I called her. No answer. I called again. No answer. So I texted her: *Please call or text me when you can. I want to make sure you're all right.*

A few minutes went by without a response and my stomach had started growling. I had no idea if I eaten anything last night—I doubt I had—so I staggered to my refrigerator. Thank the gods, I had some leftover Chinese food. I didn't even bother heating it up in my microwave; I just pulled a fork from my drawer and started chucking it down my throat. Then I chugged some water.

After taking a shower, I lay on my bed for an indeterminate length of time before getting dressed. Completing those basic tasks had drained me, so I went back to lying on my couch.

■ ■ ■

Around four in the afternoon, I received a text from Alexis. By that point in the day, I was not expecting any contact from her, so I let a little time lapse before I checked my phone.

Are you home? I'm coming over to explain. And apologize.

I was not sure how to respond. I certainly deserved an explanation, but the angry, hurt, and childish parts of me wanted to ignore her—or worse. After typing, deleting, and retyping, I merely answered, *Yes.*

There was a knock on my apartment door twenty minutes later. My hangover was gone by then, but Fred and I had been spending a lot of time together, so I was in a pretty foul mood. I hoisted myself up sluggishly and gradually navigated my way to the door.

When I peeped through the keyhole, I saw the object of my affection and my wrath. I opened the door halfway without saying anything. I just stared at her like she was a missionary who also wanted me to donate to a charity no one had ever heard of.

"May I come in?"

"Why?" I said. I was in no mood to be cooperative or mature.

"Because I'm sorry, and I want to explain." She did not appear to be anguished, which was not helping her cause.

Without saying anything, I opened the door farther and gestured for her to enter. She walked past me and sat down on the couch. I purposely did not offer her anything before I plopped down in a chair across from her. Her face reacted subtly to my refusal to sit next to her, but it was too fleeting for me to interpret.

"I'm sorry I ran out last night," she said.

"Your phone doesn't work?" I asked, my vehemence only slightly contained.

"What?"

She looked a little startled by my fury. I had mixed emotions about that. "You couldn't call me back or text me the last twenty-four hours? Or twenty-one hours, whatever it's been?"

"I'm sorry."

"You could've texted me that like twenty hours ago. Or ten, or five."

"Can you please just let me talk?"

"Sure. Start from the beginning. The part where you turned your back on me and ran away." I was not going to make this easy for her. I didn't care if I blew everything up in the process—like that German villain. Her actions the night before had hurt me more than I had thought. My emotions had shut down from pain overload, and they were only then coming back online.

"Please," she pleaded earnestly. "I'll explain."

I have always been a softie—my anger burns hot and fast like a firework. "Sure. Enlighten me." My words were condescending, but my hostility was already evaporating.

"Bill needed me. He relapsed. He was drinking."

Get out, get out, get out! my brain screamed, but I said coolly, "That's not an explanation." Like I said, my emotions were on the fritz. Anyway, I knew she had gone to see him; the reason for doing so didn't change anything. At least not yet. "You're not starting from the beginning."

"What do you mean? You wanted to know why I left last night."

"How long have you been talking to Bill? How long have you been seeing him?"

"How do you know I've seen him?"

"You don't get to ask me questions right now," I said. "If you want to stay here, you have to answer *my* questions. If you don't want to do that, just leave and go back to Bill." I had simulated the conversation in my head about a hundred times; I couldn't believe real life was somewhat tracking with how it had played out in my mind.

A spark of annoyance rippled across her countenance, but to her credit she didn't snap at me. "Okay. Bill is an alcoholic. He first reached out to me a month or so ago, as part of his AA program."

"Why? To make amends? That sort of thing?"

"Yeah, exactly that," she said. "He wanted to apologize for what he put me through."

"But obviously that wasn't the end of it, right?"

"Yeah, I'll tell you everything. Just be patient."

Sure, because you've been so forthcoming before this, I quipped in my head. But I swallowed it down and instead said, "Sure, I'll shut up. Tell me."

"I met Bill for coffee a few days after he called me so he could apologize in person. We ended up talking for an hour or so, because he had been making strides at recovery. He hadn't had a drink for six months, he was working again, and for the first time ever he genuinely apologized to me. Actual remorse. If you knew him, you'd know how significant that is."

I only wanted to know what his nose would feel like against my knuckles—or my knee.

"Anyway, when I was getting ready to leave, he asked me if I was dating someone. I told him I was in a serious relationship with a great guy. That's you, by the way." She had been looking slightly away from me while she spoke but turned to make eye contact when she delivered the last line.

"Thank you for the clarification." Despite my best efforts, I smiled a little.

"You're welcome. He said he was happy for me, and he asked if he could maybe check in with me periodically. I told him sure. He's been such a large part of my life for so long, I—I was just happy that he was recovering."

"So far, this all seems very innocent on your part," I said. "I don't understand why you hid this from me."

"I didn't mean to hide it, per se. But I had only seen him one time, and I wasn't sure if we were going to try to be friends again. So I didn't think it was a big deal, and I knew you wouldn't be happy to know I had seen him, so I didn't tell you about it."

My chilled rage was returning to a simmer. "No, you can't put this on me. You chose not to tell me because it was easier for you. Maybe you had other reasons too. Maybe you think I'm a fragile little weakling who can't handle bad news. But you didn't tell me because you chose the low road." It felt so good to get that out, but I didn't want to push too hard and make her leave.

"Don't tell me what my reasons were. You don't know what I was thinking." Apparently, she hated people assuming her intentions as much as I did.

"Okay, you're right. Sorry. But don't use me as a reason not to tell me things. Especially this—I want to know what's going on with Bill. I don't want to be kept in the dark."

"All right, I'm sorry too. I should've just told you from the start. But I don't think you're a weakling either. Don't accuse me of things that aren't true."

"Fine," I said with a partial smile. "I'll only accuse you of things that are true."

"I'd rather you not accuse me of anything," she said with a return Mona Lisa smirk, "but I'll take it."

"All right, so you met him once, and he asked if he could check in with you. Did you see him again before last night?"

"No, I didn't see him again. He texted me a few times just to say hi, and that he still hadn't had a drink, but nothing beyond that."

"So what happened last night?"

"He texted and said he needed help. That it was an emergency. I asked him to explain, and he said he had had a drink. He didn't want to have another, but he didn't think he could stop by himself. He asked me to meet him at the bar where he was and walk with him."

"Why did he need *you*, though? Isn't that what AA is for? Isn't he supposed to have a sponsor who helps him in those types of situations?" That's what happens in the movies and TV shows, anyway.

"I didn't think about that right then. I just wanted to help him. But his sponsor wasn't available last night to help. I found that out later."

"So you get his texts and then you just run away? I still don't get why you couldn't tell me what was going on."

"James, if I couldn't tell you I had heard from Bill a month ago, what makes you think I'd be able to tell you I was leaving a party to go see him? I couldn't tell you about Bill, not like that. So I just rushed out so I wouldn't have to make up a lie." Then she added, "And I was a tad drunk, so I probably didn't make the best choice given the circumstances."

Her explanation sounded plausible, but it didn't fix anything. She should've told me something, anything—or at least texted me later to let me know she was okay. "Fine, we can talk some other time about the appropriate way to bail on each other. Although the next time you do this—"

"There won't be a next time," she said. "I promise."

"Okay, well, if you ever have to leave in a hurry or under mysterious pretenses again, at least let me know you're okay. All right?"

"Yeah. I will. I'm sorry. I kind of feel like a broken record with the apologies."

You owe me like a hundred more. "Okay. So back to what happened. You had to go find him at a bar?"

"Yeah. Someplace in Lakeview."

"What the hell was he thinking?"

"Being in Lakeview?"

"Huh? No." There's nothing wrong with Lakeview. "What I mean is, if he's an alcoholic, why's he going to a bar on one of the craziest nights of the year?"

"That's exactly what I asked him! He said he'd been doing so well, he thought he could handle going out with some friends and not be tempted to drink. He also wanted to test himself, which is definitely something he would do. Obviously, he failed his test."

"So you get to the bar, and then what?"

"I had told him to stand outside to wait for me, so he did. We walked to an all-night diner, and I stayed there with him until like three a.m., so he could come to grips with his relapse, and so I could keep him away from booze. Then I took him back to his place in a cab and made sure he went into his building, and then I went home to my place. I was exhausted, so I fell asleep immediately."

"Are your feelings coming back for him?" I didn't want to ask the question because I hated revealing any insecurities, but I had to do it. Otherwise, Fred would conceive his own opinion.

"No, I swear. I mean, I love him as a person, I told you that. But I don't want to be with him; last night only confirms that."

She had told me what I wanted to hear, but her delivery was not as persuasive as I would have liked. Maybe there was no way she could have said it that would have dispelled all my fears. "You probably will see him again, though?"

She grimaced faintly. "Yeah, I guess so. I mean, he's trying so hard to stay sober, and it seems like he needs a friend. I know him better than pretty much anyone else, so I think I can help him—especially now that I'll be acting as his friend instead of his girlfriend." She hesitated briefly, then continued. "I don't think I'll see him that often. Just when he genuinely needs me."

"Maybe you guys could just be pen pals?" I said. She only smiled slightly in response. "Online chat buddies?" Just a dead stare that time.

I figured she would be seeing him again. If she never intended to see him after the coffee shop rendezvous, she would have told me about it in the first place. That fact also undercut any ultimatum I could have made. If I demanded she never see him again, I would only be asking for her to resent me. At the same time, I needed her to understand how much this hurt and how much I cared for her.

"Alexis," I said somberly.

"Yes, James?" she replied, matching my tone.

"Will you promise to tell me whenever you see him?"

"Yes, I promise."

"Say it again slowly, more solemnly."

"I promise to tell you, immediately, if I ever see Bill again," she said.

"Because if I'm going to be okay with that—with you seeing him, that is—I need you to be clear with me."

"Okay, I can do that. I promise, James."

"And, Alexis?"

"Yes?"

"There's something else I need to tell you." *Gulp. What am I doing?* "I realize this is not ideal timing, but it's something I've been thinking about for a long time—pretty much every day."

I inhaled a deep breath to collect myself. Here went nothing. "I'm not an expert in relationships, and I don't have anything to compare to—I know you know that—but I think about you all the time. Before you, I was sad and lonely. But then you gave me a chance, and every day since you've made me happy. You mean everything to me. What I'm trying to tell you is, I love you."

There it was. I had laid my cards on the table like a Texas hold'em player going all in, hoping against hope for a straight on the river. All I could do was wait and see what happened.

"Oh, James,"' she murmured as she stood to walk toward me. I followed her lead and got up as well. "Come here." She beckoned, and I noticed she had tears welling up in her eyes. So I did as requested, and she held my neck while she kissed me.

"You mean so, so much to me," she said. "I want to say it back to you; I do. But I'm not ready yet. My heart isn't fully healed. When I say it again, I want it to be to the last person I'll ever say it to. I'm sorry, but I hope you can understand."

My head and heart were uncertain on how to proceed. They hadn't heard what they wanted to hear, but Alexis's words amounted to an acceptable second-place finish.

"I understand. And that's fine with me," I said with a smirk, "just as long as I end up being that person." Then it was my turn to kiss her.

Chapter 32

THANKSGIVING BLUES

The next day, I arrived at the office extra early as promised, although not bright-eyed and bushy-tailed. Despite the silver lining at the end of Alexis's visit, Fred had been going bananas the previous night, oscillating between seething rage toward Bill and absolute misery that Alexis had once again lied to me. I tossed and turned in bed for eons, dreaming up various calamities and pondering whether someone could physically die from a figuratively broken heart. I didn't have a broken heart, but it was best to be prepared. After staring interminably at the shapes that formed on the inside of my eyelids, I fell asleep for a few hours.

I had been in the office for only a half hour when Francis knocked on my door.

"Kept your word. Good," he said as he entered.

That statement was in the top ten nicest things he had ever said to me—maybe top five.

"Yes. Morning, sir. What can I do for you?"

"Morning," he said gruffly. "Did you enjoy your Halloween party?"

"I did. Thank you. Did you have any plans, sir?"

"Hrumph," he replied. He really said "hrumph." I'm not just spelling out the sound phonetically. "Just a small party with the missus. No costumes for me."

He's tailor made for a perfect costume, and he didn't take advantage of it? Manuel would be sad to hear that.

"I have good news for you," he said. "I need someone to go to Dallas for the next few weeks. Based on what I've seen so far, I think you're best suited to handle it."

That was definitely a top-five statement, but it was anything but good news. It was good news like learning that your school snow day was being downgraded to a late start instead. I was in a dogfight for the love of a beautiful woman, and I was going to lose by default because I'd be in Dallas.

Was he punishing me for having the audacity to ask for one half of a weekend? Or was he entrusting me with a critical assignment? Either way, it didn't matter: it was terrible freaking timing.

"All right. When do you need me to go?"

"Have your assistant book a flight out for first thing tomorrow morning. Come to my office in an hour, and we can talk about what I need you to do while you're there."

"Yes, sir."

"And, James."

"Yes, sir?"

"You smell like booze. Get some mouthwash or gum or something."

"Yes, sir."

■ ■ ■

My three weeks in Dallas were dreadful. The whole time I was there, I only came home for one weekend in the middle; otherwise, I was working essentially around the clock. There had been zero time to write in my diary, and any entry would have been terribly melancholic anyway. I saw no point in writing "this sucks" over and over again.

Alexis claimed not to have seen Bill during my banishment to Dallas, but my instincts and Fred had some doubts about the veracity of that claim. In fact, when Fred hadn't been sending a torrent of doubt and angst my way, his presence had been seeping into all my cracks. So much so that I was beginning to wonder whether I had progressed at all with Dr. B and her therapist. I requested my medical records from her office so I could see for myself. I should have them in hand in a week or two.

To add to my apprehension, Alexis didn't seem quite herself the one weekend I did see her. She was affectionate, but not as loving as she had been the night after Halloween. Nor were we burning the midnight love oils like we had been leading up to Halloween. Our flaming saganaki passion had been reduced to a barely melted grilled cheese. Our previously unbridled ardor could now be contained by shoji screens. Oh, you understand? The picture has been painted, retouched, and reproduced in print? I'll move on.

Anyway, upon my return to Chicago, we entered a brief lull in our larger project at work, so I took advantage of the rare slow period by taking a few days off. Since Thanksgiving was around the corner, I flew to Pittsburgh to be with my mom and Rachel; Andrew and Leslie were set to arrive the next day.

Despite Fred's siege and my misgivings about Alexis, I'm a sucker. I love her so much, and I couldn't rebottle my feelings after I had thrown open my vault. In fact, I was missing her right as I started to write this, so I texted her.

Hi, beautiful, I sent. *What are you doing?*

I received one of those automatic driving responses. She must have started her trek down to the Champaign-Urbana area to visit with her family. At least she doesn't text and drive, so she never has to worry about my thermite grenades—assuming I ever get Miles's buddy to make them for me.

Speaking of Miles, I hadn't seen him recently either, but we had been texting a decent amount. The guy was definitely growing on me more and more—smart, funny, and a little weird, but in an amusing way. Since I was bored, I typed a text to him.

Hey man, how's it going?

I'm good, came the reply within seconds. The appropriate response time for a text. *I think Steve is done for though.*

Huh? I responded. *How so? What'd he do? Eat somebody's dog? Threaten to blow up a school?*

I don't know. He left a few days ago and I haven't seen him. But FBI agents just came by.

What? Come on, you're just messing with me.

Dead serious. They left like five minutes ago.

Crazy. What'd they say?

Just that they wanted to talk to him. They left a card and told me to call them if I see him.

What kind of agents do you think they are? I asked. *Antiterrorism? Cybersecurity?*

How the heck would I know? They look like regular people.

Apparently Miles was not a natural detective like me. *You tell them anything?*

Huh? No. I have nothing to tell.

That's good. Steve's probably monitoring everything you do. Keep up the charade.

Ha. You're so witty. I have no charade to keep up.

You get a new hard drive yet?

Shut up, he replied. *He didn't do anything to my computer.*

You better hope so. It's too late now. You destroy anything, they'll put you in Abu Ghraib and pee on you.

I'm regretting my decision to tell you about this.

I hear that a lot. It's true, unfortunately. *Update me when something happens next.*

No.

Please?

Fine.

I'm a master of persuasion. *What are you doing for Thanksgiving?* I asked.

Just going to the suburbs to see family. You?

I'm in Pittsburgh with family. Enjoy the holiday!

You too. See you when you get back.

And Miles, I said, and then waited for a response.

Yes?

Wipe my prints from your apartment. Better yet, burn that place down.

You know that sweatshirt you left at my place?

Damn, I had totally forgotten about that. *Yeah?*

I'm going to put it in Steve's bed.

You wouldn't.

Bye, James.

I didn't have much leverage, but the last thing I wanted was the FBI thinking I was Creepy Steve's lover. *You do that, and I place an anonymous phone call about the human head I saw in your freezer.*

You didn't see a head in my freezer.

The cops don't know that.

Bye, James.

■ ■ ■

On the Wednesday night before Thanksgiving, being the family that we are, we went out to the bars together. We used a car service because we're responsible drinkers. Our first stop was Butcher and the Rye, a split-level bar and restaurant known for unique, time-intensive cocktails and fantastic food—or so my mom told me. I could see for myself that the bar had two levels, but when I was of drinking age and home from school for the summer, I wasn't going to swanky places. The downstairs area was well lit and featured an impressive two-story wooden wall stocked with liquor. We climbed the stairs to the darker lounge area on the second level and eventually swooped in for a table when another party left. Our drinks arrived soon thereafter.

"I'm so happy you're all here," my mom told us. "It's so rare that I get you in the same place. I love you all so much."

"You're not going to cry, are you, Mom?" Andrew asked.

His wife Leslie responded by giving him the most withering of looks. Her stock had just risen one thousand points in my book.

"No, I'm not going to cry. I just love having all my babies together. Is that so bad?"

"Not at all, Mom," I said, sucking up to her. Although I wouldn't have minded if Andrew had been stuck back at the house, working on some last-minute brief or expert report—or "entering his time." He's always whining about having to log his work history by the tenth of the hour, which is every six minutes for the layman. "Rachel and I are thrilled to be back in the 'Burgh."

"I can speak for myself," Rachel said, "but yes, I am happy to be back. Plus, this Black Dahlia drink is terrific."

"Andrew's buying the first five rounds, right?" I asked. "That's what we agreed on before he got here?"

The flight he and Leslie had been on was delayed, and they only had a few minutes to get ready before we left for the bar.

"That was my understanding," Rachel quickly said. She may be as quick-witted as me. Maybe.

"I'll buy everyone's drinks except James's," Andrew said. "He's had a job for a while now. He can afford it."

"Yeah, but you like buying things for people," I countered. "And I like to drink pro bono."

"Not for you, I don't."

That was not very nice. He didn't even laugh at my lawyer joke.

"Leslie, can you buy my drinks?" I asked. "Your husband reneged on the deal we committed him to."

She actually chuckled! "Sure, I can do that. What's your next drink? Something infused with eighteen-karat gold leaf?"

And she made a joke! She was like a whole new person. "That sounds great," I said.

"So I have some news about tomorrow," my mom announced.

"Dad's coming over for Thanksgiving?"

"Please, James. Don't joke about that."

"Sorry, Mom."

"You're forgiven. No, he's not coming, although I hope he has plans. But I do have a special guest coming. It's the man I've been dating. His name is Gary." Her face and neck flushed when she revealed her secret. It was charming for her, which was annoying, because on me it looks like I've contracted a painful skin disorder.

I turned to make squinty-eyed contact with Rachel, but she didn't reciprocate. She barely even reacted. Wait a second—she already knew about this development! Why hadn't anyone given me my detective's badge yet? Seriously! I would have to talk to Rachel about this later—find out whatever else she knew about this Gary.

"I didn't know you were dating someone," Andrew said. Of course he didn't. He knows nothing about anyone who is not him. "How long has this been going on?"

"You did too!" my mom insisted. "I told you I was seeing someone a few weeks ago." Just like I said: Andrew was clueless. "We've been seeing each other for about seven months, I think."

"That's right," he said, trying to save some face. "I remember you saying something about it now."

Doubtful. Anytime a conversation isn't about him, his brain turns his ears off to conserve energy.

"I like him, so I want you all to meet him," my mom said. "Of course, I also want your thoughts on him. This relationship goes nowhere if my babies don't like him."

"If you like him, Mom, I'm sure we all will," Rachel assured her. "I'm excited to meet him!"

"Does he like talking about billable hours and discovery motions? If so, Andrew will love him."

"Shut up, James," Andrew said. "You're always so negative. Can't you go one night without complaining or trying to put somebody down?"

I was about to escalate this quarrel to level two, but Rachel kicked me hard in the shin. At the same time, my mom placed her hand on my forearm and said, "All right, boys. Enough. It's the day before Thanksgiving. No fighting."

I liked my mom's soothing techniques more than Rachel's. I squeezed Rachel's thigh under the table to let her know how I felt.

"Can't I defend my honor against his scurrilous attacks?" I asked.

"No. You can tell us about Alexis, though. How are things going with her?"

"Who's Alexis?" Andrew asked. "Does James have an internet girlfriend?"

"Andrew, I mean it!" my mom exclaimed. "Stop the bickering!"

"All right, sorry. But seriously, who's Alexis? I've never heard her name before."

"She's my girlfriend. We've been dating since May. Things are going pretty well, I guess." Now was not the time to go into the recent developments concerning Bill. "She's still hanging out with me, anyway."

"Sounds like you guys are getting serious," Andrew quipped.

"Andrew, enough," my mom exhorted.

"What's she like?" Leslie said at the same time, cutting Andrew off from further insulting me.

She was asking me a question about my personal life too! What a turn of events. "She's great: smart, beautiful, and we seem to play off each other well." *When she's not hanging out with Bill*, Fred uttered from the margins of my consciousness. *Damn you, Fred*. He had been swooping down a lot lately, like a fat pigeon who was too accustomed to city life to care that people were kicking at him to make him fly away.

"That's great. I'm happy for you." What trickster spirit had taken over Leslie's body? I didn't know how to process her being so nice. "Will we get to meet her this weekend?"

"Sadly, no. She's in southern Illinois visiting her family."

"That's too bad. Maybe we'll come to Chicago and see her then."

"Yeah, sure, that sounds great." *Please don't bring Andrew with you.*

■ ■ ■

We went to a second bar but didn't stay out too late. Leslie was tired from traveling, Andrew was spent from sucking the fun out of life, my mom wanted to get up early to prep food and watch the parade, and Rachel and I planned to be up early the next morning to run the Turkey Trot together. We had made it a tradition the past few years; there was no question we were going to be stuffing our faces later, so we might as well burn a few calories in advance. Plus, Rachel loves to insist that we both wear roasted turkey hats while we run. It's fun because it makes her happy, but for some-one who sweats like a corpulent old man wearing a sweat suit in a sauna, sporting a stuffed animal on my head while I run is not ideal. Even when it's cold outside.

We ran the race together at a pretty good pace, but one that allowed us to talk a little too. We had agreed not to compete; we were just out there for fun and to prepare our bodies for gluttony.

At one point during the run, Rachel asked, "So how are things really going with Alexis? Have you confirmed your suspicions about Bill?"

"I never know how things are anymore. I haven't seen her much lately, but we talk on the phone and text a decent amount. One day, she acts like she's head over heels for me. The next day, I barely hear from her. And who knows about Bill. She did see him, but she supposedly hasn't seen him since that one night, because she's supposed to tell me if she does see him. And she hasn't done that. But I don't trust her anymore."

"Hmm," she intoned. "I'm sorry."

"It's fine. Don't get me wrong, I'm crazy about her. But I don't trust her. Not about Bill anyway."

"I get that. I wouldn't trust her either."

"I'll just have to see how this plays out, but I wish I saw her more frequently. Being away in Dallas didn't help, and still being stupidly busy with work is not helping."

"Well, I'm always here for you," she said.

"I know. You're the best, Rach."

"Love you too."

With a tenth of a mile to go, Rachel dropped a glove, and I stopped to pick it up. Then I saw her hauling ass toward the finish line in a dead sprint.

"So much for not racing," I said when I caught up to her after the finish line.

"I didn't race," she said innocently. "I could've gone faster. But I didn't say I wasn't going to beat you."

"Do you feel good about yourself now?"

"I feel great. Body and mind—a well-oiled machine."

"Good enough to run all the way home?"

"Nice try. You'd never ditch me."

"You better hope so."

■ ■ ■

Gary came over around noon. He had a full head of wavy salt-and-pepper hair—I hope I have a shock like that at his age—and a wiry frame. His square jawline and pronounced cheekbones made him good-looking—if you cross your eyes like with Manuel—and he was well-dressed in a thin navy sweater over a button-down shirt and slim-fitting chinos. I don't like to go shopping, but if I did, I'd go shopping with that guy. His handshake was solid too. In the first impressions department, Gary was pulling a 9.9 out of 10. I deducted a tenth of a point because he said hello to Andrew before he said hi to me. It was simply a matter of spatial relation-ships—Andrew was closer when he entered the house—but it could not be overlooked.

"It's nice to finally meet you three," Gary said to Andrew, Rachel, and me. "And of course you too, Leslie. I didn't mean to leave you out."

"No offense taken," Leslie assured him.

An awkward lull then began, and it lasted an interminable five sec-onds. Because I had drunk a beer or two—to celebrate the TV parade, of course—I took it upon myself to get the conversation going.

"So, Gary, who is your daddy, and what does he do?"

"James," my mom exclaimed with a half smile, "don't be weird right off the bat. Gary doesn't know your inside jokes."

"Sorry, Gary. What I mean is, tell us a little about yourself. Mom has been intentionally cryptic. The usual stuff like where are you from, what do you do, and which of the three of us does Mom talk about the most?"

"Gary," said Rachel, "don't hurt their feelings by answering the last question. Just start with where you're from and what you do."

"Sure," Gary said with a casual air I couldn't pull off if I practiced. "I'll start with my job. I'm an IT director for a law firm here in the city, so I know a little bit about the life Andrew leads." Ugh. *You're blowing it, Gary.* Another tenth of a point lost. "And I'm from here, born and raised. So not that exciting, I have to say."

"IT stuff, huh? You and I should talk later," I suggested to him. "I have a friend who may need to destroy a few hard drives, if you know what I mean."

"James has an active imagination, if you couldn't tell," Andrew said.

"His roommate is being investigated for being a hacker, and maybe for being an anthropophagus," I said.

"See what I mean?" Andrew asked.

"I do see," Gary said, somewhat siding with Andrew and forever in-curring my wrath in the process. Three more tenths of a point deducted. "Although I have no idea what word he just said."

"Yes, James is very special," Rachel said, as if I were a simpleton who couldn't comprehend they were talking about me, as she put her arm around me. "You'll get used to him. Anyway, tell us how you met Mom. She wouldn't give me the details."

"You'd think it was online because of my job, but you'd be wrong. Well, half wrong. I went on an online date with a woman who happened to be friends with Diane."

"Diane is our mom's name," I interrupted to tell Andrew. He just sneered at me in response.

"Yes," Gary said, politely ignoring my jest. "My date with your mom's friend was okay, but we knew we weren't right for each other. However, she said she knew someone who was perfect for me, and she set me up with your mom. So far, she's been right." Gary grasped my mom's hand when he said this, and they both had beaming smiles plastered to their faces. I wanted to hug her and vomit at the same time.

"That's so sweet!" Leslie proclaimed.

"I know!" Rachel said. "I love it!"

The interrogation into what made Gary tick continued for some time, especially since we all snatched beers and plopped ourselves in front of a muted football game, and more proximately in front of several appetizers. Gary seemed like a pretty good guy, and he managed to make me laugh a little.

At some point, my mom broke up our questioning by assigning us various tasks to get ready for dinner. "Dinner" was really a late lunch so that we would have plenty of time to eat dessert and then second helpings later in the evening.

Throughout the rest of the day, I studied how Gary acted around my mom. He was attentive to her, they made each other laugh multiple times, and he proactively looked to help her whenever he could. She definitely had never received assistance like that from my dad. I even saw his hand dip once when he had it on the small of her back, which caused me to gag, but I was glad my mom had someone who was interested in her and found her attractive.

As happy as I was for her, Gary's displays of affection also sent pangs of pain through me, as they reiterated that Alexis wasn't with me—then and possibly long term. I shouldn't have let Fred render me so defeatist, but sometimes the writing on the wall was written in neon letters that glowed in the dark.

■ ■ ■

Alexis texted me in the early evening, *Hey sexy! Miss you! I'd call but we're busy with family stuff. Lots of aunts, uncles, and cousins over!*

That's okay, we're busy also, I texted back. *Miss you too. Say hi to your parents for me.*

Will do. Do the same for me. Do you want to talk to my dad about his guns again? ☺

I had almost forgotten about that. *No thanks. I heard enough about his guns. Talk tomorrow?*

Sure. Bye, hon.

Bye, you. Still no pet names.

That ended the conversation, I thought. Forty-five minutes later, however, she sent me this message: *Miss you too, sweetie!*

The hair on the back of my neck began to tingle. If I was a vampire, I would've bared my fangs and hissed. Clearly, the message was not meant for me; I didn't even need to employ my advanced detective skills. One, we had already said we missed each other. Two, she said "too," implying I had just said it to her. Three, she never called me sweetie. Ever.

Fred suggested she was texting dirty-bathroom-floor Bill. I was inclined to agree, but there was a chance she was texting a female friend or cousin. Given her string of half truths and lies by omission, I was not disposed to giving her the benefit of the doubt.

I texted her *???*

The first question mark signified my confusion. The second indicated I was impatiently awaiting an explanation. The third was just gratuitous.

I waited a couple minutes before she responded. *Sorry babe,* she said. *Meant to send that to my cousin Melissa. She didn't come home for Thanksgiving—still in college and couldn't afford it. We're all missing her.*

I temporarily rescinded my proscription on "the lady doth protest too much." She could've stopped at *Melissa*—or even *Thanksgiving*. Tacking on the extra details to her message suggested she was feeling guilty.

No problem, was all I said back.

Then I headed to the kitchen to make myself a stiff drink while Fred whispered sweet nothings to me.

■ ■ ■

It was around ten on Friday morning. I refused to participate in Black Friday—or any other ridiculous holiday sale, for that matter—because people are at their worst when they're fighting for highly discounted things they don't need. But Rachel, my mom, and Leslie were out shopping. Andrew was working upstairs, thank the gods, so I didn't have to interact with him.

My phone started playing *La Cucaracha*, which meant Manuel was calling.

"*Hola*, Manuel."

"Hey, *mano. Qué tal?*"

"Yeah, I'll take four." I knew he was asking me how I was doing.

He ignored my nonsense. "How was your Thanksgiving?"

"Pretty good. Rachel came here with me, and my mom's doing well. I met her boyfriend, who seems like a good guy. I've even been having a good time with Andrew's wife! Imagine that."

"Sounds great. I didn't know your mom was dating a new guy."

"I only sort of knew before I got here. I'll tell you more about him later. How was your Thanksgiving?"

"It's been great so far. We're in New York. Sam came with me. She's getting along well with my parents and Reina."

"That's good. Although I'm sure you weren't worried about Sam getting along with anyone."

"No, definitely not. Actually, I have something to tell you."

"Okay. Don't leave me hanging. What is it?"

"I asked Sam to marry me."

"No way! That's so awesome, Manny! Congrats!" I was beyond elated for him.

"Thanks. We're pretty excited."

"Yeah, I'm sure. I bet your parents are ecstatic."

"Ha, you have no idea."

"You don't think it's too soon, do you?"

"Nah. We've been a thing since like February, and officially a couple since May. Besides, what does the timing matter when you know you're in love?"

"Makes sense to me," I said. "Just thought I'd check. Did she like the ring you picked out?"

"I think so. Honestly, she didn't even look at it for like ten minutes. She was too excited; I had to wait until she calmed down to put it on her."

"I assume you guys don't have a date set, right? Way too early for that kind of stuff?"

"Yeah, no date set; we're going to wait until at least next summer. But along those lines, I do have a question to ask you." He paused again.

"Okay. So what is it?"

"You're my best friend, *mano*. I call you that for a reason. We've been through a lot together, good and bad, and I see you as my brother. You've always had my back—ever since that second week in school."

"Stop it, Manny. You're going to make me cry." I was joking, but that was to hide the fact that tears were welling up in my eyes. It was his tone of voice that did it—so genuine and raw.

"I'm serious. Don't joke for once. I know you've had your share of problems—and so have I. But through it all, we're always there to help each other out. I love you, man, and I want you to be my best man. The wedding wouldn't feel right if you weren't."

Dammit, now I did have a tear or two coming down. "I love you too, man. You're like the brother I never had."

"You have a brother, James."

"I know. But he used to beat me up all the time, and now he looks down on me. You've never done either of those things. You've always been there for me. Even at times when I know it wasn't fun to be around me. I know I'm not always easy to deal with." I was dangerously close to a waterworks situation.

"Shut up, *chacho*. I don't have to deal with anything. I wouldn't be friends with you if you were hard to deal with. Besides, like I said, everybody has problems."

From the sound of his voice, I didn't think his eyes were clear either. I presumed we would never speak of this part of the conversation ever again. I was already locking it up in my man vault.

"Thanks, Manny."

"So will you do it?"

"Do what?" I was messing with him again.

"Will you be my best man?" he asked with frustration.

"Of course I will. I'd be honored, Manny."

"Thanks. Sam is going to be excited too—even though we both assumed you'd say yes."

"Cool. When do you need me to provide you with bachelor party plans? Does next week work? Or do you need a general outline this weekend?"

"Ha, relax, *chacho*. Nothing that soon."

"Okay, I'll stand down for now. But I call dibs on having Reina walk down the aisle with me."

"I'm already regretting my decision."

"Oh, don't say that, Manuel. You just said you loved me. I'm going to get us a pair of those best-friend split-heart necklaces."

"Yeah, as much as I'd love to see where else this conversation goes, I need to make some more phone calls. Happy Thanksgiving, *mano*."

"You too, *guapo*."

"Still didn't look it up, did you?"

"No, I forgot. Later, man."

After I hung up the phone, I tapped into the feeling I had been experiencing that wasn't pure joy. It was a strong undercurrent of sadness. Manuel was moving on with his life with someone he loved. My mom and Gary were building a strong relationship. Even Andrew had maintained what seemed like a loving marriage with someone who was turning out to be much more enjoyable than I originally thought.

And I have...what? A beautiful and fun girlfriend whom I can't trust as far as I can throw a Batwing shuriken—which so far is undetermined but is probably not far.

Chapter 33

THE TRUTH WILL SET YOU FREE

Three weeks had passed since Thanksgiving. I hadn't been doing any traveling, fortunately, but I hadn't had any spare time for fun either. Alexis and I got coffee and lunch a handful of times, but setting up evening plans had proved too difficult most of the time. She still maintained she hadn't seen Bill, but at this point I had zero faith in her proclamations concerning him. Although I never did try to interrogate her about that errant text message.

In the early afternoon on Friday, I stopped by her office to see if she wanted to do something low key that night.

"Hey sexy," I said as I entered. It didn't exactly roll off my tongue like a Spanish *r*, but I did manage to use a pet name.

"Hey you, how are you?"

"Slammed, like usual."

"Me too," she said.

"Yay for both of us. I just wanted to stop by to see what you're doing tonight. Thought maybe we could watch a movie or something at one of our places?"

"I wish I could, hon. It feels like it's been so long since we hung out. But I have a girls' night planned with a bunch of volleyball friends I haven't seen in a while."

I couldn't get a good read on whether this was the truth or a lie to cover up other plans she might have had. At this rate, it probably didn't matter. The less I saw her, the less likely I was going to keep her.

"Damn. Well, have fun with your friends," I told her. "Maybe we can do something tomorrow. I'll check in with you in the morning."

"Okay, sounds good. Have a good night."

"You too. See you later."

These continued rebuffs from Alexis, however polite or true they might have been, were starting to take their toll. I can ignore Fred when he only has a fingerhold or two, but Alexis's snubs were turning me into a beginner's climbing wall for him. If I hadn't been drowning in work, I would've taken the rest of the afternoon off to hide under my covers.

Rather than walk back to my office, I meandered to a rarely used stairwell and began to walk down the two flights to my floor. Because I was dejected and generally have the silent stalking skills of a jungle panther, I heard and then saw a man and a woman groping each other a floor below me: some sloppy kissing and thorough heavy petting. I ducked down to better hide myself as the man pressed his jumbo-sized body even closer to the woman, his gelatinous composition threatening to engulf her like an amoeba surrounding protozoa. Slowing my breath like a sniper behind a rifle scope, I obtained a distinct view of the stairwell gropers and their identities.

They were none other than Francis Mason and Elizabeth Foster. The married workaholic and the EEOC succubus, seemingly trying to fuse their bodies together. I temporarily went on autopilot, because my brain was threatening to seizure as it tried to ascertain what was most repulsive about their obscene tryst. Then, as I came back online, I had the presence of mind to take a discreet picture of the taboo liaison—a defensive hand grenade in case Elizabeth ever filed a real discrimination suit against me.

To keep myself from vomiting while the action continued, I pretended I was a *National Geographic* photographer capturing rare footage of two different species engaged in anatomically awkward foreplay. After several more minutes, Francis finally backed away, probably because he was close to an asthma or heart attack. Then they both straightened their clothes, whispered something to each other, and kissed once before Elizabeth walked back onto the office floor from whence they must have come. Francis staggered his entrance a few minutes behind hers.

■ ■ ■

I rushed down the stairs and ran-walked over to Manuel and Miles's office to tell them the news. Manuel wasn't there when I walked in, unfortunately, but Miles was, with his back to me.

"Miles!" I shouted, startling him. "You have to hear this!"

"Goddam, James," he yelled after he had jumped out of his seat. "Sometimes you're the most annoying person in the world."

"I know."

"Just knock next time."

"I will not. But I have something important to tell you." I purposely waited to make him ask what me it was.

"Okay? So tell me."

"Francis Mason, a.k.a. Sgt. Slaughter. You know him, right?"

"Yes, especially since you complain about him all the time."

"Exactly. And Elizabeth Foster, aka Medusa, a.k.a. Booby Traps, a.k.a.—"

He cut me off. "I know who she is too. Because of you. Get to the point."

"I just saw them dry humping in the hallway."

"Shut up. No way."

He seemed way more interested than I thought he would be. "I have proof. Do you want to see it?"

"I don't know," he admitted. "Do I?"

"Yes."

"Okay, then show me."

I showed him the photo of their bodies merging like one fat candle melting over one beautiful candle.

"That's so disturbing—but captivating at the same time. How did her bones not break? Or her lungs collapse?"

"Those are excellent questions," I said. "I have no idea."

"What are you going to do with the photo?"

"I'm not sure. Probably nothing, unless Elizabeth comes after me with HR."

"Whatever you do, don't try to extort one of them. I think that would end up biting you in the ass."

I was just thinking the same thing. "I agree, Miles. That's why you're going to extort them."

"The hell I am," he said.

"I'm just kidding. I'll probably do nothing with it."

I paused and was about to leave when Miles asked, "What are you doing tonight?"

"No plans." Because my girlfriend, to whom I had said *I love you*, wouldn't hang out with me. I wasn't bitter about it.

"You want to hang out?"

"Sure."

"My place okay?"

"There's been no sign of Creepy Steve, right?"

"No, none," he said. "It's weird. He's gotta be on the run. As far as I know, the FBI hasn't found him."

"Given his attitude toward hygiene and his lack of need for sunlight, he's probably hanging out in a pit, like Saddam Hussein did."

"Could be. So you want to come over or not?"

"Yeah, I do. But on one condition."

"What is it?"

"Besides playing video games, we have to get sloppy drunk."

"Fine," he said.

"And also throw your Batwing shuriken."

"That's two conditions."

"Okay, then on two conditions."

"Fine."

"Nice. See you tonight."

■ ■ ■

I got to Miles's place around eight o'clock with some beer and a handle of Maker's Mark.

"Special delivery," I announced as he pulled the door open.

"Damn, you weren't kidding about getting drunk, were you?"

"I never kid about that, Miles. Plus, it's been a rough few weeks. And I can't unsee the whole Francis and Elizabeth thing."

"She's so hot," he said. "I just don't get it. Why Francis?"

"She's not that hot, Miles. She just has a killer body that she only slightly conceals behind the slimmest of fabrics, and she's a master of seduction."

"I'm not sure you disagreed with me. But anyway, what do you want to drink to start?"

"One shot to start, and then let's make up a drinking game. Whoever loses a round in whatever we're playing has to take a shot or half shot, depending on the game length. We can drink beer in between like civilized chaps."

"Works for me. Why was it a rough week?"

"Let me have a few drinks and kick your ass in a few video games first, and then we can discuss my lady drama."

"Fighting words, huh? I can wait to hear your story," he said, "but you won't be kicking anyone's ass."

"We shall see. If you beat me too many times, I'll call the FBI about the crap that's on your computer."

"There's nothing illegal on my laptop!"

"See? You've already lost. I'm under your skin."

■ ■ ■

We had a few drinks and played video games for a few hours before we took a short break.

"All right, man," Miles said. "Tell me why you've had a rough few weeks. I assume it's about Alexis."

He might have been slurring his words a little, but I had no idea, because I was probably slurring my own.

"You're mostly right. Work has been a nightmare the last few months, but I'm somewhat adjusted to my crazy schedule. And someday the craziness will end. What bothers me about Alexis isn't what you think, though."

"It's not about Bill?" he asked. "It's not about Bill and how she lied to you about him?"

"No, it is those things. But those aren't the biggest thing," I said. "The biggest thing is that I've come to realize that my happiness is entirely dependent on Alexis. Honestly, man, before her, my life kind of sucked. Well, not kind of sucked. It did suck. I don't talk about this much, but I suffer from a form of depression. Nothing really lifts my spirits. I have good days here and there, and of course friends like you and Manuel make me laugh. But before Alexis, I always felt like something critical was missing from my life. And for the life of me, I couldn't figure out what. But then, like I said, Alexis came along, and that mostly went away. I was happy for days, weeks, maybe months at a time. Until Bill reared his ugly-ass head, anyway. Now all the doubt and fear and depression are back. With some rage thrown in too. So much rage."

"I don't think that's all that uncommon, man."

That was not a response I was expecting. "What's not uncommon?"

"Depression," he said. "I think more people deal with it than you think."

"Oh yeah? Like who? Creepy Steve?"

"Nah, man. Like me. I deal with it."

I probably should've seen that coming, but I didn't want to be presumptuous. And I was drunk. "Depressed like you don't want to get out of bed every once in a while? Or depressed like you take medicine and stuff? Or depressed like you've written a will?"

"Yeah, some of that, and other things. I've been taking an antidepressant for years—it seems to keep me even. And it's not something I talk about much either, but I've definitely wondered, on more than one occasion, whether life is worth it. What the point is. You know?"

"Yeah, I know." Boy, did I know.

There was a short silence that eventually he broke. "You ever think about killing yourself?"

I thought hard about how to answer that question, which was not easy to do in my inebriated state.

"I dunno, Miles. Maybe, yeah, sort of. But if I ever thought about killing myself, I mean really killing myself, it's not something I would talk about with anyone. It has nothing to do with you. It's just that if someone wants to do it, they shouldn't threaten to do it, they should just do it. And if they don't want to do it, then they should shut up about it and try to work on their problems."

"No problem, man," he said, using his hands to signal surrender. "But let me tell you this. A few years ago, I did think about it. I came close to trying it a few times too. But there was always someone around to stop me or help me get through whatever pain I was trapped in at the time."

"I'm sorry to hear that," I said. I was. I get choked up when I hear about other people who suffer to the same extremes that I do.

"I don't want any pity, James," he admonished. "I'm still here, after all. I'm doing just fine. What I'm trying to tell you is really just a message for you: if you ever feel that way, call me, and I'll come help. No questions asked, no judgments made. Got it?"

"Got it. Thanks, Miles." I appreciated the sentiment, but my attitude was less than committal.

"I mean it," he stressed.

"Thanks. I mean that too."

■ ■ ■

I woke up around ten thirty in the morning and took some probing steps to establish how bad my hangover was going to be this fine Saturday morning. The answer was not that bad. I was amazed.

Then I texted Alexis, *Hey sexy. What are you doing?*

After a couple minutes of staring at Alexis's lack of a response, I jumped into the shower. Well, hopped into it, I guess. I wasn't feeling *that* good. Taking my time, I maximized Alexis's opportunity to not let me down. She did not avail herself of my magnanimity.

So I texted her again. *I'm gonna be in your neighborhood in a little while. Let me know if you want to meet up.*

This wasn't untrue. I was going to walk in the direction of her place. Even if I didn't hear from her, there was a sandwich place I wanted to hit up that was close to her apartment building.

I dressed and did a few more things around my place to kill time. Alexis's response time continued to climb toward infinity. Left with no choice, I threw on some layers, my coat, hat, and gloves, and then headed out into the blustery winter day.

Too engrossed in my thoughts to be aware of my surroundings, which was impressive given the low temperature and howling winds, I arrived at Alexis's place before I knew it. I checked my phone and confirmed what I already knew: she was ignoring me.

I walked into her building, and Raul was sitting at the lobby desk.

"Hey, James," he exclaimed enthusiastically. "It's been a while."

"Hey, man. I know. A few weeks at least."

"At least," he stressed. "Where you been?"

"Dallas for a few weeks, and otherwise working all the time."

"I hear that. I feel like all I do is work."

"Sorry to hear that. One of us should be having a good time."

He chuckled. "Yeah, if only. You here for Alexis, I assume?"

"Yeah. Have you seen her today?"

"Mm hmm. She left a few hours ago. I'm not sure if she came back. Let me call up."

I watched while he called, waited, then hung up. "She's not answering," he said. "Must not be back."

"Okay. Could you just let me into her apartment, and I'll wait there?"

He laughed this time. "Nice try. You know I can't do that." Then he leaned toward me and craned his neck for maximum extension, whispering, "Unless you have five hundred bucks. Do you have five hundred bucks?"

"Not on me," I said, playing along. "Let me run to an ATM, and I'll be right back."

"Shut up, dude. I'm not letting you in."

"Fine. Be that way, Raul." I didn't want to leave there with nothing, so I turned back to him and played a hunch. "Do you know her ex-boyfriend Bill? The guy she dated last year?"

Recognition appeared on his face. "Yeah. Why?"

"Has he been around here lately?"

"I can't answer that for you. Sorry, man. I'm not supposed to talk about the tenants."

He had no problem a second ago when he told me Alexis had left the building this morning. "Make an exception. Please," I begged. "I'm not some creep you don't know."

I wasn't sure he was going to answer, but then he said, "You didn't hear anything from me. You got it?" I nodded my head. "But you're a good guy, so you deserve to hear this. He's been around here a lot lately. Just yesterday even."

"What's a lot?"

"I don't know for sure, man. I only work certain hours," he said, "but I've seen him at least three or four times in the last couple of weeks."

Dirty-bathroom-floor Bill was a dead man.

"And don't kill the messenger, but I feel like I gotta tell you the whole story." I just stared at him in silence, waiting for his hangman's ax to drop. "I'm almost positive he stayed the night here once a few weeks ago. I—"

He was about to explain, but a resident approached him with some quasi emergency concerning something in the parking garage. He left with her, and I was left wondering what it was that made him think Bill had slept over.

Bowel-shaking earthquakes of doubt and remorse, assail him, impale him with monster-truck force. The song wasn't apropos, but the stanza was. I could feel Fred pacing back and forth like a boxer who smelled blood, just waiting for the sound of the bell to restart the match.

My rage was climbing fast, and I was already overheating in my full winter garb, so I stomped outside to plan my next move. Did I drop a boulder on Bill, Wile E. Coyote style? Run him through with a rusty pipe? Throw him in a bathtub of acid?

All options were on the table. Like swallowing a salty, slimy oyster, I was willing to maim or disfigure Bill, but I would want to do it quickly, and I wouldn't enjoy it.

■ ■ ■

After learning the hard way that winter gloves did little to dampen the pain of punching a brick building, I decided to walk home in an effort to eliminate my murderous wrath, or at least diminish it. I considered calling Alexis while I was walking, and I pulled out my phone a few times, but I resisted the urge. I needed to be cold and calculating like the six-fingered man when I spoke to her.

When I entered my apartment, I was no longer visualizing the minute details of flaying Bill's demonic flesh. But I was hungry because I had forgotten to go to that sandwich place. Dammit! That alone almost whipped me back into a frenzy.

I sat down on my couch and started writing about the morning's events. Then I took a break, and with my phone in hand, I prepared to craft a carefully written missive to Alexis. But after a few minutes of staring at my phone while my hand autonomously tried to strangle it, I texted her: *WE NEED TO TALK! NO MORE LYING!*

That should get her attention. I assumed she wouldn't respond immediately, even if she read it instantly. Who would? Since I had some time on my hands, I ate some leftover stuff from the back of my fridge.

Alexis called within an hour, while I was playing a video game involving shooting people. I knew it was her because my phone started playing "In the Air Tonight" by Phil Collins. I had changed my ringer before I started playing.

"Hello?" I answered coolly and slightly affected, like a slightly perturbed robot. So far, so good on the keeping-it-together front.

"Hey," she said tentatively. "What's going on?"

Fred wanted me to scream at her. I wanted to scream at her. But my voice caught in my throat, stifling the compulsion.

"We need to talk" was all I managed to utter.

"I gathered that from your text," she said haughtily, "which is why I called. So what's going on?"

"Can we talk in person?"

"I need to meet a friend soon, so no." *Gee, wonder who that is.* "Also, based on your text, I'm not sure I want to see you right now."

"That's rich. You're angry with me." I couldn't help but emit a little bit of scorn.

"James, what is this about? This isn't like you!"

"It's about Bill!" I yelled, a few decibels lower than a scream. "It's always about Bill!"

"What's about Bill? What are you talking about?" Her voice had risen reflexively.

I swallowed to get my volume under control. "I know you've been seeing him, and you've been lying by not telling me."

A few seconds of silence followed on her end, and then, "What are you talking about? Who told you that?"

So she was not going to fold easily. "I know you saw him last night. True or false?"

Another pause before the predictable "How do you know that? Are you following me?"

I'd had a hunch I would have to provide sources before she coughed up the truth. It was her style. Which left me no choice but to throw Raul under the bus. I felt a little bad about it, but one, we were only pseudo-friends—we had yet to slice our hands and shake while our dripping blood intermingled—and two, he was not going to get in trouble. There was no way Alexis was going to confront him or call her building's office to complain that he had told her boyfriend she was seeing another guy. There were no universes where that call went smoothly for her.

"No, I'm not following you," I said, punctuating every word with disdain. "I stopped by your place today, and Raul told me. He said you saw Bill yesterday, and you've seen him a bunch of times in the last few weeks."

Prolonged silence ensued as her brain's emergency cogs kicked up to a higher RPM. This was a trap from which she could not escape, and I had not even started the timer. Faced with this reality, she chose a partial confession.

"Okay, I've seen him a few times, but so what? I'm sorry I didn't tell you, but I didn't want you to make a big deal out of nothing."

I had heard this song before, and it didn't get better the longer I listened to it. "So how many times has he stayed the night at your place?"

The door was slammed shut, and the timer had started. All she could do now was watch as it counted down. No response was forthcoming.

"Alexis?" I prodded. "It's a simple question. How many times has he slept in your bed lately?"

"I'm not going to dignify that with a response," she finally lashed out at me. "He stayed over one night because he almost had a drink again and needed help. It's none of your business, but he slept on the couch."

I had little reason to believe her, but I didn't have to judge the veracity of her claim.

"It doesn't matter," I told her. "You keep lying to me, and for what? So you can save the soul of a drunk that you broke up with a year ago? Why does he mean so much more to you than I do? Can you answer that?"

"That's not true," she shouted back. "And it's not fair! I care about both of you! How many times do I have to say that?"

"Do you want to be with me? Or do you want to save Bill? You can't have both anymore."

"So that's what this is?" she growled at me. "You're forcing me to choose between two people I love?"

That was the first time she had told me she loved me—in any form. Rather than soothe my anguish, I sensed my heart break a little more. She couldn't have told me she loved me at any point in the past, in a tender and, I don't know, loving way? Instead, she told me as I was yelling at her about betraying me?

"Yes," I said with steely resolve. "You have to choose. Now. I'm done being lied to about Bill."

"That's not fair, and you know it."

"I don't give a rat's ass what's fair, Alexis. This is life. Be a big girl and make a decision for once."

Perhaps taunting her based on her gender was a mistake.

"Fine! You want me to choose?" she screamed. "I choose Bill!"

Somehow I had not seen that coming. My voice faltered as my heart shriveled into a prune. She took my muteness as an invitation to berate me.

"I'm so sick of you whining about him! And being mopey when you're not. Grow up! Bill's a part of my life. He's someone I care about. If you're too insecure or too weak to handle that, then we shouldn't be together."

Each barb she threw at me hit the mark with force, and I was not recovering.

"Say something," she said. "You started this fight, and now you have nothing to say?" She paused again, and then, because I remained quiet, she continued. "We're finally talking about Bill. Isn't that what you wanted? But now you're quiet? Say something!" she shrilled.

The tears in my eyes shamed me, even though she couldn't see them. I knew they were there. I had never felt so small, and I did not revel in the experience.

"You made your point," I whimpered meekly to her. "I get it. I'm sorry I've been so unbearable to you."

She sounded like she was about to scream something else, but she stopped herself. "James," she said with much less amplitude. "I'm sorry. I didn't mean those things. But I don't want to keep fighting about Bill! You need to get over it," she said.

"I don't need to get over anything, Alexis. We both have said how we feel, and I can't be with you anymore."

"Wait, what? *You're* breaking up with me?" she asked incredulously. "Is that what you're doing?"

"Yes," I muttered.

"Seriously?"

I had started to regain my ability to speak. "Not by choice. But you've made it clear Bill is more important to you, and he probably always will be. I'm not going to keep living in fear that one day you'll leave me for him."

"You're kidding me. Are you really doing this?"

"I have to. I'm sorry."

"James, I swear to God—"

"Goodbye, Alexis." Then I hung up.

She called five or six times in a row, but I didn't pick up.

Then she texted me. *You're an idiot. Did you not just hear me say I love you? But you're throwing us away anyway?*

Too little, too late, I typed back, while tears still streamed down my face.

My heart had been exposed to the open air since I first told her I loved her, and she had done nothing to protect it from the elements. In fact, just now she had trampled all over it while wearing boots.

You're an idiot, she said again in response.

Probably. I felt completely hollow inside and not at all certain I had made the right decision.

■ ■ ■

I have spent the past few hours crying and fighting the compulsion to text or call Alexis. I still don't know for certain whether my drastic decision was necessary. However, I have learned a truth about me these past few months. By myself, I am not a happy person. I should have known that my whole life, but it wasn't until I started dating Alexis and experiencing prolonged contentment that I realized just how bad life had been before her. It was like eating flavorless porridge every day, and then one day life decided to give you steak and lobster. How do you go back to porridge when steak and lobster decide they don't care about you anymore?

To be content in life, I need to hitch my train car to someone else's locomotive. Alexis is a beautiful, high-speed model, but who knows when she'll decide to uncouple my car for good?

I do not want to live a life full of misery and darkness. I do not want to live a life dependent on someone else's light.

I think Fred is going to win after all.

Chapter 34

THE ENDING NO ONE WANTED

Four days ago, James was walking along Lake Michigan near Ohio Street Beach, alone on Sunday night. The temperature was hovering around freezing. The surface temperature of the lake registered about the same.

James jumped right in. He had bound his ankles in duct tape to hinder his ability to tread water.

Approximately ten minutes before he threw himself in, he had called Mom. According to her, she said hello, and then James immediately blurted out, "I'm sorry, Mom. I'm so sorry."

She was confused at first. "What are you sorry for, honey? What's wrong?"

"I'm sorry because I can't do this anymore," he said through tears. "I can't do it."

She had an inkling as to what he meant. Given his history, she started to panic. This was the call she had always dreaded getting from James. But she had been planning for it.

"What can't you do, James? I'm here for you," she said.

Gary was with her. After speaking those words, she covered the phone and ordered Gary to call me. I didn't recognize the number. It had a 412 area code, though, so I answered on the second ring.

"Rachel, it's me, Gary. Your mom's boyfriend."

"Hi," I said, unsure why he was calling me.

"Your mom told me to call you. Please stay on the line. She's talking to James, and I think something's wrong."

"Okay."

I could hear bits and pieces as Mom continued to talk to James. She later filled me in on the details.

"I'm not meant for this, Mom," he told her through sobs. "I'm broken."

She could hear wind rustling where James was, and what sounded like waves.

"James, honey, where are you? Are you outside?"

He hesitated for a moment before answering. "What? Yeah, I'm by the lake. I'm going in. I'm sorry, Mom."

She covered the phone again and yelled to me, "Rachel, call nine-one-one, now! Tell them your brother is trying to commit suicide by jumping into Lake Michigan!"

I hung up with Gary and dialed.

"Nine-one-one," a woman answered. "What is the nature of your emergency?"

"My brother. He's going to commit suicide!"

"What is your location?"

I gave her my address, but then I added, "But he's not here. He's walking along Lake Michigan. He's going to jump in!"

"Where along Lake Michigan, ma'am?"

"I don't know. He's on his phone talking to my mom right now. All we know is that he's near the lake. He's probably somewhere between North Avenue Beach and the Loop."

"What is his name?"

"James Wright."

"What does he look like?"

"Tall, blond, thin, young. In his twenties."

"How do you know he's going to commit suicide?"

"He told my mom he's going to jump in."

"But you don't know where along the lake he is?"

"No! Please, you have to look for him!"

"Does he have a history of depression or suicide attempts?"

"Yes."

"Okay. Hold on, ma'am."

Then she came back thirty seconds later. "Are you there, ma'am?"

"Yes."

"I have a unit nearby that's going to drive down the lakeshore path to look for him. Can I get a callback number for you?"

"Yes." I told her my number.

"Okay. We're going to look for him. I'll call you if we find him."

"Thank you."

"And call us back if you get more information."

"I will. Thanks. Please find him."

I texted Gary to tell him I had called. Then I started praying like I had never prayed before. My face was a river of tears.

While this was going on, Mom was still talking to James. "What do you mean you're going in, James? It's freezing outside."

"I know, Mom," James said through chattering teeth and snivels. "That's the point. I don't want to be here anymore."

"James, honey," Mom said in her best hostage negotiation voice. "Please go inside somewhere and talk to me. You don't need to hurt yourself. Whatever it is, I can help you."

"You can't help me, Mom!" James shouted back at her. "That's the whole point!"

"James, please, just go inside and keep talking to me. We can figure out this out."

"I already figured it out! I'm not happy, Mom!" Up until that point, Mom said it was difficult to understand him because he was crying so hard and shouting. But then his breathing slowed, and the sobbing ebbed. "I'm never going to be happy, Mom. That's what I figured out. There's no point to sticking around here anymore. I'm only a burden for everyone."

"James, you're not a burden on any of us. I love you so much. Your family loves you so much. You can't leave us! You can't leave me!"

"I'm sorry, Mom. I love you. Tell Rachel I love her. And Andrew."

"James, you are not getting off this phone! Not until we work through this! Do you hear me?"

She was doing whatever she could to keep him talking.

"There's nothing to work through, Mom. I already did that. This is the only way."

"James, no, listen to me," she pleaded. "There's always another way."

"I'm sorry. Bye, Mom. I'm sorry."

"James! James!" she cried, but he had already hung up.

She was certain, right then and there, she had failed to save her son. She had never experienced anything more painful in her life.

■ ■ ■

Unbeknownst to us at the time, our efforts to alert emergency workers had not been in vain. The squad car drove down the lakeshore path, its high beams illuminating a large swath in front of it. The officer noticed something thrashing in the water near the edge. God must have been guiding his way. From where he was, he couldn't tell who or what it was, but he pulled his car over to investigate.

The officer approached the water's edge on foot, and he spotted James's head bobbing out of the water. He alerted dispatch and then removed his outer winter gear and his boots. Then, probably in violation of department policy and training, he jumped right in to save James.

It's not entirely clear how the officer got James out of the water. Nor do we know whether he needed assistance to do it. But we know two things for sure: that man is a hero, and James was still conscious when he was removed from the lake.

But James was not in the clear. While being strapped into an ambulance, his heart stopped beating. Or maybe it stopped before he was loaded into the back. Either way, James was dead.

■ ■ ■

I got a call on my cell phone. "Hello? This is Rachel."

"This is nine-one-one dispatch. Am I speaking with Rachel Wright?"

"Yes, speaking." My heart was fluttering. I thought I might faint.

"Ma'am, an officer found your brother. He's being transported to Northwestern Memorial Hospital."

Thank you, God. Thank you, I mouthed. "Is he alive?"

"I don't know, ma'am. I only know he's headed to the emergency room at Northwestern."

"Thank you."

"I'll pray for you and your brother," she said. And then she hung up.

Her small act of kindness snapped the situation back into focus. I started bawling my eyes out again, and then I called Mom. She was already on her way to the airport to get on the first flight she could. Then I took a cab to the hospital.

■ ■ ■

I sat in the emergency waiting room for at least a half hour before I heard any news about James. A nurse or a physician assistant—I didn't know who she was—told me he was alive. She had no other details to provide despite my efforts to glean more information. I didn't know if he was conscious, if he was injured, if he had suffered brain damage. I only knew he was alive. I thanked God and continued to pray. It was maybe another hour before I was allowed to go back to visit him.

When I first put eyes on him, I almost didn't recognize him. He looked so small and haggard. But he was awake! Then he noticed me and gave me a small, sad smile. I flew to his side and hugged him. Then I stepped back, and we both cried for several minutes before I interrupted the sounds of our sobs.

"How could you, James? How could you do this to yourself? To us?"

"I'm sorry, Rach. I'm so sorry. I wish I had a way to explain this."

"I'm so mad at you. I'm relieved you're alive. I want to punch you in the face. I...I don't know what to feel." I was on emotional overload.

"Please don't punch me in the face. I almost died, you know." He had a tiny smile on his face. I wanted to punch it off. I also wanted to hug him again. Then his face changed, and his voice grew somber. "It wasn't supposed to be this way. I'm not supposed to be alive. I don't want you, or Mom, or anyone else to have to worry about me anymore. I'm sorry."

"Are you apologizing for being alive?"

He didn't say anything.

"James," I demanded. "Are you apologizing for being alive? Because I will punch you."

"I don't know, Rach. Yes? No? I don't know what to say. I'm sorry."

■ ■ ■

They kept James overnight. I stayed there with him and slept on a chair that folded out to become a passable bed. Before that, I of course called Mom to tell her James was alive. She had a similar reaction to me. She wouldn't be able to make it to Chicago until first thing in the morning.

I know I wasn't being completely honest when I said James was dead, but I wasn't lying either. He did jump into icy water with the sole intent to end his life. And as a result, his heart stopped beating. For however long it lasted, he was clinically dead. Only then he was revived.

I couldn't tell you from the start that James was alive and recovering. You would not have had the slightest clue what Mom and I went through. This way, you could experience at least a fraction of a fraction of the sheer dread and limitless agony we had to endure. Complete terror while we waited for any updates on what had happened to him.

■ ■ ■

The following afternoon, James's primary care physician came to evaluate him. So did his psychiatrist, Dr. Bhattacharya. I met them both, but Mom and I were not permitted to stay in the room during their evaluations. They both asked if James had left a suicide note. It turned out he did. James asked that I retrieve it from his apartment, because the doctors wanted to include it in their medical files.

While I was at James's apartment, I noticed he had attacked more than a few walls and personal items. I didn't spend too much time examining the damage. I found his handwritten suicide note on his coffee table next to his laptop. Next to both was a large envelope from Dr. Bhattacharya's office. I peeked inside and saw that it seemed to contain his medical records.

I read the suicide note first, but I am not going to describe it here. I promised James I would not. I will always respect his wishes, as long as they do not put him in harm's way. I will say the note left me more pissed off than anything else. I couldn't get over what he had put us through. Not right then anyway. His note didn't offer anywhere near enough contrition to make me feel even microscopically better.

Although I must make one exception to not describing the contents of his suicide note. It contained the password to his computer and a request to finish his book. Of course I would do that for him. After I made sure my excerpts were included. At this point, you have read them.

Before I left his apartment, I read his medical records and took them with me. The time for respecting his privacy was over, and the contents were illuminating. For instance, I knew he had been in a horrible place roughly one and a half years ago. However, I had no clue he had tried to kill himself by overdosing on pills. I'm not sure what's scarier: that he did it, or that he was able to hide it for so long. I also saw he was supposed to be taking a medication called Abilify. He never mentioned it to me once. I checked his medicine cabinet and found four completely full bottles inside. He stopped taking his medication at some point, and according to his records, he never told his psychiatrist.

Those are the kinds of secrets my family and I need to know going forward if we're going to help James. If we're going to keep him alive. I also think the medical records are necessary to understand more of his situation. So I inserted some of the more significant entries into his book where appropriate, again, as you have already seen.

■ ■ ■

When I got back to the hospital, Manuel and a guy I later learned was Miles were visiting with James. Mom and Andrew were hanging out in a nearby waiting area. I was glad his friends had come. James was going to need all the support he could get.

The hospital held on to James a second night. That gave us enough time to make temporary plans for his discharge. When he was released, he returned to his place, with Mom and Andrew to watch him. Andrew can only stay for a few days, but Mom is going to stay out here for several weeks. That will give our family enough time to come up with a long-term solution to keeping James healthy. Dad is planning to come out in a few days and will stay with me.

I do not know what the future has in store for James, but I am going to put my worries off for a while. I am going to be thankful that James is still with us. That he has another chance to seek happiness in this world. He deserves to find it. We all do.

Chapter 35

You should have known you couldn't get rid of me that easily. I'm as annoying as those horror movie monsters that reanimate after being decapitated, or after their thoraxes have been crushed by multiton trucks. Or the plantar wart on the bottom of my foot I thought was long dead. I freeze it, I burn it, I scrape at it, and it still lives! It's the juggernaut of skin maladies.

Anyway, I digress. It's been a few weeks since my "suicide-related behavior." I had thought my plan was painless and foolproof. The universe apparently wanted one more chance to prove me wrong. So I guess I should try to explain everything.

The first phase of cold-water immersion is the cold shock response. When the skin rapidly cools, as it does when plunged into ice-cold water, the body gasps reflexively for air, and sometimes people hyperventilate. If your head is underwater, you breathe water into the lungs, which naturally results in drowning. I vaguely recall that when I first jumped in, I sank but didn't gasp for air until my head had bobbed up to the surface. Panic had set in almost instantaneously, though, so I can't be sure.

If you don't breathe in water and drown immediately, which apparently I did not, the second phase is cold incapacitation, which sets in within five to fifteen minutes. To preserve core body heat, your arteries narrow to decrease blood flow to your extremities—a process called vasoconstriction. Without the heat from your blood, the muscles in your hands and feet lose functionality, followed by your arms and legs. Obviously, it's difficult to perform physical activities like swimming when your arms and legs aren't working properly.

Hypothermia is the third phase. It takes way longer than one would expect for moderate hypothermia to set in, like thirty minutes or more. At a body temperature of ninety-five degrees Fahrenheit, you merely shiver. Below ninety degrees, which occurs after roughly thirty minutes in icy water, you lose consciousness and drown without a flotation device. Around eighty-three degrees, you risk cardiac arrest.

I was never counting on hypothermia to do me in. With my legs wrapped together with duct tape, I figured muscle fatigue or vasoconstriction would force my head to drop below the surface and drown me well before my core temperature dipped low enough to render me unconscious.

The fourth phase is circum-rescue collapse. The body is literally struggling for its continued existence, so senses are heightened and adrenaline is pumping. While in the process of being rescued, or after having been rescued, the brain relaxes, which can simultaneously cause the body to cease its output of stress hormones. Without stress hormones stoking the fire, blood pressure drops and muscles fail. Cardiac arrest can also occur, which is apparently what happened to me.

At some point before they placed me in the ambulance, my heart stopped. It took a minute or two of resuscitation before my heart kicked into gear again. It probably would have started sooner, but Alexis had broken it.

Of the whole ordeal, however long it lasted, I only remember fragmentary details: jumping in, resurfacing, panicking. Once panic fully set in, despite my intentions, I started thrashing my arms and kicking my bound legs to stay afloat. I think I recall someone yelling at me and grabbing me while I was in the water, but I can't be certain. I don't remember anything else, vividly or not, until being in a hospital bed.

Rachel was the first face I recognized when I regained my faculties.

I realize I'm reciting the details of my suicide attempt in a flippant manner, but my plan was to be dead. I never expected to have to describe this particular fragment of my life. I never wanted to have to defend the indefensible. In fact, I felt two emotions most acutely when I first awoke: anger I was still alive after having resolved to end everything, and sorrow that my family would have to persist in carrying the burden that is my continued existence.

Those two sentiments passed quickly, within a matter of seconds or minutes, but I distinctly recall having them. I'm not going to evaluate whether they were appropriate responses—it's too soon for that—I'm only noting what I felt.

Then the feelings one would expect me to have after surviving certain death came rolling through my body like tsunami waves: gratitude for being saved, shame for being so emotionally weak, regret for putting my family through this trauma, and a general sense of being overwhelmed by their love and concern for me.

For a guy who daydreams all the time and thinks about death on a fairly regular basis, one would think that I would have had some visions of heaven or hell, or purgatory, or any form of the afterlife. But nope. Nothing.

Of course, there can certainly be hell here on earth, and I have not come to terms with the hell I put my family and friends through. I've discussed it a little with Dr. B, since I just started a biweekly schedule with her, but I am loath to begin that journey in earnest right now. One day I will, and then I will apologize to each of them appropriately. But not just yet. Besides, at this time, I cannot find the words to express my gratitude for the plan my mom, Rachel, and Gary implemented—or for the love and concern they, Andrew, Manuel, and Miles demonstrated when they came to see me in the hospital. And I'm more than a tad bit ashamed of myself.

My mom is still out here staying with me, although that will end soon. Miles's lease is expiring, and with no sign of Creepy Steve returning, we agreed to get a place together. I tried to give him an idea of what he has in store for himself, but he'll never know the full brunt of his new burden until we move in together.

At least Rachel will always be around as well to help keep an eye on me. She has always been my rock, and these past few weeks have been no exception. Manuel too. If nothing else, I need to pull myself together so I can carry out my best-man duties with the gravitas and élan they deserve.

My dad even came here for a few days and stayed with Rachel while he was in town—like I said, he can't be in the same place as my mom. He didn't say anything to make me feel worse than I already do, so I guess it was a positive visit.

As for my job, I have to say, my office was compassionate with me throughout this post-suicide-attempt ordeal. Everyone I talked to seemed concerned and encouraging, especially the people in HR. But I let them know yesterday I would not be returning to the firm, regardless of when I feel ready to resume working. The job is not going to help me find happiness—it's just not what I want to do with my life—so I need to rip it off like a bandage.

Before I officially quit, I spoke to Yasmin and Richard. They joked there had to have been an easier way to get Francis to back off a little. I'll miss them, especially after we had a good laugh about Francis and Elizabeth getting it on in the stairwell.

Dr. B has also been hugely supportive throughout this whole mess. Besides the biweekly visits, we're working on the right combination of medicine to keep me sane while not turning me into a zombie. It remains to be seen how successful we will be.

As for what I will do with my life going forward, time will tell. Looking back on the past ten or so months, besides the temporary highs I had with Alexis, the one thing I looked forward to doing was writing this memoir. Besides being proud of the finished product, I enjoyed the process itself. So I don't know exactly what I'll do, but I'm going to try my best to do some kind of professional writing—either blogging or working at a small paper for starters, or maybe going back to school to get a master of fine arts in creative writing.

Other than that, as the cliché goes, I will take things one drunken stumble at a time. Except I won't be drinking, because everyone says that's no bueno for me anymore—particularly if I adhere to my prescribed medication regimen, whatever it may be.

I haven't talked to Alexis, nor do I want to. I do hope she finds happiness, whether it's with Bill or as a nun in a convent on some remote mountaintop. If I'm being honest, my preference for her is the high-altitude nunnery.

As for Fred, I know he's still around, but everyone around me is helping to exorcise him for good. The world let me hit reset one time. It's time to come back twice as strong.

THE END

ACKNOWLEDGMENTS

I couldn't have written this novel without the support of my wonderful, brilliant, and talented wife, Jenny. With grace and patience, she allowed me to spend nights and weekends working on this book while I occasionally neglected some household chores—and her. And when I was done, she provided critical feedback and gave me the confidence to see this book through to publication.

After my wife, I can't thank enough my cousin-by-marriage, Rita. She instantly fell in love with the manuscript, and her enthusiasm convinced me that others would love it too. This book is published because of her.

Finally, I have to thank the friends and family who read early versions of my manuscript and gave me indispensable advice and critiques: Zak, Jennifer, my mom and brothers, Uncle Bill, Chris, Laura, Shannon, Luttrell, and Jeff.

SUICIDE PREVENTION

If you know someone in crisis, call the National Suicide Prevention Lifeline (Lifeline) at **1-800-273-TALK (8255)** or text the Crisis Text Line (**text HELLO to 741741**). Both services are free and available twenty-four hours a day, seven days a week. The deaf and hard of hearing can contact the Lifeline via TTY at 1-800-799-4889. All calls are confidential.

Chapter 23

SLEEPING ON JAMES'S COUCH, JUST LIKE OLD TIMES

Imagine my surprise when James called me in the afternoon, just to hang out. I couldn't believe he was willing to spend a precious Saturday night away from his beloved Alexis. Whatever the reason, I took it. They had been inseparable almost since they started dating. If I wasn't so happy for him, I would have been annoyed. Especially because it was mid-August, which meant Chicago had precious few days of summer left. No more summer meant no more outdoor beer gardens and restaurant patios.

Seeing him that night was perfect timing. Besides missing James, I needed a laid-back evening. I had gone to a happy hour the night before with coworkers and then met some friends later in the evening. It wasn't until 3:00 a.m. that I realized I had skipped dinner. Chugging water and eating a frozen pizza at 4:00 a.m. didn't stave off my hangover Saturday morning.

After I didn't feel like death anymore, I ran a few errands and then started to make my way toward James's place. He had suggested we walk somewhere nearby for food and then go back to his place to watch a movie.

When I arrived at his apartment, no one answered the door. I checked the handle, and it was open. In I went.

"Hello? James? It's Rachel," I called out.

I heard a muffled "Be out in a minute." He must have been in the bathroom.

The place appeared to be clean! I was shocked. It seemed having a girlfriend was the right motivation for James not to live in squalor. As I snooped around, I didn't notice anything out of the ordinary. No signs of excessive drinking or melancholy. Except for the slow-paced song playing, which I did not recognize. The refrain had something to do with familiar faces going nowhere.

"Hey," he said as he came out of his bedroom. "How are you?"

"I'm good! My hangover is gone as of an hour ago."

"That long of a hangover, huh? Must've been a good night."

"It was. I went to happy hour with coworkers and then met Sarah and some other friends. And I forgot to eat food for a long stretch of last night."

"Sarah?" he asked. "Brown hair, English major, likes boy bands?"

"She's my roommate, James."

"That's the one."

"Yes, you've met her several times now."

"I know. I was just testing you. You want to head out for food?"

"Sure." As we started walking, I asked him, "So what'd you do last night? How did you escape Alexis's clutches? I never see you anymore."

"Nothing last night. I had to work super late and then the same most of today. Work is out of control right now. I'm not sure I can keep up this pace for the next nine months." Then as an afterthought he added, "I think I'm going to see Alexis tomorrow night for dinner. She's been busy, too, and has a ladies' night tonight. Which is fine with me, I guess. I kind of need to decompress."

"And you were overdue for hanging out with me?"

"Yes, of course that," he said with a smile. "So what's new? Job is still going well?"

It was going well, and I was loving it, but it isn't exciting to write about. As we ate, I told him mostly about work, and about the few dates I had had, none of which had gone well. Guys my age seem so immature. I'm not looking to hook up, which is the opposite of what 99 percent of them want to do.

As we were talking, I began to notice James wasn't as jovial as he had been in the recent past. Either in person or through his text messages. He was not in a James-level funk. Certainly not as gloomy as he was in the era I call Pre-Alexis. But something seemed off kilter. It took me a while to re-alize he hadn't mentioned Alexis once. Unless he was giving pithy answers to direct questions about her. The jig was up; I was onto him. Time to get the full scoop.

"So, besides your hectic schedules, how are things going with you and Alexis? Usually every time we talk, you can't stop raving about her."

He started to speak but then paused to reflect. A rare course of action for James. It's not that he typically speaks out of turn. He just normally doesn't backtrack when he has something to say. "On the whole, I think things are going really well," he said. "Being with her is easy. I can be myself and not worry about her judging me. She's caring and smart. And likes my jokes." Another rare pause, then, "She makes me want to be a better person."

"But?" I asked.

"But what?"

"You started by saying 'on the whole.'" I'm a good listener. "I was waiting for you to make some kind of qualifying statement, but everything you listed was positive."

"Yeah, I guess these past few weeks haven't been the best."

"Did you guys have a fight or something?"

"No. Not a fight. It just hasn't been a great couple of weeks."

That wasn't much to go on, but we were making progress. "Because you were so busy?" I asked.

"No. Well yeah, but that's not it."

"So what is it? Did something happen that you haven't told me?"

Something registered on his face. I had a clue to chase down now. "Nothing bad happened, no. But I found out Alexis was engaged."

"Oh." That was kind of a big deal. "How long ago?"

"About a year ago, to a guy named Bill."

"How'd she bring it up? It doesn't sound like an easy conversation to have."

"She didn't. Her friend told me."

"Hmm. Are you upset she didn't tell you?" They had only been dating a few months. It wasn't crazy she had not told him yet, but I held my tongue.

"Yeah, I guess so. And about how she reacted when I asked her about it."

"Ah. How did that go?"

"Well, not great," he said. "We talked on Sunday afternoon about it, and she didn't say much. We haven't talked about it since."

"Have you tried to?"

"No, not really. I've only seen her a few times over the past couple weeks. Sgt. Slaughter is taking up all my time."

"Huh?"

"Oh, a partner at work. He's driving me into the ground. Plus, I had to travel this past week."

"That sounds not so fun," I said.

"It's not. The only silver linings are my coworkers Richard and Yasmin. They make the project slightly bearable."

"Well, at least you have that."

"Yeah."

"Back to Alexis and Bill. Are you worried maybe she still has feelings for him?"

"Bingo. Give this girl all the money."

"Is there any reason to suspect she does?"

"I dunno. No? Maybe?" he said. "Except...except when I told her I knew about Bill and that I was worried about her having feelings for him, she ignored that aspect of it. She didn't try to reassure me at all. Instead, she started interrogating me about who told me and what exactly I knew."

"Erm," I said eloquently. Taking a defensive posture from the start was no good. But I didn't know the full context either, since I was not there. I would never take her side over James's, but I didn't want to jump to any extreme conclusions without hard evidence. "Did you tell her everything you know?"

"No. I would have, if she had wanted to talk about it, instead of ignoring the substance and asking me what I knew and how I knew it."

That made sense to me. "So what didn't you tell her?"

His expression was growing glummer by the second. I hated seeing him sad. "Bill's an alcoholic," he said. "Apparently, she gave him every chance to get better, but he couldn't do it, so she eventually left him. Her friend says it tore her up for months afterward. Even Alexis admitted she still loves him." He halted for a second and then said, "All of that wouldn't without understanding the actions of the *sans-culottes* of Paris, the French nobility and the peasants of rural France. But this assumes (if unselfconsciously) the idea of *typical actors* – each acting with materials at hand.

The *AJS* debate suggests that there remains considerable unreflective empiricist philosophy still afoot even in highly self-conscious and sophisticated writers. If the foregoing analysis and criticism are near to being correct, all sides to the debate, while nominally "realist," fail to see the deep difference between a realist notion of causality and the conventional Humean constant conjunction view. Indeed, the consequences as regards theory and explanation are enormous. Similarly, while Kiser and Hector rightly insist on the causal priority of agency in explaining social outcomes, rational choice theory as a "general" theory cannot do the job that they intend. Finally, then, Somers is quite right to reject general theory and to insist on the importance of history in explanation, but her "relationalism," which certainly seems agentless, would also seem to create more problems than it solves.

Appendix D   The neo-classical model

For the interested reader, this appendix adds some detail and argument to the discussion of neo-classical economics. Following Hausman (1984), it may be convenient to distinguish "equilibrium theory" from "general equilibrium theory." Static equilibrium theory may be defined in terms of the following fundamental assumptions. These comprise the core of mainstream micro-economics:

1. For any individual A and any two options x and y, one and only one of the following is true: A prefers x to y, A prefers y to x, A is indifferent between x and y.
2. A's preferences among options are transitive. (If A prefers x to y and y to z, A prefers x to z.)
3. A seeks to maximize his or her utility where the utility of an option x is greater than the utility of an option y for A if and only if A prefers x to y. The utilities of options are equal just in case the agent is indifferent between them.
4. If option x is acquiring commodity bundle x' and option y is acquiring commodity bundle y' and y' contains at least as much of each commodity as x' and more of at least one commodity, then all agents prefer y to x.
5. The marginal utility of a commodity c to an agent A is a decreasing function of the quantity of c that A has.

The foregoing postulates define the rationality of actors. The following define the assumptions of production.

6. When we increase inputs into production, other things being equal, output increases, but, after a certain point, at a decreasing rate.
7. Increasing all inputs into production in the same proportion increases output by that proportion. The production set is weakly convex and additive.
8. Firms attempt to maximize their profits by minimizing costs relative to revenues.

As Hausman points out, this brief summary is both rough, misleading and incomplete: rough because the theory can be stated more precisely, misleading because neo-classical economists do not always make use of all these postulates, and incomplete for two reasons. First, as part of the background, commonly used mathematical techniques are assumed. Indeed, the full power of the theory is the fact that it can be represented mathematically. This is a feature of what is sometimes attributed to "physics envy," where the understanding of physics is in terms of positivist theory of science. Second, and more obviously, a host of strong, but narrower assumptions must be made. On the competitive market model, one must assume that there are many buyers and sellers in every market and that each may enter and leave easily. These are relaxed in conditions of "imperfect competition." This includes monopoly, the limiting case of "imperfect competition," and oligopoly, where several large firms dominate the market, there are barriers to entry and the suppliers produce relatively similar products. General equilibrium theory assumes further that everyone has all the relevant information, that there is an interdependence among the many markets, and that commodities (including labor) are infinitely divisible. This last is critical insofar as calculus is the indispensable tool for writing and solving simultaneous equations which define equilibrium. But, for example, if labor does not have a marginal product, but only an average or step-wise product, the marginal productivity of labor is a mathematical fiction, useful for calculation but lacking empirical reality.

In exemplary "deductivist" fashion, many propositions may be strictly deduced from the foregoing, for example, that the price will rise when demand exceeds supply. Let us sketch how this works.

As noted, propositions 1–5 define rationality. We then construct "indifference curves" which represent preferences of actors between bundles of two items, for example, apples and bananas. In a two-person exchange, equilibrium is reached (the invisible hand) when both persons are rational and pursue a minimax strategy. If, for example, we measure apples on the vertical line and bananas on the horizontal line (figure 1) there is an infinite series of bundles of apples and bananas to which O is indifferent. Every bundle further from point O is preferred (curve O_2 is preferred to O_1). The curves are convex because we assume that apples and bananas have diminishing marginal utility. That is, after some amount – one cannot eat that many bananas – there is a decreasing utility for each additional consumption of the good. The same as regards X, drawing his indifference map for this bundle convex to point x. If they are rational they will not stop trading at either P or S since one or the other will see that the

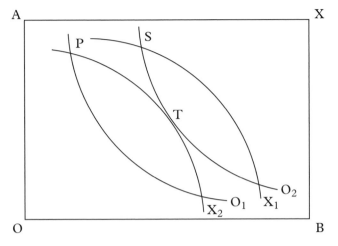

Figure 1.

exchange is not to his advantage. They reach equilibrium at T: there is no way for either to get more without the other getting less, the definition of a "Pareto optimum."[1]

If we introduce money as "numeraire," we represent the price of (say) apples on the vertical axis (figure 2). This is O's demand curve for apples, what she will buy at what price. It slopes down since buyers are rational. Price represents opportunity cost, what other goods must be sacrificed. Given some fixed amount of income (a budget), O's problem is to allocate her money so as to maximize utility (in accordance with the postulates of rationality). We can represent a supply curve for X, what she will supply at what price. Since she is also rational (and in a condition of pure competition), the supply curve slopes up. The supply curve slopes up as a condition of diminishing marginal productivity.

The concept of elasticity is pertinent here. A curve is elastic when the quantity demanded (or supplied) is very responsive to price. Oxenfeld offers that the contribution of the economist's idea of elasticity of demand "may be far below zero." First, although theory acknowledges that this

---

[1] Indifference curve analysis is owed to the economist-cum-sociologist Wilfredo Pareto. As Dyke shows, in order to construct an indifference curve, one must assume that choices are made pairwise and that this assumes the independence of irrelevant alternatives, that preferences can be arranged ordinally. Thus, choices depend only on comparing one bundle with another. The point is that we are rarely in such conditions. For example, the choice between two breakfast cereals may be a "pure preference" but the choice between a needed medication and a breakfast cereal generally is not. As Dyke points out, there are many reasons for choosing one thing over another, including availability, future needs, budgetary constraints, etc. Dyke's account (1981: 114–116) is excellent.

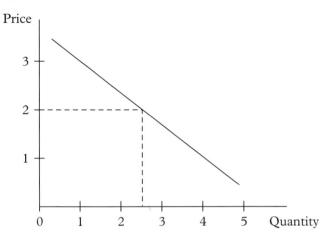

Figure 2.

elasticity is not uniform over the relevant stretches of the demand curve (where it is not either vertical or horizontal) simplifying assumptions are always made. This is a source of considerable mischief. Second, businessmen use an alternative and far simpler method: "the effect of price reductions on unit sales can be stated as the number of added units that would be sold as a result of given dollar 'expenditures' in the form of price reductions"(Oxenfeld, 1963: 73).

Imperfect competition

But worse, in conditions of imperfect competition, not only is elasticity not uniform across the relevant stretches of the supply and demand curves, but in "the short run" the curves will be very *inelastic:* for some goods, electricity, for example, there is a public monopoly and consumers have no choice but to purchase the service. Similarly, producers infrequently increase output in response to higher demand in the short run: they take windfall profits instead.[2] But the point here is not whether monopolies or oligopolies are inefficient as defined by the theory (below); only that in imperfect competition, the competitive equilibrium model does not hold and that, accordingly, price is not the intersection of the sloping demand and supply curves as these are constructed by the theory.

[2] The "long run" is a wonderful escape for theory, but as Keynes observed: "in the long run, we are all dead."

As is generally acknowledged, there is no adequate economic theory of oligopolistic competition which explains how prices and output are set, except to say that corporations do not engage in what would be manifestly mutually destructive price-competition and that they remain in a competitive environment in which they must constantly employ a host of forms of non-price competition (Galbraith, 1968; Baran and Sweezy, 1968). On the other hand, since for the mainstream, imperfect competition continues to be considered "the special case," the absence of a rigorous theory is not seen to be a disaster.[3] But of course, the behavior of corporations which are not engaged in price competition is of considerable importance to understanding contemporary market capitalism, including "consumerism," global inequalities and continuing problems with the stability of the system.

In a purely competitive market, mainstream theory tells us that there would be no payoff for advertising which provided more than information since firms responding to market demand would produce the same products and sell all their output at the equilibrium price. Similarly, on the mainstream view, all costs – including accordingly, the enormous costs of the sales effort – are "necessary." But this provokes the question, raised by Thorstein Veblen, of the rationality of the system: He wrote:

The producers have been giving continually more attention to the saleability of the product, so that much of what appears on the books as production-cost should properly be charged to the production of saleable appearances. The distinctions between the workmanship and salesmanship have been blurred in this way, until it will doubtless hold true now that the shop-cost of many articles produced for the market is mainly chargeable to the production of saleable appearances, ordinarily meretricious.[4]

---

[3] Schumpeter remarks that "from all the infinite variety of market patterns pure or perfect monopoly and pure or perfect competition stand out by virtue of certain properties – of which the most important is that both cases lend themselves to treatment by means of relatively simple and (in general) uniquely determined rational schemata – and on the other hand, that the large majority of cases that occur in practice are nothing but mixtures and hybrids of these two, then it seems natural to accept pure monopoly and pure competition as the two genuine or fundamental patterns and to proceed by investigation how these work out" (1954: 975). Unfortunately, reality was sacrificed for rigor. See Schumpeter, 1954: 962–985, 1150–1152. See also Brakman and Heijdra (eds.), 2001. The editors note that there were two "revolutions" in the theory of monopolistic competition, the first initiated by Robinson (1969) and Chamberlin (1962) in the 1930s and the second by Dixit and Stiglitz in 1977. The first failed, according to them, because it lacked an adequate model. The second attempt "introduced a formalization that had all the characteristics of monopolistic competition but was easier to handle" (Brakman and Heijdra, 2001: 1–2). But they note also that there are serious problems with this formalization, even if, for them, it shows promise.

[4] Veblen, *Absentee Ownership and Business Enterprise in Recent Times*, p. 300, quoted by Baran and Sweezy (1968: 133). The account of Baran and Sweezy, which also draws on Chamberlin (1962) and Kalecki (1965), remains very useful.

Veblen, writing in 1923, saw only the beginning of this "blurring" which, with the astronomical growth of advertising in the recent past, makes the production unit the handmaiden of the marketing division. Baran and Sweezy quote a sympathetic defender of this dramatic change:

In fact, broadly defined as it properly can be, to include the whole range of marketing operations from product design through pricing and advertising right on to doorbell pushing and the final sale, selling or marketing is not only a symbol of a free society, but is in ever-increasing measure a working necessity in our particularly free society.[5]

To be sure, consumerism is a measure of "our particularly free society," and is "a working necessity," but an explanation was already in Marx, hinted at by Keynes and is the central theme of Baran and Sweezy. Common sense tells us that commodities produced must be sold if the system is to reproduce itself, that unless consumption is somehow guaranteed, the system falls into crises. The problem, as noted by Henry Ford, was that it is not only necessary that wage earners want to buy what is being produced, but that they have to have sufficient income to do this. For Marxists, of course, this was a problem for which capitalism could provide no permanent solution (Harvey, 1987).

Micro- and macro-theory

This is a good place to include Keynes's contribution. Despite what may be an excusable misunderstanding of Keynes, he was no radical in his theorizing, conserving most of the elements of the legacy derived from Marshall and Pigou. Indeed, despite its pertinence to his main concerns, his work shows no evidence of influence from attacks in the early 1930s on traditional price theory by Joan Robinson and E. H. Chamberlin. "As Robert Lukas repeatedly pointed out even in the early 1970s, graduate students were taught one thing during their Monday / Wednesday microeconomic courses and another thing on Tuesdays and Thursdays in the macro-economic courses" (Boettke, 1997: 36).[6] Samuelson (1947) was here the key figure in making the system seem to work. But his synthesis of the neo-classical tradition and Keynes was, contestably, coherent. As Boettke writes: "Samuelson's synthesis created a rather strange mix of general equilibrium economics with Keynesian macroeconomics"

---

[5] Dexter M. Keezer and Associates, *New Forces in American Business,* p. 90, quoted by Baran and Sweezy (1968: 124). By contrast, one thinks of Vance Packard's important *The Waste Makers* (1960).

[6] Rational choice theorists tend to take a more optimistic view and hold that in economics, the micro–macro gap has been closed.

(1997: 36). Indeed, for Baran and Sweezy: "the effects of a thoroughgoing reintegration of the two levels of analysis – the substitution of a monopolistic price system for the traditional competitive system, and the analysis of its implications for the whole economy – are nothing short of devastating to capitalism's claims to be considered a rational social order which serves to promote the welfare and happiness of its members" (1968: 56).

The link between the classical theory and Keynes's view was in the labor market. Presumably, on the standard view, where commodity and labor markets are perfectly competitive, a wage reduction expands employment which expands consumption. There would always be a wage rate, no matter how low, which produced full employment. The most critical departure from the neo-classical tradition was Keynes's demolition of Say's law, the idea that in competitive markets general glut or unemployment could not occur because supply creates its own demand.[7] But, as Boettke points out: "if the labor market was in competitive equilibrium, this implied that the full-employment output level had been achieved, i.e., there was no macroeconomic problem" (1997: 36). This is Keynes's summary of his rejection of this idea:

When employment increases, aggregate real income is increased. The psychology of the community is such that when aggregate real income is increased aggregate consumption is increased, but not so much as income. Hence employers would make a loss if the whole of the increased employment were to be devoted to satisfying the increased demand for immediate consumption. Thus, to satisfy any amount of employment there must be an amount of current investment sufficient to absorb the excess of total output over what the community chooses to consume when employment is at the given level. For unless there is this amount of investment, the receipts of entrepreneurs will be less than is required to induce them to offer the given amount of employment. It follows, therefore, that, given what we shall call the communities' propensity to consume, the equilibrium level of employment . . . will depend on the amount of current investment. The amount of current investment, in turn, will depend on what we shall call the inducement to invest; and the inducement to invest will be found to depend on the relation between the schedule of the marginal efficiency of capital and the complex rates of interest on loans of various maturities and risks . . . There is no reason in general for expecting [the equilibrium level of employment] to be *equal* to full employment. The effective demand associated with full employment is a special case, only realized when the propensity to consume and the inducement to invest

---

[7] The "law," named for Jean Baptiste Say (1803) was a lynchpin of both classical and neoclassical theory. In Ricardo's crisp formulation: "No man [*sic*] produces but with view to consume or sell, and he never sells but with an intention to purchase some other commodity . . . By purchasing them, he necessarily becomes either the consumer of his own goods, or the purchaser and the consumer of the goods of some other person . . . Productions are always bought by productions, or by services" (quoted from Robert Lekachman, 1964). This is a most useful introductory volume.

stand in a particular relationship to one another . . . But it can only exist when, by accident or design, current investment provides an amount of demand just equal to the excess of the aggregate supply price of the output resulting from full employment over what the community will choose to spend on consumption when it is fully employed. (Keynes, 1960: 27)

The "propensity to consume" is, of course, profoundly influenced by what Keynes terms "subjective factors," or "those psychological characteristics of human nature and those social practices and institutions which, though not alterable, are unlikely to undergo a material change over a short period of time except in abnormal or revolutionary circumstances" (Keynes, 1960: 91). Of course, the existence of "subjective factors" leaves enormous room for some concrete empirical work. But Keynes paid no attention, for example, to how advertising and the manipulation of wants affect these "subjective" factors. In his book, Keynes, not untypically, takes the subjective factors as "given," and assumes that "the propensity to consume depends only on changes in the 'objective factors'," on, that is, the "variables" defined by neo-classical theory. But to his credit Keynes was not, in contrast to Samuelson, a formalist who was committed to mathematical economics. Keynes wanted models, but for him, building them required "a vigilant observation of the actual working of our system." Indeed, "to convert a model into a quantitative formula is to destroy its usefulness as an instrument of thought" (Keynes, 1984). That conclusion can be strongly endorsed!

Keynesian state policies follow: governments can affect total spending and total employment either by monetary policies, which lower interest rates (for example, increasing the supply of money) or fiscal policies which expand total spending by increasing public spending, without raising taxes, or decreasing taxes without reducing public spending. This limited intrusion of government did not in any way threaten capitalist markets as these were theorized by mainstream theory. Similarly as regards direct "public spending" – as long as it was in the interest of national defense – so-called "warfare capitalism" (in contrast to "welfare capitalism"). But the consensus which formed on this view of the matter did not last.

While the point cannot be pursued here, Samuelson's neo-Keynesian model managed to "square the circle" "by means of 'wage stickiness' and 'the money illusion'" (Boettke, 1997: 37). But here again the assumptions were not only ad hoc, but implausible, leaving the model vulnerable to the Chicago School's "hyperformalist attempt to purify the synthesis by purging it of its Keynesian contaminants" (Boettke, 1997: 38). The Neo-liberalism of the recent past was the consequence. Boettke summarizes matters well:

Samuelson's reconciliation of the micro-economic ideal type with involuntary unemployment was repudiated, along with Keynesian prescriptions, in favor of a view that there could be no involuntary unemployment, hence that government action was unnecessary. The result was a doctrinaire derivation of the laissez-faire conclusions that had been overturned by the formalist revolution; economics was now cleansed of Keynesian impurities that had been introduced in the interest of realism. (1997: 38)[8]

Market efficiency according to the model

But to return, supply and demand curves of commodities are simply aggregations of the curves of an infinite number of individuals (as either producers or consumers). The equilibrium price is the price where the two curves intersect (see figure 3). At this price, the market will "clear": everything brought to the market will be purchased.[9]

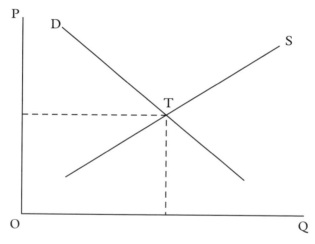

Figure 3.

---

[8] Rational expectations theory also played a role. Human capital theory (invented by Gary Becker) was the effort to place labor back within the price-auction framework. See Thurow, 1983: chapter 7.

[9] Thurow (1983) argues that the question is not whether or not markets clear or even whether they are competitive. He insists that the real question is whether markets clear based on fluctuations in prices (1983: 9). Similarly, as Hicks argues, we can assume competition, but once we take seriously the idea that inventory plays a critical role in pricing, we can see that:

The traditional view that market price is, at least in some way, determined by an equation of supply and demand [has] now to be given up. If demand and supply are [no longer to be] interpreted, as had formerly seemed to be sufficient, as flow demand and supplies coming from outsiders, it is no longer true that there is any tendency, over any particular

Equilibrium is, by definition, a condition of efficiency ("getting the price right"). Efficiency is Pareto optimality. "A distribution of goods or a scheme of production is inefficient when there are ways of doing still better for some individuals without doing any worse for others" (Rawls, 1971: 67). We can separate the two components here. Production is efficient when there is no way to produce more of some commodity without producing less of another. Since, however, there is "consumer sovereignty," where markets are competitive, consumers have decided on the bundles to be produced. But since we are at equilibrium, the distribution will also be efficient: there will be no distribution which improves the circumstance of at least one with someone's situation being worsened.

We need to see first there are many efficient configurations. Assume a fixed stock to be distributed between x and y.

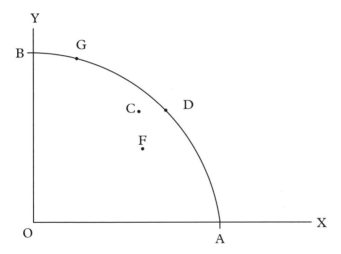

Figure 4.

By definition for all the points in the convex set within AOB, excepting those on line AB, it is possible to improve either x or y (or both) without worsening their opposite with the change (figure 4). At C, for example y's condition has been improved without change to x. At D, both x and y are better off than they were at F. D is efficient but so is G. Indeed, all the points on line AB are efficient since for any point on that line

period, for them to be equalized; a difference between them, if it were not too large, could be matched by a change in stocks. It is of course true that if no distinction is made between demand from stockholders and demand from outside the market; demand and supply in that inclusive sense must always be equal. But that equation is vacuous. It cannot be used to determine price, in Walras's or Marshall's manner. (Hicks, 1989: 11) it is impossible to alter the distribution so as to make some persons (at least one) better off without at the same time causing the other's situation to worsen. If (say) x has it all (point A), then he must lose if y were to get any. Indeed, "the willingness to trade shows that there is a re-arrangement which improves the situation of some without hurting anyone else" (Rawls, 1971: 70). A is efficient, since where x gets it all, y has nothing to trade![10]

A powerful motivation for policy choice in modern political economy is the idea that markets are efficient. However, it is not difficult to show that even if the theoretical conditions are met, it is highly dubious that we would have efficiency. Many different lines of argument are available.

One line of argument regards externalities. Roughly, externalities are side-effects, spillover costs or benefits for third parties. Polluting smoke from a steel mill is a negative externality. Plainly, with externalities there will be a misallocation of resources. Thus the (real) costs of producing steel are not included in the supply schedule and thus, social utility is not optimized. We can introduce a point made earlier about markets. We need to know the type of property relation to determine if some "externality," for example, air pollution, is Pareto-relevant. This is nowhere a given: it is always decided and raises the question of who decides?[11]

Second, there are various forms of micro-rationality which lead to macro-irrationality. The Prisoner's Dilemma, for example, shows that two rational economic actors (actors who satisfy 1–5) will not end up with the best result. One needs to show, accordingly, that such situations never or rarely arise, for example, that inflationary pressure is not best

---

[10] Thus, Samuelson: "The Invisible Hand will only maximize total social utility *provided the state intervenes so as to make the initial distribution of dollar votes ethically proper*" (quoted by Lachman, 1984: 310). Followers of Hayek are on the right track when they write: "There is, of course, no such thing as an 'initial distribution' before the market process starts [as is assumed by mainstream theorizing]. The distribution of wealth in terms of asset values at any point of time is the cumulative result of the market process of the past" (Lachman, 1984: 310). I say "on the right track" here because Lachman (like Hayek) assumes, with Samuelson, that the market process is always a competitive market process. It is for this reason, accordingly, that the Invisible Hand maximizes total social utility only if the State does *not* seek to make "the initial distribution of dollar votes ethically proper" (Lachman, 1984: 310).

[11] Similarly as regards transaction costs. Boettke argues that "Coase's project . . . has been largely misunderstood by formalist neoclassical economics. Instead of highlighting the functional significance of real-world institutions in a world of positive transactions costs, Coase's work has been interpreted as describing the welfare implication of a zero-transactions-cost world" (1997: 21). On the contrary, it should lead to a consideration of how the constitution of markets through the use of law may address the many problems created by existing markets. As Boettke notes, Coase's work must be contrasted with the work of Posner (e.g., 2004) who is engaged in the opposite task of applying neo-classical theory to issues in law.

explained in terms of rational strategies pursued by workers and consumers.

Similarly, if one assumes neo-classical theory, then in a perfectly competitive market, "although all the firms have a common interest in a higher price for the industry's product, it is in the interest of each firm that the other firms pay the cost – in terms of the necessary reduction in output – needed to obtain a higher price" (Olsen, 1971: 9). Indeed, "the only thing that keeps prices from falling in accordance with the process . . . is outside intervention. Government price supports, tariffs, cartel agreement, and the like may keep the firms in a competitive market from acting contrary to their interest" (Olson 1971: 10).[12] But if, for example, lobbying efforts are thought to be necessary to get the government's help, an identical problem arises: just as it is not rational for a producer to restrict his output, it is not rational for him to assume any of the costs of hiring the lobbyist – the so-called "free rider problem."

Finally, there is what Hirsch (1976) has called the "adding up" problem. For "positional goods," for example, driving your private car to work, or high-rise development to attract buyers who want an ocean view, "opportunities for economic advance, as they present themselves serially to one person after another, do not constitute equivalent opportunities for economic advance by all. What each one can achieve, all cannot" (Hirsch, 1976: 4). There is an immediate advantage to standing on tiptoe to get a better view, but if everyone does this, everyone is worse off. At some point, as new drivers get on the freeway, the initial gains are lost in traffic jams. More generally, for a host of "positional goods," since "the standard concept of economic output is appropriate only for truly private goods, having no element of interdependence between consumption by different individuals" (Hirsh, 1976: 7), there is no way to translate individual improvement to overall improvement. Hence, individual maximizing behavior in these contexts is counter-productive. For each of us the scramble is rational since individually we never confront "the distinction between what is available as a result of getting ahead of others and what is available from a general advance shared by all" (Hirsch, 1976: 10). More than a distributional issue is here involved. Wider participation affects not only what one gets from winning the game, but the nature of the game itself. If the goal of a bachelor's degree is a better job and

[12] Of course, this all assumes that corporations are engaged in price competition. But we should not assume this. Indeed, not only are cartels and non-price competition rational, but in many industries, to prevent either extra-large profits (by a monopolist) or extremely low profits, for example, in agriculture, government will gladly step in with regulatory commissions, price supports, acreage controls, etc. to assure that these "deviant" industries maintain healthy profit ratios. See Baran and Sweezy, 1968: 64–66.

better income, then while getting a bachelor's degree remains rational, the consequence is the diminishing value of the degree. At some point, in terms of costs and gains in income, everyone is worse off. We would like to believe, of course, that the effort was not wholly instrumental and that the educational experience bought more than a credential (Thomas, 2004).

More generally, Adam Smith and the tradition which followed him was wrong. As Hirsch concluded: "Competition among isolated individuals in the free market entails hidden costs for others and ultimately for themselves. These costs are deadweight cost for all and all involve social waste" (Hirsch, 1976: 5). And indeed, as with *all* of the foregoing problems, collective action provides the only solution.

A third line of argument is Arrow's paradox. On the neo-classical view, we have individual preferences which via the mechanism of the market result in a social preference. Arrow established a series of conditions, "social choice functions," which restrict ways that the social preference could be derived from individual preferences. All are fairly obvious: rationality, the idea that as more people prefer some alternative, then this alternative ought not to lose ground as a social preference; that "irrelevant alternatives" must be independent (above); and there is "non-dictatorship," – no individual's preference automatically defines social preference. The independence condition says that "the social choice made from any environment depends only on the orderings of individuals with respect to alternatives in that environment." (This precludes substitutes and duplicates and is assumed in postulate 1, above.) Arrow demonstrated that "no social choice function fulfilling these conditions could guarantee satisfactory results when there were more than two individuals in the society and more than two alternatives to choose from" (Dyke, 1981: 113). This has implications for democratic theory; but it shows, I think, now uncontestably, that a fundamental error of equilibrium theory is the assumption that market behavior consists of simply pairwise choices between bundles: the assumption of the independence of irrelevant alternatives.[13]

Finally, neo-classical theory assumes that efficiency can be defined in terms of exchange values. But surely this is not a reasonable notion. An economy could produce "efficiently" (as defined above) *and* wastefully *and* destructively. Destructive but efficient production violates the environment, perhaps making it unfit for human life. Wasteful but efficient production generates commodities which fail to serve human needs and

---

[13] Conversely, there is the question of whether there ever is "market failure." See Pitelis, 1991.

wants, or fails to do so as well as it might. Star Wars technology is a good example of the former; poor quality housing an example of the latter. But, of course, since, contrary to neo-classical theory, consumers are not sovereign, this is to be expected.

But as argued in this appendix and in chapter 6, mathematical economics is hardly the best choice as model of a successful social science. Paradoxically, the reason for this is exactly what has made it so attractive: it seems to be more like physics than any other social science. This volume has argued, however, that the actual practices of the successful natural sciences are poorly described by empiricist philosophy of science and that the individuals who constitute the social mechanisms which would give us an understanding are badly mis-theorized by mainstream theory.

References

Abrams, Philip (1983) *Historical Sociology*. Ithaca: Cornell University Press.

Achen, Christopher (1982) *Interpreting and Using Regression*. Beverly Hills: Sage.

Achinstein, Peter (1981) "Can There be a Model of Explanation?" *Theory and Decision* 13. Reprinted in David-Hillel Ruben, *Explanation*, Oxford: Oxford University Press.

Alexander, Jeffrey (1987) "The Importance of the Classics," in Anthony Giddens and Jonathan Turner (eds.), *Social Theory Today*. Oxford: Polity Press.

(1998) *Neofunctionalism and After*. Oxford: Basil Blackwell.

Anderson, Perry (1974) *Lineages of the Absolutist State*. London: New Left Books.

Anderson, P. W., Arrow, Kenneth J. and Pines, David (eds.) (1988) *The Economy as an Evolving Complex System*. Redwood City: Addison-Wesley.

Appadurai, Arjun (1996) *Modernity at Large: Cultural Dimensions of Globalization*. Minneapolis: University of Minnesota Press.

Archer, Margaret (1995) *Realist Social Theory: The Morphogenetic Approach*. Cambridge: Cambridge University Press.

Aronson, Gerald (1984) *A Realist Philosophy of Science*. New York: St. Martin's Press.

Ashley, Richard K. (1989) "Living on Border Lines: Man, Poststructuralism, and War," in James Der Derian and Michael Shapiro (eds.), *International / Intertextual Relations*. Lexington, MA: Heath.

Atkins, Peter (2003) *Galileo's Finger*. New York: Oxford University Press.

Augier, Mie (1999) "Some Notes on Alfred Schütz and the Austrian School of Economics: Review of Alfred Schütz's *Collected Papers*, Vol. IV. Edited by H. Wagner, G. Psatha and F. Kersten," *Review of Austrian Economics* 11.

Bakan, Joel (2004) *The Corporation: The Pathological Pursuit of Power*. New York: Free Press.

Balough, Thomas (1982) *The Irrelevance of Conventional Economics*. New York: Liveright.

Baran, Paul A. and Sweezy, Paul M. (1968) *Monopoly Capital: An Essay on the American Economic and Social Order*. New York: Monthly Review Press.

Barnes, S. B. (1977) *Interests and the Growth of Knowledge*. London: Routledge & Kegan Paul.

Barnet, Richard J. and Cavanaugh, John (1994) *Global Dreams: Imperial Corporations and the New World Order*. New York: Simon and Schuster.

Barnet, Richard J. and Müller, Ronald E. (1974). *Global Reach: The Power of the Multinational Corporations*. New York: Simon and Schuster.

Barone, Enrico (1908) "The Ministry of Production in a Collectivist State," in F. A. Hayek (ed.), *Collectivist Economic Planning*, London: Routledge & Kegan Paul.

Bauman, Zigmunt (1998) *Globalization: The Human Consequences*. New York: Columbia University Press.

Bendix, Reinhard (1976) "The Mandate to Rule: An Introduction," *Social Forces* 55.

(1978) *Kings or People*. Berkeley: University of California Press.

(1990) *Force, Fate, and Freedom: On Historical Sociology*. Berkeley: University of California Press.

Berger, Peter L. and Luckmann, Thomas (1967) *The Social Construction of Reality*. New York: Anchor Books.

Berle, Adolf A. and Means, Gardiner C. (1968) *The Modern Corporation and Private Property*, revised edition. New York: Harcourt, Brace and World.

Bhaskar, Roy (1975) *A Realist Philosophy of Science*. 2nd edition, 1978. Atlantic Highlands: Humanities Press.

(1978) "On the Possibility of Social Scientific Knowledge and the Limits of Naturalism," *Journal for the Theory of Social Behavior* 8, 1.

(1979) *The Possibility of Naturalism*. Atlantic Highlands: Humanities Press.

(1986) *Scientific Realism and Human Emancipation*. London: Verso.

Bickerton, Derek (1990) *Language and Species*. Chicago: University of Chicago Press.

Biggart, Nicole Wesley (2002) *Readings in Economic Sociology*. Oxford: Blackwell.

Blau, Peter (1964) *Exchange and Power in Social Life*. New York: John Wiley.

Bloor, David (1976) *Knowledge and Social Imagery*. London: Routledge & Kegan Paul.

Boettke, Peter J. (1997) "Where Did Economics Go Wrong? Modern Economics as Flight from Reality," *Critical Review* 12.

Bohm, David (1984) *Causality and Chance in Modern Physics*. New edition. London: Routledge & Kegan Paul.

Bonham, Vence L., Warshauer-Baker, Esther and Collins, Frank S. (2005) "Race and Ethnicity in the Genome Era: The Complexity of the Constructs," *American Psychologist* 60, 1.

Boudon, Raymond (1998a) "Social Mechanisms Without Black Boxes," in Peter Hedström and Richard Swedberg (eds.), *Social Mechanisms: An Analytical Approach to Social Theory*. Cambridge: Cambridge University Press.

(1998b) "Limitations of Rational Choice Theory," *American Journal of Sociology* 104, 3.

Bourdieu, Pierre and Wacquant, Loïc, J. D. (1992) *An Invitation to Reflexive Sociology*. Chicago: University of Chicago Press.

Brakman, Steven and Heijdra, Ben J. (eds.) (2001) *The Monopolistic Competition Revolution in Retrospect*. Cambridge: Cambridge University Press.

Brenner, Robert (1977) "The Origins of Capitalist Development: A Critique of Neo-Smithian Marxism," *New Left Review* 104.

(2003) *The Boom and the Bubble: The US in the World Economy*. London: Verso.

Brodbeck, May (ed.) (1968) *Readings in the Philosophy of the Social Sciences*. New York: Macmillan.

Brown, Harold I. (1977) *Perception, Theory and Commitment: The New Philosophy of Science*. Chicago: University of Chicago Press.

Bourgois, Phillipe (1997) "In Search of Horatio Alger," in Craig Reinerman and Harry G. Levine (eds.), *Crack in America: Demon Drugs and Social Justice*. Berkeley: University of California Press.

Bunge, Mario (1979) *Causality and Modern Science*. New York: Dover.

(1996) *Finding Philosophy in Social Science*. New Haven: Yale University Press.

(2003) "How Does it Work? The Search for Explanatory Mechanisms," *Philosophy of the Social Sciences* 34, 2.

Burawoy, Michael (1989) "Two Methods of Search in Science: Skocpol versus Trotsky," *Theory and Society* 18.

(1998) "The Extended Case Method," *Sociological Theory* 16, 1.

Burian, Richard (1989) "The Influence of the Evolutionary Paradigm," in Max Hecht (ed.), *Evolutionary Biology at the Crossroads*. Flushing, New York: Queens College Press.

Calhoun, Craig (1996) "The Rise and Domestication of Historical Sociology," in Terrence McDonald (ed.), *The Historic Turn in the Human Sciences*. Ann Arbor: University of Michigan Press.

(1998) "Explanation in Historical Sociology: Narrative, General Theory, and Historically Specific Theory," *American Journal of Sociology* 104, 3.

Calhoun, Craig, Gerteis, Joseph, Moody, James, Pfaff, Steven and Virk, Indermohan (eds.) (2002) *Contemporary Social Theory*. Oxford: Basil Blackwell.

Camic, Charles (1987) "The Making of a Method: A Historical Reinterpretation of the Early Parsons," *American Sociological Review* 52.

Campbell, D. A. and Misanin, J. R. (1969) "Basic Drives," in P. H. Mussen and M. R. Rosenzweig (eds.), *Annual Review of Psychology*, vol. 20.

Cartwright, Nancy (1989) *Nature's Capacities and Their Measurement*. Oxford: Oxford University Press.

Cavalli-Sforza, Luigi Luca (2000) *Genes, Peoples and Languages*. New York: North Point Press.

Cavalli-Sforza, Luigi Luca and Cavalli-Sforza, Francesco (1995) *The Great Human Diasporas*. Cambridge, MA: Perseus Books.

Chai, Sun-Ki (2001) *Choosing an Identity: A General Model of Preference and Belief Formation*. Ann Arbor: University of Michigan Press.

Chakrabarty, Dipesh (1989) *Rethinking Working Class History: Bengal 1890–1940*. Princeton: Princeton University Press.

Chamberlin, E. H. (1962) *The Theory of Monopolistic Competition: A Re-Orientation of the Theory of Value*. 8th edition. Cambridge, MA: Harvard University Press [1933].

Chandler, Alfred D. (1962) *The Visible Hand: The Managerial Revolution in Modern Business*. Cambridge: Belknap Press.

Chisholm, Roderick (1946) "The Contrary to Fact Conditional," *Mind* 55.

Clifford, J. and Marcus, G. E. (eds.) (1986) *Writing Culture: The Poetics and Politics of Ethnography*. Berkeley: University of California Press.

Clough, P. T. (1992) *The Ends of Ethnography: From Realism to Social Criticism*. Newbury Park, CA: Sage.

Coase, R. H. (1995) "The Institutional Structure of Production," in R. H. Coase, *Essays on Economics and Economists*. Chicago: University of Chicago Press.

Cole, Stephen (1994) "Why Sociology Doesn't Make Progress Like the Natural Sciences," *Sociological Forum* 9.

Coleman, James S. (1988) "Social Capital and the Creation of Human Capital," *American Journal of Sociology* 84.

(1990) *Foundations of Social Theory*. Cambridge, MA: Belknap Press of Harvard University Press.

Collier, Andrew (1994) *Critical Realism: An Introduction to Roy Bhaskar's Philosophy*. London: Verso.

Collingwood, R. G. (1969) "The A Priori Impossibility of a Science of Man," the title given to a section of his *The Idea of History*, excerpted in Leonard J. Krimerman (ed.), *The Nature and Scope of Social Science*. New York: Appleton-Century-Crofts.

Collins, Patricia Hill (2000) *Black Feminist Thought: Knowledge, Consciousness, and the Politics of Empowerment*. 2nd edition. London: Taylor and Francis, Inc.

Collins, Randall (1979) *The Credential Society*. New York: Academic Press.

(1980) "Weber's Last Theory of Capitalism: A Systematization." *American Sociological Review* 45, 6.

Conley, Dalton (2001) "The Data in Your Lap: How to Interpret Naturally Occurring Experiments," http://chronicle.com/weekly/v50/i17/17b02001.htm

Craver, Carl F. (2001) "Role Functions, Mechanisms and Hierarchy," *Philosophy of Science* 68.

Davis, Mike (2001) *Late Victorian Holocausts: El Niño Famines and the Making of the Third World*. London: Verso.

Davis, William L. (2004) "Preference Falsification in the Economics Profession," *Economic Journal Watch* 1.

Debreu, Gerard (1984), "Economic Theory in a Mathematical Mode: The Nobel Lecture," *American Economic Review* 74, 1.

Delanty, Gerard and Esin, Ingin F. (eds.) (2003) *Handbook of Historical Sociology*. New York: Sage.

Denzin, Norman and Lincoln, Yvonne S. (eds.) (1994) *Handbook of Qualitative Research*. Thousand Oaks: Sage.

Dobbin, Frank (ed.) (2004) *The New Economic Sociology: A Reader*. Princeton: Princeton University Press.

Drechsel, Emanual (1991) "The Invalidity of the Concept 'Race,'" in M. Tehranian (ed.), *Restructuring for Ethnic Peace*. Honolulu, Hawai'i: Matsunaga Institute for Peace.

Dretske, Fred (1977) "Laws of Nature," *Philosophy of Science* 44.

Dugger, William M. (1992) *Underground Economics: A Decade of Institutionalist Dissent*. Armonk: M. E. Sharpe.

Duhem, Pierre (1954) *The Aim and Structure of Physical Theory*. Princeton: Princeton University Press.

Durkheim, Emile (1972) *Selected Writings*, ed. introd. Anthony Giddens. Cambridge: Cambridge University Press.

(1982) *Rules of Sociological Method*, ed. Steven Lukes, trans. W. D. Halls. New York: Free Press,

Duster, Troy (2004) "Selective Arrests, an Ever-Expanding DNA Forensic Debate and the Spector of and Early Twenty-First-Century Equivalent of Phrenology," in D. Lazer (ed.), *The Technology of Justice: DNA and the Criminal Justice System*. Cambridge, MA: MIT Press.

(2005) "Race and Reification in Science," *Science* 307, 5712.

Dyke, Charles F. (1981) *Philosophy of Economics*. Englewood Cliffs: Prentice-Hall.

Eisenstadt, S. N. (1961) *Essays on Sociological Aspects of Political and Economic Development*. The Hague: Mouton.

Elias, Norbert (1939) *The Civilizing Process*, vol 1. New York: Pantheon.

(1982) *The Civilizing Process*, vol 2. Oxford: Basil Blackwell.

Elson, Diane (1988) "Market Socialism or Socialism of the Market," *New Left Review* 172.

Etzioni, E. and Etzioni A. (eds.) (1973) *Social Change*, New York: Basic Books.

Etzioni, Amitai and Lawrence, Paul R. (1991) *Socio-Economics: Toward a New Synthesis*. Armonk: M. E. Sharpe.

Fabian, Johannes (1991) "Ethnographic Objectivity Revisited: From Rigor to Vigor," *Annals of Scholarship* 8, 3–4, ed. by Allan Mcgill.

Feinberg, Gerald (1973) *Social Philosophy*. New York: Prentice-Hall.

Feyerabend, Paul K. (1975) *Against Method*. London: New Left Books.

Frankfort-Nachmias, Chava and Nachmias, David (1992) *Research Methods in the Social Sciences*. 4th edition. New York: St. Martin's Press.

Franklin, R. L (1983) "On Understanding," *Philosophy and Phenomenological Research* 43, 3.

Friedman, Michael (1974) "Explanation and Scientific Understanding," *Journal of Philosophy* 81, 1.

Friedman, Milton (1968) "The Methodology of Positivist Economics," in May Brodbeck (ed.), *Readings in the Philosophy of the Social Sciences*. New York: Macmillan.

(1991) "Old Wine in New Bottles," *The Economic Journal* 101.

Galbraith, John Kenneth (1968) *The New Industrial State*. Boston: Houghton Mifflin.

Gambetta, Diego (1998) "Concatenations of Mechanisms," in Peter Hedström and Richard Swedberg (eds.), *Social Mechanisms: An Analytical Approach to Social Theory*. Cambridge: Cambridge University Press.

Gemes, Ken (1994) "Explanation, Unification, and Content," *Nous* 28, 2.

Geneen, Harold, with Moscow, Alvin (1984) *Managing*. New York: Doubleday.

Geertz, Clifford (1956) *The Development of the Javanese Economy: A Socio-cultural Approach*. Cambridge, MA: MIT Press.

(1973) *Interpretation of Cultures*. New York: Basic Books.

(1983) *Local Knowledge: Further Essays in Interpretative Anthropology*. New York: Basic Books.

Giddens, Anthony (1976) *New Rules of Sociological Method*. London: Hutchinson.

(1979) *Central Problems in Social Theory*. London: Macmillan.

(1981) *Contemporary Critique of Historical Materialism*. Berkeley: University of California Press.

(1984) *The Constitution of Society*. Berkeley: University of California Press.

Giddens, Anthony and Turner, Jonathan (1987) *Social Theory Today*. Oxford: Basil Blackwell.

Gillespie, Alex (2005) "G. H. Mead: Theorist of the Social Act," *Journal for the Theory of Social Behavior* 36.

Gilroy, Paul (2000) *Between Camps: Nations, Cultures and the Allure of Race*. London: Allen Lane.

Glassner, Barry (2000) *The Culture of Fear*. New York: Basic Books.

Glennan, Stuart S. (1996) "Mechanisms and the Nature of Causation," *Erkenntnis* 44.

Goffman, Erving (1961) *Asylums*. Garden City: Anchor Books.

Goldstein, Paul, Brownstein, Henry H., Ryan, Patrick J. and Belluci, Patricia (1997) "Crack and Homicide in New York City," in Craig Reinerman and Harry Levine (eds.), *Crack in America: Demon Drugs and Social Justice*. Berkeley: University of California Press.

Goldstone, Jack A. (1998) "Initial Conditions, General Laws, Path Dependence, and Explanation in Historical Sociology," *American Journal of Sociology* 104, 3.

Goldthorpe, John H. (1991) "The Uses of History in Sociology: Reflections on Some Recent Tendencies," *British Journal of Sociology* 42. See also the special issue discussion of Goldthorpe's essay in the same volume.

Gould, Roger V. (ed.) (2004) *Rational Choice Controversy in Historical Sociology*. Chicago: University of Chicago Press.

Gould, Stephen Jay (1981) *Mismeasure of Man*. New York: W. W. Norton.

Gowan, Peter (1999) *The Global Gamble: Washington's Faustian Bid for World Dominance*. London: Verso.

Granovetter, Mark and Swedburg, Richard (eds.) (1992) *The Sociology of Economic Life*. Boulder: Westview.

Granovetter, Mark and Tilly, Charles (1988) "Inequality and Labor Process," in Neil Smelzer (ed.), *Handbook of Sociology*. Beverly Hills, CA: Sage.

Grathoff, Richard (ed.) (1978) *The Theory of Social Action*. Bloomington: Indiana University Press.

Green, Donald and Shapiro, Ian (eds.) (1996) *Pathologies of Rational Choice Theory: A Critique of Applications in Political Science*. New Haven: Yale University Press.

Grossman, Sanford (1989) *The Informational Role of Prices*. Cambridge, MA: MIT Press.

Hacking, Ian (1983) *Representing and Intervening: Introductory Topics in the Philosophy of Natural Science*. Cambridge: Cambridge University Press.

(1992) "The Self-Vindication of the Laboratory Sciences," in Andrew Pickering (ed.), *Science as Practice and Culture*. Chicago: University of Chicago Press.

(2000) "What about the Natural Sciences?" in *The Social Construction of What*. Cambridge, MA: Harvard University Press.

Hall, John R. (1999) *Cultures of Inquiry: From Epistemology to Discourse in Sociohistorical Research*. Cambridge: Cambridge University Press.

Hall, Peter and Soskice, David (2001) *Varieties of Capitalism*. Oxford: Oxford University Press.

Hamouda, O. F. (1993) *John R. Hicks: The Economist's Economist*. Oxford: Basil Blackwell.

Hannaford, Ivan (1996) *Race: The History of an Idea in the West*. Baltimore: Johns Hopkins University Press.

Hanson, Norwood (1958) *Patterns of Discovery*. Cambridge: Cambridge University Press.

Harré, Rom (1970) *Principles of Scientific Thinking*. Chicago: University of Chicago Press.

   (1986) *Varieties of Realism*. Oxford: Basil Blackwell.

Harré, Rom and van Langenhove, Luk (1999) *Positioning Theory: Moral Contexts of Intentional Action*. Oxford: Basil Blackwell.

Harré, Rom and Madden, Edward (1975) *Causal Powers*. Oxford: Basil Blackwell.

Harré, Rom and Secord, Paul (1973) *The Explanation of Social Behavior*. Totowa, NJ: Littlefield, Adams.

Harris, Judith Rich (1998) *The Nurture Assumption*. New York: Free Press.

Harvey, David (1987) *The Condition of Post-Modernity*. Oxford: Basil Blackwell.

Hausman, Daniel (1984) "Are General Equilibrium Theories Explanatory," in Daniel Hausman (ed.), *Philosophy of Economics*. Cambridge: Cambridge University Press.

Hayek, F. A. (ed.) (1935) *Collectivist Economic Planning*. London: Routledge & Kegan Paul.

   (1978) *New Studies in Philosophy, Politics, Economics and the History of Ideas*. Chicago: University of Chicago Press.

Hedström, Peter and Swedberg, Richard (eds.) (1998) *Social Mechanisms: An Analytical Approach to Social Theory*. Cambridge: Cambridge University Press.

Hempel, C. G. [1950] (1965) "Theoreticians Dilemma," in C. G. Hempel, *Aspects of Scientific Explanation*. New York: Free Press.

Henningsen, Manfred (2004) "Die europaeische Schrumpfung der Menschheit. Die Aufklaerung und die Entstehung des transatlantischen Rassismus," in Aram Mattioli, Markus Ries and Rudolph Enno (eds.), *Intoleranz im Zeitalter der Revolutionen. Europa 1770–1848*. Zürich: Orell Fuessli Verlag.

Hernes, Gudmund (1998) "Real Virtuality," in Peter Hedstrom and Richard Swedberg (eds.), *Social Mechanisms: An Analytical Approach to Social Theory*. Cambridge: Cambridge University Press.

Hesse, Mary (1970) *Models and Analogies in Science*. Notre Dame: University of Notre Dame Press.

Hexter, Jack H. (1971) *The History Primer*. New York: Basic Books.

Hicks, J. R. (1989) *A Market Theory of Money*. Oxford: Clarendon Press.

Hintikka, Jaako and Halonen, Ilpon (1995) "Semantics and Pragmatics for Why-Questions," *Journal of Philosophy* 92.

Hirsch, Fred (1976) *Social Limits to Growth*. Cambridge, MA: Harvard University Press.

Hirshman, A. O. (1985) "Against Parsimony," *Economics and Philosophy* 1.

   (1997) *The Passions and the Interests*. Princeton: Princeton University Press.

Hobbs, Jesse (1993) "Ex Post Facto Explanations," *Journal of Philosophy* 90, 3.

Holton, Gerald (1970) "Mach, Einstein and the Search for Reality," in R. S. Cohen and R. J. Seeger (eds.), *Ernst Mach, Physicist and Philosopher.* Dordrecht: Reidel.

Hull, David (1974) *Philosophy of Biological Science.* Englewood Cliffs, NJ: Prentice Hall.

Hume, David (2000) *A Treatise of Human Nature,* eds. David and Mary Norton. Oxford: Oxford University Press.

Jorde, Lynn B., and Woodling, Stephen P. (2004) "Genetic Variation, Classification and Race," *Nature Genetics* 36, 11.

Kalecki, Michal (1965) *Theory of Economic Dynamics.* London: G. Allen & Unwin.

Kantor, Rosabeth Moss (1977) *Men and Women of the Corporation.* New York: Basic Books.

Kemp, Stephen and Holmwood, John (2003) "Realism, Regularity and Social Explanation," *Journal for the Theory of Social Behavior* 33, 2.

Keynes, John Maynard [1937] (1960) *General Theory of Employment, Interest and Money.* London: Macmillan.

(1984) "Economic Model Construction and Econometrics," excerpts from correspondence of Keynes to Roy Harrad [1938]. In Daniel Hausman (ed.), *Philosophy of Economics.* Cambridge: Cambridge University Press.

Kim, Jaegwon (1987) "Causal Realism and Explanatory Exclusion," *Midwest Studies in Philosophy* 12. Quoted from the reprint in David-Hillel Ruben (ed.), *Explanation.* Oxford: Oxford University Press.

Kirzner, Israel M. (1985) "Prices, the Communication of Knowledge, and the Discovery Process," in Kurt Leube and Albert Zlabinger (eds.), *The Political Economy of Freedom: Essays in Honor of F. A. Hayek.* Munich: Philosophia Verlag.

Kiser, Edgar and Hector, Michael (1991) "The Role of General Theory in Comparative-Historical Sociology," *American Journal of Sociology* 97, 1.

(1998) "The Debate on Historical Sociology: Rational Choice Theory and Its Critics," *American Journal of Sociology* 104, 3.

Kitcher, Philip (1976) "Explanation, Conjunction, and Unification," *Journal of Philosophy* 73.

(1981) "Explanatory Unification," *Philosophy of Science* 48.

Knorr-Cetina, Karen (1981) *The Manufacture of Knowledge: An Essay on the Constructivist and Contextual Nature of Science.* Oxford: Pergamon.

(1999) *Epistemic Cultures: How the Sciences Make Knowledge.* Cambridge, MA: Harvard University Press.

Kripke, Saul (1982) *Naming and Necessity.* Cambridge, MA: Harvard University Press.

Kuhn, Thomas (1970) *The Structure of Scientific Revolutions.* Chicago: University of Chicago Press.

Lachman, Ludwig M. (1984) "Methodological Individualism and the Market Economy," in Daniel Hausman (ed.), *Philosophy of Economics.* Cambridge: Cambridge University Press.

Langlois, Richard N. (ed.) (1986) *Economics as a Process: Essays in the New Institutional Economics.* Cambridge: Cambridge University Press.

Latour, Bruno (1987) *Science in Action*. Cambridge, MA: Harvard University Press.

Latour, Bruno and Woolgar, Steve (1979) *Laboratory Life: The Social Construction of Scientific Facts*. Beverly Hills: Sage.

Lawson, Tony (1997) *Economics and Reality*. London: Routledge.

Lazarsfeld, Paul F. and Rosenberg, Morris (eds.) (1955) *The Language of Social Research: A Reader in the Methodology of Social Research*. New York: Free Press.

Lazonik, William (1991) *Business Organization and the Myth of the Market Economy*. Cambridge: Cambridge University Press.

Leamer, E. E. (1983) "Let's Take the Con out of Econometrics," *American Economic Review* 73.

Lekachman, Robert (1964) *Keynes and the Classics*. Boston: D. C. Heath.

Lentin, Alana (2004) *Racism and Anti-Racism in Europe*. London: Pluto Press.

Leontief, Wassily (1971) "Theoretical Assumptions and Nonobserved Facts," *American Economic Review* 61.

   (1982) Letter in *Science* 217.

Lewis, David (1987) "Causal Explanation," in David Lewis, *Philosophical Papers*. New York: Oxford University Press. Quoted from the reprint in David-Hillel Ruben (ed.), *Explanation*. Oxford: Oxford University Press.

Lewis, Paul (2000) "Realism, Causality and the Problem of Social Structure," *Journal for the Theory of Social Behavior* 30, 3.

Lewis, Paul and Runde, J. H. (forthcoming) "Subjectivism, Social Structures and the Possibility of Socio-Economic Order: The Case of Ludwig Lachman," *Journal of Economic Behavior and Organization*.

Lewontin, Richard (1974) "The Analysis of Variation and the Analysis of Causes," *American Journal of Human Genetics* 26. Reprinted in Richard Levins and Richard Lewontin (1985) *The Dialectical Biologist*. Cambridge, MA: Harvard University Press, and in Ned Block (ed.) (1976) *The IQ Controversy*. New York Pantheon.

   (1982) *Human Diversity*. New York: Scientific American Library.

   (2004) "Dishonesty in Science," *New York Review of Books* 52.

Lindbloom, Charles E. (1977) *Politics and Markets*, New York: Basic Books.

Lipset, Seymour Martin and Richard Hofstadter (eds.) (1968) *Sociology and History: Methods*. New York: Basic Books.

Littlechild, S. C. (1988) "Three Types of Market Process," in Richard N. Langlois (ed.), *Economics as a Process: Essays in the New Institutional Economics*. Cambridge: Cambridge University Press.

Lorenz, Edward (1996) *The Essence of Chaos*. Washington: University of Washington Press.

Luhmann, Niklas (1997) "Limits of Steering," *Theory, Culture and Society* 14, 1.

Lukes, Steven (1972) *Emile Durkheim: His Life and Work*. New York: Harper & Row.

Lynch, M. (1985) *Art and Artifact in Laboratory Science*. London: Routledge & Kegan Paul.

Lynch, M., Livingston, E. and Garfinkel, H. (1983) "Temporal Order in Laboratory Life," in C. Knorr and M. Mulkay (eds.), *Science Observed: Perspectives on the Social Study of Science*. Beverly Hills: Sage.

Mach, Ernst (1959) *The Analysis of Sensations.* New York: Dover.

Machamer, Peter, Darden, Lindley and Craver, Carl F. (2000) "Thinking about Mechanisms," *Philosophy of Science* 67.

MacRaild, Donald M. and Taylor, Avram (2004) *Social Theory and Social History: Theory and History.* London: Palgrave Macmillan.

Mahoney, James (1999) "Nominal, Ordinal, and Narrative Appraisal in Macro-Causal Analysis, *American Journal of Sociology* 104.

Mahoney, James, and Rueschemeyer, Dietrich (eds.) (2003) *Comparative Historical Analysis in the Social Sciences.* Cambridge: Cambridge University Press.

Mandel, E. (1986) "In Defense of Socialist Planning," *New Left Review* 159.

(1988) "The Myth of Market Socialism," *New Left Review* 179.

Manicas, Peter T. (ed.) (1977) *Logic As Philosophy.* New York: Van Nostrand.

(1981) "Review Essay of Skocpol, *States and Social Revolutions,*" *History and Theory* 10.

(1987) *A History and Philosophy of the Social Sciences.* Oxford: Basil Blackwell.

(1989a) "Explanation and Quantification," in Barry Glassner and Jonathan Moreno (eds.), *The Qualitative–Quantitative Distinction in the Social Sciences.* Dordrecht: Kluwer.

(1989b) *War and Democracy.* Oxford: Basil Blackwell.

(1989c) "Comment on Burian, 'The Influence of the Evolutionary Paradigm,'" in Max Hecht (ed.), *Evolutionary Biology at the Crossroads.* Flushing, New York: Queens College Press.

(1992) "Nature and Culture," *Proceedings and Addresses of the American Philosophical Association* 66, 3, reprinted in John Ryder (ed.) (1994) *American Philosophical Naturalism.* Amherst, NY: Prometheus Books.

Manicas, Peter T. and Rosenberg, Alan (1985) "Naturalism, Epistemological Individualism and 'The Strong Programme' in the Sociology of Knowledge," *Journal for the Theory of Social Behavior* 15, 1.

(1988) "The Sociology of Scientific Knowledge: Can We Ever Get it Right?" *Journal for the Theory of Social Behavior* 18, 1.

Manicas, Peter T. and Secord, Paul (1984) "Implications of the New Philosophy of Science: A Topology for Psychology," *American Psychologist* 38, 4. http://www. geocities.com/Athens/5476/ N_T_abs.htm

Mann, Michael (1986) *The Sources of Social Power.* Cambridge: Cambridge University Press.

Margolis, Joseph, Manicas, Peter T., Harré, Rom and Secord, Paul (1986) *Psychology: Designing the Discpline.* Oxford: Blackwell.

Marx, Karl (1970) *Capital, Vol 1.* London: Lawrence and Wishart.

Marx, Karl and Engels, F. (1956) *The Holy Family: A Critique of Critique.* Moscow: Foreign Language Publishing House.

Mauss, Marcel (2000) *The Gift: The Form and Reason for Exchange in Archaic Societies.* New York: W. W. Norton.

May, Tim *et al.* (2002) "Symposium: Rom Harré on Social Structure and Social Change," *European Journal of Social Theory* 5, 1.

McAdam, Doug, Tarrow, Sidney and Tilly, Charles (2001) *Dynamics of Contention.* Cambridge: Cambridge University Press.

McDonald, Terrance J. (ed.) (1996) *The Historic Turn in the Human Sciences.* Ann Arbor: University of Michigan Press.

McLean, Scott L., Schultz, David A. and Steger, Manfred B. (eds.) (2002) *Social Capital: Critical Perspectives on Bowling Alone*. New York: New York University Press.

Mead, George Herbert (1967) *Mind, Self and Society*. Chicago: University of Chicago Press.

Merton. Robert K. (1957) *Social Theory and Social Structure*. Glencoe: Free Press.

Mills, C. Wright (1956) *The Power Elite*. New York: Oxford University Press.

(1959) *The Sociological Imagination*. Middlesex: Penguin.

Mirowski, Phillip (1991) "The When, the How and the Why of Mathematical Expression in the History of Economic Analysis, *Journal of Economic Perspectives* 5, 1.

Mittleman, James H. (2000) *The Globalization Syndrome: Transformation and Resistance*. Princeton: Princeton University Press.

Moore, Barrington (1966) *Social Origins of Dictatorship and Democracy*. Boston: Beacon Press.

Morgan, John P. and Zimmer, Lynn (1997) "The Social Pharmacology of Smokeable Cocaine," in Craig Reinerman and Harry Levine (eds.), *Crack in America: Demon Drugs and Social Justice*. Berkeley: University of California Press.

Mulkay, Michael (1985) *The Word and the World: Explorations in the Form of Sociological Analysis*. London: Allen & Unwin.

Münch, Richard (1987) "Parsonian Theory Today: In Search of New Synthesis," in Anthony Giddens and Jonathan Turner (eds.), *Social Theory Today*. Oxford: Basil Blackwell.

Murray, Martin (1998) *Methodological Approaches to Historical Inquiry*. Perseus Books.

Nagel, Ernest (1961) *The Structure of Science*. New York: Harcourt Brace.

Nelson, Benjamin (1981) *On the Roads of Modernity*, ed. T. Huff. Totowa, NJ: Rowman and Littlefield.

North, Douglas C. (1981) *Structure and Change in Economic History*. New York: W. W. Norton.

(1990) *Institutions, Institutional Change and Economic Performance*. Cambridge: Cambridge University Press.

Nove, Alec (1989) "Socialism, Capitalism and the Soviet Experience," in E. F. Paul *et al.* (eds.), *Socialism*. Oxford: Basil Blackwell.

Nussbaum, Martha and Glover, Jonathan (eds.) (1995) *Women, Culture and Development: A Study of Human Capabilities*. Oxford: Clarendon.

Ogbu, John (1978) *Minority Education and Caste: The American System in Cross-Cultural Comparison*. New York: Academic Press.

Olsen, Wendy and Morgan, Jane (forthcoming) "A Critical Epistemology of Analytic Statistics: Addressing the Sceptical Realist, *Journal for the Theory of Social Behavior*.

Olson, Mancur (1971) *The Logic of Collective Action*. Cambridge, MA: Harvard University Press.

Outhwaite, William and Bottomore, Tom (1992) *Blackwell Dictionary of Social Thought*. Oxford: Basil Blackwell.

Oxenfeld, Alfred R. (ed.) (1963) *Models of Markets*. New York: Columbia University Press.

Paige, Jeffrey M. (1999) "Conjuncture, Comparison and Conditional Theory in Macrosocial Inquiry," *American Journal of Sociology* 105, 3.

Pareto, Wilfredo (1909) *Manual of Political Economy*. New York: Augustus M. Kelly.

(1935) *Mind and Society*, 4 vols. New York: Harcourt.

Parsons, Talcott [1937] (1968) *The Structure of Social Action*. New York: Free Press.

Passmore, John (1957) *A Hundred Years of Philosophy*. Harmondsworth: Penguin Books.

Pendergast, Christopher (1986) "Alfred Schütz and the Austrian School of Economics," *American Journal of Sociology* 92, 1.

Pickering, Andrew (ed.) (1992) *Science as Practice and Culture*. Chicago: University of Chicago Press.

Pitelis, Christos (1991) *Market and Non-Market Hierarchies: Theory of Institutional Failure*. Oxford: Blackwell.

Polanyi, Karl (1971) *Primitive, Archaic, and Modern Economies: Essays of Karl Polanyi*. Boston: Beacon Press.

(1992) "The Economy as an Instituted Process," in Mark Granovetter and Richard Swedberg (eds.), *The Sociology of Economic Life*. Boulder: Westview.

(2001) *The Great Transformation*. 2nd edition. Boston: Beacon Press.

Polanyi, Karl, Arensberg, C. M. and Pearson, H. W. (eds.) (1957) *Trade and Market in the Early Empires: Economies in History and Theory*. Glencoe: Free Press.

Pomeranz, Kenneth (2000) *The Great Divergence*. Princeton: Princeton University Press.

Porpora, Douglas (1989) "Four Concepts of Social Structure," *Journal for the Theory of Social Behavior* 19, 2.

Posner, Richard A. (2004) *Catastrophe: Risk and Response*. New York: Oxford University Press.

Putnam, Robert D. (2000) *Bowling Alone: The Collapse and Revival of American Community*. New York: Simon & Schuster.

Quine, W. V. [1950] (1961) "Two Dogmas of Empiricism," in W. V. Quine, *From a Logical Point of View*. New York: Harper Torch books, revised edition.

Ragin, Charles, and Zaret, David (1983) "Theory and Method in Comparative Research: Two Strategies," *Social Forces* 61, 3.

Ravetz, Jerome (1971) *Scientific Knowledge and its Social Problems*. New York: Oxford University Press.

Rawls, John (1971) *A Theory of Justice*. Cambridge, MA: Harvard University Press.

Reinerman, Craig, and Levine, Harry (eds.) (1997) *Crack in America: Demon Drugs and Social Justice*. Berkeley: University of California Press.

Ridley, Matt (2003) *Nature Via Nurture: Genes, Experience and What Makes us Human*. New York: HarperCollins.

Ringer, Fritz (1989) "Causal Analysis in Historical Reasoning," *History and Theory* 28.

(1997) *Max Weber's Methodology: The Unification of the Cultural and Social Sciences*. Cambridge, MA: Harvard University Press.

(2002) "Max Weber on Causal Analysis, Interpretation, and Comparison," *History and Theory* 41.

Ritzer, George (2004) *The Globalization of Nothing.* Thousand Oaks: Pine Forge Press.

Robertson, Roland (1992) *Globalization: Social Theory and Global Culture.* London: Sage.

Robinson, Joan (1969). *The Economics of Imperfect Competition.* 2nd edition. London: Macmillan.

Rorty, Richard (1981) *Philosophy and the Mirror of Nature.* Princeton: Princeton University Press.

Rosaldo, R. (1989) *Culture and Truth: The Remaking of Social Analysis.* Boston: Beacon Press.

Rosenberg, Alex (2005) "Lessons from Biology for Philosophy of the Social Sciences," *Philosophy of the Social Sciences* 35, 1.

Roth, Guenther and Schlucter, Wolfgang (1979) *Max Weber's Vision of History: Ethics and Methods.* Berkeley: University of California Press.

Rothstein, Richard (2004) "Must Schools Fail?" *New York Review of Books* 51.

Rotimi, Charles N. (2004) "Are Medical and Non-medical Uses of Large-scale, Genomic Markets Conflating Genetics and 'Race'?" *Nature Genetics* 36, 11.

Ruben, David-Hillel (ed.) (1993) *Explanation.* Oxford: Oxford University Press.

Sahlins, Marshall (2004) *Apologies of Thucydides: Understanding History as Culture and Vice Versa.* Chicago: University of Chicago Press.

(2005) *Stone Age Economics.* 2nd edition. London: Routledge.

Salmon, Wesley (1978) "Why Ask 'Why?' " Presidential Address. American Philosophical Association 51.

(1984) *Scientific Explanation and the Causal Structure of the World.* Princeton: Princeton University Press.

Samuelson, Paul (1947) *Foundations of Economic Analysis.* Cambridge, MA: Harvard University Press.

Sassen, Saskia (1999) *Globalization and Its Discontents: Essays on the New Mobility of People and Money.* New York: New Press.

Sawyer, R. Keith (2003) "The Mechanisms of Emergence," *Philosophy of the Social Sciences* 34, 2.

Sayer, Andrew (1992) *Method in Social Science.* London: Routledge.

Sayer, Derek (1979) *Marx's Method: Ideology, Science and Critique in Capital.* Sussex: Harvester Press.

(1987) *The Violence of Abstraction.* Oxford: Basil Blackwell.

Schor, Juliet B. (1992) *The Overworked American.* New York: Basic Books.

(1999) *The Overspent American: Why We Want What We Don't Need.* New York: Perseus Books.

Schumpeter, Joseph A. (1954) *History of Economic Analysis.* New York: Oxford University Press.

Schütz, Alfred (1954) "Concept and Theory Formation in the Social Sciences," *Journal of Philosophy* 51, 9.

(1970) *On Phenomenology and Social Relations*, ed. and introd. Helmut R. Wagner. Chicago: University of Chicago Press.

Scriven, Michael (1959) "Truisms as Ground for Historical Explanations," in P. Gardiner (ed.), *Theories of History*. New York: Free Press.

(1962) "Explanations, Predictions and Laws," in H. Feigl and G. Maxwell (eds.), *Minnesota Studies in the Philosophy of Science*, vol. 3. Minneapolis: University of Minnesota Press.

Searle, John R. (1983) *Intentionality: An Essay in the Philosophy of Mind*. New York: Cambridge University Press.

(1992) *The Rediscovery of Mind*. Cambridge, MA: MIT Press.

(1995) *The Construction of Social Reality*. New York: Free Press.

Sellars, Wilfred (1963) *Science, Perception and Reality*. London: Routledge & Kegan Paul.

Sen, Amartya K. (1977) "Rational Fools: A Critique of the Behavioral Foundations of Economic Theory," *Philosophy and Public Affairs* 6.

Sewell, William H. Jr. (1992) "A Theory of Structure: Duality, Agency and Transformation," *American Journal of Sociology* 98, 1.

(1996) "Three Temporalities: Toward an Eventful Sociology," in Terrance J. McDonald (ed.), *The Historic Turn in The Human Sciences*. Ann Arbor: University of Michigan Press.

Shelling, Thomas C. (1998) "Social Mechanisms and Social Dynamics," in Peter Hedström and Richard Swedberg (eds.), *Social Mechanisms: An Analytical Approach to Social Theory*. Cambridge: Cambridge University Press.

Shonfield, Andrew (1965) *Modern Capitalism: The Changing Balance of Public and Private Power*. London: Oxford University Press.

Simon, Lawrence H. (1994) *Karl Marx: Selected Writings*. Indianapolis: Hackett.

Skocpol, Theda (1979) *States and Social Revolutions*. Cambridge: Cambridge University Press.

(1984) "Emerging Agendas and Recurring Strategies," in Theda Skocpol (ed.), *Vision and Method in Historical Sociology*. Cambridge: Cambridge University Press.

(1994) *Social Revolutions in the Modern World*. Cambridge: Cambridge University Press.

Skocpol, Theda and Margaret Somers (1980) "The Uses of Comparative History in Macrosocial Inquiry." *Comparative Studies in Society and History* 22.

Slater, Don and Tonkiss, Fran (2001) *Market Society: Markets and Modern Social Theory*. Oxford: Polity Press.

Smelzer, Neil (1964) "Towards a Theory of Modernization," in A. Etzioni and E. Etzioni (eds.), *Social Change*. New York: Basic Books.

Smelzer, Neil and Swedberg, Richard (eds.) (1994) *The Handbook of Economic Sociology*. Princeton: Princeton University Press.

Smith, Charles W. (1989) *Auctions: The Social Construction of Value*. New York: Free Press.

(forthcoming) "Markets as Definitional Mechanisms: A Robust Alternative Sociological Paradigm."

Smith, Dennis (1991) *The Rise of Historical Sociology*. Cambridge: Polity Press.

Solow, Robert (1980) "On Theories of Unemployment," *American Economic Review* 70, 1.

Somers, Margaret (1998) " 'We're No Angels': Realism, Rational Choice, and Relationality in Social Science," *American Journal of Sociology* 104, 3,

Steele, Claude (2004) *Young, Gifted, and Black: Promoting High Achievement Among African American Students.* Boston: Beacon Press.

Steger, Manfred B. (2005) *Globalism: Market Ideology Meets Terrorism.* 2nd edition. Lanham: Rowman and Littlefield.

Stewart, A., Prandy K. and Blackburn, R. (1980) *Social Stratification and Occupations.* London: Macmillan.

Stiglitz, George (1994) *Whither Socialism.* Cambridge, MA: MIT Press.

(2002) *Globalization and Its Discontents.* New York: W. W. Norton.

Stinchcombe, Arthur (1978) *Theoretical Models in Social History.* New York: Academic Press.

(1983) *Economic Sociology.* New York: Academic Press.

(1998) "Monopolistic Competition as a Mechanism," in Peter Hedström and Richard Swedberg (eds.), *Social Mechanisms: An Analytical Approach to Social Theory.* Cambridge: Cambridge University Press.

Suppe, Frederick (1977) *The Structure of Scientific Theory.* 2nd edition. Urbana, IL: University of Illinois Press.

Swedburg, Richard (1993) *Explorations in Economic Sociology.* New York: Sage.

Tawney, R. H. [1912] (1998) *Religion and the Rise of Capitalism.* New Brunswick, NJ: Transaction Books.

Thomas, Scott L. (2004) "Globalization, College Participation, and Socioeconomic Mobility," in Jaishree K. Odin and Peter T. Manicas (eds.), *Globalization and Higher Education.* Honolulu: University of Hawai'i Press.

Thompson, E. P. (1978) *The Poverty of Theory and Other Essays.* London: Merlin Press.

Thurow, Lester (1983) *Dangerous Currents.* New York: Random House.

Ticktin, Hillel (1992) *Origins of the Crisis in the USSR.* Armon, New York: M. E. Sharpe.

Tilly, Charles (1982) *As Sociology Meets History.* New York: Academic Press.

(1984) *Big Structures, Large Processes, Huge Comparisons.* New York: Russell Sage.

(1992) "Coercion, Capital and European States," in Craig Calhoun *et al.* (eds.), *Contemporary Social Theory.* Oxford: Basil Blackwell.

(1995) "To Explain Political Processes," *American Journal of Sociology* 100, 6.

(1997) *Roads From Past to Future.* Lanham: Rowman and Littlefield.

(2001) "Mechanisms in Political Processes," *Annual Review of Political Science* 4.

Tilly, Chris and Tilly, Charles (1997) *Work Under Capitalism.* Boulder: Westview.

Tobin, James (1972) "Inflation and Unemployment," *American Economics Review* 62.

Toulmin, Stephen (1953) *The Philosophy of Science.* New York: Harper & Row.

(1961) *Foresight and Understanding.* New York: Harper and Row.

Turner, Jonathan H. (1987) "Analytical Theorizing," in Anthony Giddens and Jonathan Turner (eds.), *Social Theory Today.* Oxford: Basil Blackwell.

Varela, Charles, and Harré, Rom (1996) "Conflicting Varieties of Realism: Causal Powers and The Problem of Social Structure," *Journal for the Theory of Social Behavior* 26, 3.

Voegelin, Eric [1933] (2000) *Race and State*. Baton Rouge: Louisiana State University Press.

Wagner, Helmut (1983) *Alfred Schütz: An Intellectual Biography*. Chicago: University of Chicago Press.

Wagner, Peter, Wittrock, Bjorn and Whitely, Richard (eds.) (1991) *Discourses on Society: The Shaping of the Social Science Disciplines*. Dordrecht: Kluwer Academic Publishers.

Wallace, William A. (1974) *Causality and Scientific Explanation*, 2 vols. Ann Arbor: University of Michigan Press.

Wallerstein, Emmanuel (1974) *The Modern World System: Capitalist Agriculture and the Origins of the European World*. New York: Academic Press.

Weber, Max (1949) " 'Objectivity' in Social Science," in Max Weber, *On the Methodology of the Social* Sciences. New York: Free Press.

(1958) *The Protestant Ethic and the Spirit of Capitalism*. New York: Charles Scribner's Sons.

(1968) *Economy and Society*, ed. Guenther Roth, 3 vols. New York: Bedminster Press.

(1975) *Roscher und Kneis*, trans. Guy Oakes. New York: Free Press.

(2003) *General Economic History*. New York: Dover.

Weiss, Paul A. (1968) *Dynamics of Development: Experiments and Inferences*. New York: Academic Press.

(1971) *Hierarchically Organized Systems in Theory and Practice*. New York: Hafner.

(1972) *Order and Understanding: Three Variations on a Common Theme*. Austin, TX: University of Texas Press.

Whitfield, Keith E. and McClearn, Gerald (2005) "Genes, Environment and Race: Quantitative Genetic Approaches," *American Psychologist* 60, 1.

Wight, Colin (2003) "Theorizing Mechanisms of Conceptual and Semiotic Space," *Philosophy of the Social Sciences* 34, 2.

Williams, Malcolm (2005) "Situated Objectivity," *Journal for the Theory of Social Behavior* 35, 1.

Williams, Terry (1989) *The Cocaine Kids: The Inside Story of a Teenage Drug Ring*. New York: Addison-Wesley.

Willis, Paul E. (1981) *Learning to Labor: How Working Class Kids Get Working Class Jobs*. Morningside Edition: Columbia University Press.

Wimsatt, W. C. (1976a) "Reductionism, Levels of Organization and the Mind Body Problem," in G. G. Globas, *et al.* (eds.), *Consciousness and the Brain: A Scientific and Philosophical Inquiry*. New York: Plenum Press.

(1976b) "Complexity and Organization," in Marjorie Grene and E. Mendelsohn (eds.), *Topics in the Philosophy of Biology*. Dordrecht, Holland: Reidel vol. 27, Boston Studies in the Philosophy of Science.

Woodward, James (1984) "A Theory of Singular Causal Explanation," *Erkenntnis* 21. Quoted from the reprint in David-Hillel Ruben (ed.), *Explanation*. Oxford: Oxford University Press.

Woolgar, Steve (ed.) (1988) *Knowledge and Reflexivity: New Frontiers in the Soci-ology of Knowledge*. Beverly Hills: Sage.

Zafiroski, Milan (2003) *Market and Society: Two Theoretical Frameworks*. New York: Praeger.

Ziliak, Stephen T. and McCloskey, Deirdre N. (2004) "Size Matters: The Stan-dard Error of Regressions in the *American Economic Review,*" *Economic Jour-nal Watch* 1, 2.

Index